ALL MY KISSES FOR YOU

ALL MY KISSES FOR YOU

NEW YORK TIMES BESTSELLING AUTHOR

MONICA MURPHY

Entangled Publishing, LLC
644 Shrewsbury Commons Ave., STE 181
Shrewsbury, PA 17361
rights@entangledpublishing.com

Amara is an imprint of Entangled Publishing, LLC.

Visit our website at www.entangledpublishing.com.

Edited by Rebecca Barney
Proofreader Sarah Plocher
Cover design by Bree Archer
Stock art by Preto_perola/GettyImages, and Stella Photography/shutterstock
Interior design by Britt Marczak

ISBN 978-1-64937-712-8

Manufactured in the United States of America

First Edition June 2024

10 9 8 7 6 5 4 3 2 1

ALSO BY MONICA MURPHY

THE LANCASTER PREP SERIES

Things I Wanted To Say
A Million Kisses in Your Lifetime
Promises We Meant to Keep
I'll Always Be With You
You Said I Was Your Favorite

FOR TEEN READERS

Pretty Dead Girls
Saving It
Daring the Bad Boy

PLAYLIST

"Kerosene!" - Yves Tumor

"So It Goes…" - Taylor Swift

"To Be So Lonely" - Harry Styles

"HARD ROCK LULLABY" - Noah Guy

"My Girl 2020" - Valley Boy

"i die when u cry" - New Body Electric

"Late Checkout" - Hotel Ugly

"Hand As My Arrow [Feat. BROODS]" - Zella Day, BROODS

Find the rest of the **ALL MY KISSES FOR YOU** playlist here: https://bit.ly/42GBHvU

To those who love lollipops, art, lipsticks and Chanel bags…
this one is for you

PROLOGUE

CREW

She approaches me slowly, her tiny feet shuffling across the bare wood floor, her long, dark hair, so much like her mother's, tumbling past her shoulders in a haphazard mess. I know for a fact Wren brushes our daughter's hair after a bath every night. If she's not doing it, I am.

Somehow, our sweet Willow makes a mess of it in those twilight minutes between bath and bed. Every single time.

"Daddy." Her big blue eyes that match mine shine up at me, her little rosebud lips pursed into a perfect pout. She is truly the most beautiful little girl in the entire world, but I'm her father so I'm biased. "Can you put me to bed?"

I glance over at my wife, who's standing in the doorway of the living room, a soft smile on her face, cradling our baby boy in her arms. Another Lancaster to carry on the family name.

"Just performing our expected duties," I said to Wren when she told me she was pregnant. She rolled her eyes and gave me a gentle shove, which caused me to pull her down onto our bed and perform more of those duties on her…

But I digress.

"I thought you asked Mama to put you to bed." I'm already rising to my feet, holding my hand out to our daughter, and she takes it, curling her small fingers around mine.

"I want you instead," Willow says firmly.

Wren watches us, her expression a little weary. Our son is keeping her up at night because he's always hungry and she's breastfeeding. "She specifically requested her daddy."

"I don't mind." I stop beside my wife, leaning in to brush a kiss to her cheek before I murmur close to her ear, "Are you feeling all right?"

She nods. "A little tired. Row is finally asleep."

Our son. Rowan. He doesn't like to take naps and isn't the best sleeper in general. Wren says it's because he never wants to miss a thing and I tend to agree with her.

"Go to bed." I deliver another kiss, this time to her lips. "I'll join you in a few minutes."

"After you tell me a story," Willow demands.

We go to her bedroom, the light on her nightstand already on, as well as the light we installed to highlight Wren's favorite art piece, which is in our daughter's room. I tuck Willow into her fluffy princess dream of a bed, brushing her dark hair from her eyes, and she scoots away from me, patting the empty spot beside her.

"Sit."

I do as she says because this little girl owns my heart like her mother does and settle in beside her, slipping my arm around her slender shoulders and scooping her closer to me. She tilts her head back so our eyes meet, her lips parting, and I have a feeling I know what her request is going to be.

"Tell me the story about you and Mama."

My gaze goes to the piece hanging on the wall, smiling as the memories wash over me, one after another. Willow has already heard this story countless times and she's barely three. But she can't get enough of it.

"Wherc shall I start?" I ask.

"When Mama didn't like you." Willow wrinkles her nose then bursts out laughing. "It's funny."

"That would make you laugh." I tickle her and she giggles uncontrollably, so loud that Wren calls from our bedroom.

"What's going on in there?"

We both go silent, sharing a secret look, and I press my finger to Willow's lips.

"Nothing. I was just telling her a story," I respond.

"Uh huh." The doubt in my wife's voice is obvious and I smile.

So does Willow.

"We need to be quiet," I whisper.

"Don't tickle me," Willow says, sounding completely logical.

My girl is smart. Much like her mama.

Clearing my throat, I lean against the headboard and stare at the art piece, telling the story about watching for Wren every day before school started. How I didn't know her, but I wanted to, even though she never wanted to give me the time of day. How we were forced to work together on a school project and we slowly got to know each other.

And swiftly fell in love.

"What about the kisses?" Willow stares at the piece with me.

"What about them?"

"You owe her two million." She remembers that. She remembers pretty much every detail of our story. "How many do you give her?"

"A lot."

"How many?"

"We're probably only a quarter of the way in," I say, and my poor little daughter frowns, confusion etched in her delicate features. "Let's just say Daddy still owes Mama a lot of kisses."

The frown disappears, just like that. "I want kisses."

I give her one on her forehead. Her nose. Each cheek. "All the kisses you could ever want, you deserve."

"I wanna husband who gives me kisses too." Her gaze turns dreamy as she stares at the art piece once more.

Over my dead body, is what I want to say, thinking of my own self not too long ago and how completely over the top I was.

How badly I wanted Wren and went after her with a dogged determination that still surprises me. I've never chased after someone like I chased after Wren.

And look at me now. I got her. I love her. I love our little girl and I love our son. Life is pretty great.

"Someday," I tell Willow, dropping another kiss on top of her head. "But for now, save your kisses for your mama and daddy. And your brother."

"Okay, Daddy. I'll save all my kisses for you." She tilts her head back to look at me, and for a moment I think she looks older. Wiser than she should. "But someday I'm going to kiss someone else. Like Mama kisses you."

"Uh, sure." I swallow hard, hating the thought of her being so grown up. She's still my baby. My first child. My daughter. "Just... don't give your kisses away too easily."

She frowns. "Doesn't everyone need a kiss?"

I say nothing, unsure of how to explain myself. She's unreasonable a lot of the time, but she's still a toddler so it's expected. She's also naturally fiery and hotheaded—Wren calls that the Lancaster in her.

She's right. I can't deny it.

"Kisses are the best. They're so pretty." She turns toward the art, a little sigh escaping her. "I want it."

"Want what?"

"Kisses." She turns a toothy grin on me. "Lots of them."

Shit.

I'm in trouble.

CHAPTER ONE

WILLOW, AGE 18

LABOR DAY WEEKEND

"Why are we starting back at school so late again?" I'm sitting at the baroque-style vanity table that's in my cousin Iris's room, dotting my face with a highlighter stick almost aggressively.

"I already told you." Iris rises from her prone position on her bed, her dark blonde hair in the perfect messy bun I can never, ever duplicate, no matter how hard I try. "You leave for a year and everything changes."

She loves to remind me of this.

"Oh, I know." I turn away from the mirror, glaring at her like I'm mad, even though I don't mean it. She's not only my cousin, but she also happens to be my very best friend. "But we used to start in August."

"And now we start in September." Iris shrugs her slender shoulders, the strap of her tank top slipping. She shoves it back into place and plops backward onto the unmade and downright chaotic bed. Total symbolism for the complete disarray that is her mind and life. "Only fifteen minutes was added to our school day, but that's enough to allow us to start school later *and* end it sooner. Doesn't Westscott have the best ideas?"

My face turns into a grimace. I can feel it, and from the look on Iris's face, she can see it. Even though she's lying down and staring at the ceiling. "I haven't even met this mythical new headmaster and he's all you can talk about."

"That's not true. I don't talk about him all the time." She rises up into a sitting position as if she's rising from the dead. Even points an accusatory finger at me. "You're just mad because you've been gone and so much at Lancaster Prep is different now. Face it. You don't like change."

I return my focus to the mirror and start patting the highlighter into my skin with my fingertips. "You're right. I hate change."

"Well, then you're going to hate your senior year because *everything* is different." Iris sounds almost gleeful. I think she's enjoying this—torturing me over how things are all switched up at school. She'd never admit it, but she was a little jealous, a lot sad and plenty angry with me for abandoning her during our junior year of high school. That's the word she always uses—abandoned. Like I'm her deadbeat mom and I dropped her off on an orphanage doorstep. "You might freak out and feel like you're at a different school, but you'll be fine." She pauses. "Hopefully."

My cousin/bestie has always had a flare for the dramatic.

"Iris." I jump to my feet and whirl around to face her, resting my hands on my hips. "You have to stop holding my leaving you against me. I went to Italy. I was gone for almost a year and I missed you terribly, but now I'm back and we're together again. Please stop being angry with me over it."

The best thing about my relationship with Iris is how loyal we are to each other, yet we also can fight like sisters and make each other cry. I think we act like this because we're the same age and there are hardly any girl cousins in the family. The few that exist are a solid five years younger than us and we have nothing in common. As in, we can barely tolerate hanging out with them because they're so young and annoying.

Once we started at Lancaster Prep our freshman year and were in the same grade, Iris and I clung to each other and eventually became inseparable. No one talked about us in a singular way—it was always Iris and Willow. Or Willow and Iris. Until I applied for a foreign exchange program our sophomore year and surprisingly enough, got accepted. Oh, she was so mad at me.

I think she might still be.

"You know I love to hold a grudge." She's staring at the ceiling again, stretching her long, enviable body across the mattress. She's tall and lithe while I'm short with too big boobs. "Mom reminds me all the time that I'm just like my father and we all know how he is."

Grumpy. Quick to judge—but always willing to admit when he's wrong. Fiercely loyal and protective but once you wrong him, you're dead to him. Whit Lancaster is a man most don't want to cross. His children are basically the same way—all three of them.

"But my father always says Mom knows how to hold a grudge like no other so I'm doomed." Iris sighs. "I come from a grudge-holding, revenge-seeking set of parents. Whoever wants to tangle with me, they better watch out."

"Revenge seeking. Give me a break." I march over to my bed—we've shared a room at Iris's house since I was little—and grab a pillow, tossing it at her. It bounces off her forehead, making her laugh. She can never stay in a bad mood for long. "Come on already. Get dressed so we can go downstairs."

"Get dressed? I am dressed." She slides off the bed, effortlessly chic in a cropped white tank that shows off her tan and dark brown leggings that showcase how long her legs are. She slides her feet into a pair of furry Louis Vuitton slides and throws her arms out. "Dressed and ready to go!"

I sort of hate her.

No, that's a lie. I absolutely *adore* her. These are my own insecurities rising up and threatening to choke me.

We leave Iris's bedroom, her slides slapping against the sleek white marble floors extra loud as we head for the staircase. The sound echoes throughout the cavernous corridor and I'm surprised her mother isn't screaming at her to walk properly. I know I'm tempted to tell her just that.

"I'm starving," I murmur, thinking of all the yummy breakfast food Marta will have prepared. She's their housekeeper and we all adore her. She's been with the family so long that we consider her an honorary member and she acts like one too.

Always bossing us around and telling us what to do. We all roll our eyes and most of the boys talk back to her, but we all end up doing exactly what she wants.

"I ate an orange earlier." My side-eye is strong and aimed right in her direction, making her shrug almost helplessly. "What? I woke up at seven and couldn't go back to sleep. The light was so bright since you forgot to close the drapes last night."

"You have hands too, you know."

"I guess I was too excited to sleep any longer." Iris shrugs, shooting in front of me as she calls, "Race ya to the bottom of the stairs."

We run down the endless steps, but Iris shot ahead of me at the top, which means she's going to win. If my mother could see us now, she'd be furious. These are the very stairs where Sylvia Lancaster tumbled to her death—she was Iris's grandmother and her funeral was held on the day Iris was born so we didn't even know her. I've heard the family stories though. She was awful and abusive toward her daughter Sylvie, but no one really talks about her.

Typical. Iris and I are always griping about the family secrets and how no one will share them with us.

"You seem off this morning. Are you about to start your period?" Iris jumps from the second to the last step, her slides slapping the floor and echoing throughout the entire foyer. "We used to be synced up. One more thing we lost."

Her winsome tone is as good as any actor I've heard.

"Dramatic much?" I tease back, making her laugh. The sound of it warms my heart and I reach for her, locking her in a hug. She struggles to get out of it, but I won't let her go. I'm a touchy-feely Lancaster and she is most decidedly not. "Come on, let me hug you."

"Ew no. Hugs are for wimps." She starts to run ahead of me, those vaguely annoying—but very cute—shoes smacking on the cold marble floor. "Better hurry or you might miss breakfast. Marta starts clearing plates at nine-thirty!"

Ugh, she's such a liar. Marta's not the one clearing plates from the buffet table in the dining room. There are servants for that task and Marta is the one who manages them.

My steps slow at the thought and I sort of hate myself for having it. Being away from my family for the school year showed me how the other half lives—the term my mother used when I was first accepted to the exchange program and my father was dead set against letting me leave. I had to beg and plead and cry for him to finally give in and let me go.

I'm a self-admitted daddy's girl, which means I know how to get my way with him almost always, but convincing him to let me leave the country and live with another family for a school year? That was difficult. He didn't want me away from them for that long. He also thought I was too young, too sheltered, too…I don't know. Too naïve? He never said those words out loud, but I'm fairly certain that's what he was implying.

I am my mother's daughter in many, many ways, but I would never consider myself as naïve as she was. He would've been proud to see me hold my own while I was away, which I did. I learned a lot, and I pushed myself out of my comfort zone just by going there, and I'm proud that I lasted the entire school year. It would've been so easy to give up, to go home, but I refused. I wanted to have an experience on my own, without all of those Lancaster expectations attached to it.

It's really good to be back home though.

Eventually I end up in the dining room—all the breakfast food is still out, shocker—and I'm behind Iris as we fill our plates with fluffy scrambled eggs and colorful pieces of fruit. I also add one slice of bacon and a chocolate croissant while Iris ignores both items and we settle in at the table with a few of our cousins. Not a single parent is in sight. They all get up far earlier than we do and I'm sure the majority of them are outside already. The men are probably golfing at the nearby country club and Iris's mom is tending to the garden because that's her new favorite thing.

"Where's Row?" Iris asks me as she pops a square of honeydew melon into her mouth.

"He's heading back to campus today, remember?" My younger brother brought a friend along with him to the house, and from what I can tell they've had a great time swimming and hanging out together, but they're both on the football team and have to go back to school early for practice.

It's still unbelievable to me that Row plays football. That he actually wants to do it. Our family has never really been into competitive sports before, but I guess there's a first for everything.

"Oh right. Because of football." She digs into her food, practically shoveling endless pieces of melon into her mouth while I nibble on my single piece of bacon, mulling over my younger brother's choice to leave early. "He's really good at it, Willow. They've made him the quarterback and everything."

"I know—I've heard all about it," I murmur, still a little stupefied over the fact that Lancaster Prep now has a winning football team.

Look, our school is known for a lot of things. Only the elite of the elite have attended the private high school for hundreds of years, but the new headmaster has made a lot of changes since he took over, and he implemented those changes in a rapidly short amount of time. Like our sports department. We always had one, but it wasn't necessarily award-winning. Our lacrosse team did well years ago. Oh, and the girls' volleyball team always wins division championships.

But never football.

"The team is going to kill it this season." At my amused look, Iris huffs out a sigh and rolls her eyes. "You're such a snob. There's nothing wrong with going to a football game on a Friday night and screaming your guts out because you're so excited that we're winning."

"*We're* winning?" I repeat. "We had nothing to do with it."

"It's called school spirit." She smiles. "And the entire campus has it. Trust me, you're going to love the vibe when you come back. I know you will."

She's just trying to reassure me because as she already pointed out, I don't like change. I should've known some things would be different when I came back from Italy, but it turns out *nothing* is the same. My little brothers both grew like three feet—okay, a total exaggeration, but they are both so tall now—and from what I've heard so far, my school has changed a lot. Even Iris seems to be different. More mysterious. Which makes me wonder if she might be holding on to something that she doesn't want to tell me…

Or maybe that's just me being paranoid. I've definitely not brought up a certain someone because I'm worried over what she might say. Mom told me a long time ago when I was having trouble with a friend back in middle school that the truth hurts but sometimes, we need to hear it.

She's right. The problem? Sometimes I don't want to hear the truth, especially if it doesn't align with my secret wishes.

I remain quiet as we finish our breakfast, listening to the nonstop chatter from our younger cousins and siblings. Our family likes to get together for almost every holiday, Labor Day being no exception. Both Iris and I have brothers that are the same age, and Vaughn and Beau are talking about video games and a Marvel movie they went and saw yesterday afternoon. Then there's Prudence and Paris, Aunt Carolina's twin girls, who also went to the movie yesterday and keep trying to interject their opinions. The four of them won't stop talking and when Iris finally sends me a look, I know she's telling me she wants out of here.

August strides into the room just as we're pushing back our chairs, a look of complete disdain on his face when he sees the younger cousins sitting at the table. "You're leaving?" he asks his sister.

Iris nods. "You can hang out with them. I'm sure you'll have so much fun."

She knows her brother can barely tolerate anyone, even relatives.

"Fucking Christ," he mutters as he heads for the side table to grab some breakfast, his irritation coming off of him in palpable waves.

"He's so grumpy," Iris says to me. "I thought college would put him in a better mood but apparently he hasn't changed a single bit."

"Apparently," I agree, shaking my head.

We promptly exit the house, the younger cousins' laughter still ringing as we make our way outside, and the moment that I pull the door shut, there's nothing but blessed silence, save for the occasional seagull squawking as one of them flies overhead.

"God, our little brothers are annoyingly loud," Iris mutters as she heads toward the closest table. The bright white and navy striped umbrella is open above it, leaving plenty of shade, and there's a warm breeze blowing, making the ends of my hair dance. "Never any peace and quiet when they're around."

"I don't mind it," I admit. "I missed having so much family around."

Our parents seemed to make some sort of pact when they all started having children that they wanted to stay connected. When Iris's parents took over the Rhode Island house, the one that's been in the Lancaster family since basically the dawn of time, it was decided that it would become the family compound. The one central place where everyone got together for every family celebration and holiday. Throughout the summer. Spring break. All of it.

Iris and her family reside here full time and my family bought a house not too far after my youngest brother Beau was born. But our house isn't nearly as big as the original Lancaster estate.

"You missed all of us?" Iris ducks her head, her blue gaze meeting mine. She's got those Lancaster eyes, just like mine. Physically it's the only part of my father that I have. Otherwise…

I am the spitting image of Wren Lancaster.

"Of course, I missed everyone. Especially you." I lean into her, pressing my shoulder to hers.

"You didn't even come home until a week ago," she points out. "You were gone for what felt like forever."

"My parents wanted to travel all around Europe as a family for the summer." I shrug, remembering how upset my mother was when my brother Rowan insisted on going home early so he wouldn't miss football practice. He's only a sophomore, but the second he becomes interested in something, he takes it seriously. To the point of obsession sometimes.

It's the Lancaster in him, Daddy said. I suppose he's right.

"Did you have fun? Meet any boys on your trip with the fam?"

I slowly shake my head, wondering if I should tell her the boy I'm actually wanting already goes to our school and she knows him very well. "How could I? I was with my parents the entire time."

"No fun." She mock pouts. "Did you at least get to drink?"

"I turned eighteen when we were there, so yes. But I didn't get drunk or anything." My birthday is in July and we celebrated it in Paris, which was wonderful, but I missed my friends and the rest of my family.

I was eager to get home. I'd been gone long enough.

"I suppose it's not as much fun getting wasted with your parents." Iris sighs and I can't help but laugh.

"No, it's not much fun at all," I agree, laughing. "But none of that matters now. I'm home, we're together once again, and we're ready to have the best senior year of our lives." I smile.

Iris smiles too. "It's going to be epic."

"You really think so?" I hear the worry in my voice and I hate it. I shouldn't have a care in the world. I am a Lancaster, after all. I'm back on this campus where I belong.

"I know so." Iris's nod is firm, her eyes sparkling. "It's going to be amazing. Just wait until you're back on campus. You're going to love it!"

If she says so.

We hear clattering footsteps on the stairwell that leads down to the gardens and the beach just beyond it and two heads suddenly appear. One is my brother. The other is his friend that he brought with him.

Callahan Bennett.

"Iris!" Rowan shouts when he spots us. "Go to the front and entertain Rhett for a minute while we grab our shit."

Iris's brows shoot up. "What in the world is Rhett doing here?"

"Who's Rhett?" I ask, looking between her and my brother.

"Only the best quarterback I've ever witnessed in my life," Row proclaims.

Callahan smiles broadly at me. "Rhett's my brother. He came here to pick us up and take us to school."

"Please, Iris." Row makes a prayer gesture with his hands folded in front of him. "I'll owe you."

"Come on, Willow." Iris rises from the chair, sighing loudly. "Let's go meet the hottest guy on campus."

"Ew," Cal says as he walks past us, trailing after Row, who's already halfway in the house.

We enter the house after them, headed for the front, while the boys race up the stairs to grab their things, their heavy footsteps sounding like a herd of elephants barreling through the house.

"Who's the hottest guy on campus?" I ask Iris as we briskly walk through the massive living room, drawing closer to the front door. I can hear the blare of loud music coming from outside and I wince.

"You'll see," Iris says cryptically, stopping in front of the massive door and turning the locks before she swings it open and strides outside. "Rhett! Darling!"

Darling? What?

I follow her out onto the front terrace, shading my eyes from the sun. There's a car in the drive. A sleek white Porsche 911 with tinted black windows and a loud, rumbling engine. The driver's side door is cracked open and this Rhett person has one leg out with his foot braced on the ground, as if he's poised and ready to leap from the car at a moment's notice.

"Iris." His deep, commanding voice seems to tug at something low in my belly and I drop my hand, watching breathlessly as he emerges from the car, his hand braced on top of the door. Wow, he's tall. "Where's my brother and Row at? We gotta get going."

"Calm down, they're coming," Iris says with an unfamiliar laugh. I send her a strange look, but she's not paying any attention to me. "Where's your friend?"

Rhett appears genuinely confused. "Who are you talking about?"

"Brooksie."

"Wait a second—are you referring to Brooks Crosby?" I ask Iris.

She shushes me and I take a step away from her, annoyed.

"He's already at school. And he hates riding in my car. You know this. Says he's too big for it." Rhett laughs, the sound rich and deep, and I shade my eyes again because I can't make out a single feature, thanks to the blazing sun above our heads.

My heart stops as I drink in his handsome face. No wonder Iris is laughing and flirting with him. I would be doing the same thing if I knew who this boy was. He's tall, with golden brown hair that gleams in the sun, and while he's wearing sunglasses that cover up half of his face, that doesn't diminish his good looks. He's got great facial structure. Prominent cheekbones and a sharp jawline that is just begging to be kissed.

I shake my head a little at the thought. What in the world?

"Sorry, Rhett!" Callahan emerges from the front door in a full sprint, Row right behind him. They're both carrying unzipped gym bags that are bulging with clothing and a sock falls out of Row's bag, landing at my feet.

"Get your skinny asses in the car, pronto," Rhett demands, turning toward his seat and flipping it forward. "You can take the back, Cal."

"Aw, man." Callahan groans as he folds his lanky body into the back seat.

"Row, you forgot this!" I wave the sock above my head, grateful it's clean and doesn't smell like sweaty feet.

"I don't need it," Rowan yells as he rounds the front of the beautiful—and dangerous looking—Porsche.

I ignore what he says. I also ignore Iris, who asks me what I'm doing as I run down the steps without thought. Gravitational pull, I think as I approach Rhett. He's larger than life, bigger than I realized, and my gaze lands on his arms—his biceps in particular. He's got muscles for days and his chest is wide, that navy Lancaster Prep T-shirt he's wearing stretched to the absolute limit.

My breaths come faster and I skid to a stop, holding out the sock lamely. "This is my brother's."

Rhett slowly lowers his glasses down the bridge of his nose, blatantly checking me out with what looks like hazel-colored eyes. "Who are you?"

"I'm Row's sister." I wave the sock at Rhett again, feeling like a fool. "Can you give this to him for me, please?"

"Anything you want, pretty girl, I'll do for you," he drawls as he slides the glasses back up, covering his eyes.

"Jesus, don't flirt with my sister, Rhett!" Row screams from the passenger seat.

"Yeah, yeah. Whatever." Rhett completely ignores him, sliding his hands into his shorts pockets. "You go to Lancaster?"

I nod.

"Huh. With that gorgeous face of yours, I'd definitely remember you." A pained expression suddenly appears on his face. "Please tell me you're not a freshman."

"I'm not," I say with a breathless laugh, my heart fluttering at him calling my face gorgeous.

"Thank God," he mutters.

"I'm a senior," I tell him. "I was in Italy last year. On a foreign exchange program. But now I'm back."

Oh God, am I rambling? He probably doesn't care about any of that.

"Wait a minute." He snaps his fingers, pointing at me. "You're the infamous Willow Lancaster."

I blink at him, shocked he'd know me. "You've heard of me?"

"Everyone knows who you are—except for me. Looks like we need to change that." He grins, the sight of it blinding me worse than the late summer sun. He snags the sock from my grip, our fingers brushing, and I feel his touch all the way down to my soul.

Now I feel as dramatic as Iris.

Rhett climbs back into the car, tossing the sock at Row's face before he shuts the door. I take a step back, wincing at the roar of the engine. The tires squeal when he pulls out of the driveway and takes off like a shot, hitting the horn twice as a goodbye.

In a complete daze, I turn to find Iris watching me with a giant smile on her face. "Um. Wow."

She giggles. "Tell me all about it."

CHAPTER TWO

WILLOW

The morning air is downright crisp as I head for the auditorium where the first day assembly is being held. A breeze sweeps through the trees, making the leaves rattle, and I shiver inside my jacket, thinking of the other first days I've experienced at Lancaster Prep. They were always warmer, with the August sun blaring down, making all of us sweat.

Starting school a few weeks later than we used to is already bringing plenty of change, and I try my best to accept it.

Iris is walking beside me, keeping up a constant stream of chatter as she waves and speaks to almost everyone around us, but all I can do is nod and smile. I'm the quieter Lancaster, the more observant one. Iris is the social butterfly while I need to test someone out before I give in and share bits of myself.

Some may think of me as secretive or worse, aloof, but I can't help it. I'm not about to blab my business to just anyone. Having the Lancaster name makes it hard for me to trust people. I always wonder what their motives are when they try to get to know me.

"Where's Alana?" Iris asks, her question breaking through my thoughts.

"I haven't seen her yet." Alana Kirkpatrick is our other best friend. The three of us have hung out together all through high school and I can admit to myself that I was jealous when Iris would send photos and Snapchats and share stories of her and Alana laughing and screaming over something trivial and silly throughout the school year while I was gone. They looked like they were having fun—without me.

I missed them so much sometimes my heart would physically ache.

"How weird. She texted me last night asking me what I was wearing." Iris laughed. "I told her, 'um, the uniform?' Like we have a choice. But she was talking about accessories I suppose."

"She didn't text me." I'm frowning. That's what Alana and I have in common—a love for fashion. I was always her go-to when she needed an opinion on what to wear.

I'm almost a little offended she didn't reach out.

"Did I tell you that you look amazing this morning?" Iris is smiling at me and I can tell she's trying to change the subject.

"No, you didn't. And thank you." I do a quick twirl, my uniform skirt flaring out. I have the waistband rolled up because that's what we all do and Iris's skirt is even shorter than mine, so I don't feel bad.

"What was your inspiration?"

"I found this scrapbook my mom made a long time ago and the pages were filled with photos of my mom and dad. Polaroids mostly." I remember some of the photos that shocked me. Of my dad shirtless with lipstick kisses all over his back. His chest. His face, his neck. Mom's face turned red when I brought the scrapbook to her and asked about it and she even took it from me, stashing it in her closet.

I won't mention those particular photos to Iris.

"Oh yeah? Your mom is such a fashion icon."

She still is and she was as a teen too. "The uniforms were pretty much the same back then, but she'd always wear a bow in her hair and Doc Marten Mary Jane shoes." I kick out my feet. "You can't find them in that style anymore, but I thought these

Mary Janes were cute."

They're Chanel and they're adorable because of course they are—Chanel is my mother's favorite fashion label.

"Cute. Love the knee-high socks too."

"My mom didn't do the knee-highs. I had to put my own spin on it." Instead of wearing my hair down, I have it in a high ponytail with a white satin ribbon tied in a bow at the base. "I wanted to rock the same vibe, but make it my own."

"I'm liking the red lip too." Her smile is knowing as she points at my mouth. "You never wore such a bold color before. Are you trying to get Silas's attention?"

I press my red lipstick-covered lips together, hopeful I'm not blushing. Finally, she says his name out loud. Silas. Silas Fortner. My sixteen-year-old self was madly in love with him. Well, maybe not *love* because that's a strong word and emotion, but I definitely had a huge crush on him for almost the entirety of our sophomore year, and I thought he felt the same way about me.

Oh, at first he was completely oblivious. I don't know how he didn't see it because I pretty much followed him everywhere, laughed extra loud at his jokes, and always tried to sit next to him during lunch, during class, in the library, any chance I could get.

Eventually, he started to notice. We would talk. Conversations in the hall, or in class. Sometimes after school. We started hanging out together during lunch sometimes, which Iris barely tolerated because I don't think she likes him that much. We'd even message each other at night, especially toward the end of our sophomore year. We'd send each other funny memes or videos, but it never went beyond that. We weren't confessing any sort of feelings toward each other, and he never asked me to do anything with him, like a date. I'd hoped he was into me, but nothing ever happened.

Like…nothing at all.

He's nice. Polite. Handsome. Comes from a good family and that's important to me. For whatever reason, I always found myself clamming up every time I was around him though. Like I would stutter and everything, which Iris thought was just hilarious.

I can't wait for her to fall head over heels for some poor soul. She claims no one interests her, but I don't know. I think she likes to throw up walls and pretend nothing affects her because she wants to protect her heart. I might do that too, but in a different way—she's bold where I'm hesitant. Loud where I'm quiet. I let some people—a particular person—get too close, and then he disappeared. Iris wouldn't have let him get close in the first place.

"You think it's too dark?" It's a classic red shade from Chanel that my mother has always worn, and since we have the same coloring, she told me it would look good on me and I believed her.

Now Iris is making me self-conscious. I'm not one to wear such a bold color so this feels like I'm making a statement, which I guess I am. I haven't been here for a year and now I've returned. Iris and I plan on fully ruling this school, but I don't know. Maybe I've lost some of my power because I've been gone. People might've forgot all about me.

"I love it. It looks good on you." We both pause as she reaches for me, rubbing at the corner of my mouth with her thumb. "You had a tiny smudge."

"Thank you," I murmur just as we approach the double doors that lead into the auditorium. Plenty of other students are ahead of us and we're all in a line, shuffling inside. "I hope this assembly doesn't last too long."

"They're not dry and boring like Matthews' speeches were, so don't worry. It's going to be fun." Iris hooks her arm through mine and we eventually enter the cavernous auditorium. She drags me to the senior section and we settle into the front row, dead center, practically having to crane our necks to see the stage directly in front of us.

"Couldn't we sit a couple of rows back?" I glance over my shoulder, doing a double take when I spot Silas ambling down the walkway, heading straight toward us.

I quickly face forward, my cheeks going hot, my heart starting to race.

"What's wrong?" Iris glances in the direction where I just saw Silas, but she keeps looking, not really saying anything at all.

"Stop staring at him," I practically hiss at her, embarrassed. "Please."

Her gaze shifts to mine and I see the uncertainty there. Alarm bells start going off in my brain. "What is it?"

"Um…you'll never believe this, but." She bites down on her lower lip for a brief second. "Alana just appeared at Silas's side and now they're…holding hands."

I whip my head around to catch Silas and Alana walking side by side down the aisle, my gaze dropping to their connected hands. Their interlocked fingers clutching tight. I lift my gaze to their faces, noting the way Silas is staring at her, a dazed expression on his face. As if she's the most beautiful thing he's ever witnessed in his life.

My heart crumbles into a million tiny pieces. Seriously?

Seriously?

"Did you know about this?" My voice squeaks. My heart pounds. God, if Iris knew all this time and never told me…

"No, of course not! You know I would never keep something like that from you. I had no clue. She pretty much ghosted me the last month of the summer, but I figured she was out of town. I only just heard from her last night." I glance over at Iris to find her staring them down with narrowed eyes. Her Iris-is-pissed expression is in full force. "Did she conveniently forget you had a massive crush on him and that you two were talking?"

"I've been gone for a year."

"Doesn't matter. She stole your man." We both turn in our seats and face forward. "If she even dares to sit close to us, I'll—"

"You'll what?" I rest a gentle hand on Iris's arm, noting how tense she is. "Are you going to beat her up for me? Come on, Iris."

"It's such a bitch move on her part." Iris shakes her head. "What kind of friend does that?"

I barely look over my shoulder just in time to watch them sit to the right of me, three rows back but still in the senior section. She won't even look in our direction, though I'm sure she saw us. Silas is oblivious, too enamored with Alana to care. He's currently reaching out to touch her cheek, but she bats his hand away.

My heart hurts for him, which is dumb. But I would never push away his touch. I would welcome it. Revel in it because that's all I want. To find a great love like my parents did when they were in high school. To find someone who falls so madly in love with me, he can't see anything else. And I'd feel the same exact way. Just completely gone over him. That's what I want more than anything else, and I believed I could find it with Silas. I guess I was wrong.

Silas being with Alana doesn't necessarily feel like a betrayal. No, it's more like a revelation. It's obvious he wasn't the right guy for me. My heart still aches at the loss though.

"It's okay. I'm not going to blame her," I say as a sense of calm settles over me. "Like I said, I was gone. I didn't expect him to wait for me. He was fair game. He didn't even know I had a crush on him."

"She knew how gone you were for him, though. You wasted all of your sophomore year wishing he'd notice you," Iris complains, crossing her arms and slumping in her seat.

Some of this past year too, even while I was in another country, but I can't dwell on that now.

"What's done is done. I wish them well." I straighten my shoulders and lift my chin, hoping I appear as if I don't have a care in the world. Doing my best to hide the turmoil currently swirling inside me.

If I'm not going to spend my senior year with Silas as I'd hoped—oh what a silly little girl I was, and that's a difficult realization to have—then I guess I'll spend it with friends, which isn't a bad thing. And it's not that I need a boyfriend to make me happy. I've never had one in the first place, but it would be nice…

Disappointment floods me and I mentally push it aside. I don't need to get depressed over Silas's new relationship with my friend. I should've known nothing was going to happen between us. He never contacted me when I was in Italy beyond the occasional like on a social media post. Once I was out of sight, I was out of his mind.

It does hurt though, what Alana has done. I thought we were friends. She was my closest friend after Iris. Now I'm not even sure I can trust her, let alone remain friends with her.

Iris starts talking to the girl sitting next to us and while I smile and nod and pretend to keep up with the conversation, my mind, and my gaze, are wandering. Scanning all of the male faces that fill the auditorium, trying my best to stick to the ones closest to me since they're in my grade.

While I see a few familiar ones, there aren't a lot of boys sitting with us, which is…odd. Where are they?

"Where is everyone?" I whisper close to Iris's ear just as the curtains start to pull back, revealing the new headmaster standing behind a podium, a giant smile on his enthusiastic face as he throws his arms up at the same time loud music begins to blare through the giant speakers flanking him on the stage.

"If you're meaning the boys, just wait," Iris tells me out of the side of her mouth when she starts to clap. She even yells along with everyone else. The entire auditorium erupts into cheers, which I don't think I've ever seen happen at Lancaster before.

I guess she wasn't lying.

The school definitely has a new vibe going on.

CHAPTER THREE

RHETT

We're waiting on the side of the stage, me in front of the rest of the football team since I'm their QB. My younger brother Callahan is behind me and I can hear his big mouth rambling on like he does, but I don't tell him to shut up, which is my usual response when I get sick of his nonstop talking.

I'm not about to start a fight with him in front of everyone. There's no point. Besides, he's chatting up his new best friend Rowan Lancaster and considering that kid's family owns the damn school, I'm not looking to start any trouble. Talk about rich…

My mind shifts to that massive house I picked them up at. Most everyone who goes to this school is from real money that's generations old. My family is wealthy, but we've got nothing on the Lancasters. And then there's Row's sister.

Gorgeous. Long, silky dark hair. Big tits. Wide eyes that gobbled me up while she held out that stupid sock. I wanted to yank on her hand, drag her into my car and take her with me, but I repressed the urge. I had more important things to take care of that morning.

Like football.

Tugging at the front of my jersey, I look down, glaring at the khaki uniform pants I still have on. At my old school we could wear whatever we wanted along with our jerseys during game days or when there were rallies. I come to this fancy prep school and it requires uniforms on a daily basis. Still can't get over the fact that I go to this damn school and this is my second—and final—year here. Thank God.

Someone bumps into me and I send him a dirty look, which has the kid panicked and apologizing. I don't remember his name—he's new to the organization and a sophomore. We've got a junior varsity team this year so I don't deal with them as much as I used to. Every single one of these guys standing with me though, they'll do pretty much whatever I say. It wasn't easy, taking command of this newly rejuvenated team, but I eventually won them over.

"Stop scaring the JV team," Brooks says out of the side of his mouth. He's my closest friend at this school and we make a great team on the field. He's the best wide receiver we've got and the one I like to throw the ball to more than anyone else.

"They need to calm the fuck down," I mutter, shaking my head, glancing over my shoulder yet again, my gaze narrowing. They go quiet, even Cal, and once I'm satisfied with their behavior, I face forward once more, eager to get this rally over with and get on with my day.

I know exactly what helped me take over the team and become their leader, despite only transferring to this school last year. It's my last name, and the fact that my dad is a former NFL QB and is now a coach for an NFL team. I come from a long line of football players. Like it's fucking crazy how many are in my family, in the bloodline, including my own father. He married into it, but the Callahans are a powerhouse of football and have left a legacy that reaches generations.

I hope to be one of the stars of the new generation, and my little brother does too. We didn't actually believe playing at this stupid, snotty-ass prep school would be the answer, but I've gained so much attention thanks to attending Lancaster Prep and being on their football team, it's kind of wild.

And awesome. Totally awesome.

"Wish Westscott would introduce us and get it over with," Brooks mumbles and I silently agree with him. Though I can't deny our headmaster knows how to hype the team up.

I rest my hands on my hips, waiting for Westscott to run through his happy first day of school spiel. He goes hard, boasting about his efforts to turn Lancaster Prep around and bring more school spirit to our campus. He even gets everyone to yell, "Go Lions!" on repeat.

The football team yells it right along with them, high fives all around, and finally, it's our time to shine.

"And now, let's give a hearty welcome to our league champions, the Lancaster Lions football team!"

I give the signal and we all run out on stage, crowding around Westscott, me still in the front, Brooks just to my right. The headmaster detaches the microphone from its stand to say, "Here's our team captain and quarterback, Rhett Bennett. Give us an update on the team, Rhett."

Westscott thrusts the mic in my face and I lean forward to speak into it since I tower over the dude. "We've been practicing like crazy and we're ready to take the team all the way to the state championships this year, sir."

"That's the spirit!" Westscott screams, making the entire auditorium scream along with him.

I gaze out at the crowd, seeing so many of my classmates yelling and clapping and whistling. I scan the first row, locking in on one girl in particular who's watching us with a confused look on her face.

Her brows are drawn together, her deep red lips pursed. She's got long, dark hair pulled into a high ponytail that shows off her delicate bone structure and I don't want to look away.

It's like I can't.

Goddamn, she's beautiful.

I know the exact moment our gazes actually connect because

it feels like a bolt of lightning shot straight through me, fiery hot and settling in my balls. I stare at her, Westscott's booming voice growing distant, the screaming crowd now nothing but a dull roar.

I recognize her. Rowan Lancaster's sister. She tilts her head to the right, her ponytail swinging, and I'm gripped with the image of me grabbing hold of her hair and tugging her head back, kissing the fuck out of her.

Blinking, I pull myself out of my stupor and say something into the mic that's suddenly in my face again. Whatever it was I said, it's got the crowd yelling even louder, and I tear my gaze away from the girl, realizing she's sitting right next to Iris.

She's cool. Cousin to Rowan. Probably the most popular girl in my class and completely untouchable. Not like we talked much last year, but we had a couple of classes together. I like her as a friend, but that's it. She's too blonde for me to ever be interested.

I'm surrounded by blondes. My sister Kenzie is a blonde and so is my mom, and I'm just like…nah. I prefer dark-haired girls.

Like Rowan's sister, who's studying me blatantly, her brows still drawn together like I might confuse the shit out of her. I wonder if she felt that bolt of lightning too when we locked eyes. If she's electrified as I am. It's like I can feel every part of my body—every hair standing on end, the blood pumping through my veins, my heart throbbing in my chest.

I flex my fingers. Shake my hands out and tilt my head to the left, then the right, savoring the satisfying sound of my neck cracking. Westscott is giving me an odd look, unsure of what I'm doing, and without warning, I swipe the mic right out of his hand and stride toward the front of the stage, standing almost on the edge of it.

Directly in front of her.

"We're going to dominate this season! By the end of the year, everyone in this country will know who the Lancaster Lions are. I guarantee it!"

Everyone leaps from their seats. Even Iris. It's like my words pushed everyone right over the edge and they've all lost their damn minds.

Except for her. She's still sitting in her seat, clapping lightly, her head turning to the left, then the right, the confusion remaining in her expression. The applause is obligatory but does she even know why she's clapping? I'm guessing no.

Our gazes lock yet again and I smile at her. She doesn't smile back, but she keeps watching me with those big, startling blue eyes. Just before I look away, her lips curve up the slightest bit, not showing any teeth. A Mona Lisa smile if I've ever seen one.

Never understood that saying before until this very moment. This girl is mysterious. I may know her name, but I want more.

And I'm going to make it my mission to find out every little thing about her.

CHAPTER FOUR

WILLOW

"What did you think?" Iris asks once we've finally exited the auditorium with the rest of the students pouring out. "Can't help but get swept up in the school spirit, am I right?"

My nod is reluctant, as are my feelings, which I can't even explain. "It's definitely something."

Iris's steps slow and I can feel her staring at me, but I refuse to look at her. "Seriously, Willow? You didn't like it?"

"What do you want me to say? That I'm a Lancaster Lion until the day I die?" My sarcastic tone makes me laugh, but I clamp my lips when I see the look on Iris's face. It's obvious she's displeased with my reaction.

"Well, you're exactly that. We're more Lancaster than anyone else on this campus. Shouldn't we show that we have school spirit?"

"It's just so…rah rah, go team." I shake my hand in the air like I have a pom pom in it. "That's never been my thing. That's never been our school's thing either."

"It is now," Iris says firmly. "And I think it's fun. We needed things shaken up around here after having Matthews in charge for so long. He wasn't one for change."

"True." I don't want to talk about it anymore. I'm afraid I'll just offend her further and right now, I need as many allies as I can get, considering I feel like I might've lost one. "What do you think is going on between Silas and Alana?"

As if conjured up by my question alone, the crowd parts ahead of us and I see them. Walking hand in hand yet again, Alana glances up at Silas, laughing when he says something to her.

Curiosity courses through me and I wish I knew what he told her.

"I hate to say it, but they look pretty serious to me." Iris touches my arm lightly, and I know she's trying to comfort me, which I appreciate. "Forget him. Forget the both of them. How dare she pretend I don't even exist when she gets a boyfriend? I'm still pissed about it."

"I would be too, but maybe she just got wrapped up in—him." I get it. I would ditch all my friends and spend every waking second with the boy of my dreams too. I just didn't figure one of my best friends would steal him from me.

What am I even thinking? Not like I owned him. He wasn't mine to steal. Maybe in my mind he was, but that's it.

"Still shouldn't ditch your friends for some guy. Boyfriends only last so long. Friends are forever," Iris points out.

"You're right," I say, my mind drifting to the football player on the stage, the one who showed up at the house a few days ago. He stared at me like I was a tasty steak and he was craving red meat. "Rhett Bennett is pretty popular, huh?"

Iris goes right along with my subject change. "Definitely."

"His jersey number is one? Isn't that…arrogant?" I wrinkle my nose. I don't really understand how numbers are chosen for team sports, but if the guy is walking around with the number one on his jersey, I'm thinking it could go to his head.

"His dad is a retired quarterback, but now he's a coach. His dad's number was always number one. He's just following in his father's footsteps," Iris explains.

"How do you know this?"

"Row told me. If you spend any amount of time with your

brother, you find out all he wants to talk about is football."

He wasn't like that at all last year. It feels like everything has gone haywire and nothing's the same. It's so weird.

"Rhett is a great football player, much like his dad according to Rowan. Rhett took the team all the way to the league championship, but they lost in the playoffs. He's popular, too. Flirts with every girl on campus, including me," Iris continues. "You saw how he was a few days ago when he came to pick up his brother and Row."

I did. Touching him was electrifying. Having him watch me so carefully from where he stood on the stage was much the same. Like a shock to my system. Not that I'm anything special. He just has really good flirting skills.

"I did," I confirm, not wanting to delve too deeply into it. "He flirts with you too, huh?"

"Nothing beyond flirting," she reassures. "He's not my type."

I think about his handsome face. Sharp jaw and cheekbones, lush, kissable mouth. I think of the photos I found of my parents and the kiss marks all over my dad. Embarrassing, yes, but also…

Rhett is extremely good looking. And for whatever reason, I can imagine doing the same thing to him that Mom did to Dad. Lipstick stains all over his face. Weird considering I don't know him at all, but it's there, lingering in my brain. Teasing me.

"Why isn't he your type? You don't like football players?"

"Nope." Iris lets the *P* pop. "Why are you asking anyway?"

"No reason," I say way too quickly.

Iris catches on because of course she does. "Wait a second. Are you suddenly into football players, Willow?"

"No, of course not. He just—he looked at me when he was on stage," I admit, my voice hushed as I glance around. I don't want anyone to hear, but no one is really paying attention to us.

"Oh yeah?" She bumps her shoulder against mine. "And how, exactly, did he look at you?"

Like I was the most beautiful girl he's ever seen. As if he was undressing me with his eyes. "Like he was trying to figure me out."

"Maybe he couldn't place you at first. You two did just meet after all, and did you even tell him your name?"

"No. I don't know. I can't remember."

"That must be it then. He has so many girls throwing themselves at him. You're just one more face he's trying to recognize." She laughs.

Iris sounds perfectly logical and I just nod, trying to push him out of my thoughts. I need to focus on my new classes. My schedule in Italy was so lax compared to here. I never felt like I was behind, but we definitely focused on subjects that we rarely study here.

The program I was accepted into had a section that was solely devoted to art. Roman art. Medieval. Renaissance and Baroque art. We traveled all over the country, visiting various museums and art galleries, and I was in absolute heaven. That is why Mom convinced my father to let me do it. She's just as into art as I am, and my grandmother too. It was so much fun, but now, I'm back to work.

Iris and I already compared schedules the minute we got them, and we don't have first period together so we part ways and I head toward the building where my honors English class is. Iris is in college prep English since she's more of a science and math girlie, which works out nice for the both of us. We're always helping each other out with our classes.

I missed that last year. It'll be nice to be back into my normal routine. One more year here.

And then the possibilities are endless.

When I enter the classroom, I stop short, my gaze landing on Silas and Alana sitting right across from each other in the middle of the rows of desks. Alana's gaze catches mine and she offers me a tight smile and a tiny wave.

I wave back, mouthing the word hi, and turn on my heel, stumbling and losing my footing. My face goes hot as I realize in a split second that I'm falling. I want to die of mortification, especially when I land in someone's lap.

A male someone's lap.

"If you're trying to catch my attention, it worked." His voice is deep and delicious and makes my stomach twist in anticipation.

I jerk my head up, my gaze meeting twinkling hazel eyes. A knowing smile spreads across his face and I leap out of his lap, not even sure how I managed to fall into it, but oh my God, I so did.

"Sorry," I mumble, scurrying away from Rhett Bennett and collapsing into a desk in the next row over, across from his.

He swivels in his seat, and I don't look up from my task, though I can feel his gaze on me, hot and intense. I'm unzipping my backpack and pulling a notebook out, hoping he'll look away. Hoping Silas and Alana didn't witness me falling on him. There aren't that many people in here yet, including the teacher, and maybe everyone will forget this ever happened.

"Wanting to sit next to me, huh, new girl?" Rhett asks.

A wave of giggles fills the room and I finally dare to glance up to find him still staring at me.

He ditched the jersey and is now wearing the requisite school uniform. His tie is crooked and loose around his neck, the white shirt wrinkled. The blue jacket clings to his shoulders, emphasizing how wide they are, and when my gaze finally meets his, I can see the amusement there.

My heart sinks into my stomach. I'm funny to him. Like I'm a joke. He probably loves that I fell into his lap. Might even think I did it on purpose.

He pats the desk directly behind him. "Sit with me."

I slowly shake my head.

His disappointment is obvious. He even rests his hands over his chest, like he might be clutching his heart. "Come on, new girl. Do me a favor."

"I'm not new," I murmur.

He leans forward, as if he's trying to hear me. "What did you say?"

"She said she's not new." I'd recognize that voice anywhere, and I sort of want to die. “She’s a Lancaster, dumbass.”

It’s Silas.

Glancing over my shoulder, I send him what I hope is an evil glare before I turn forward, clearing my throat. “I was gone last year. Part of a foreign exchange program.”

“I remember you telling me that.” Rhett doesn’t seem affected at all by Silas calling him a dumbass, which was really…cruel of Silas to say. “You’re Row’s sister. We met a couple of days ago.”

“Right.” I frown. “I must not have been that memorable if you already forgot me.”

“I didn’t forget you. I was just teasing.” His gaze is warm and his expression is kind. Maybe he really was teasing me.

“Oh.” I swallow hard, not knowing what else to say.

“For a sophomore, your brother is pretty good. I’ve been giving him tips since he’s a quarterback like I am.” Rhett contemplates me, his gaze roaming, and my skin grows warm all over from his blatant examination. “We talked about you.”

My heart falls. God, what did they say? What did Row tell him? We haven’t talked much since we returned from our European vacation. The moment he came back here, he was all about practice. We talked some on vacation, but we haven’t had any deep conversations like we used to.

There’s a distance with Rowan and me that started when I left for Lancaster Prep to start high school. He came to campus last year while I was gone, so this is the first—and only—time we’ll be at Lancaster Prep together during high school. Meaning, right now, Row almost feels like a stranger. Things are happening in his life that I’m not privy to and I wish we were closer.

“Come sit by me, Lancaster.” Rhett’s tone is inviting and for a moment I’m tempted.

But I remain rooted in place, unable to move. It would probably be a mistake, sitting closer to him. Aren’t I close enough already?

“Don’t do it.” Again, this comes from Silas and I turn around in my seat to face him, noting the way Alana is watching our interaction, annoyance filling her gaze. “He’s just toying with you, Willow.”

Like you did with me, is what I want to say to Silas, but I don’t. “I’m a big girl,” I reassure him with a sniff. “I can handle myself.”

I shift my attention to Alana, whose expression turns faux friendly the moment our gazes connect. “Willow, it’s so good to see you back.”

Her voice is warm, but her eyes are dead. Like she’s merely going through the motions versus actually meaning what she says.

“I sent you a text when I got home,” I remind her. “You never responded.”

And that hurt. She was avoiding me and I didn’t know why.

Now I do.

“I’m sorry. I’ve just been *so* busy this summer.” She shares a quick look with Silas before returning her attention to me. “Want to catch up at lunch?”

“Actually, I would love to,” I say just as our English teacher Mrs. Patel enters the classroom at the same time the bell rings. I turn to face forward once more, not looking in Rhett’s direction, though I can still feel him watching me. Can almost sense the disappointment he’s experiencing because I didn’t rush to sit next to him.

I don’t even know him. Just because he’s attractive doesn’t mean I’ll do whatever he wants when he snaps his fingers. I need to play it cool, which I’ve never really had to do before. I’m just… who I am, accept me or not. With Rhett though? It feels different. If I act like I’m into him, he might blow me off because from what I’ve seen and heard, lots of girls are into him. No way do I want to be just another girl who has a crush on Rhett Bennett.

I want to stand out.

CHAPTER FIVE

WILLOW

By the time it's lunch period, I've already filled Iris in on Alana joining us, and she's all fired up.

"I have a few questions for her myself," she mutters as we enter the dining hall. "Though she probably won't like what I have to say."

"Please don't start a fight." Iris's personality default is fiery and she's always ready to argue at a moment's notice while I avoid confrontation.

"I don't want to fight with her. I just want to ask her why she avoided me most of the summer, especially after we spent so much time together during school. It was rude." I know Alana's disappearance hurt Iris's feelings too.

We both get in line for the salad bar, Iris ahead of me.

"It was totally rude," I agree, validating her feelings. "But maybe there were other things going on in her life."

I'm all for trying to figure out why someone behaves the way they do. Sometimes it's nothing personal. They've got their own problems they're trying to deal with and it affects their relationships. Friendships. Whatever.

"I sent her texts, Willow. Multiple times. Or I'd send her funny TikToks like we always used to do, and when summer first started, she'd respond, but eventually, she ignored me." Iris tosses lettuce into her empty bowl like she's mad at it.

"Well, please don't attack her. We don't know what was going on in her life. Let her explain herself first."

Iris shakes her head. "I don't know how you can be so calm about it. It's obvious why she avoided us—she was too busy with Silas. Meaning, she did you dirty, hooking up with him. They're a bona fide couple, you know. Bronwyn told me."

"Who's Bronwyn?" I've never heard Iris mention that name before.

"Oh, we became friends last year. She's a junior. Really sweet. She has Spanish with Alana during second period and she asked her about Silas. Alana basically told her everything," Iris explains, her tone casual.

I remain quiet, my mind turning over what my cousin said. I want every stupid detail about Alana and Silas, but then if I ask for all of those details, I'll look like I care. And I don't.

Not really.

Okay, I care a little bit but only because I'm curious. I think anyone in my position would feel that way, right?

By the time we find a table to sit, I feel like I'm going to burst. I can't take it any longer.

"What exactly did Bronwyn tell you about Alana and Silas?" I tap the edge of my salad bowl with my fork, my stomach twisted up in knots over what she might reveal.

So stupid, but I can't help myself.

"That they got together at the beginning of summer, right after school ended. Silas supposedly approached her, but I don't know if I believe that. According to Alana, they've been inseparable ever since." Iris stabs at the lettuce, gathering up as much as she can on her fork before she shoves it into her mouth.

"Since the end of junior year then," I say, my voice soft, my brain calculating how many months that is. It's simple math—three months, give or take.

"They're serious. That's what Alana told Bronwyn," Iris says after she swallows. "She could tell that Alana was all gaga and in love. Like, barf, right?"

"Right." My voice is distant, my lunch forgotten as I spot Silas and Alana together in line to scan their meal cards for their lunches.

If Alana brings him over to our table, I don't know what I'll do. It was weird enough what he said to me during English. Warning me off Rhett Bennett, which was odd. What does he care who I'm talking to?

It shouldn't matter to him. *I* shouldn't matter to him.

They part ways once he drops a kiss on her cheek and Alana's striding toward us, an overly bright smile on her face as she sets her tray onto the table and pulls a chair out, plopping into it. "Hey, guys!"

Her enthusiastic voice grates and I put on my best smile, though it feels more like I'm baring my teeth. It's not even close to genuine either. "Hi, Alana."

Iris says nothing and I have to kick her under the table to get her to respond. "Oh." She sniffs. "Hi."

A sigh leaves Alana and she slumps in her chair. "I know you're mad at me, Iris."

"You do? Then why didn't you text me like two months ago, hmmm?"

Here we go, Iris starting a fight when I asked her not to. I push my salad bowl away, knowing I'm going to be starving later, but I can't eat. Not right now.

"I don't know. I guess I just got—caught up in Silas. If you were in a relationship, you'd understand." Alana shrugs, and I can tell she feels superior to us because she has a boyfriend. That's so lame. "I'm sorry. It wasn't very nice of me to ignore you."

The surprise on Iris's face is obvious. I'm sure she wasn't expecting an apology so quickly. "You're right. It wasn't."

"I know. And like I just said, I'm sorry. I didn't mean to hurt you." Alana's expression is contrite as her gaze shifts to mine. "I'm sorry I didn't reach out to you either, Willow."

"It's okay." I shrug, wincing when I feel Iris's loafer kick into my ankle.

I glance over at Iris to see her glaring at me, most likely for saying it's okay so quickly. I'm too forgiving, according to her, and I'm sure she's right. But I can't help myself.

"It's not just that." Alana presses her lips together for a second before she says, "I should've warned you I was dating Silas."

The sentence just sits in between the three of us like a bomb about to detonate. I don't say anything and neither does Iris. Neither does Alana. We're silent for so long I can tell Iris can't take it any longer.

"It's serious between the two of you, then?" Her tone is downright hostile. All on my behalf, I might add.

"Um, yeah." Her cheeks turn pink. "I think I'm in love with him."

Ouch. Like a stab to my heart. Not that I know what being in love with someone feels like, but the crush I was nursing for Silas throughout our sophomore year was pretty intense.

"And he's in love with you?" Now Iris sounds like she's full of disbelief.

"Well…yeah." Alana glances around before she leans over the table, her voice lowering. "We've already done it. Like, a lot."

"Done what?" I ask, blinking at her. Playing dumb on purpose.

"Seriously, Willow?" Iris nudges my foot with hers again and I shift away from her, not wanting to get bruised. "She means they've had sex."

"Oh my God, I know, Iris. I was just teasing." My gaze finds Alana and her expression is nothing short of concerned. "I'm happy for you."

"Happy that they're having sex?" Iris asks, sounding incredulous.

I send her a measured look before I turn my attention to Alana.

"That the two of you are together and in love. You deserve it."

"Are you sure?" Alana winces, and I realize in this moment that she's known exactly what she's done from the start. It didn't matter that I liked Silas first. I wasn't around last year so she was going to go for it. "I know you crushed on him big time. Like since we started high school."

I laugh but it sounds false so I stop. "It wasn't for that long."

"Only sophomore year," Iris adds.

Now it's my turn to kick her, making her grunt in pain.

Good.

"The whole year though," Alana says, and she's right because we were hanging out together all the time. She would know and remember all of that, I'm sure. "And he never did a thing about it."

I'm frowning, a hint of anger rising inside of me but I tamp it down. "What exactly are you implying?"

"Yeah, what are you trying to say, Alana? Because if you ask me, it sounds like you're being kind of shitty right now." Iris sends her a hard glare and in this very moment, I love my cousin more than anyone else I know.

No one else has my back like Iris does.

"Oh, I don't mean to be shitty at all!" Alana rests her hand on her chest, her eyes wide. Like she's innocent, but I don't know.

Iris is right. She's being a little gross.

"It's just that if Silas actually liked you, Willow, he would've done something about it, right? Because that's what he did with me." That overly bright smile is on Alana's face again and I sort of want to smack it off.

And I'm not one to resort to violence. I leave that to other members of my family. Like Iris. Both of her brothers. My little brother, who can have a nasty temper sometimes.

"Are you trying to tell us that you're oh-so-special and we're not? Because seriously, what's so special about Silas?" I ask, my tone vaguely snotty.

I clamp my lips together, dropping my gaze to the tabletop

for a brief moment. I shocked myself by saying all that. And I can feel Iris's amusement. I'm surprised she's not blatantly laughing.

Alana's eyes narrow and I know I pushed her too far, but I couldn't help myself. "Why don't you tell me since you wanted him so badly for the last two years of your life?"

My jaw drops. Did she really just say that?

"Okay, this is getting hostile, Alana, and I thought you were our friend." Iris stresses that last word extra hard. "Maybe you should take your petty ass away from this table and leave."

Alana jumps to her feet, her hard gaze sweeping over the both of us. "I knew I was better off staying away from you two. You're nothing but a guard dog, Iris. Always watching out for your weak cousin and, Willow, why don't you grow a pair for once in your life and actually form a personality? You're boring."

With that, she grabs her lunch tray and marches off. Heading straight for Silas, no doubt.

"Did you hear her just now? What the hell? A guard dog? I mean, I don't even think that's an actual insult but whatever." Iris resumes eating her salad, the fork action still vaguely stabby and violent. "What a bitch."

Alana's words run through my head on a continuous loop. According to her…

I'm weak.

I have no personality.

I'm boring.

"Do you think I'm boring?" I whisper.

Iris's expression turns incredulous, her fork clattering in the now mostly empty bowl. "Boring? Absolutely not. You're one of the most interesting people I know."

She's just saying that. She has to say that because she is my cousin. We're blood. Practically sisters.

"Uh huh." I push my salad bowl farther away from me, until it's practically in the center of the table. "I hate everything she just said."

"She's a bitch," Iris says vehemently. "And she knows just how to get under your skin because we've been friends with her for so long."

"Alana wasn't that mean toward you. She only called you a guard dog," I point out.

"Because her real beef is with you."

"I don't fight with anyone."

"Don't be dense, Willow. This is about Silas. I'm guessing the only reason she's acting that way toward you is because for whatever reason, she's insecure about her stupid relationship with him and wants to keep you away from him. Talk about boring." Iris actually snorts, slouching in her chair and crossing her arms in front of her. "They deserve each other because they're both so pathetic."

"I appreciate you standing up for me all the time," I say, my voice still soft, my thoughts all over the place.

Iris watches me and I know she can tell I'm stressing out. "Don't let what she said bother you. Seriously. I didn't know being in a relationship would turn her into such a witch."

"She's awful," I agree, grabbing my backpack before I stand. "I think I'm going to go to the library."

Iris sits up straight, but I see the misery on her face. She's not a fan of the library or books, which I don't really get. "You want me to go with you?"

I can tell by her tone that she doesn't want to go, but she'll do it for me. And I'm realizing she does a lot for me. After being on my own for almost a year in a foreign country, I come back to Lancaster Prep and fall right back into my old habits. They probably weren't such great habits either. Maybe Alana is right. I need to learn how to stand on my own two feet.

"I think I need some alone time." I offer Iris a reassuring smile. "But thanks."

"Don't dwell too much on what she said. I mean it, Willow. She was just trying to be mean, and look—it worked."

"Okay, sure." I walk away before she can say anything else, gripping the strap of my backpack extra tight as I exit the dining hall.

First day of school and I'm already miserable, which was not what I expected. I figured I'd be welcomed back with open arms. Everything would be the same, and Iris and I would be on top of the world. Living our best lives as seniors—finally.

I've been waiting for this moment since I started high school, and instead it's all different. I've lost a friend—and she stole the guy I had a crush on, which she knew.

Meaning, she knew what she was doing. Alana probably went after Silas on purpose. And if that isn't the bitchiest thing ever...

"Hey, Willy!"

I come to a stop at the familiar male voice, pausing in the middle of the walkway, waiting for that same voice to say something else. He doesn't disappoint.

"Where you going in such a hurry? Lunch barely started."

My eyes fall closed for a hot second and I count quickly to five before I open them and slowly turn around to face who's questioning me.

It's Rhett. Sitting on top of one of the picnic benches that are in the quad just outside the dining hall, a big grin on his handsome face. He's shed the uniform jacket, clad in only the white button-up and he's got the sleeves rolled up. Revealing tanned, strong forearms dusted with golden brown hair.

I stare at those stupidly attractive arms for a moment too long and when I finally lift my gaze to his, I see the smirk on his face. Like he knows what I'm doing.

How embarrassing.

"Never call me Willy again," I tell him, my voice flat. Realizing I sound rude and I just dealt with someone who said awful things to me, I immediately gentle my tone. "Please."

His smile doesn't slip whatsoever. "Isn't that your name?"

"No one calls me Willy." I hesitate. "Like ever."

"Why not? I think it's kind of cute." His tone turns flirtatious and I almost roll my eyes. "Though your full name is cute too. Willow."

My heart squeezes at hearing him say my name and I tell myself I'm being ridiculous. This boy is nothing like the type I'm usually attracted to.

"Willow is such a long name though," he continues, and I brace myself for insults. How is Willow too long? Just because his name is only one syllable, what? He can't handle two? "I think I'm gonna call you Will."

I wrinkle my nose. "That's a man's nickname."

"There is nothing manly about you at all, Will. Trust me," he drawls.

My skin tingles at the way he's looking at me, his gaze roaming everywhere. All over me. "No one has ever called me that before in my life."

"Really?" He sounds surprised. "Well, I guess it's my special nickname just for you, then. And I don't do that for just anyone."

"He doesn't," says the guy sitting next to him. It's Brooks Crosby. I've gone to school with him for what feels like my entire life. He's just always there in the background, and he's perfectly nice. "This is kind of a big deal."

Rhett slaps him in the shoulder. "Don't tell her that. She'll get a big head."

"No, I definitely won't." I smile and I wonder what in the world I'm doing flirting with this boy.

"Being a Lancaster and looking like you do, you don't have a big ego, Will? Really?" He sounds like he finds that hard to believe.

"Looking like what?" I ask, my voice faint. Is he complimenting me? Am I so pathetic I need to hear him praise me further?

Yes. Right now, with the verbal beating I just took, thanks to Alana, I definitely do.

CHAPTER SIX

WILLOW

Anticipation ripples through me as I wait for him to say something. Anything. Feels like I'm hanging on the edge of a cliff at the moment, which is silly.

Of course, Rhett takes his time. As if he knows he has me dangling by a thread, just dying to hear him compliment me.

I am not this girl. I don't think I've *ever* been this girl. The one who needs validation from a boy in order to feel better about herself, but I'm hurting from Alana's casually cruel treatment and wondering if she laughed at me with Silas.

That hurts. More than I'd ever care to admit.

"Do you really need me to tell you?" he finally asks, his brows shooting up. They're darker than his hair, which is a golden brown, though not as light as the hair on his arms. He's a mass of various colors. "You look in the mirror every day, don't you?"

Disappointment fills me and I can't help but sigh. "Right. Sorry." Why did I just apologize? I'm only making things worse.

I turn on my heel, ready to walk away with my virtual tail tucked between my legs because this is embarrassing.

"Hey, whoa. Where you going, Willy?" I can hear him calling out to me, which only makes me walk faster.

But then I hear footsteps coming up behind me and next

thing I know, he's touching my arm. The moment his fingers make contact—even through my jacket and shirt—my skin sizzles where he touches me. I jerk away from his hold and turn on him, the ball of anger growing inside my chest about ready to burst out of me.

"Oops, I mean Will," he corrects, no doubt after he saw the feral look in my eyes. "Why'd you take off?"

"Our conversation was going nowhere." I offer him a wan smile, trying to play off the fact that not even five seconds ago I was furious at him.

My emotions are all over the place. I need to take a couple of deep breaths and regain my composure.

"You wanted to hear me tell you how fucking beautiful you are, right?" His tone is so serious, as is the look on his face.

I suck in a sharp breath, startled by his brutal honesty. The curse word. I'm used to bad language because both of my brothers are the worst, which they get from Dad, but I'm more like Mom. She rarely uses foul language and I'm the same.

I'm also not used to gorgeous boys making such bold statements about…

Me.

"I…" The words die on my lips and my entire mouth goes dry.

"It's true, you know. That you're beautiful." He takes a step back, shoving his hands in his pockets. "You should come watch me practice sometime."

I'm frowning. I can feel the crease between my eyebrows deepen. "Is that a thing?"

"Watching me play? It's definitely a thing. I promise you won't be disappointed." He grins.

The ego on this boy…

"I don't know if I have time." I shrug, trying to play this off. And really?

Watching him play football sounds boring.

"You should try and fit me into your busy schedule." His smile is faint, just a gentle curve of one side of his mouth, not revealing any teeth, and I can't help but smile back. "I'll make it worth your time."

"You don't even know me..." My voice drifts and I slowly shake my head, a huff of laughter escaping me. "Who put you up to this?"

The smile fades. Now he's frowning. "What are you talking about? Put me up to what?"

"Talking to me."

"Nobody put me up to anything. Maybe I wanted to." His frown deepens. "What, are you trying to tell me that guys at this school don't talk to you?"

I shrug, feeling helpless. Wishing I had Iris with me.

No. I don't need Iris to have a conversation with a boy I don't know. I can do this on my own. I don't need my "guard dog" taking care of me all the time.

"They're idiots," he mutters when he realizes I'm not going to give him a verbal answer. "You're like, the hottest girl I've ever seen on this stupid campus."

My cheeks go hot and he notices.

"I'm serious," he tells me. "I mean, look at you."

"There is nothing special about me," I murmur, and he actually bursts out laughing.

I stand there, waiting for him to finish, but he just keeps laughing. To the point that I start to feel uncomfortable and I'm shuffling my feet. Ready to make my escape when he finally says, "You look pretty fuckin' special to me."

"Is that a compliment?"

"Definitely."

"Are you—flirting with me?"

"If you can't tell, then I'm doing a shit job of it." He grins.

My heart trips over itself.

"Willow! There you are!"

I turn to see Iris making her way toward us, her eyes full of curiosity at finding me talking to Rhett.

"Hey," I say weakly to my cousin, scared her appearance might make him leave.

Though maybe that's a good thing. My stomach is currently tied up in knots over this weird conversation.

"Rhett, leave my cousin alone," Iris tells him, her tone faintly teasing. I send her a dirty look, though she doesn't even notice.

"No harm in me talking to Will here." His smile reaches his eyes and they're sparkling when they meet mine. God, he's handsome. He has a nice smile. Straight white teeth. "See ya later this afternoon?"

"Maybe," I tell him, nibbling on my lower lip.

"A girl of mystery. I like it." He starts walking backward, heading away from us, his gaze never straying from mine when he says, "See you around, Lancaster."

He finally turns and strides away, his steps brisk.

Iris remains quiet until there's plenty of distance between us and Rhett before she finally says something.

"What was that about?"

"Nothing." I start toward the creative arts building, where my next class is. The lunch period is practically over anyway so I may as well head on over. "We were just—talking."

"Flirting?"

That single worded question fills me with disappointment. The fact that she automatically assumes he was flirting with me tells me he does this often. "Not really."

"He's a giant flirt. Player. Whatever you want to call it. Just watch out for him. He's already got a reputation." Iris laughs, shaking her head. "He had one within the first couple weeks starting here last year."

"Seriously?" I don't want to know anything about this.

All lies. Of course, I want to know.

"Yep." Iris nods.

"Did he date every girl on campus or what?"

"The minute he showed up, all of the senior girls were on him. You know how it is when there's new meat." Iris rolls her eyes.

I sort of do. I experienced it myself when I first arrived at the school in Italy. Plenty of the boys were interested in me, but that wasn't my intention when I was there. I was all about being a serious student, learning more and focusing on my classes. Oh, and making friends, which I did.

Get a boyfriend though? Not really. I had a few makeout experiences with boys when we would go out to the nightclubs, but nothing major. No boy made me feel all shivery inside—those kissing sessions were more exploratory and I was always worried I was doing something wrong. When I tried to explain it to Iris, she told me I was too much in my head, and I'm sure she's right.

I've never had a kiss that made me forget all my thoughts. Where I could just lose myself and…feel.

"Rhett went out with a bunch of senior girls?" I try my best to keep my voice causal. Like I don't really care, even though I totally do. I want all the details. Why, I'm not exactly sure. To torment myself?

He's not my type, but he is pretty to look at.

"I don't know if I would define what he did with all of those girls as 'going out.'" Iris makes air quotes and she knows how much I hate that.

"What do you call it then?"

"Hooking up? Fucking around? Getting laid?" Iris starts to laugh, no doubt thanks to the horrified expression on my face. "Stop acting like a prude."

"I'm not a prude." My face is warm and I wish I wasn't so prone to blushing. "I just can't believe he would hook up with so many girls."

"You know how rumors can be. The number is probably inflated. He's really charming though. Like, he knows just what to say." We slow our steps as we draw closer to the building. "You know we've never discussed in depth what happened when you were in Italy."

"Trust me, it wasn't that big of a deal." I shrug. "You know pretty much everything that I did."

"Did you have sex with anyone over there?"

"What?" I swivel my head left and right, making sure no one is nearby to hear her ask that question. "No. Of course not. You'd be the first person I told if I did."

"I was kind of hoping you were keeping a dirty little secret." Her disappointment is obvious. "What a bummer."

"Did you—have sex when I was gone?" I'm whispering so low I can barely hear myself.

"Nope. But I might've messed around a bit." Her knowing smile tells me she definitely messed around.

"With who?"

"I can't tell." She practically starts to run away from me. "See ya after school!"

I watch her go, letting my curiosity get the best of me about everything. Who did Iris hook up with and why wouldn't she reveal his name? She's being so secretive and it's a little shocking, considering we normally tell each other everything.

Not that I've said much to her either since I've come home. I just haven't gotten the chance yet, though I don't have a lot to tell.

Ugh. I'm boring. Just like Alana said.

As I make my way across campus, I can't stop thinking about Rhett Bennett's playboy reputation and how many girls he might've possibly hooked up with. The way he flirted with me. Calling me Willy. Hated that. Telling me I'm fucking beautiful—didn't hate that part one bit. But who does that? Is he just saying that sort of thing to get in my panties or does he actually believe it?

I rush into the building and head straight for the girls' bathroom, relieved to find it empty when I enter. I stare at my reflection in the old, slightly foggy mirror, trying to see myself through Rhett's eyes.

All I see is the same old me. I have a few stray tendrils flying around my head and I turn on the faucet, wetting my fingers before I smooth them back into submission. My lipstick is long gone, faded to a faint red that doesn't look great, and once I've turned off the faucet, I'm rustling through the front pocket of my backpack. Finding what I'm looking for, I open the Chanel lipstick my mom gave me for my birthday and slick it on my lips, rubbing them together when I'm done.

There. Much better.

I'm okay. I know I'm not a hideous troll, and sometimes, when I put a lot of thought and attention into my outfit, I can look pretty. Fashionable even. When I was in Italy, I was photographed a few times, especially when I went to the Milan fashion shows with my mother. Some of the headlines declared me the next "it" girl.

Whatever that means.

It's like I returned to Lancaster Prep and I became lazy again. We don't need to put much effort into anything since we wear the same uniforms day in and day out. I don't feel like I'm anything special here. I'm definitely not an "it" girl. Being stuck at a boarding school with everyone else wearing the same thing humbles you real quick.

By the time I leave the bathroom, the corridor is filled with students heading to their next class and I grab my schedule out of my backpack, checking for my room number. I push my way through the crowd, slipping into the classroom at the last second, right as the bell rings and the teacher strides in directly behind me, slamming the door.

I breathe a sigh of relief as I fall into the closest available desk, dropping my backpack at my feet. I bend over to unzip the top and pull a notebook out when I hear that same familiar voice whisper my name.

"Will."

And when I look up, my gaze locks with Rhett's. He's sitting right next to me.

Great.

CHAPTER SEVEN

RHETT

Fuck me running, how did she do that? She actually looks even better than she did only a few minutes ago when we were talking. Flirting.

Whatever you want to call it.

She's extra hot with the red lips and the slicked-back dark hair. That damn ponytail swinging, tempting me to grab hold of it and wrap those silky strands around my fist. It's so long, I bet it would wrap around twice…

"You're taking this class?" she asks, her voice breathless. Her brows are drawn together and she's frowning slightly. Like maybe she's not thrilled at the idea of me being in another class with her.

"Definitely." I lean back in my seat, blatantly checking her out. The skirt is a little short, showing off her slender thighs and smooth knees. She has pretty legs. I've always been more of an ass man, but I'll convert for Willow Lancaster.

"Photography and film making?" Now her brows are shooting up in question.

"Thought it would be an easy A." I shrug. May as well be truthful with her. "Is that why you're taking it?"

"Noooo." She draws the word out, shaking her head. "It fits right in with what I want to do in college."

"And what do you want to do in college?"

"I want to major in art history."

"This class is more about making history than studying it," I point out, feeling the need to keep up this conversation. The teacher is still at his desk, shuffling through papers, so I'm making the most of this moment.

"I'm hoping it'll help me cultivate my eye." I must give her a look because she further explains herself. "My artistic eye. Like how I see things. Photography definitely hones your view and makes you look at the world in a different way."

I'm nodding along with her, but I've never thought of photography that way. I've heard the teacher prefers we use our phones to take photos and film stuff, and he gives mostly A's as long as you turn in your assignments on time. Talk about easy. Everyone raves about this class and how you can coast right through it.

I need that. Every easy class I could find at this school, I've taken. Sometimes I still can't believe I'm here, but my parents convinced me and my brother that this would be a good move. At my previous high school, I never got a chance to play football much because it was such a big team and ultra-competitive, from the students to the parents to the coaches. Everyone wanted to go there because the team won championship after championship—eight out of the last ten seasons. That's fucking huge.

Being on that team was stressful as hell. There were three quarterbacks that were older and better than me. And I was second-string QB on the JV team because the number one guy was the little brother of the first-string quarterback on the varsity team.

It was bullshit. I knew it. My dad definitely knew it. When Mom suggested I go to another high school, I was reluctant at first. Then Dad took a job coaching an NFL team on the East Coast and it sort of fell into place. This has turned out to be the best move for my future as a football player.

Because I will have a future playing football. I'm working my ass off to ensure it, and last season we almost took it all the way.

This year, we're on track for more. I can feel it in my soul. We're going to be state champions if I have anything to do with it. And considering I'm the team captain and the QB, we're gonna make it happen. Coach Turner demands nothing less than excellence, and the way we've looked during practice, we're going to deliver.

"Your artistic eye, huh?" I finally ask, realizing that I haven't responded to her yet.

She nods, the ponytail swinging. A constant temptation. "Yes. Definitely. But I'm sure you don't want to hear me ramble on about art."

I could listen to her sweet voice all damn day if she wanted to keep talking to me. "I don't mind."

"You're humoring me. It's okay." She waves a hand and twists her body so she's facing toward the front of the class. "I know I can be boring sometimes."

My mouth drops open and I'm ready to tell her she's the furthest thing from boring to me, but the teacher starts talking, effectively ending our conversation. Willow isn't even paying attention to me any longer. Her focus is one hundred percent on the teacher, which means my focus is one hundred percent on her.

Boring. Does she really believe that? I wonder if someone said that to her just to try and tear her down. Maybe some jealous bitch who views her as competition because…yeah.

There is nothing boring about this girl. All that long dark hair I'd like to see down. The deep blue eyes and red, red mouth. Her lips are currently parted as she hurriedly scribbles something down in her open notebook and I realize I've got nothing out. Not a piece of paper, not even a pencil.

First day of school we don't really take notes—at least I don't. All the teachers pass out a syllabus and go over expectations. Isn't that good enough? Especially in a class like this. It's not about note taking and written tests. We'll have to turn in photos and extremely short videos. How hard can it be?

Leaning forward, I tilt my body to the left, drawing closer to her so I can peek over her shoulder to see what she's written so far. Her handwriting is perfect of course. I can read it clearly.

Willow catches me spying on her notes and sends me a faint dirty look. "What are you doing?"

Her whisper settles right in my balls. I'm not even deterred by the vague irritation I hear in her question. "Making sure I'm not missing anything."

The person sitting in front of Willow hands her a syllabus at the same time I receive one too. And on that syllabus is the same thing Willow already wrote down.

"I guess I don't need to take notes. It's all here," Willow seems to murmur to herself as she scans the class expectations and upcoming assignments.

"You sound almost disappointed."

She says nothing. Just keeps reading the syllabus.

"You coming to my practice today?"

Willow shoots me the quickest look. "Probably not."

"You should."

"Why?"

"You can watch me." I thrust out my chest. She'll want to watch me. I'll put on a show just for her.

Well, and all the other girls that'll probably be out there. But everything I do today will be only for my new friend Will.

"I don't think so." Her tone is haughty. It kind of turns me on. "I've got other things to do."

"Better than watching me play?"

She turns her head, her gaze meeting mine directly. "Definitely."

I rest my hand on my chest. "I'm wounded, Willy."

"I told you not to call me that." She sends me a death glare.

"Do you have a question for the class, Miss Lancaster?"

Oh damn. The teacher just called her out and from the look on her pretty face, she doesn't like it.

“I’m fine, Mr. Chen. Just answering a question that he had.” She jerks her thumb in my direction.

“Well, Mr. Bennett, do you have a question for me?”

“No, sir.” I shake my head, sitting up straighter.

The teacher moves on, turning off the lights and turning on the overhead projector to explain the various parts of an iPhone camera compared to an Android.

A snooze-fest. Though Willow seems totally into it, her expression enraptured as she stares at the image shown on the white board.

“You’re really enjoying this, aren’t you?”

She shushes me, which only makes me want to talk to her more.

“Maybe you should come to my practice and take photos,” I suggest.

“I’m not going.”

“You’ll be there.” I say this with complete confidence. She might not show up today, but she will.

Eventually.

Damn, I really do love a challenge.

“No, I won’t.” She won’t even look at me and I’m tempted to get in her face, but that’ll just piss Mr. Chen off and I don’t feel like dealing with him.

“You’ll regret it if you don’t show up,” I practically taunt.

“Doubtful.” Her lips curve upward though, like what I said was funny.

“Hey, it’s your loss.” I lean back in my seat once again, kicking my feet out. She’ll show up.

They always do.

CHAPTER EIGHT

WILLOW

Of course, I don't go to his practice. Why would I? I'm not about to become a total fangirl. I don't even know this guy. Not really.

But after school, I do walk by the field to see what's going on.

The first thing I notice is how many girls are already sitting in the stands, watching the football team play with stars in their eyes—I can practically see them from where I stand. Their phones sit idly beside them on the bench, unless they're taking photos of the boys scrambling around like chickens on the field.

And the longer I watch everything unfold, the more I notice that the girls do that a lot—take photos of the boys playing. Or they take selfies together, making sure they get the team on the field behind them because I'm guessing it's a flex, to hang out and watch them practice? It makes no sense.

I pause for a moment, focusing my attention on the boys out on the field. I have no idea what they're doing, and I've never really cared before either. I don't pay attention to sports. My father watches football sometimes—even more now because of Row being on the team—but I couldn't tell you who his favorite team is. Does he watch college football or professional? I have no clue. It never really mattered before.

Rhett removes his helmet and I watch as he faces the stands, his head slowly moving like he's scanning the crowd. A few girls wave at him and when he waves back, it hits me.

He probably invites every single girl he talks to to come watch him play. Talk about arrogant.

I push away from the fence and hurriedly walk away, heading back to my dorm suite, battling the disappointment swirling within me. For a second, I thought maybe, just maybe, I could be special, but I'm not.

Not to Silas. Not to Rhett.

Not to anyone.

• • •

The next day in Honors English, I try my best to keep to myself, but I can feel his presence the moment he enters the room. The air shifts, filling with an electric warmth that seems to radiate toward me. The temptation to turn around and see if he's there is strong, but I resist the urge.

Barely.

Remaining still, I focus on the blank page of my notebook, startling when I feel a gentle tug on the end of my ponytail.

I whip around, ready to say something, when I spot the forlorn expression on Rhett's face. The words die on my tongue. He looks downright…sad.

"You didn't come to practice," he accuses, sliding into the desk directly behind mine.

Oh, come on. He had an entire fan club out there supporting him.

I part my lips, unsure how I might explain myself, but he keeps talking.

"I looked for you and everything, but you weren't there."

The retort escapes without hesitation, as if I have no control over it. "I'm surprised you noticed, considering there were so many girls in the stands."

The smile that spreads across his face is blinding. Oh, he's so pleased with himself. "You were there."

I lift my chin, hating that I just ratted myself out. "I walked by the football field after school."

"Uh huh." He doesn't believe me, and I suppose I can't blame him.

"You didn't need me there—you had enough support." I turn back around to face forward, wishing the bell would ring.

Silas and Alana enter the classroom, Alana's gaze meeting mine before she rises up on tiptoe and kisses Silas on the cheek.

"No public displays of affection in class, Miss Fitzpatrick," Mrs. Patel chastises.

I send a quick smile to the English teacher before I duck my head, pleased that they got in trouble.

"I still missed you," Rhett says from behind me.

Turning my head to the side, I murmur, "I'm not so sure about that."

"It's true. I really wanted you to watch me play."

"It sounds boring."

He scoffs, leaning forward. Close enough that I can stare into his eyes and see that they're shot through with little strips of green. "You wouldn't be bored watching me."

I go still, momentarily mesmerized by the look on his face. The words he just said. Having his entire focus on me is the slightest bit disconcerting.

"Big ego much?" I blink at him.

He settles back in his chair, smirking. "Just stating facts."

"It must be nice living such a delusional life. Believing you're just that amazing." The sarcasm is thick, but he barely acknowledges it.

"I'm not delusional, Will. I just know what I'm capable of."

"And what exactly are you capable of?" I arch a brow, something I've practiced in my mirror for years before I somewhat perfected it.

"Impressing you."

The bell finally rings and I face the front of the room once more, clutching my hands together, those two words running through my mind on repeat.

Impressing you.

He's full of it. He has to be. I cling to what Iris said about him yesterday. He's a giant flirt. He's obviously arrogant and thinks he can do no wrong. And that anyone will do what he says. All he has to do is ask.

A streak of pride runs through me. I didn't do what he asked, and I can't help but be proud of myself. I bet girls fall at his feet every time he flashes that magnetic smile in their direction, but not me.

Not that I'm special or above everyone else, I just…I don't have time to deal with someone like Rhett Bennett. I don't like arrogant boys, which is kind of funny because they run rampant all over this campus.

Maybe that's why I was drawn to Silas. He's quiet and kind and never boastful—at least to me. I don't remember a single moment where he bragged or showed off in front of me. Not like Rhett.

That's all he does. That's all he's ever done since the moment I met him.

I feel something jostle one of my chair legs and I glance down to find Rhett's legs stretched out, his loafered feet on either side of the chair. I'm half tempted to kick him out of the way, but I refuse to acknowledge him, even violently.

"The first book we're going to read this semester is *The Great Gatsby*," Mrs. Patel announces, holding up a copy of the book.

Oh good. I've never read that one.

Rhett groans behind me, the sound closer than I expected. "Snooze fest."

"There's a stack of books on a table in the back of the classroom," Mrs. Patel explains. "I'll release you by rows to go pick up your copies."

I wait with nervous anticipation to go grab my book, offering Alana a smile when she walks past me to return to her desk, but she looks away, her lips curled in the faintest sneer.

Okay then.

"Damn," Rhett mutters.

I frown at him and he shrugs. "She snubbed you."

"She definitely did," I agree.

Our row is finally released to go grab our books and I slowly rise from my desk, shocked to find Silas at my side. Since he sits in the same row, I suppose I shouldn't be surprised at all, but I figured he'd avoid me like Alana just did.

Rhett seems to be waiting for me, his gaze roving over Silas, his lip curling with disgust.

"You have a good first day of school yesterday?" Silas asks me as we sail right past Rhett, heading for the table of books.

I nod, telling myself this means absolutely nothing. Silas is just being his usual, kind self. "It felt weird, being back."

"I bet. We're all glad you're here, though." Silas's smile grows and he reaches out to grab a copy of the book from the table, handing it to me.

"Thank you." I clutch the book to my chest, wanting to say more. But my gaze shifts to where Alana sits to find she's already watching us.

And she doesn't look pleased.

"You don't want that copy."

I turn to find Rhett standing in front of me, thrusting a less battered copy of the book toward me. "This one doesn't have a ripped cover."

"Oh." I glance down at the book I'm holding to see that the cover is barely hanging on. "Thank you."

Rhett takes the book Silas gave me and tosses it on the table, placing the newer copy in my hands. "You're welcome."

The two boys glare at each other while I stand in the middle and I study Silas's face.

Then Rhett's.

It's obvious they don't like each other, but why?

"Silas! Come here," Alana demands, breaking the tension.

He does as she bids, scurrying back to sit across from her, and she leans over the aisle, her lips moving rapidly. I wish I could hear what she was saying.

"Those two deserve each other," Rhett says.

"You don't like Alana?" I ask him.

He grabs his own copy of *The Great Gatsby*. "I don't know her."

"Then why would you say that?"

"I don't like the way she treated you." We start walking back to our seats, Rhett just behind me. "And he acts like he might like you a little too much for a guy who has a girlfriend."

"We're just friends—" I start, but Rhett speaks over me.

"Nah. I know when a guy is into a girl. He's into you." Rhett falls into his seat while I carefully sit down in my mine, tucking my skirt under my butt, my mind filled with nothing but riotous thoughts.

Silas shouldn't like me. He's got Alana. They have sex all the time—and that's a direct quote from her. Why would he be interested in me? I, for one, haven't had sex with anyone, so Alana has got me beat on experience. And supposedly they're madly in love?

I am seriously so confused.

• • •

At lunch, it's just me and Iris sitting at the table at first, and I'm trying to work up the courage to ask her the questions that have been lingering in my mind for hours since Rhett said what he said.

"Do you think Silas is happy with Alana?"

Iris grimaces. "I guess he is. According to her, they're having sex nonstop, and what boy wouldn't be happy with that?"

"Right." That's the same thought I had. "That makes sense."

"Why are you asking anyway? Please don't tell me you've still got a crush on him. I hate to be mean, but you're wasting your time."

I lean in close and explain everything that happened today, leaving out the part where Rhett said he wanted to impress me. I want to hold on to that moment privately for a little while longer.

"Maybe he's talking to you to make Alana jealous," Iris suggests when I finish speaking.

"I suppose so, though that doesn't seem like something Silas would do." I chew on my lower lip, wishing I could read minds. Wondering for about the hundredth time why Silas never made a move on me.

Wondering even more why he chose Alana.

"You don't know him that well, Willow," Iris points out. "Don't forget you were gone all last year. I'm sure he's changed."

I hate believing that he's changed that much, but I suppose she's right. "Oh, I definitely won't forget. You won't let me."

Iris leans her shoulder into mine. "And then there's the fact that Rhett said what he said."

"What do you mean?" I sit up straighter, my gaze going to where he's sitting outside in the quad. I can see him perfectly through the window, and he's laughing at something one of the boys is saying to him, his attention going to the window. It's like our gazes meet even through the tinted glass and he stares for a moment too long, the smile fading.

He can't see me. There's no way.

"I think he likes you, and I understand why. He doesn't know you at all."

"What are you implying? He'll get to know me and not be interested anymore?" Is that what happens with boys? Are they drawn to me because of my family name and then once they realize what I'm about, they lose interest?

My heart pangs. The realization is…painful.

"No, of course not! I was referring to you being…new meat, for lack of a better term," Iris explains.

I wrinkle my nose. "Gross. And I'm not new meat."

"You are to him," she points out. "And I'm guessing he finds you entertaining."

"Entertaining? You make me sound like a show he enjoys watching." And I don't think anyone has ever described me as entertaining before. Not my parents. Not my friends or my family or teachers.

"A pretty girl Rhett hasn't seen around campus is definitely entertaining to him." Iris laughs when I send her a withering look. "It's okay though. He's harmless."

"You warned me yesterday that he's a player," I point out.

"Right, but Rhett is like a…harmless player. He's a fun guy. Not a serious bone in his body. Life is fun and games for him and he's just here to enjoy it," Iris says.

"Yeah, I could kind of tell." My gaze lingers on Rhett. He's not staring through the window any longer and I forget all about my lunch. I watch him, curiosity running through my blood, making me wish I could talk to him more, which I can.

Next period.

CHAPTER NINE

RHETT

I watch Willow Lancaster pause in the doorway of our class, seemingly scanning the room. I take note of her uniform, and how she's put her own spin on it. All that lush, glossy dark hair is pulled into a ponytail again with a dark blue ribbon looped into a bow. She's got her jacket on and it dips in at the waist, the buttons undone, almost showcasing the fact that her tits strain against the front of her white shirt.

The girl has got curves for days. I curl my fingers into a fist, fighting the urge to go to her and touch her. If I even made the attempt—hell, if I merely mentioned it to her—she'd most likely flip the fuck out and tell me to kiss her ass for all eternity.

And why does that have such an appealing ring to it?

The bell rings, jolting her of the seeming trance she fell into, and she takes a step forward, stumbling a bit when a couple of dudes barge through the door, knocking right into her.

I leap to my feet and rush toward her, glaring at the dumbasses who pass by me.

"Watch the fuck out." I growl at them before turning my attention to Willow. "You all right? Did they hurt you?"

When I touch her sleeve, she takes a step back, like she needs the distance. I let my hand drop, my gaze sweeping over her to make sure she's in one solid piece. "I-I'm fine. It was no big deal."

"You almost fell." I lighten my tone, telling myself to chill out. "You keep doing that around me."

"I don't know why I'm so clumsy." Her smile is shaky. "Thank you for watching out for me."

"No problem. I got your back, Will." I glance around, my gaze touching on everyone already seated at their desks, most of them blatantly watching us.

Willow notices too. "We're causing a scene."

"Who cares?" I shrug.

She starts walking and I keep pace with her. "I do. Like I said, it was no big deal."

Without another word, she settles into her desk, her backpack landing by her feet. She bends forward, that ponytail swinging as she unzips her backpack and pulls out her notebook and a set of colored pens and highlighters.

Damn, this girl is serious. It's a photography class for Christ's sake. Why does she need to take that many notes and make them fancy?

Because she's a fancy chick. That's her deal. A beautiful, rich but prissy girl who wants things to look a certain way, and I'd bet big money she'd expect whatever guy she's with to act a certain way too.

That's not me. I don't conform to anyone. I am who I am and I know sometimes I can be a lot.

Scratch that, I know most of the time I'm a lot, but my parents never tried to stifle me or expected me to act like someone I'm not when I was a kid. If anything, they indulged my individual quirks. My dad is pretty outrageous. That's part of his charm. Anyone who knows my dad even in passing has something to say about him.

I want that too. Not that I want to be a duplicate of my dad, but I want to be memorable. I don't want people to forget me.

Most of the people who go to this school are like Willow. Wealthy beyond anything I've ever witnessed or lived with. And my family is rich. My dad is a retired NFL quarterback who made millions back in the day, but we've still got nothing on a lot of the families whose kids go here.

Especially the Lancasters.

But I don't let any of that bother me. I can hold my own with this group, and pretty successfully. I know I'm a solid football player and they've never seen anything like me play for their school team. Lancaster Prep was known for being an elite high school that only the richest of rich attend. They focused on academics but never sports. Not really. Not until Westscott became the new headmaster and changed things up.

And brought me in.

Mr. Chen starts talking, droning on about landscapes and catching certain light. I shift in my seat, already bored, and when I glance over in Willow's direction, I realize she is too.

Her head is bent, her chin almost touching her chest, the ends of her ponytail sliding around the side of her neck. Her rosebud lips are parted and her eyes are closed.

Is she…sleeping?

I watch her for a few more seconds and she doesn't move a muscle, save her chest rising and falling with each breath she takes. Little Miss Studious is definitely asleep. And I find that oddly…

Cute.

"You all seem a little distracted this afternoon so why don't we go outside and I can show you what I'm talking about?" Mr. Chen announces. There's a lot of shuffling as everyone starts to move, save for Sleeping Beauty right next to me. "Bring your backpacks. I doubt we'll go back to the classroom before the bell rings."

Nice. I prefer being out of the classroom anyway. Being stuck at a desk and not able to move for fifty minutes sucks big time.

People are rising to their feet, grabbing their stuff. Chatting loudly as they all start heading out of the room, following Mr. Chen. Only when someone laughs does Willow startle, lifting her head and glancing around the room in confusion.

I'm standing right next to her desk, waiting for her to notice me. And when she does, the puzzled look on her face is almost funny. But I don't laugh. I don't think she'd like that.

"What's going on?"

"We're headed outside. Chen's gonna show us what he's talking about versus just give us a boring lecture." I nod toward her backpack. "Grab your stuff."

She glances down, her movements slow as she reaches for the strap of her backpack.

"Mr. Bennett? Miss Lancaster? Are you coming with us?" Mr. Chen lets his irritation bleed into his tone. Grumpy asshole.

"We're coming," I answer for the both of us.

Willow scrambles, sliding out of her desk almost too quickly, and I swear, she's gonna fall again. Luckily, I grab her arm, my fingers curled around her elbow, keeping her steady. She sends me a grateful look, shaking her head at herself. "I don't know what's wrong with me."

"You were napping, Sleeping Beauty." I try to keep most of the amusement out of my voice because I don't want her to think I'm making fun of her.

"I was not." She sounds downright indignant. "I don't fall asleep in class."

With that final statement, she starts walking, heading for the door. I'm so dumbfounded by her response it takes me an extra second or two to launch into action, but once I do, I'm chasing after her, surprised at how fast she is.

"Here's the thing," I say once I'm right beside her. We're all walking down the hallway toward the double doors that are on the east side of the building. Willow and I are the last stragglers behind everyone else, and no one is paying attention to us. Not even Mr. Chen. "You were sleeping. I saw you."

She sends me a scathing look, clearly irritated. "I'm sure you'll go tell everyone too. How Willow Lancaster fell asleep in class."

I rear back a bit, the anger in her voice telling me she's already written me off as a snitch. "I wouldn't do that."

"Why not?"

"Because I'm not an asshole." I push open the door for her. "Who hurt you to make you so damn defensive?"

Willow comes to a stop at the top of the steps, her shoulders sagging. I stand next to her waiting for a response and the one she gives me is unexpected.

"I'm sorry. I guess I'm being a little…ridiculous."

"It's cool." Shoving my hands in my pockets, I head down the stairs, skipping a couple of them and jumping to the ground. "Maybe you're grumpy when you first wake up."

"I am not," she insists as she scurries down the steps, picking up her pace to keep up with me. "I think you enjoy giving me grief."

"Can't lie, it's kind of fun." I grin at her.

She scowls at me.

"You need to lighten up, Lancaster. Life doesn't have to be so damn serious all the time."

"How am I being too serious?" Her voice rises and I glance toward the rest of our class ahead of us, wondering if they can hear us. No one is paying us any attention though. They're all laughing and having a good time.

"You act like you have a…" My voice drifts, and I reconsider what I'm going to say.

Yeah. I shouldn't say that at all. Knowing her, she'll get pissed at me. And I think she actually likes being angry with me.

"I act like I have a what?" she prompts when I go quiet.

"It's nothing." I shake my head. Smile at her.

That scowl remains on her face. It's a good look for her though. She's beautiful. Like, I could stare at her face for hours beautiful and it still wouldn't be enough.

"Oh, it was definitely something. You should just say it, Rhett."

I stand a little taller at her saying my name. I like how it sounds coming from her, even if she's irritated with me. "You don't want to know."

"I really, really want to know."

A ragged exhale leaves me and I stroke my chin, knowing I'm going to regret the choice I'm about to make.

"I was going to say you act like you've got a stick up your ass all the time."

CHAPTER TEN

WILLOW

I gape at Rhett, shocked he would say something so crude. Now granted, I have two younger brothers and a father who can all talk crudely at one point or another and I hear them, but they very rarely direct that sort of talk at me.

While this boy—this obnoxious, full of himself boy—just flat out said he thinks I have a stick up my butt. What a jerk.

"I knew you wouldn't like that," he says after I remain silent for way too long.

We're outside and the sun is warm on my face, making me squint, wishing I had sunglasses on. The majority of our class is ahead of us, listening to Mr. Chen talk about light and sun placement. And while I'd prefer listening to him rather than having a conversation with Rhett, I'm still standing here. Glaring at him.

Then I remember what he did earlier, when those boys knocked into me in the doorway and I almost fell. How he didn't hesitate to tell them to watch it. He might've been a little rude toward them, but he did it in my defense and that was...

Nice.

I don't think he's a bad person. I just don't believe he's *my* type of person.

"You're right. I didn't," I retort, trying my best not to look at him. My gaze gets stuck on his handsome face and then I can't think, which is annoying.

Everything about him is annoying, especially that gorgeous face of his. Ugh. I hate myself for even thinking that.

"It's not that big of a deal that you fell asleep in class," he says, keeping up with me even though I'm walking faster. Like I want to get rid of him, but he doesn't take the hint. "It happens to me all the time."

I come to a stop and so does he. "Really?"

"Well…no." He shrugs those broad shoulders of his and I study them for a moment. He's big. Tall. He might even be taller than my father. "But I've wanted to. Plenty of times. A lot of the shit they talk about is boring."

Rolling my eyes, I start walking once more, fighting the embarrassment that wants to swoop over me. That's my issue with this entire moment. With my every interaction with Rhett Bennett, really. He's always catching me at my worst. Or when something awful happens to me. And it's only the second day of school. How much more humiliation must I endure?

"This conversation is pointless," I tell him when I realize he's not leaving my side. "We should go pay attention to what the teacher is saying."

"Why? He'll only put me to sleep."

"I want to learn more about photography." I tilt my chin up, my nose in the air, putting on my best snotty expression that I can muster. May as well lean into my rich girl attitude because I know he already thinks of me like that. Why else would he say I act like I have a stick up my ass?

"I've seen your photos on Insta. Seems like you've already got that handled." He says this so casually, like it's no big deal, but yet again, I come to a complete stop.

So does he.

"Are you…stalking me?" I shade my eyes from the sunlight with my hand. Rhett is backlit by the sun, which shadows his face and that's a good thing.

He makes a dismissive noise. "Of course not. It's pretty normal to check out someone's social media after you meet them."

"Oh." He's not wrong, but I didn't think he'd ever admit to doing it.

I know I wouldn't.

"Your photos look—good." He's nodding, trying to…what? Seem casual?

"Most of them I didn't take," I admit. "Someone else did."

"Iris?"

"No." I shake my head. "Well, sometimes she does. I also have a professional take them for me on occasion."

His brows shoot up. "Really?"

My cheeks start to burn. A surefire indication I'm embarrassed. Yet again. "I was trying to grow my social media presence."

"With a professional photographer."

I shrug.

"You're just a regular girl who goes to high school," he points out. Incorrectly, I might add.

"I am the oldest child of Crew and Wren Lancaster. High society knows who my parents are, and they keep track of them—and their children. I've been a part of their social circles since I was born," I explain.

"Hanging out with a bunch of old people?" He sounds amused.

"People around my age. Your age. Some of those people even go to this school."

"Let me guess—like Silas."

My cheeks go even hotter if that's possible. "Not quite."

"Oh yeah? He's not part of your fancy social circle?" His tone is snide, and I try my best to ignore it.

"No. His parents move in different circles compared to mine."

Rhett doesn't say anything for a few seconds. Just watches me with his hand on his jaw, stroking his chin slowly. The droning sound of Mr. Chen's lecture reaches my ears and I realize I'm not missing a single thing.

"You're snobbier than I thought," Rhett finally says.

My mouth drops open. "You have zero problems with saying rude things, hmmm."

"I'm just calling it like I see it." He shrugs.

"Maybe you should learn how to repress some of the things you say."

"And miss out on witnessing your reactions? Hell no. It's been worth it so far." He's smiling again, his head turning in the direction where everyone else is standing with Mr. Chen. "Think we should go over there?"

"Definitely." I'm already walking and he falls into step beside me yet again, but this time I successfully avoid him for the rest of class. He ends up going to talk to two boys that are in our class, and I turn my back on all three of them, secretly hoping they aren't talking about me.

Of course, they're not. According to Alana, I'm too boring to talk about anyway.

• • •

"Sweetheart, what's wrong?"

Just having Mom ask me that question in her sweet, concerned mother voice I recognize so clearly has me near tears in an instant. Worse, we're on FaceTime together and she can see me. I'm sure my uncertainty and sadness are showing like a thick winter coat wrapped all around me.

"I'm fine." I offer her a weak smile, shaking my head.

"You say you're fine yet you're shaking your head no, which is sending mixed signals." Mom's gaze sticks with mine and I can't look away. She's got me all figured out. "Is everything okay? Are you struggling since returning to school?"

It's finally Thursday afternoon. Only one more day and then

it's the weekend and I've never been more grateful. I just want to hole up in my dorm suite and be alone. I don't even want to hang out with Iris, even though I'm sure she's making plans for us at this very moment and won't tell me about them until the last minute.

"It's been…weird. Coming back," I admit, struggling to swallow past the lump in my throat.

"Weird how?" Mom's brows draw together in confusion. "I know things have changed on campus, but it's all good things, according to your brother. Have people changed? Iris is treating you nicely, isn't she?"

"I have zero problems with Iris," I reassure her. "She's perfect. It's everyone else…"

"Like who?"

I launch into my explanation. How everything on campus is different compared to when I was last here, and how the new headmaster is the one heralding all of the change. I mention classes and football and school spirit and Mom just sits there, a faint smile curling her lips the entire time.

"I don't like it," I say with determination, ignoring the expression on her face. I can tell she thinks I'm being silly, when I don't feel silly at all. This all feels so important to me. I was excited to come back to something familiar, and instead, it feels like I started at a new school all over again.

I hate it.

"Well, your brother is thriving," Mom says once I'm finished. "He loves the football program and their coach. He loves how the school has so much more spirit. And he likes the new headmaster a lot. Your father and I like him as well."

"You don't get it," I say morosely, throwing myself across the bed. "Then, there's Silas."

"Silas? The boy you used to have a crush on?"

I turn to look at Mom on my phone, grabbing it and holding the screen up in front of me. "He has a girlfriend."

"Oh no."

"It's Alana."

Mom's quiet, blinking at me as if she needs to absorb this information. "Your best friend?"

I nod, frowning. Maybe even pouting. "She won't talk to us."

"Well…that's just awful. What kind of friend is she?"

"I suppose I shouldn't be mad at her. I mean, I get it. I wasn't around for an entire school year. If Silas showed that he liked her, what was she supposed to say? No, you have to wait for Willow to come home?"

"Yes!" Mom sounds positively indignant with just that one word. "I know Iris would never."

She's right. Iris wouldn't go for Silas because she knew how I felt about him. But do I feel that way about him still?

A little bit.

Maybe?

Rhett's face magically appears in my brain and I banish it. I am definitely not interested in him.

Am I?

"Yes, Iris would never, but Alana would. And did." I sigh. "It's okay. I don't think I'm that interested in him anyway."

"You don't sound very convincing to me."

The doubt in Mom's voice is obvious and I appreciate her supporting me. "Really, it's okay. There are plenty of other boys on this campus."

"Don't settle for just any boy though, Willow. Make sure he—respects you," Mom warns.

"Is that what you did with Dad?"

"What do you mean? Settling with your father? Oh my." She laughs, her expression turning wistful. As if she's remembering when she was my age and they first met. "There is no settling for Crew Lancaster. Want me to be truthful?"

"Yes, please." I crave any bit of information they share about the early days of their relationship. I loved hearing my father tell me the story of how Mom hated him. Or so he thought. She was actually just scared of him.

Scared of any boy really. Mom was a bit of a self-admitted prude, and I kind of am too.

"Your father put on an act. He was rude and acted ridiculous when he was around his friends. In public in general, he was kind of awful. But when it was just the two of us? He was as sweet as he could be." Mom smiles. "Though I think he also enjoyed antagonizing me."

Yet again, I think of Rhett. He seems to enjoy antagonizing me every chance he gets. "Do you mean Dad enjoyed teasing you?"

"Well, yes. And being rude." Mom wrinkles her nose. "He sometimes said the most awful things. You know how boys are."

"Considering I have two brothers and plenty of boy cousins, yes, I do."

Mom laughs. "You also know that a lot of what they do and say is just for show. I don't know why they act that way, but they do. Sometimes it's our job to get to the core of them. Figure them out."

"That seems unfair."

"Oh, but they have to do the same to us, don't you think? Our public personas are different compared to our private ones," Mom points out.

"I guess you're right," I say, my voice soft.

"Maybe you should try to talk to Alana. Is it worth losing a friendship over a boy?" Mom asks.

"She's not being very nice."

"Maybe she feels threatened by you."

That is such a mom thing to say. "Why in the world would she be threatened by me? Alana is beautiful and confident and interesting. I can see why Silas fell for her."

"Willow. Darling. You are beautiful and confident and interesting too. And so incredibly smart. Sweet. You have many wonderful qualities. Why wouldn't she feel threatened?"

I roll my eyes. "You're just being a mom."

She laughs. "I suppose I am."

We talk for a little while longer and once we end the call, I remain on my bed, staring at the ceiling. Ruminating over everything we discussed. Even if Alana is threatened by me, she should know I would never stoop so low as to try and steal her boyfriend. I'm not interested in Silas like that. I can't be—he's taken. And besides.

I think I have a new distraction.

CHAPTER ELEVEN

WILLOW

"We're going out tonight," Iris declares the moment we see each other in the hall Friday morning.

All Lancaster children who attend Lancaster Prep reside in a different building versus the dorms where everyone else stays. Our suites are larger and more private. The perks of being a Lancaster.

Withholding the sigh that wants to leave me, instead I ask, "Where exactly are we going?"

"There's going to be a bonfire out by the old ruins," Iris explains once I catch up to her. She falls into step beside me and we exit the building via the double doors. "The football team puts it all together. A way to celebrate the beginning of school and the start of football season."

"Looks like it might rain," I point out, frowning when we step outside. It's cloudy and the air is chilly, which is disappointing.

I was hoping for sunny skies all weekend. Feels too early for clouds and rain.

"Rain or shine, they're having this party. They did it last year too," Iris explains. "It's a lot of fun."

"Will there be drinking?"

"Duh. Of course." Iris grins.

"I don't know..." My voice drifts and I startle when Iris makes a frustrated sound.

"Don't think you can back out. You're going." Her voice is firm.

"Do you think Alana and Silas will be there?" I ask, my voice hushed as I glance around. I don't want anyone hearing me.

"If they are, who cares? You're going to ignore them." She sends me a pointed look. "And flirt with other boys."

"Like who?"

"Anyone but Silas. Forget that guy. He made his choice. Forget her too." I can hear the vague pain in Iris's voice and I recognize it because I feel the same way.

Is it worse because we lost a friend? I think so. Boys come and go, but a betrayal from a friend hurts the most. At least in my opinion.

"I wouldn't flirt with him," I say, practically running to keep up with her because suddenly, Iris's stride is eating up the ground. She's either mad or hungry. Maybe a combination of both—dangerous.

"Good. You need to forget about him and take a look around." She abruptly stops and so do I, watching as she waves her arm around in a sweeping gesture. "There are plenty of boys on this campus who would die for a chance to talk to you."

"Like who?"

"I don't know." Now she's throwing both arms up in the air, her frustration obvious. I bet she didn't expect me to ask that question. "We're going to dress up and look freaking hot and make them chase after us all night. You in?"

This sounds like a nightmare, but I can't refuse her. She won't let me. "I'm in."

The grin is back and she lunges toward me, wrapping me up in a tight hug. "We're going to have so much fun tonight. You won't regret going, I promise."

"I hope not." My voice is muffled against her chest since she's taller, but I don't think she heard me.

We enter the dining hall still laughing, ignoring everyone

else as we each pick out our usual breakfast: wheat toast for me, sometimes with avocado but today, they don't have it, and a double chocolate chip muffin for Iris. We always get the same coffee order too—iced caramel white chocolate mocha is Iris's and I get a vanilla latte with skim milk.

I have to watch what I eat because it's easy for me to gain weight, unlike Iris, who consumes whatever she wants and never gains an ounce. I envy her ability to eat like complete garbage and still manage to look stunning.

Once we're seated at our usual table and I've had a few sips of coffee and am feeling somewhat human, I start glancing around the cavernous room with a critical eye. Iris is oblivious, too busy picking at her muffin and scrolling her phone, searching for hairstyle ideas for tonight.

I'm checking all the boys out, hoping I can see them in a new light. I realized Mom is right—there are plenty of boys who go to Lancaster Prep, those who are in my grade that might interest me. But who? So many of them I've gone to school with for what feels like forever, though I suppose that shouldn't matter.

As I scan each table, noting the familiar faces, I realize they don't do anything for me. I've known so many of them for so long, I can't imagine feeling anything beyond a friendly fondness for any of them. The only one who I was interested in now belongs to someone else.

I spot him because of course I do. They're seated together. Silas and Alana. Clear across the room sitting on one side of the table, right next to each other. It's the perfect table where everyone can see them. Like me.

Did they do that on purpose? Knowing Alana, the answer is yes. She resented the fact that Iris and I are Lancasters and would always gripe that people were drawn to us because of our last name.

Not like we can help it. And she doesn't even know what it feels like to have people want to spend time with us only because of our last name and what we can possibly do for people.

Alana catches me staring at them and she leans in toward Silas, curling her hand around the nape of his neck before she pulls him in close, her lips settling over his. I jerk my gaze away, embarrassed to be caught, mad at myself that I let her get to me.

I keep my gaze focused on my lap for a beat, taking a deep breath before I lift my head to find someone watching me a couple of tables over.

Rhett Bennett.

His expression is sleepy, his hair mussed. As if he just rolled out of bed, threw his uniform on—not all of it, he's not wearing his jacket or tie—and stumbled into the dining hall to eat something. His plate is full of food and there's a small chocolate milk carton to the right of his tray.

He drinks milk. How…cute.

His white button-down stretches across his chest and is tight around his biceps, showing off just how muscular he is, and I can't help but get caught up in his stare. And when he smiles at me, this closed-lipped, one-sided curve of his mouth, my stomach dips.

I'm suddenly breathless.

"Hey, I think we should do your hair like this." Iris's voice tears my attention away from Rhett, her sharp elbow seemingly digging into my ribs as she jabs me to get my attention. I glance down at her phone screen, studying the image she's showing me. "Do you like it?"

"Sure." I return my focus to Rhett, but he's no longer looking at me. He's laughing at something Brooks said, the joyous sound carrying over to our table, and I wish I knew what he thought was so funny.

"You okay, Willow?" When I frown at Iris, she continues, "You seem distracted."

"I'm excited about tonight," I tell her.

And I mean it.

The morning goes by like usual. By the time I'm entering my English class, I'm feeling anxious. Even a little nervous? It all has to do with seeing Rhett, which might be silly, but I can't help it.

Could I actually like him? Everything is happening so fast and maybe I'm just getting caught up in it all. He certainly seems determined to get my attention, and while I suppose he's like that with plenty of girls, maybe I really do interest him. Or maybe not.

He can be rude sometimes. Pushy. Arrogant. But there's something just beneath it all—like he wants to get to know me. He doesn't seem to care about the Lancaster name either, which is downright refreshing.

I've arrived in English relatively early, since my last class is so close to this one, and I settle in at my desk, pulling out *The Great Gatsby* from my backpack and setting it on my desk, along with my notebook.

"Hey, Willow."

I glance up to find Silas standing next to my desk, a friendly smile on his face. I fight the disappointment filling me, hoping it doesn't show. "Hi, Silas."

"How are you? Glad it's Friday?"

Alana isn't with him, which is odd. They always seem to come to this class together, but there's no way I'm asking him where she is. "Definitely," I say with a nod.

"Same." He shifts his feet, briefly glancing over his shoulder before he returns his attention to me. "Look, I was hoping we could talk sometime."

I rest my hands on top of my desk, curling them together. Us talking is probably a terrible idea. I'm sure Alana wouldn't like it. "What is there to talk about?"

His brows draw together and he seems adorably confused. Ugh, I hate that I just mentally used the word adorable about him. "I-I thought you might want to talk about—"

"Yo, Lancaster. Looking good this morning."

Rhett's familiar voice washes over me, making butterflies flutter in my stomach, and I look to my left to see Rhett standing on the other side of my desk, a fierce expression on his face that is the complete opposite of his friendly tone.

"Hi, Rhett. And, um, thank you." I smile at him, noting that he's wearing his uniform jacket, but his tie is still missing.

"You interrupted us," Silas tells him, sounding vaguely out of sorts. Even mad.

"Whoa, didn't know you were having a private conversation." Rhett throws his hands up in a defensive gesture, completely unfazed.

"Well, we were."

Rhett's gaze meets mine for the briefest moment, questioning. I just shrug, which seems to please him. "Where's your girlfriend?"

Silas's cheeks turn ruddy at Rhett's question. "None of your damn business."

"Maybe you should go find her."

"Maybe you should go sit down."

"There's no need for the two of you to get angry," I say, trying to diffuse the situation. Because seriously, what is happening right now?

"Stay out of it, Willow." This comes from Silas, and his dismissive tone lights something within me that isn't pleasant.

No, more like I'm pissed.

Leaping to my feet, I turn toward him, eager to let him have it. "There's nothing to stay out of, Silas. I agree with Rhett. Maybe you should go find Alana."

The wounded look on Silas's face isn't adorable. Not at all. With one last scathing glare cast in Rhett's direction, Silas leaves us alone, settling into his desk at the front of the classroom. Alana glides in within seconds, sitting next to him and keeping up a steady stream of one-sided conversation, oblivious to the tension that filled the room not even ten seconds ago.

"Damn, Lancaster. You're hot when you're angry."

I whirl on Rhett, trying to ignore the way my skin prickles with awareness at his casual compliment. "He was being a jerk."

"For real."

"You were too," I'm quick to point out. "Sort of."

"He needs to stop sniffing around you." Rhett sits in the desk behind mine, his big body sprawled out like he can't contain himself into such a small space. I suppose he can't, considering how tall and broad he is.

What he just said slowly sinks into my brain and I gape at him for a moment, at a loss for words. "Did you just say that Silas is *sniffing* around me?"

"Yeah." He shrugs his broad shoulders. "I did. And he needs to stop. He's got a girlfriend. He doesn't need to lead you on or whatever the hell it is that he's doing."

"He's not leading me on," I insist as I sit back down. I'm agitated by the near fight between them. Were they fighting over…me?

No. Impossible.

Rhett actually snorts. "If you say so."

I keep my back to him, watching our teacher enter the room and head straight to her desk, my brain going over what Rhett said again and again until finally I can't take it anymore. Turning in my seat, I find he's already watching me, one brow lifted in question. "Why would he lead me on anyway?"

"Why wouldn't he? If the most beautiful girl on this campus acted like she was into me, I'd want to lead her on too. Though I wouldn't be leading her on. I'd be just as interested, and what makes it even better? I don't have a girlfriend." He smiles, like what he just said was no big deal.

While I gape at him, shocked by pretty much every word that came out of his mouth, I snap my lips shut, about to ask him another question when the bell rings, and Mrs. Patel immediately starts talking.

Effectively ending the most interesting conversation I've had with Rhett yet.

I reluctantly turn around in my seat, facing forward, offering a weak "here" when my name is called. Rhett shifts in his seat, drawing closer. Close enough that I can smell him, and as subtly as I can, I breathe him in, savoring his scent before I slowly exhale.

"You coming to the bonfire tonight, Will?"

His voice is low, his warm breath brushing against the back of my neck, making me tremble. "Yes."

"Good." He sounds pleased. "Maybe we can talk more then. Unless you plan on continuing your conversation with Silas there."

I glance over my shoulder, glaring at him as he settles back into his seat. "Did you invite him?"

"It's not up to me. It's a blanket invitation to anyone who wants to come. If he shows, he shows." Rhett shrugs. "If I had my way, he wouldn't be there."

"Why not?"

"Then I wouldn't have to worry about him sniffing around you."

I make a face. "That's such a gross term. Sniffing around."

"What else would you call it? Oh, I know. Something more polite. Like, showing interest in you. That sounds way nicer."

I straighten my shoulders, vaguely offended. "It does."

"Look, I'm just calling it like I see it, Will. And that guy is definitely interested in you. I don't care if he has a girlfriend. I think he'd like to have you too."

A week ago, this would've given me hope, even if the entire situation is completely hopeless. I still would've been tempted by the idea of Silas wanting to be with me, though there's no way I would've agreed to see him if he was with Alana. I'm not a cheater, and I'm not about to be the other woman either.

The idea of Silas liking me now, though? I don't know.

Sounds like more trouble than it's worth.

CHAPTER TWELVE

WILLOW

"We can't look like we're trying too hard." I'm kind of whining as I stare at my reflection in the full-length mirror in Iris's dorm suite, contemplating my outfit. Her room is the same size as mine, and it currently looks like a disaster zone. As if a hurricane came whipping through it, causing destruction everywhere it touched. Heaps of discarded clothes cover most of the bed, and there are pairs of shoes scattered all over the floor. Iris's desk has been converted into a vanity table, with a variety of cosmetics lying open on top of it, a lipliner slowly rolling across and hanging perilously on the edge before it finally falls, landing on the floor.

Iris grabs the lipliner and puts the cap on it before tossing it onto the desk/vanity, plopping into the chair and staring at her reflection in the mirror. "Who cares if we look like we tried too hard? Isn't that the point?"

I tilt my head to the side, my pin-straight hair falling past my shoulders. Iris tried to convince me I should wear my hair in some elaborate style, but I let her straighten it instead. She even wanted me to wear a dress, but I had to draw the line somewhere. We're going to be standing around a bonfire out by the old building that burned down forever ago. The clouds never left and it's going to be chilly, though there's no rain in the forecast, thank goodness.

I'm wearing jeans and a cropped black sweatshirt, with black Adidas Sambas on my feet. Cool girl styling without looking like I'm trying too hard, my ultimate goal. My makeup is subtle—after much insistence with Iris that she not overdo it—and now it's her turn to get ready.

"We can look good but we don't want to appear...desperate. Right?" I turn to face her, watching as she leans in close to her magnified mirror and applies a thick coat of mascara to her lashes.

"As if we ever look desperate." The scoffing noise she makes tells me she believes I'm talking absolute nonsense. "Don't forget who we are."

I can't help but smile. "You sound like your dad."

"Well, Daddy dearest is right." She lifts her head away from the mirror to study me, the tube of mascara still clutched in her hand. "You've been weird since you've come back."

"Weird? How?"

"Not normal. You're unsure of yourself, like you left your confidence behind in Italy and came back a self-conscious shell of a person."

Leave it to Iris to be so casually cruel with her words. Like a true Lancaster, though our generation is trying our hardest not to be that way, just like the generation before us. "I am not a shell of a person."

"No, you're right. That's just me being dramatic." She returns her attention to the mirror, working on her left eye now. "You're definitely more unsure though."

"With what?"

"With boys. With stupid Silas." She shoves the brush back into the mascara tube almost violently. "You should tell him to kiss your ass."

I made the mistake of telling her what he said to me earlier in English. How he wanted to talk to me but only because Alana wasn't around. I failed to mention what Rhett did, or what he said because I didn't want to delve into that with her.

Considering I'm not quite sure how to feel about it yet, I'd rather hold it close to my chest and mull over it on my own. At least for a little while longer.

"I'm afraid if I tell him that, he'll actually want to," I quip, making Iris laugh.

"He probably would. I bet he regrets getting with Alana. Ugh, men." She grabs a Chanel lip gloss and twists it open, slicking on the shiny, glittery stuff along her lips and making them sparkle. "Why do they always want what they can't have?"

"Are you speaking from experience?"

"I wish," she mutters, rubbing her lips together and pursing them at her reflection in an exaggerated kiss. "I'm over the boys here."

"Here? You mean the boys we go to school with?"

"Yep." She makes the *P* pop with her lips. "I prefer older men."

"How much older are you talking about?" I think of her brother August and all of his friends. He's in college and in some sort of fraternity or secret society thing, and that means he's hanging out with all sorts of bros. Some of them he brings back to the house, and I know for a fact that Iris thinks the majority of them are gorgeous. And that's because she told me so.

I'm sure they're gorgeous. They're probably all jerks too, but that won't stop her. I think she's attracted to jerks. She comes by it naturally.

"Oh, you know. College." She shrugs, keeping her tone casual. Playing it off like usual. "There's no one in particular that I like. I'm just drawn to men."

"Iris. You're barely eighteen," I remind her.

"And legal as can be so it's not so taboo, is it? What's wrong with wanting to fuck a twenty-two-year-old?"

"Iris!" She can't go around dropping f-bombs so casually, but she just laughs.

Yikes. Maybe I'm as much of a prude as my mom was. I thought I was more liberated than her.

"What? It's true. They're all babies here. Even the seniors."

My mind immediately goes to Rhett's broad shoulders and thick biceps. In my eyes, he's the furthest thing from a baby. "Maybe not all of them."

"Ooh, Willow, who exactly are you thinking of then, hmm? And don't play like you're not talking about anyone specific. I know you." Iris's expression turns vaguely horrified. "If you say Silas, I'm going to murder you in your sleep."

"So violent!" I burst out laughing, shaking my head. Silas is... cute. But Rhett?

Rhett is something else.

He's sexy. Confident. Like he knows what he's doing, and even if he doesn't, he could figure it out really quick.

"Seriously, if it's Silas, I'm going to have to smack some sense into you." She waves her hand like she's slapping someone across the face. "He's the worst."

"Why do you say that anyway?" I'm curious. She's always got something negative to say about Silas and I wonder if she has an actual reason or if it's just because she's rushing to my defense like any best friend would.

"Why wouldn't I say that? Especially after what you just told me. I hate to say it, but he's playing you, Willow. I think he likes the idea of you waiting in the wings for him, nurturing that hopeless crush. Like you're a backup plan in case things don't work out with him and Alana." She rolls her eyes.

Ouch. If that's true, I hate it. I don't want him thinking of me like that. I'm not waiting around for him, that's for sure, and if he believes I am? He's going to be sorely disappointed.

Turning, I face the mirror once more, fixing my necklace so the clasp is where it belongs, at the back of my neck. I'm wearing the birthstone pendant that my parents gave me when I turned sixteen—a round cut ruby surrounded by tiny diamonds. It's one of my favorite pieces, not that I have a lot yet. My mother lets me borrow her jewelry most of the time, which is always fun because her collection is like a treasure chest of jewels. My father spoils her—he always has. He spoils all of us, especially me since I'm his only daughter.

Iris's father is just as bad. He lavishes his girls—his wife and daughter—with all the jewelry they could ever want, not that Iris is interested in any of it.

"Should I tell Alana that Silas is trying to talk to me?" I ask, keeping my focus on the mirror so I don't have to see Iris's face.

I know she's going to be exasperated with me and all the huffing and puffing only proves my point.

"If you tell her that, she'll just get mad at you. Or accuse you of trying to cause problems between them, when that's the last thing you want. No, don't tell her anything. Let him self-implode. If you don't show him any interest, he'll just move on to some other girl. He'll eventually slip and get caught. You don't need to get involved."

"You're right." I straighten my shoulders, thrusting my chest out and immediately wincing. God, I wish I had smaller boobs. "Maybe I should get a minimizer."

"What? Are you talking about your tits?" Iris practically screeches, leaping to her feet and running over to me. She stares at my reflection along with me, her gaze zeroed in on my chest. "You have fabulous boobs. I wish I had them."

"No, you really don't. They're big and always in the way." After my mom had Beau, she had a breast reduction because they were too big and heavy, and she was tired of being in pain. I'm sure I'll have to do the same thing one day after I have children. Something I'm definitely not looking forward to. "I wish I had your boobs."

"My tits are nonexistent. Boys love big ones."

"Oh please. I'm sure the majority of them our age wouldn't know what to do with them anyway." I start giggling. So does Iris.

"You never did tell me who you're interested in," Iris says once the giggling has subsided. "Let me take a guess."

"No."

"It's Kody."

I send her an incredulous look. "Kody? No."

"He's not bad looking."

"True."

"He's on the football team."

"I don't consider that important criteria for me to be interested in a guy." Ooh, I sound snotty but seriously. I don't give a crap about the football team. Not like every other girl at our school who has become suddenly enamored with the team members and the supposed status it brings them. I find it all silly.

"He's nice."

"He ate his boogers in the third grade." I turn to face her. "The *third grade*. We were eight. Nine. Whatever. That's way too old."

Iris is laughing again and so am I. "This is the problem with going to school with the same people for so long."

There are plenty of people who attend Lancaster Prep that we didn't go to elementary school with, but there are also so many who we grew up with and we know all of these odd little details that sort of ruin any illusion we might have about them. It's a blessing and a curse.

More like a curse.

"Wait a minute. I know who it is." Iris snaps her fingers, a sly smile curling her lips. "Rhett Bennett."

I'm blushing almost immediately. I can feel the heat in my cheeks, and yes, Iris notices.

"No, it's not him."

"Why are you lying to me? We're best friends, Willow. We tell each other everything. Are you telling me you have a crush on him now?" My cheeks grow hotter and she points at me, doing a little dance as she hops over the discarded clothing on the floor while on her way back to the vanity. "He's gorgeous."

"You think he's a bad choice though." My protest is weak. The only reason I'm bringing this up is because I want to beat her to the punch. She's mentioned to me before all of his flaws and I don't want to hear them again. I seriously don't need the reminder.

"If he's your choice, then I won't knock him. I promise." Her expression is solemn as she settles back into her chair and resumes putting on her makeup. "He'll be there tonight."

"I know."

"You're excited to see him?"

"I don't know how to feel about him," I answer truthfully. "I don't even know if I actually like him."

"Why do you say it like that?"

"How I feel about him is so confusing. Like…I can't deny he's attractive. His face. His body."

"Ooh," Iris starts, but I silence her with a look.

"But then he opens his mouth and says things that are both appealing and…kind of awful," I admit.

"You really think so?"

"Oh definitely," I say with a nod. "He can be charming but also a little…crude."

"Do you think he's interested in you?" Iris asks.

"You've told me before that he flirts with everyone."

"He sort of does." Iris winces. "But honestly? I haven't heard much about him since school started."

"It's the first week. How much could you hear?"

"A lot, especially when you take into account that it's Rhett we're talking about. He played a bunch of girls hard last year."

"That was last year," I say with a shrug, hating what she just said. "Maybe he's not like that anymore."

"But maybe he is. Just—be careful, Willow. I don't want you to fall completely for this guy and get your heart broken."

"He won't break my heart," I say with a ferocity I don't quite mean.

I hope that's true, but I don't know. Maybe he will break my heart.

Maybe I'll let him.

CHAPTER THIRTEEN

RHETT

It's around nine o'clock when the party is finally rolling along at a decent clip. There's plenty of alcohol flowing. People brought their own. Plus, Brooks has an older brother who supplied us with a couple of kegs that are currently inside the crumbling old building that used to be part of the campus back in the day or some shit like that.

I don't know much about this school, but that's the story I've always heard. It's also where the annual Halloween party is held, which is epic. I went to last year's and got drunk off my ass.

"Where are all the girls?" Brooks grumbles into his red Solo cup of beer.

I'm tempted to tap the bottom of his cup and make it spill all over his face, but I don't do it. I'm not that much of an asshole. "You know how girls are. They take ten hours to look like they just rolled out of bed."

"Wish one of them would roll out of my bed." Brooks Crosby is a grumpy motherfucker. He's always complaining about something, which I find hilarious considering he's richer than God—but not the Lancasters—and realistically shouldn't have a single thing in his life to complain about. I've never seen someone so spoiled and so fucking cranky about it all the time.

I think that's why he's on the football team. It gives him something legitimate to do—and complain about. And while I'm not big on people who gripe all the time, I do care about my friend because he's as loyal as they come and fast as fuck on the field. He's my number one wide receiver and we've made more touchdowns together than me and anyone else. Our coach loves us.

The girls love us—well, me. Brooks? Not as much.

I blame that fact on his mouth and all the shitty things it says. Since I'm pretty much the same way, I figure this is why we're such good friends.

"You start flattering them instead of giving them grief all the time and you'd find one," I tell him, sipping from my cup of beer. It's mostly foam and getting warmer by the second, but it'll do for now. It helps knowing that if we want to get really fucked up, I have a stash of liquor bottles hidden behind a pine tree.

Not that I'm looking to get fucked up tonight. I have priorities, and at the top of my list is one Willow Lancaster. I have a feeling she's not into sloppy drunk guys. Does she even drink? Or is she holier than thou when it comes to booze and drugs?

I won't touch drugs, especially during football season. Our coaching staff has a zero-tolerance policy and I'm not about to risk it. First, my dad would murder me on the spot. Second, my mom and grandpa and everyone else on the Callahan side would murder me if my father didn't do it first. I'm not about to ruin my chances. I have plans, and all of them have to do with going pro. Keeping up the legacy is important to me.

This is why I treat my body like a goddamn temple and work out morning, noon and night. So much exercise means I consume a ton of calories, and I just love when the girls say, "Where do you put it all?" when they watch me eat.

I exert it all out on the field, ladies, is what I want to tell them but I don't. They don't get it. Well, some of the girls who are also athletes do, and I tried to date a couple of them—not at the same time of course—but I ended it with all of them. Always felt like we were in competition against each other and I hated it.

Weird.

Then there's Brooks who smokes blunts and hits the occasional bong. Currently he's going through an edible stage and he's high at this very moment, but never worried about it. His family has gone to this school for generations and he knows if he was caught doing drugs, nothing would happen to him. His dad would throw money at the school and they'd have a new building under construction in no time. They'd name that bad boy Crosby too.

Wonder what it's like, to be that untouchable? I come from a privileged background, and I never deny it. I thought I had it pretty good growing up, but then I came here and realized how we live is different compared to some of the people I go to school with.

They come from big money. Generational wealth, meaning they're part of a long line of rich assholes who managed to make a fortune in the early days and the generations that came afterward managed to not fuck it up and spend it all.

Mom comes from wealth. My grandpa Drew Callahan's dad was rich as hell too, and none of us wanted for anything growing up, but there are things people do here that we'd never think to ask for, let alone receive. Hell, there was a senior last year who brought her maid with her everywhere she went. In class. At lunch in the dining hall. During P.E. That poor lady was at this rich bitch's beck and call at all hours of the day and night, and I've never seen anything like it.

"Here comes the Lancaster girls," Brooks suddenly announces, his tone snide.

I stand at attention at hearing that last name, scanning the many faces in search of the prettiest face I've ever seen. Ah, there she is.

I'm struck dumb for a moment by her beauty, my chest aching because seeing her steals my breath. I rub at the spot between my pecs absently, taking her in. She's wearing baggy jeans and a cropped black sweatshirt that shows off her tiny waist to perfection. I bet my hands could span it, she's so slender there. And curvy everywhere else where it counts. Big tits. Flared hips. Cute black sneakers on her feet. Stylish like every other girl at this party but somehow, none of them do it for me like this one does.

My gaze goes to her face. Her long, dark hair is straight and flowing past her shoulders, and she brushes a few wayward strands away from her cheek, smiling at something her cousin whispers in her ear.

"You don't like them?" I ask Brooks when I realize he's waiting for me to say something.

"Who, Willow and Iris? They're all right. I've known them forever. Our families have stories of me being in a playpen with Iris when we were infants and I pulled her hair so she nailed me in the nads with her foot."

"Seriously?" I send him a skeptical look, but he just shrugs.

"That's the story our moms tell."

"You two are friends?" I've never seen Brooks and Iris hang out together. Not once.

"I usually avoid her at all costs."

"And why is that?"

"She's fucking terrifying." Brooks's voice is dead serious and I can tell he means it. "She's too beautiful."

"I don't see it." Now it's my turn to shrug, my gaze sticking on Willow. Some guy approaches them and her smile is friendly, just before the guy yanks her into a hug. A low growl leaves me and I clutch the Solo cup so tightly, I'm worried it's going to crack and spill everywhere.

I need to chill out.

"You don't think Iris is beautiful?"

"I mean yeah, she's pretty. Definitely hot." I shrug then take a sip of my beer while I watch the guy back away from Willow and

Iris with a wave before he takes off. "Not my type though."

"I thought everyone was your type."

"Not blondes."

"Why not?"

"I'm not attracted to them. I like dark-haired girls."

Brooks follows my line of vision, figuring out that I'm watching Willow. At least that's what it seems like, thanks to the smug look that appears on his smug face. "Like Willow."

"She's all right." I play it off, but he sees right through me.

"You're watching her like you're trying to sec what she's got on underneath her clothes." He sounds amused.

"I'd love to know."

"Wouldn't every other guy at this party." Brooks is grumbling again, sipping from his cup of beer and grimacing. "This shit is awful."

"We could crack open the whiskey." I hesitate, mentally running through what he said to me only a second ago. "And what do you mean, every guy at this party wants to know what she's got on underneath her clothes?"

"They're all hot for her, dumbass. She came back to school with the plump red lips and plump round tits and they're all salivating for a chance at her," Brooks explains, his expression telling me that he thinks I'm an idiot for not noticing.

Guess I was too busy noticing her that I didn't see everyone else was doing the same thing as me.

"Who else wants her?" I sound indignant. I am indignant. I never once considered that someone else was interested in her. The moment I laid eyes on Willow Lancaster, all I could think was, *I want that one.*

Sounds like a jackass thought, but I never claimed that I wasn't a jackass.

"How much time do you have?" He chuckles, but the moment he notices my glare, he shuts up. "Come on, Rhett. She's been gone for a year and then sweeps back onto campus looking hotter than ever. You didn't think anyone else noticed?"

"Did you notice?"

"She's not my type."

"Right. You like violent blondes." I grin.

Brooks grunts, polishing off his beer in one big swallow. "Let's get fucked up."

"No way." I shake my head. "I'm working toward a pleasant buzz and that's it."

"It'll take you fifty cups of this shitty beer to even feel it, so good luck to you. I'm digging out the whiskey." Brooks starts walking away and I call out to him.

"You remember where I put it?"

He gives me the bird and nods while he keeps walking.

Okay then.

A group of girls approaches me, all of them giggly and barely able to speak. They're younger. Juniors? Maybe even sophomores and I humor them for a bit, letting them ask their dumb questions about football. It's painfully obvious they know nothing about the sport and it's fine. That's cool. But I don't want to be the one who teaches them.

"Rowan, hey!" I shout when I spot Willow's younger brother.

Row's entire face lights up when he sees I'm the one who yelled his name and he comes right over to where I'm standing, clutching a full cup of beer and wearing a big ol' grin on his face. "Hey, Rhett. How's it going?"

"Good, buddy. How are you?" I slap him on the back extra hard, making him take a step forward, the beer sloshing over the rim of his cup. "How's practice going?"

Since taking over as the JV QB, Row is looking good. He's got a decent throw that'll get better with work and he's fast. Meaning, if he doesn't spot anyone to throw the ball to, he has no qualms tucking it against his chest and trying to run it in himself.

I love a guy who's willing to take risks, and Row is definitely a risk-taker.

"Oh my God, Rowan," one of the girls squeaks, rushing up to him and throwing her arms around his neck. He stands there helplessly while she squeezes him, though he never puts his arms around her in return. He's too worried trying to save his beer from spilling any more. "I love watching you play."

I've heard he's got his own fan club during practice, not that I ever see it. Our daily practices are held at two different fields, with two different sets of coaches. Last year we were all put together because we didn't have as many players, but now?

Every motherfucker who goes to this school seems to want to play now after our fantastic season last year, even a few girls. The JV team has a female kicker and she's phenomenal. Guess she used to play soccer but got sick of the drama on her team.

"Hey thanks," Row says, flashing what is most likely a panty-melting smile at the girl who suddenly looks like she might faint.

Huh. I mean, the kid is a Lancaster. I get it. But I didn't realize he had that much rizz going on.

I try to make small talk with him, hoping to steer the conversation toward his sister, but the girls keep interrupting me, all three of them eager to gain Row's attention by asking him lots of questions. I'm all but forgotten, which isn't normal for me, but I'm cool with it in this instance. I like Row. Plus, it's smart for me to get on his good side, considering who his sister is.

I leave them be and start wandering, taking my opportunity when I see the familiar blonde and brunette standing close to each other, talking excitedly.

"Ladies." They both jerk their heads up at my greeting, a knowing smile spreading across Iris's face while Willow just stands there and stares at me mutely. Damn, she's cute. "Glad you showed up."

"We wouldn't miss this party for the world, Rhett," Iris says, her blue eyes dancing with mischief. "As a matter of fact, I was just telling Willow about what happened last year during this party."

Oh great. May as well own it. "When I got shit-faced?"

Iris bursts out laughing. "Yes. You were hilarious. Will there be a repeat performance this year?"

"Hell no." I shake my head. "I'm not interested in getting wasted again."

"Why not?" This question comes from Willow.

I turn my attention onto her, our gazes meeting. Locking. I stare into her beautiful eyes, deciding to be truthful. "I don't need to make an ass of myself tonight. I'd rather work on impressing you."

Iris nudges Willow in the side with her elbow, offering her a small smile. Willow steps aside, sending her cousin a vaguely dirty look. All of this gives me hope because it's got me thinking they've been talking about me, and that's a good thing.

I rub my hand along my jaw, contemplating Willow while Iris rattles on about something—I don't even know what because I'm not listening. I'm too entranced with the beautiful girl standing in front of me, her wide-eyed gaze shifting to the left, then the right. Like she might be looking for someone?

Someone else?

Fuck, that kills me.

"You want something to drink?" I ask, my voice low, not wanting to stop Iris from talking, which she doesn't.

Willow makes a cute little face, her nose wrinkling. "I don't really care for beer."

"You want something else?"

"You have something else?"

Iris stops talking mid-sentence, her brows drawing together. "Are you two even listening to me?"

"Nope."

"No."

We answer at the same time, sharing a smile, and Iris rolls her eyes.

"Should I leave you two alone, then?" She starts walking before

I get a chance to say, hell yes, but Willow grabs hold of Iris's hand, stopping her from going.

"No. Stay for a few more minutes." Willow sends me a look and I'm a goner. Seriously, what the hell is wrong with me? "Rhett was just offering us something to drink."

"Something besides the shitty keg beer?" Iris asks hopefully.

"I'm offended." I rest my hand against my chest, which makes Willow giggle while Iris reaches out and pushes my shoulder, though I don't move.

Wish Willow would've touched me, but I'm patient. That will definitely happen.

Hopefully tonight.

CHAPTER FOURTEEN

WILLOW

I envy Iris's ease while talking to Rhett. Like he doesn't affect her whatsoever, and maybe he doesn't. Actually, I know he doesn't. He's just another guy to her while to me, he's...

I don't know what he is, exactly, but I'm overwhelmed with a wave of unfamiliar emotion stealing over me, standing so close to him. I don't know what to say or do, and I'm nervous. My palms are sweating and so are my underarms, and oh my God, do I smell? Can he smell me? I'm mortified. Fully freaking out and ready to make my escape—

Calm. Down.

The rational voice in my head sounds suspiciously like my mother and I'm grateful for it. I need it to remind me that I'm panicking for no good reason.

Taking a deep breath, I exhale softly, shaking out my hands to hopefully get rid of the sweat coating my palms. Hoping no one paid any attention to the minor meltdown I just had.

But when my gaze goes to Rhett, I see he's watching me carefully, his focus on me despite the occasional *yeah*, and *oh damn*, he sends Iris's way as he pretends to listen to her. All the while his focus is seemingly on me.

You okay?

He mouths the words to me and I nod, offering him a faint smile while my heart flutters wildly in my chest at his thoughtful concern.

"Are you two just going to stare at each other all night or are you finally going to give in to all of this sexual tension that's currently swirling around us and do something about it?" Iris asks, as tactful as ever.

My face goes hot while Rhett just chuckles, the sexy sound settling into a low throb between my thighs. And my entire body lights up when he sends me a mysterious look, like we're sharing a secret. I part my lips, ready to say something, but nothing comes out.

It's as if I can't form words. I can barely think. What is happening?

"Yo, Brooks!" Rhett suddenly shouts, his hand shooting up in the air to gain Brooks Crosby's attention.

I've seen them hang around together, and I know Brooks is on the football team so maybe that's why they've grown close. It's an unusual pairing if you ask me only because I never thought Brooks was the overly athletic type, but Rhett seems to fit right in with everyone else on this campus, so I suppose I shouldn't be surprised.

"Oh God." Iris groans, flipping her hair over her shoulder in obvious disdain. She's always had a love/hate relationship with Brooks. As in, she loves hating him. And I think he feels the same way about her.

Their moms were close friends when they were babies, but then the Crosbys divorced and it turned into this tense custody battle that messed with Brooks's head since it dragged on for years. His mom eventually gave up and moved to Los Angeles to become a big-shot talent agent while Brooks stayed here and lives with his dad and the nanny—aka the new Mrs. Crosby—when he's not in school.

Yeah, it's twisted like that in Brooks's family, and he's turned out relatively well-adjusted, considering.

"You don't like Brooks?" Rhett asks Iris.

"I adore him, but I also hate him, and I'm fairly certain he feels the same way about me. We've known each other since we were in diapers," Iris explains.

"He mentioned that." Rhett rubs his chin, his lips curled into a mischievous smile. "Said you kicked him in the balls when you guys were hanging out in a playpen together."

"That story is so exaggerated," Iris drawls. "And how bad could I have damaged his balls anyway? He was wearing a *diaper*."

We're all laughing by the time Brooks is standing among us, and I can tell he's worried just by the look on his face. "If you're laughing about me, I'm out."

"Oh, we were," Iris declares with relish.

She really enjoys antagonizing him, the poor guy.

"And I'm out." Brooks starts to leave, but Rhett stops him, gripping his arm tightly and keeping him in place. "Or maybe not."

"I'm just joking, Brooksie," Iris says with that familiar blithe smile. The one that should induce worry in all of us because we have no idea what she's going to do or say next. "I didn't mean to destroy your manhood when we were babies. I hope you've recuperated enough and everything is okay."

She mock pouts, fluttering her eyelashes at him. Knowing all along her statement will rile him up.

"Destroy my manhood?" Brooks repeats, his dark brows shooting up.

Oh, here they go.

"Well, that's what I've heard over the years. I always thought the story was an embellishment of the truth, but now I'm starting to wonder. Like maybe your manhood could be a little…" Her voice drops to just above a whisper. "Fragile."

"What are you trying to say, Iris? Do you want to see my so-called manhood so I can prove to you that there's nothing wrong with it?" Brooks's hand drops to his crotch, where he cradles his junk in his palm and gives it a squeeze.

All Iris can do is laugh, shaking her head and waving her hands in a sure sign of denial.

"Jesus, Brooks. Please don't whip your dick out in front of Willow," Rhett mutters, his gaze going to mine, his expression apologetic. All I can do is smile weakly in return.

"Are you afraid you'll have some competition?" Brooks taunts.

Rhett scoffs. "As if."

Oh my God. Are we really talking about dick sizes right now?

There's a shift in the air and the voices around us drop to a low murmur. As if they're whispering about something. Or someone.

When I glance to my right, I realize they're whispering about a couple of someones.

Silas and Alana, who appear to be in a somewhat heated argument.

Even the conversation among the four of us dies, our attention going to Lancaster Prep's most popular couple, who seem to be engrossed in their own little world. Their mouths are moving constantly as they attempt to talk over each other, Silas's expression grim while Alana's is full-fledged anger.

I've known her long enough to recognize her emotions. She is definitely not pleased with whatever it is they're talking about.

"Ooh, Alana looks pissed," Iris says gleefully.

"You sound happy about it." My tone is faintly chastising and I can't help it. Maybe I should be glad Alana is arguing with Silas too, but she's been my friend for years, and I can't help but feel bad seeing her in distress.

"She deserves whatever grief Silas brings her," Iris retorts.

"Maybe she's giving him grief."

"Ugh, stop defending him, Willow. It's getting old." Iris rolls her eyes.

Her words don't even bother me because, deep down, she's right. I should absolutely stop rushing to his defense.

"You want to be friends with her? Then go for it! But I refuse to just stand by and watch you two get close. You *know* how she feels about you," Alana suddenly yells, loud enough for all of us to hear.

For *me* to hear, because that statement feels directed right at me.

"It's not like that, Alana. Come on—"

Before Silas can say anything else, she's stomping away from him, tears streaming down her cheeks. Silas watches her go, his hands cupped around the back of his head, arms akimbo.

"Fuck!" he yells, dropping his arms at his sides, glancing over at us.

At me.

I look away first, turning my attention to Iris to find she's already staring at me.

"Sounds like they were fighting about you," she murmurs.

"You really think so?" I'm hoping she'll say no.

"Um, yes." She grabs hold of my arm and steers me away from Rhett and Brooks, practically dragging me away from the crowd so we can have a chat. Everyone's started talking again and music begins to play, a popular song blasting at top volume from an invisible speaker. "Tell me what you're thinking right now."

I'm frowning at my cousin, confused. "I think the question is, what are you thinking?"

"After hearing their argument, I'm guessing Silas did like you, and Alana swooped in and snagged him up. Buuuuttt…" She drawls the word out, tapping her index finger against her pursed lips. "If he really is sitting around thinking about you and talking about you to his freaking girlfriend, maybe he was just settling for Alana. Now that you're back, he's realized his mistake."

I don't feel a single spark of hope at her words. "I don't want to be the cause of their fights or eventual breakup."

"I don't think you have much choice. Looks like you already are." Iris shrugs. "Maybe you should go for it."

"Iris!"

"Willow! I'm being serious."

"I can't." I shake my head, dread filling me at the mere thought.

"Why not? What's stopping you?"

"Alana is—*was* our friend."

"That didn't matter to her," Iris points out.

True. "And I don't think I like him like that anymore."

"You've never been one to turn off your feelings so quickly, Willow. I know you. Besides, that's usually my job." Iris smiles, trying to make light of the moment, but I'm not feeling it.

Glancing over at where the boys still stand, I study Rhett for a moment, smiling faintly when he slaps Brooks's chest with the back of his hand and they both start chuckling. I like that he doesn't seem to take things too seriously, but does that mean he's never serious? Like when it comes to girls?

Like would he really want to be with me if anything was ever to…start between us?

Maybe I'm just being hopeful. I'm basing my interest in Rhett on nothing but physical chemistry and that's not how solid relationships start. We should know each other better first. Chemistry just fizzles out eventually if you're not truly compatible.

And I know Silas and I were compatible at one point. We've been friendly for a while. Actual friends, though I always, always wished for more.

"I think it's a terrible idea…" My voice drifts and I startle when I feel fingers graze my arm. I glance over my shoulder to find Silas standing there.

God, did he hear our conversation? I will die of mortification if he did.

"Hey, Willow." He smiles, but it's uneasy. I'm sure he's not thrilled that we all just witnessed that argument between him and Alana.

"Hi," I squeak, clearing my throat.

"Can you talk for a minute? I don't mean to interrupt." His gaze shifts to Iris.

"You two go ahead and chat all you want. I'm out of here." Iris pats my shoulder before she takes off, heading back toward

Brooks and Rhett.

My heart pangs when she leaves. As I watch her approach the boys. How they smile in greeting at her and how she practically throws herself at Brooks and then just as quickly shoves him away, laughing. She's got her back to him and I note the way Brooks watches her with longing, his expression shifting into neutral when she turns to face him once more.

Hmmm.

"You sure you want to talk? Or would you rather hang out with them?"

I turn at the faint hostility in Silas's voice, frowning at him. His expression evens out, just like Brooks's did only moments ago, and I immediately find it off-putting.

And I never find Silas off-putting.

"I told you we could talk, so let's do it." I smile at him and he smiles in return, obviously pleased.

He reaches for me, his hand cupping my elbow as he steers me away from my cousin and the boys. I glance over my shoulder one last time, my gaze meeting Rhett's, and my heart drops at the look on his face. Realization strikes the further Silas escorts me away from them.

This was a huge mistake.

CHAPTER FIFTEEN

RHETT

I watch Willow leave with that simp prick Silas, my fingers tightening around my cup yet again. I feel the plastic give beneath my fingertips and I take a deep breath, telling myself to calm the fuck down. I suck down the rest of my beer and get rid of my cup, tossing it in a makeshift trashcan.

But it sucks, watching the girl I fully planned on flirting with all evening getting swept up in some bullshit drama. Doesn't she realize Silas is just using her to make Alana jealous? After we all witnessed their little squabble, that's what he has to be doing.

Willow is totally falling for it too.

Iris catches me staring. I can feel her watching me watch Willow as Silas leads her away, slipping into the shadows, and I'm half tempted to follow after them. Tell him to keep his hands off of her.

I do none of that though. I'm not about to become involved in their dramatic little love triangle.

"Does she like him?" The words leave me without thought, and for a second, I regret the question.

"It's hard for her to cut off old feelings," Iris answers.

I send her a questioning look. "What do you mean by that?"

A sigh leaves her. "Can I trust you with this kind of information,

Rhett? Or are you going to blab it to everyone else?" The pointed look Iris aims at me nearly has me squirming where I stand. This girl can be hella intimidating when she wants to be.

But I remain still, shoving my hands in my pockets, dying to know what she's about to tell me. "I don't blab."

"Why don't you ask me that question, huh?" This comes from Brooks, who sounds hurt. Doesn't he realize she ignores him on purpose? She knows it drives him crazy.

"I know I can trust you, Brooksie." She pats him on the chest like he's a good little boy and I swear to God, he smiles. "Come closer. Both of you."

We take a couple of steps closer to her, both of us leaning our heads down since we're taller than Iris. I don't say a word. I swear I'm holding my breath, which is stupid. This isn't a big deal. I don't gossip much with girls because…I just don't. But in this moment, I can feel the anticipation lingering in the air, and my stomach actually twists. Like I'm nervous.

Fucking weird.

"She had a giant crush on Silas the entirety of our sophomore year, but nothing happened. She goes to Italy, comes back, and for whatever reason, believes she still likes him. Despite learning that he's with Alana now, and that Alana knew Willow had a thing for him. She went after him anyway." Iris shakes her head. "But we all know this."

I mean, I didn't, but okay.

"I've been talking trash about Silas constantly, but I started to worry that maybe it was having the opposite effect on her," Iris explains. "Maybe me constantly bagging on him was only making her want him more."

"You really think so?" Brooks looks genuinely perplexed. But he's an only child so that makes sense.

I have a sister and I know how their minds work—sometimes.

"I'm not sure, so I decided to use a different approach," Iris continues. "After watching them fight, I told Willow this could be her chance to try and get Silas."

Brooks makes a dismissive noise. "Bro, that sucks. Not like they're broken up or anything."

"Did you just call me bro?" Iris's voice is sharp and whoa there. I can tell she didn't like him saying that.

"Maybe. I didn't mean to." Brooks is scrambling, which Iris seems to enjoy.

"Anyway." She focuses her attention on me. "Maybe this was her chance to see if they could become something after all, and what do you know, Silas appeared as if I conjured him up myself and now, they're talking."

"You really want them to be together?" After that convoluted explanation, I'm thinking Brooks is even more confused.

"No, I don't. Like you said, Silas is still with Alana. If he really wanted Willow, don't you think he'd go after her?"

"I don't know." I rub along the side of my jaw, contemplating the scenario. Hating that this girl that I actually like is talking to some slimeball who might want her.

"What do you not know?" Iris asks me.

"It's risky. What if they talk, he realizes he's madly in love with Willow, and then he dumps Alana for her?" That is the absolute last thing I want, but how can I stop it?

In this moment, I can't.

"I'm hoping Willow is smarter than that. She'll see through what he's saying." Iris's voice is firm, and she's nodding, crossing her arms. "I have faith."

I hope she's right.

CHAPTER SIXTEEN

WILLOW

Silas leads me deeper into the woods, heading toward the beach that's on the other side of the trees. The air grows cooler and I'm shivering, tugging on the hem of my sweatshirt and trying to cover my bare skin.

"Can't we just talk here?" I come to a stop and so does Silas, who turns to face me. He hasn't said a single thing since we left the party and he looks stressed out.

"Sure, we can." His tone is easy, but I note the frown that appears on his face when he pulls his phone out of his pocket and checks it. I see the long list of text notifications that appears when his face unlocks the screen and I just know they're all from Alana. She's probably looking for him.

I would be too if he was my boyfriend and we just got into a very public argument.

"What do you want to talk about?" I wrap my arms around myself, rubbing my upper arms to try and generate some heat.

"It's just—it's been so weird for me and Alana since you came back," he admits.

I go completely still at his confession. I'm barely even breathing, I'm so shocked.

"Over the summer we had a great time. We got really close,

really fast and she was so much fun. Now, we come back to campus and I thought things would be perfect. Even better because there are no parents around, you know? Instead, she's acting jealous over you all the time and constantly bringing you up. Then we start fighting and it spirals out of control." He shakes his head.

I gape at him, shocked he would say all of that. "Why are you bringing me into your relationship?"

"I'm not. She is."

"But why?"

He shrugs. "I don't know. Like I said, I think she's jealous of you. I can't be friends with you because she's jealous? Such bullshit. She can't tell me what to do."

"Don't you want to respect her wishes? She's your girlfriend. I would think you'd care about her feelings. And why does it matter if we're friends or not?"

"Like I just said, I don't like Alana telling me what to do. Saying who I can and cannot talk to. She's not my mom. It's not my problem if she's jealous of you," he practically spits out.

I hate that he keeps saying that. "Maybe she's not jealous. She could just be uncomfortable with you wanting to talk to me when she knows…"

I clamp my lips shut, not about to delve any further.

"When she knows what?" he asks after a few seconds of silence.

"Nothing." I shake my head.

"You used to like me, right?"

Thank God it's dark out here so he can't see how red my face must be. My cheeks are burning and I forget all about being cold. I try to speak, but the words feel like they're clogged in my throat, and besides, what would I say?

"If you love Alana, you'll focus all of your attention on her and forget about me," I tell him, standing up a little straighter. "I don't need to be brought into the middle of your relationship. You've both made your choice."

He remains quiet for a moment, and I can hear the waves

crashing along the shore in the near distance, mixed with the steady throb of the bass coming from the music playing at the party. I wish I was there, laughing with Iris. Wondering if she has a thing for Brooks. Staring at Rhett and contemplating throwing myself at him.

Not here in the dark having to listen to Silas complain about Alana and how they fight about me, which is flat out dumb.

And none of my business.

"I have to go," I tell him, turning on my heel and scurrying away from him. I launch into a full-out run when I hear him call my name. Hear his footsteps drawing closer. A quick peek over my shoulder lets me know he's chasing after me, a determined expression on his face, and I increase my pace. Keep looking backward to make sure he's not too close—

I collide with a wall. It's solid but warm and I realize that it's not just a wall, it's an actual person. A boy. A tall, broad boy whose arms immediately clamp around me, steadying me on my feet.

"Hey, everything okay?"

I'd recognize that deep voice anywhere.

Lifting my head, I stare into Rhett's eyes, sending him a pleading look. "I'm fine."

"You sure?" His voice is a low murmur and sends a zip of awareness down my spine that's only intensified when he brushes my hair away from my face, his fingers lingering on my skin.

This type of reaction never happened with Silas.

"Oh. Hey." We both turn to find Silas standing in front of us, looking vaguely sweaty as he shoves his hair from his forehead. "You all right, Willow?"

"She's fine," Rhett answers for me, his voice firm. He somehow angles me to his side, keeping his arm around my shoulders, and I wonder what we look like to Silas.

I'm hoping we look like a couple.

Silas frowns, his gaze switching from me to Rhett and then back to me. "Willow? Are you okay?"

"She's with me, you know." Rhett's arm tightens around my shoulders and he tugs me even closer. He's as solid as a rock and so warm. I lean into him as if I have no control of myself. "You can take your concern elsewhere—like maybe to your girlfriend? I highly suggest you get the hell out of here if you don't want any trouble."

"What the hell? Are you serious?" Silas's gaze meets mine. "You never mentioned that to me."

"You never gave me the chance," I murmur, going along with it.

God, what am I doing?

Silas watches us for long, silent seconds until he finally shakes his head. "Figures."

That's all he says before he turns and walks away.

We watch him go, and the moment he's out of my eyesight, I shrug Rhett's arm off my shoulders, turning to face him. "What was that for?"

"What are you talking about?" Rhett blinks, innocent as can be.

What a crock.

"That I'm with you? Like we're together?" I throw my arms up in the air, exasperated with men in general tonight.

"It seemed like the right thing to do at the time." He shrugs, as if he doesn't have a care in the world.

"It was a mistake. Now Silas is going to tell Alana, and she's going to tell everyone that we're together, when we're not." Alana has a huge mouth. Iris and I learned that the hard way a while ago when she would share our secrets with others. Secrets we fully expected her to, you know, keep secret.

"So they talk about us. So what? Might keep things interesting." He smiles, though it slowly starts to fade when I don't smile in return. "What? Are you mad at me, Will? I was just trying to help."

It's the way he says it, his voice soft. And the look on his face too.

He means it.

A sigh leaves me and my shoulders sag. "I appreciate you trying to help, but that probably just caused more problems."

"Let them talk. Everyone will forget about us when some new drama happens anyway, and I can practically guarantee that'll happen in approximately forty-eight hours, if not sooner."

He's not wrong, but still. "What if people expect us to act like a couple? If we don't, they'll accuse us of lying."

Rhett rears back. "I'm not a liar."

"I'm sure you're not, but you did just lie to Silas."

"Woman, I did it to help you." He shakes his head, incredulous. "You're infuriating."

"Funny because that's exactly how I would describe you." I storm away from him before I say something dumb, and go in search of Iris, who I find by the bonfire. It's huge, the orange flames licking at the night sky, and when I go to stand next to her, it's almost too hot, being this close.

The moment she sees my face, she knows something is wrong. "Tell me everything."

I do, furiously whispering in her ear as I spill my guts and explain the entire story. By the time I'm done, she's smiling and I'm frowning, my stomach swirling with despair over the situation.

"What am I supposed to do?" I practically wail at her when I'm finished.

"You know what I think you should do? Go along with the lie Rhett created." Iris backs away from me and grabs hold of my shoulders, giving me a little shake. "This is perfect. You pretend to be in a relationship with Rhett, and Silas will finally leave you alone."

"Oh my God, you make no sense. A few minutes ago, you said this could be my chance with Silas and now you're encouraging me to have a fake relationship with Rhett instead?" I shake my head. "I don't understand you."

"I was trying to do reverse psychology on you, but I don't think it worked." She pulls me in for a hug, her mouth at my ear. "You stay here for a few minutes, okay? I'm going to go make the rounds and see what other people are saying about this."

"No, don't leave me." I grab at her sleeve when she pulls away, keeping her from escaping. Then I remember how I want to stand on my own two feet and I let go of her sleeve, taking a step back. "What should I do if Silas tries to talk to me again?"

"He won't." Iris nods her head once. "He's over there begging and pleading with Alana as we speak."

I spot Silas on the other side of the fire, doing exactly as Iris described. Alana is standing next to him, staring off into the distance with her arms crossed and wearing an angry expression while Silas just keeps talking.

That doesn't look good.

"I'll be right back." Iris pats my shoulder before taking off, her blonde hair streaming behind her as she practically runs over to a large group of girls, most of whom are in our grade.

I watch her as she starts talking, gesturing wildly in typical Iris fashion, while I'm also trying to keep the panic that wants to flood me at bay. This is fine. Everything is going to be fine.

Maybe.

Hopefully.

I wander around the fire, smiling at people as I pass by them, trying to appear like nothing is bothering me. I eventually find an old log on the ground that's set back from the fire and I sit on it, watching the flames dance. The fire crackles and roars, the wood settling as it slowly turns to ash, sending up a fresh wave of sparks into the night. Some of the girls standing close to the fire squeal and jump back, and when a few of them spot me, I offer them a smile, wishing someone else would talk to me. Anyone else.

I need the distraction.

But none of them do. They smile in return and some of them even greet me with a wave and a hello, but then they take off, leaving me by myself once more. I don't know if I've ever felt this lonely at a party before.

One week into school and my senior year isn't going as planned.

No, more like it's a nightmare. I wonder if I could test out and graduate early. I have most of my required classes done. I can't stand the idea of being this miserable during my senior year. Iris might be disappointed, but she wouldn't miss me that badly. She spent an entire school year without me. She could do it again.

"Hey." Looking up, I find Rhett standing there, watching me. Always coming to my rescue. "Can I join you?"

I shrug my answer, and he settles in, making the log wobble a bit with his weight.

"I'm sorry I implied that we were together to Silas." My gaze quickly cuts to his, surprised he'd apologize this soon. I'm used to the stubborn men in my family who take hours if not days to utter "I'm sorry." Even my dad is bad at apologizing. Mom always says it's the Lancaster in them.

"I probably shouldn't have done that," he continues when I remain quiet. "But I wanted him to leave you alone and I didn't know what else to say. The guy is more determined than I thought he'd be."

"The guy should worry about his own girlfriend and not me," I murmur. It feels good to voice my feelings out loud.

"No shit." Rhett shifts, kicking his legs out straight in front of him and crossing his feet. He's got on a fresh set of white Nikes with a navy swoosh, and I absently wonder how he keeps them so clean. "Are you upset because you like that guy and you think I ruined your chances with him? I can go tell him I was—"

"No. Don't go to him. I don't want you saying anything to him." I grab hold of his arm and clutch it, my gaze pleading. "Just leave it alone."

He drops his gaze to my hands still on his arm before lifting it to mine. "Okay, I will."

"I just don't want people to get the wrong idea." I release my hold on his arm, missing touching him almost immediately. He's so muscular, and he's almost as hot as the fire burning in front of us. "About…us."

"Why? You don't want people thinking we're together?"

"Well…no." I squint at him. "Do you?"

"Is it that big of a deal?"

"I figured it would be a big deal to you." His frown deepens and I further explain myself. "You don't really seem like the serious type, from what Iris has told me."

"I'm not." He pauses. "Usually."

"Then there's no reason anyone would believe we're together." I stare at the fire once again, fighting the sadness that wants to overtake me.

"Right? That's perfect then."

I glance over at him. "What do you mean?"

"We can play stupid."

"Play stupid how?"

"It's our word against his. And Alana's." Rhett shrugs and I admire the line of his shoulders. They are just so incredibly broad. I bet it would feel nice, resting my head there, drawing comfort from his strength. His warmth. I remember what it felt like when he wrapped me up in his arms. "Maybe we can be friends."

I jerk my gaze to his when I realize he's waiting for a reply. "You want to be my friend?"

"Why not? I like you, Will." He flashes me one of those one-sided smiles that makes my heart flutter.

I realize I do not want to be just his friend. There's something brewing between us. I can feel it.

Can he?

"I like you too," I admit, my voice almost a whisper. "As a friend."

"Right." He nods, his gaze focused on the fire as well. "We're friendly."

"For sure." I'm nodding as well. "Keeps things simple."

"I like simple."

"Me too."

"Guess we have that in common."

"I suppose so," I murmur. "It's been rough for me since I came back."

"Rough how?"

"I've felt a little out of sorts since I came back here."

"What do you mean?"

"No one really ever tries to talk to me. Everyone feels like a stranger, except for Iris. Well, and you've been nice to me too."

"I don't intimidate easily." His friendly smile makes me smile at him in response.

"I'm sure that's not the issue when it comes to me," I say, my voice wry. Come on now, we don't need to get too carried away.

"Seriously, Will? You do know why you're sitting here alone on this log watching the fire, right?" I shake my head, both curious and dreading what he's about to say. "Everyone's intimidated by you. Even little Silas over there."

He waves a hand in Silas's direction, who is still with Alana. She doesn't seem as rigid as she did a few minutes ago.

"No way." I shake my head.

"Definitely," Rhett says with a nod. "You're intimidating as fuck."

"I don't even understand how." I find it incredibly difficult to believe that's the case. I'm just me. I haven't changed that much over the years, and it feels like I've become more invisible since returning to Lancaster Prep.

"You're a Lancaster. You're a senior. You've got this air about you that seems to say that you're…I don't know. Better than everyone else?" He lifts his brows, and oh my God…

I'm horrified by him saying that. Devastated.

"Do I act like a snobby—bitch around everyone? Is that why?" My voice is a harsh whisper and I swear, tears are threatening to spill.

"What? No. Not at all. I described that all wrong. You're just—you emit something. It's like your aura or some shit." He shifts on the log, seemingly uncomfortable, and I wonder if it's from sitting for too long or if it's what he's saying that's making him act a certain kind of way. "You're like…sophisticated. Mysterious."

"Mysterious?"

"Yeah. Very mysterious. All the mystery that swirls around you makes me want to get to know you better. Figure you out. Just as friends, though." He stares straight ahead, as if he's transfixed by the fire, and I study his chiseled profile for a moment, unsure of how to respond.

"Maybe that's what we should do then," I murmur.

His head swivels in my direction, his brows drawn together. "Do what?"

"Get to know one another better. Figure each other out." I pause. "As friends."

CHAPTER SEVENTEEN

WILLOW

I wait for his answer, holding my breath. Worried he'll reject me or worse, laugh at me and then reject me. This entire night has been surreal, and I'm low key terrified of what his response might be.

If he tells me no, I'll die on the spot. Right here on the log in front of everyone. At least that means I won't have to worry about facing everybody at school after the rumor gets out that Rhett and I are supposedly together.

"You really think we could keep things friendly between us?" he asks me, sounding amused.

"I don't want to fight with you—"

"I'm not talking about fighting," he says, interrupting me. "I'm talking about how much I'm attracted to you."

I go silent. All I can hear is the pounding of my heart. I wonder if he can hear it too.

"But I'm thinking you don't feel the same." He's staring at the fire again, the disappointment written all over his face.

"Rhett..." I clamp my lips shut, unable to find the right words.

He shifts his position, trying to get comfortable, which is impossible on this stupid log. "You're going to let me down easy. It's fine. I get it."

Let him down easy?

"Just know that I'd never give you a reason to feel confused or conflicted. If we were together, you would know how I feel about you. I'm an upfront kind of guy, even if I've never done this sort of thing before."

"What sort of thing?" I whisper.

"Work so hard to get a girl to admit she's interested in me." A low laugh escapes him and the sound of it makes me tingle. "You're tough."

"I don't mean to be." I pause again for a moment, deciding to just go for it. "Have you ever wanted someone you can't have?"

"No." He grins. "If I want something, I go after it."

"And do you usually get it?"

His grin grows, if that's possible. "Always."

I stare at the fire once more, though I can feel Rhett's gaze on me. "I never do."

"Oh, come on now." He sounds like he doesn't believe me. "Don't pull a poor little rich girl act on me."

"I'm not trying to," I start, but he shakes his head, cutting me off.

"Maybe you're going after the wrong things."

The way he says it, so simple, so logical, makes me realize that he's probably right.

"You think so?"

"I'm sure of it. Sometimes what you want is sitting directly in front of you, but you don't even see it."

I stare into his eyes, wondering if he's referring to himself. Wondering more if he's doing it on purpose.

"Have you ever had a girlfriend?" I ask, curious.

He shakes his head. "Never."

"Hmm."

"What about you? How many boyfriends have you had?"

"None."

"Seriously?"

"Seriously." I nod. "My number is zero."

"Ever been kissed?" His gaze drops to my lips as he leans his body closer to mine, our shoulders brushing.

That brief contact sends a scattering of tingles up my arm.

"Yes," I admit, my voice soft. "A few times. Briefly."

"No full-on makeout sessions?"

"Why are you so interested in how long I've kissed someone?" This is embarrassing. I should've had a beer. At least that would've given me a little liquid courage.

"Want me to be honest?"

"No."

Rhett ignores my answer. "You look like a girl who hasn't been kissed much."

My lips part and my throat goes dry. "Is that an insult?"

"Just an observation. Definitely not an insult. You have a sweet, innocent way about you."

Oh God.

Oh.

God.

I know he didn't mean it as an insult, but it kind of felt like one.

I jump to my feet, eager to get out of here. "I need to go."

He tilts his head back, his expression confused. "Where are you going?"

"Anywhere but here."

I leave him where he sits, determined to head back to my dorm suite and be done with this night once and for all, but by the time I'm rounding the front of the old ruins, I can hear Rhett shouting my name as he chases after me. I can feel him draw closer.

It's no shock at all when I feel his long fingers clamp around my upper arm, and I go easily when he spins me around to face him.

"What the hell, Lancaster? Why'd you run like that?"

"I hated what you said to me," I admit, my voice low. I cross my arms in front of me yet again, cold once more.

"What? About you not being kissed much?"

That wasn't the worst part.

"When I called you sweet? Every girl I know wants to be called that." He sounds frustrated with me, but he's still here. Talking to me. I take that as a good sign.

"The innocent part," I tell him. "I just—I don't know. It set me off."

"I'll say." He practically snorts. "You stormed off like a snake bit your ass and you needed to see a doctor, stat."

I roll my eyes. Sometimes he says crazy stuff. "I don't want to be known as a sweet, innocent girl. I just spent a year abroad, drinking wine and learning about art. Growing up and doing things on my own, you know? But here, I'm the same person I was before. You didn't even know me then, and you described me exactly how everyone else sees me."

Well, I lied a little bit. I only drank wine like twice, but I felt terribly sophisticated when I did it, even though it tasted kind of awful. Rhett doesn't need to know any of that though.

He shifts his stance, leaning back against the old building, which makes him almost at eye level with me. He's so tall, it's kind of nice to face him without having to tilt my head back. "What exactly do you want everyone to see?"

"I don't know." I do, I'm just embarrassed to admit it out loud.

"Here's what's funny, Will." He levels that gaze on me and it's like he can see right through me, which is unsettling. "I think you know exactly what you want everyone to see when it comes to you. You're just afraid to voice it out loud."

I remain quiet, vaguely disturbed that he's able to figure me out so easily. No one else takes the time to do that. Not even Iris, though I don't blame her for it. We've known each other since birth. I'm sure she believes she knows everything there is about me.

But she doesn't. Not everything. Just like I'm sure she has a few secrets of her own.

"Come here," he murmurs when I don't respond, tilting his head to the side. He settles onto the slight ledge that sticks out of the building, his expression expectant. He's waiting for me to do something. Say something.

Hesitating, I part my lips, confused. Part of me wants to reprimand him for trying to tell me what to do because he doesn't own me, but the bigger, more secretive part of me wants to immediately give in to his gently-spoken command.

He has a confidence I aspire to. Like he fully expects everything to work out for him because he's just that lucky. Or maybe he doesn't even believe in luck. Confident people don't need to—things happen because they want them to.

"Come on, Will. Get your pretty ass over here." He actually pats his thigh like I'm going to…what? Sit on his lap? In his dreams.

Hmm, in mine too.

I take a tentative step toward him. Then another. When I draw close enough, he lets out a frustrated growl and grabs my hand, yanking me to him. I collide with his big body, a soft "oh" emitting from my lips, and I almost squeal when he whips his arm around my waist and settles me on his thigh, having me sit on his lap, just as I imagined.

"What are you doing?" I whisper, bracing my hand on his chest when his thigh dips lower, jostling me around.

"Go ahead. Act like you're into me." He leans forward, his mouth settling at my ear, murmuring. "Your friend is watching us right now."

I freeze for a moment, just about to check and see who he's actually referring to when his arm tightens around my waist like a band.

"Don't look," he warns before he slowly pulls back a little bit so I can see his face again. "We need to play it cool."

"What do you want me to do?" I lift my chin, staring into his eyes. This close, I can definitely see the flecks of green, and the golden-brown mixing in. Oh, his eyes are beautiful.

Everything about him is beautiful.

"Go ahead." His voice sounds like a dare, resonating inside me. "Give in to what you want, Willow."

My skin prickles at him calling me by my full name, something he rarely says, and it's just the fuel I need to do exactly what he's telling me.

I lightly touch his face. Can feel the faint stubble on his cheek prickling against my palm. I slowly streak my fingers downward, my gaze wandering, blatantly drinking him in. Lingering on a tiny scar that I see on the left corner of his mouth.

"What happened here?" I trace the tiny scar, coming perilously close to his lips.

His smile is lopsided, not revealing his teeth. "Accident when I was five. Fell off my bike."

"Must've been bad."

"I barely remember it." His gaze drops to my lips. "I'm not kissing you tonight."

Disappointment floods me. "Maybe I didn't want you to."

"You do." His lips curve.

"You're terribly confident."

"I know you want it." He leans in once more, his mouth brushing my ear lobe, making me shiver. "I want it too, but not out here in front of everyone. I want to do it right."

Rhett pulls away and I'm breathless at his words. Mindless. Confused and exhilarated and all of the things. "What do you mean, do it right?"

"If you have to ask, Will, then I'm assuming you haven't experienced it yet." He smiles, the look on his face reminding me of a devil.

Because only a devil could tempt me this badly, and we haven't even done anything.

CHAPTER EIGHTEEN

WILLOW

I feel like I'm floating on a cloud as I get ready for school. While I eat in the dining hall, semi-listening to Iris and Bronwyn chatter away, me nodding at the appropriate moments, though I'm not paying attention to anything they're saying.

I'm too caught up in my own thoughts. Memories. Friday night out at the ruins. The things Rhett said to me. The way he touched me. How he looked at my mouth while he told me he wasn't going to kiss me in front of everyone. His hot gaze lingering on my lips felt like a kiss, though I know that was nothing.

The idea of him kissing me, what it might feel like…

I shiver just thinking about it.

"You okay over there?" Iris snaps her fingers in front of my face, making me blink.

"Rude." I push her hand away, making her laugh. "I'm fine. Just…tired."

"Thinking about Rhett?" Iris's brows shoot up before she shares a knowing glance with Bronwyn.

"Maybe." I let my gaze wander around the dining hall in search of him but he's nowhere to be found.

"They're at practice," Iris says, because of course she's figured out what I'm doing. "Preparing for this week's game."

"Already?" Bronwyn asks.

"They're always preparing, meaning, they're always practicing." Iris takes a sip of her coffee.

"How do you know all of this?" I ask, curious.

Panic flares in Iris's eyes for the briefest second before it's gone, like I never even saw it. "I just…we all know. You barely have to pay attention and you'll hear everything you never wanted to know about the football team around here."

Huh. I don't agree, and I spend the majority of my time with Iris. Unless I'm in a class we don't share. But whatever. I think she's secretly fascinated with the football team. Maybe even a specific player, though I'm not quite sure who that could be. For once in her life, she's keeping everything quiet—meaning, she's not telling me anything about a crush. Normally this would hurt me, but I think I understand more now.

I don't want to share too many details about my feelings for Rhett. One, because I'm still trying to process them. Two, I don't want to get too ahead of myself. This could be nothing.

So why does it feel like it has the potential to be…everything?

Trying to be logical, I shove that thought from my brain. I had the same thoughts floating through my mind when I had a crush on Silas and look how that turned out. Speaking of…

He's sitting two tables over from ours with Alana practically in his lap, their heads close together, a faint smile on her face when he touches her cheek. I'm kind of grossed out by their obvious display of affection and I start to tear my gaze away from them only for Alana to catch me staring at the last minute.

That satisfied smile on her face when she does catch me? Infuriating.

"I need to go." I grab my backpack and push my chair away from the table, leaping to my feet.

Iris and Bronwyn tip their heads back, watching me.

"Where are you going?" Iris sounds confused.

"I need to stop by the library before class starts." I offer them a quick wave, fleeing the dining hall as fast as I can. I make sure I don't look in Silas and Alana's direction because that's the last thing I want, though I assume she'd guess they're the reason I'm leaving so quickly.

And she'd be sort of right. It's not that I wish I was in her place—I don't. After everything that happened between Rhett and me Friday night, I know I'm not interested in Silas.

Maybe I'm a little jealous of how easily affectionate they are together though. Hopefully, I'll get something like that. Or do I even want something like that?

See? My mind is a confused jumble of emotions. I don't know what I want and I'm still trying to figure it out.

My stride is brisk as I head for the library, though I really have no purpose going there beyond me telling the girls that's where I was headed. Class doesn't start for another ten minutes and the campus is slowly coming to life. Students are wandering along the paths, some of them scurrying toward the dining hall for a last-minute breakfast. There are a few people hanging out in front of the library, most of them clutching coffee cups in their hands as they chat with their friends.

I approach the library on the north side, rounding the building so I can enter through the front doors when I spot a familiar someone. I come to a complete stop, taking him in.

Rhett.

He's in his uniform, even the jacket, but his tie hangs around his neck completely undone, the buttons at the top of his shirt open. His light brown hair is damp, like he just got out of the shower, and he's just about to shove half a muffin into his mouth when he spots me, doing a double take.

I'm frozen in place, unsure how to react, feeling like a fool when I don't do anything at all. I don't even smile. It's like I can't move and I watch as he goes ahead and pushes the muffin into his mouth, chewing as he makes his approach.

"Willow Lancaster." He says my name like we barely know

each other, when I was sitting on his lap Friday night and his hands were on me, his mouth at my ear and saying all of those things that leave me a trembling mess just thinking about them.

"Rhett Bennett," I return because I have no clue what else I should say.

"You're looking good this morning." His gaze sweeps over me slowly, lingering on what feels like every part of me, and a hot flush coats my skin at his obvious perusal.

"Um, thank you." I did nothing special. I am in my uniform, my hair pulled back with a hunter green bow that matches the green in our plaid skirts. My lips are red but otherwise I'm not wearing much makeup except for a light coat of mascara on my lashes. I've got my usual Mary Jane shoes on my feet too—this version is made by Miu Miu.

Meaning, I am dressed as my usual self and looking the best that I can considering it's a Monday, yet he still seems wowed by my appearance. This is definitely more than Silas ever gave me.

"Where are you going?" he asks after a few seconds of me remaining quiet while I absorb his words. His overwhelming presence.

"The library." I wave a weak hand in the direction of the massive building we're standing in front of. "What are you doing?"

We didn't talk over the weekend because I didn't think it felt right. Besides, I don't have his number so I don't know how I could get a hold of him. I suppose I could've reached out via the school app we have on our phones because we have access to every teacher on it, as well as students, but I thought that might be weird.

And I didn't have the courage.

"Just got done with practice. Cramming food in my mouth before class." He pinches off a piece of muffin and pops it into his mouth. "Still thinking about Friday night."

I blink at him, shocked he'd admit such a thing. "Excuse me?"

Rhett swallows and grins. "Come on now, Will. Don't play cool with me."

"I…" The words disappear on my tongue when he takes a few steps closer to me, his body brushing against mine, his scent filling my head. The boy has no business smelling so delicious.

"You still thinking about it too?" he asks, his gravelly voice settling in my stomach, warming me up.

I shrug one shoulder, sucking in a breath when he grabs my hand, interlocking our fingers. His palm is wide and slightly rough, his fingers long, and a thrill streaks through me at him holding my hand.

This boy makes me weak.

"Come on now, Will. Be real with me."

"I am still thinking about it." I lift my head, our gazes locking. His eyes are a beautiful swirl of brown and green and I lose myself in them for a bit. "I feel awkward."

The words blurt out of me like I have no control over myself.

He smiles, reaching with his other hand to tuck a stray strand of hair behind my ear. "You don't look awkward. Why do you feel that way?"

"I'm afraid I'm going to say the wrong thing." I swallow hard. "Do the wrong thing."

His expression softens. "You can't do anything wrong in my eyes."

I actually snort, which is embarrassing. See? I can do something wrong. "Please. You're just saying that."

"Nope. Pretty sure I mean it." He smiles and the sight of it makes my breath catch. The bell rings and he releases his grip on my hand, taking a step away from me. "See you in English?"

I nod slowly, like I'm in a trance. "Definitely."

"I'll let you get to the library then. Bye, Will."

I watch him walk away, impressed by his long stride and how it eats up the ground. He's so fast. And tall. And broad.

The realization hits me so hard it nearly takes my breath away.

I've got it so bad for him.

With a wistful sigh I turn and collide with someone, a loud oof coming from the both of us when our bodies make contact. I take a hurried step back, the apologies already falling from my lips only for me to cut them off when I realize who I've run into and see the glare on her face.

Alana. It's like I can't shake her.

"Watch where you're going," she says, her tone haughty. Like I ran into her on purpose.

"I suppose I could say the same to you," I return, my voice just as snotty. I'm tired of dealing with her rude looks and obvious laughter at my expense. Or maybe that's just my insecurities shining through but I don't know. I'm pretty certain she enjoys rubbing her relationship with Silas in my face.

"Look, I can't help it if he liked me better," she says, lifting her chin. "You were gone. What was I supposed to do? Tell Silas no, that he should wait for you to come back? You two danced around each other for months during sophomore year and nothing happened."

I flinch, hating how she says that, even though it's the truth. But I'm not about to let her continue talking down to me. I'm over it.

Over her.

"You can do whatever you want. It's a free country," I say, my voice remarkably calm.

"You're right. It is. And we can do whatever we want." Alana is about to walk away when I speak again, making her pause.

"I don't care what you two are doing. It's like you're sitting close to me and putting on a show so I can't help but notice. Let me reassure you that it's completely unnecessary. There's someone else I'm interested in now." When she turns to face me, I continue. "And he's a thousand times better than Silas."

Okay, that was mean, but I can't help myself. I got a teeny bit of satisfaction of seeing the irritation cross her face too. That's what she gets for always trying to put me down. I can do it too, even though I feel like a mean girl.

"God, you're so annoying. Thinking you're something special just because you're a Lancaster," Alana mutters as she practically runs away.

I watch her go, her words on replay in my head. That's always been her problem. She's jealous of me. Did she get with Silas because it makes her feel like she stole him from me? If that's the case…

That's really messed up.

CHAPTER NINETEEN

RHETT

The day is a grind, but that's expected for a Monday. Weight training at six in the morning, followed by a short but intense practice isn't the easiest way to start the week, but according to Coach, it's necessary. Can't lie, it felt pretty good pushing my body to the limit with training. Having the guys surround me, yelling their encouragement as I increased my bench press weight. They cheered me on when I lifted the heaviest weight yet for me, and I enjoyed every moment of it.

Not as much as I enjoyed spending my Friday night with Will, though.

Catching her in front of the library had been a pleasant surprise. Swear to God she gets prettier every time I see her. What's even better? She doesn't seem to realize what her body or her sway has over me.

Girl has a lot of sway. Might even go as far as to call it power. She could snap her fingers and I'd come running, willing to do whatever she needed from me. Does that make me whipped when we're not even in a real relationship yet? Is that wrong? If so, then I don't want to be right.

I've never felt this way about a girl before. Like I can't stop thinking about her. Like I'm obsessed with her. Because I am—

obsessed with Willow Lancaster. I want to know every little thing about her. What she likes, what she doesn't like, what makes her laugh, what makes her cry. Once I find that out, I will do my damnedest to never risk seeing her tears. They'd probably destroy me.

Man, I'm overdramatic on this fine Monday morning.

By the time I'm strolling into English class, I spot my pretty girl sitting in her usual desk, a faint smile on her face as she stares at her phone screen. I just stand in the open doorway, people pushing past me to enter class, waiting for her to notice me. As if she can sense me staring, she lifts her head, her gaze finding mine, and the secret smile that curls her scarlet lips has my heart picking up speed.

Willow ducks her head like she's shy, her hair falling over her face, shielding her. Damn, that's cute.

I enter the classroom, catching that one chick Alana watching me, her upper lip curled in disgust. I send her a dismissive glance, not in the mood to deal with unwarranted bitchiness on a Monday morning, and I settle into the desk right behind Willow's, tugging on a strand of silky dark hair to get her attention.

"Hey." I drop my backpack at my feet, leaning forward so I can catch a whiff of her sweet scent. Whatever perfume she wears or lotion or whatever it is reminds me of candy. As in, the girl smells good enough to eat.

"Hi." She turns to the side, almost facing me but not quite, her lips curled into a closed-mouth smile. "How are you?"

"Better now that you're in front of me." Speaking nothing but the truth, which has her cheeks turning pink.

Adorable.

"Did you see your friend glaring at me?" I ask her.

Willow's gaze goes immediately to Alana before returning to mine. "We had a minor confrontation this morning in front of the library."

"When? How did I miss this?"

"It was after you left. I ran into her and she immediately started saying snotty, hurtful things toward me."

The wounded look on Will's face is like an arrow to the heart—and not a good one either. "What did she say?" I sound pissed.

I am pissed.

"It really doesn't matter." She waves a dismissive hand. "She hates me. I accused her of putting on a show in front of me with Silas to make me jealous."

"She probably does," I say gruffly, annoyed. Why anyone would want to fuck with Willow is beyond me. "I hope you put her in her place."

"I did." Willow waves her hand again, like she wants to sweep this conversation away. "How's football going?"

I like how she's asking about it. And how she phrases it kind of awkwardly too. "Practice was intense. We're prepping for our first game, which is an away game and I hate that."

"You hate away games?" She's frowning like she doesn't get it.

"Well, sort of. It's always better to have homefield advantage, but what I really don't like is when the first game of the season is away. I prefer to kick off the season at home," I explain.

"Why is it an away game then?" She sounds genuinely curious.

"The schedule switches every year. Last year, our first game of the season was at home. Actually, the first two were, and then we played three away games. It's always changing every year."

"Oh. I have no idea how any of it works." She nods, smiling faintly. "I hate to admit it, but I know absolutely nothing about football."

"Not a problem, Will. I can teach you *everything* I know," I drawl, pleased to see her cheeks turning that rosy shade of pink again.

More than willing to teach her whatever she wants to know.

CHAPTER TWENTY

WILLOW

The week goes by quickly. Homework starts to get a little more intense, and I have my first quiz in American Government on Friday. I spend a lot of my time after school holed up in my room or at the library with Iris, working on our assignments that are due.

Well, I work on them. Iris has a hard time concentrating sometimes. She's such a social butterfly and she looks at us hanging out at the library as a chance to talk to lots of people. Meaning, she's a complete distraction.

Gotta love her though.

Rhett and I talk in class and we even spoke during lunch today, but he told me he wouldn't be around school tomorrow because they have to leave early to travel to their away game, which filled me with disappointment. And while he's not asking for more—like my phone number or to go out on a date—he is chatting with me in my DMs at night. Flirtatious messages that leave me blushing and wondering if he's telling the truth.

You looked hot today.

Do you ever wear any other color lipstick?

Wish you could go to my game Friday. I want to see you in the stands.

That last message gave me way too much hope. He wants to

see me cheering him on? He wants me to go to the game? Why can't I? Just because it's far? I'm sure we could leave after school and watch them play.

It's Thursday night and Iris is in my room, tapping away at her phone screen while sitting on my bed, not bothering to study for our upcoming test.

Typical.

I'm at my desk hunched over our textbook, my eyes crossing as I skim the first two chapters over and over again, trying to absorb what I'm reading. Highlighter pen in hand and running it over what seems like something vitally important and might appear on a quiz.

I hate studying.

"I hate studying," Iris proclaims, as if she lives in my brain.

I glare at her from over my shoulder before returning my attention to the book. "Funny. Doesn't look like you're studying."

"I'm not. I hate it, remember." She sets her phone onto the mattress beside her and lets loose a long, forlorn sigh. "I am so ready for the weekend."

"Are you doing anything special?" I don't know why I bother asking. We'll most likely be together but sometimes she goes home while I stay here, or I go to my house.

"Spending it with you on campus, most likely. I'm just ready for the break. School is such a drag." She stretches her arms above her head and rolls over onto her side, staring at the wall. "I wish I'd graduated early."

"You probably still could."

"But that means I'd have to study extra hard and take exit exams. That sounds like a nightmare."

"You can't wish for one thing but not put in the work in order to achieve it," I tell her.

She goes silent for long seconds. To the point that I turn in my chair to check on her. She's staring at me as if I've lost my mind.

"Since when did you become an inspirational poster hanging

on a classroom wall?" she asks.

"I'm just speaking truths, Iris." I study her, noting how she keeps moving and shifting, like she can't stay still. "Are you okay? You seem restless."

"I *am* restless. I don't know why, but everything around here is bugging me. I want out." She scratches at the side of her neck, then gathers her hair and piles it on top of her head, holding it there with one hand. "Is it hot in here or is it just me?"

"It's just you. And what do you mean, you want out? Where do you want to go?"

"Anywhere but here? I'm not sure. I just feel ready to spread my wings and fly right off this campus, never to see it again." She drops her hand, her hair falling around her face, and she shoves it out of the way with a frustrated sigh. "Don't you ever feel that way?"

Not particularly, but I don't want to say that out loud and make her feel bad, or worse, get into an argument over it. Besides, I had my chance to leave and while I enjoyed spending time in Italy, I also missed this place. And her. Plus, I don't want to leave, not when something is starting to form between me and Rhett. That's exciting. Why would I want to walk away from him now?

"You probably don't ever feel that way," she says when I still haven't answered her. "You had your shot and lived it up in Italy. Honestly, I'm surprised you came back. I don't think I would've been able to leave Europe to return to this mundane place." Her tone is bitter and full of disappointment.

Hmm. Iris doesn't act like this unless something or someone is bothering her. And I would love to know what this is all about. Who she might be referring to—or what. Not sure what occurred to make her talk like this, but I'd love to know what's really going on.

"Did something happen to make you feel this way?" I ask her, not wanting to push, but not really wanting to talk in circles either. "You seem extra disappointed tonight."

Iris sits straight up, throwing her arms in the air. "My dad happened, is what."

Ah. That makes total sense. Sometimes they have conversations and the outcome isn't what Iris was looking for. My father is extremely overprotective but Whit Lancaster takes it to another level.

"I'm sorry," I murmur, going to her and wrapping her up in a hug. "Did you guys get into a fight?"

"Not really. There's no point in fighting with him. I'd never win. He's so stubborn." Iris presses her face against my old, faded T-shirt, rubbing it against the soft fabric, and I hope she's not crying. That's something she doesn't really do.

"What did you talk about?"

"I told him I wanted to go to Europe over winter break, and he said absolutely not." She sniffs but still doesn't lift her head. "He's such a jerk."

"What do you mean, go to Europe over winter break? I didn't know you were planning this."

"I didn't either. I just threw it at him to see how he'd react. I don't know what possessed me to come up with such an idea, but I thought it sounded fun." Her tone is glum. "He responded just like I thought he might."

"Who were you going with on this European trip?" I sound vaguely jealous because I am kind of jealous. She's never mentioned any European plans to me and I feel left out.

"No one! You, hopefully? I don't know! I really want to go this summer, not over winter break. That's coming up too soon. Or maybe I could go next year." She sounds tentative. Unsure. And that is so not like Iris. "My father said a gap year was a bad idea and that I should go to college first. That he doesn't want me to be 'galivanting across Europe' by myself because he'd worry about me the entire time. Like I can't take care of myself." Oh, she sounds sour.

"He's just worried about you," I start but she cuts me off, leaping to her feet so she can start pacing.

"I can't be babied my whole life! I'm already eighteen. By the time I'd want to leave after graduation and everything else, I'll be nineteen. Still with a leash on me thanks to my overprotective dad. He never does this sort of thing to August, and it's so unfair. My brother can do whatever he wants and no one stops him." Iris rests her hands on her hips, glaring at me. "And look at you! You went to Italy when you were only seventeen! All alone, doing your thing."

"I was staying with a host family who took care of me like I was one of their own," I remind her, my voice gentle. I don't want to stir her up more. "I was going to school, was very much on a schedule similar to here. There weren't a lot of differences."

"But did you feel free? No one hovering over you, asking what you're doing. That's what I want. Freedom. As long as I'm living under Whit Lancaster's rules, I will never be truly free. I've realized that." Her face starts to crumple. "And it's depressing."

I leap to my feet and pull her into my arms, holding her close while she sobs into my hair. I've never seen her this upset before, and I wonder if this has to do with something else? Yes, she gets upset with her dad sometimes, but for the most part they always get along. She usually writes off his overprotectiveness as something amusing. A burden she has to bear, but like it's a joke. And Iris definitely isn't a crier.

"Maybe we should do something tomorrow," I suggest.

"Like what?" she mumbles as she pulls away, wiping her tears away from her cheeks almost angrily.

I've been thinking about this for days, but I didn't know who to ask to see if it's an actual thing. Or I didn't want to be too obvious to Iris either. "We could go to the football game."

Her mouth drops open for a couple of seconds before she snaps it closed. "You want to go to the football game?"

"It might be fun." I shrug.

"It's an away game."

"I know." I hesitate. "Does the school put together a bus for students to attend those games?"

"Well, yeah. Sometimes. I don't know if they're doing one for tomorrow's game." Iris makes a face. "Do you really want to go?"

Yes. Yes, I am absolutely dying to go. "Maybe."

"I don't know." She shakes her head, that grimace still on her face. "I don't think I want to. Sounds like a long night."

Disappointment crashes through me. "Oh. Well, that's okay. It was just a suggestion."

"But you could go," she says. "Maybe Bronwyn is going too. I'm sure you two would have a great time. Or I know, you can go with your parents. They're probably going to watch your brother play."

That doesn't sound like as much fun. I love my parents and I'd like to watch my brother play football, but it would be weird without Iris there. And I really don't want to go with just Bronwyn. She feels more like Iris's friend versus mine, though we get along perfectly fine.

I'm being ridiculous, but I was really hoping Iris would want to tag along. I also don't want to push and ask too many questions over why she's saying no. Iris reveals only what she wants. If someone keeps badgering her, she'll shut down completely.

"It was just an idea. Something different, like you mentioned earlier."

"Something different for you, since you weren't here last year," Iris points out.

"Oh yeah. Right." I return to my desk and settle back in for more studying, trying to ignore how sad I feel about not going to watch Rhett's game. "I need to focus on studying for this quiz."

"I should too." Iris's smile is faint. "Maybe we could help each other? Read sections out loud and try to absorb all of this pointless info in our brains?"

"Yeah." I smile at her, trying to pretend I'm not disappointed. "That sounds like a good idea."

• • •

I'm on campus Friday morning when I run into him. Rhett. He's headed for the dining hall like I am, and I'm alone since Iris still isn't out of bed yet. She always seems to run late on Fridays for some reason.

"Hey, Will," Rhett greets me, stopping to wait for me to catch up to him. "Looking fine this morning."

He's given me compliments every morning all week, and I'm starting to look forward to them more and more. "Good morning. Ready for today's game?"

"You know it." His grin, his entire demeanor oozes confidence. I could just stand here and let him smile at me like that all day, basking in his presence. "We're going to crush them."

"Yeah, you will," I tease, murmuring a thank you when he holds the door open for me as we enter the dining hall. "I thought you had to leave this morning."

"I'm grabbing something to eat before we go." He slows his pace so I can keep up with him. "The rest of the team is going to show up at any minute so I wanted to beat them and get the best selection."

A laugh escapes me. "Sounds like a solid strategy."

"You should grab something too before they all barge in here," he encourages.

I get my usual bagel order and watch as Rhett piles a variety of food—including a breakfast burrito, a cup of mixed fruit, a banana, a blueberry muffin and two small cartons of chocolate milk—onto his tray. We're headed to the checkout line, me laughing at whatever Rhett is saying because he is extremely entertaining, when we both hear someone call out his name.

It's Headmaster Westscott, approaching us with an affable smile on his face, his attention all for Rhett.

"Ready for tonight's game?" Westscott slaps Rhett on the back, his attention going to the overflowing tray Rhett is carrying. An amused smile curves his lips. "Looks like you're gathering resources."

"That's one way to put it." Rhett sends me a quick look. "You know Willow Lancaster, right?"

Westscott barely looks at me. "Of course, I do. Nice to see you again, Willow."

"You too," I murmur, surprised at how dismissive he is of me when he resumes his conversation with Rhett. I'm not used to that kind of treatment at Lancaster Prep.

"Do you mind giving us some privacy?" Westscott asks me once we've checked out with our meals. "I'd like to speak to Rhett here one-on-one."

"Of course." I'm about to say something to Rhett but Westscott grabs his arm and steers him away from me, leaving me standing there alone.

I watch them go, Rhett glancing over his shoulder with an apologetic smile, his gaze practically pleading with me to understand. Which I totally do. He has nothing to do with this. Westscott was the one who pulled him away from me. So rude.

I wonder what his problem is.

"Hey, Willow."

I turn to see my brother coming toward me, his tray overflowing with as much food as Rhett's. "Hi, Row. I didn't see you come in."

"Too busy talking to Rhett and Westscott." Row smiles, and I think for about the hundredth time that my brother looks almost exactly like my dad. Only difference is he doesn't have the Lancaster blue eyes. They're green, like our mom's.

"He was weird to me." When Row frowns, I add, "Headmaster Westscott."

"What do you mean?"

"He barely acknowledged me. Was downright dismissive."

"Westscott isn't that impressed with the Lancaster name, if that's what you're referring to." Row shrugs one broad shoulder. "Don't take it personally."

Ugh, we're so spoiled, expecting people to bow down to us

because we're Lancasters. I don't actually feel that way, but I am surprised when something like this happens.

"Besides, he's obsessed with the football team, and Rhett in particular. He's all about winning," Row further explains. "And he loves that Rhett is too."

Odd. For some reason, I don't like hearing that Westscott is obsessed with Rhett. Seems weird. And I'm still not over how Westscott treated me either. My gut feeling says there's something going on with his behavior toward me.

And I always trust my gut.

CHAPTER TWENTY-ONE

WILLOW

I receive a message notification from Headmaster Westscott via our school app first thing Monday morning. It was sent before I even woke up, at five in the morning, and I frown when I read it, my head still fuzzy from sleep.

Miss Lancaster, please come to my office before school begins. I would like to have a word with you.

Why does he want to talk to me? I feel like I'm in trouble and I haven't done a thing.

I'm reluctant to start my day, worry gnawing at my insides, and I tell myself to get over it. Crawling out of bed, I take a quick shower and get dressed, deciding it's better to face this meeting head-on than dawdle and make myself sick with nerves.

I slip out of my dorm suite, ready to sneak past Iris's door, but it swings open just as I approach, her blonde head popping out. She's not even fully dressed yet, which isn't surprising. She thrives on being last minute at everything.

"Where are you going? It's still so early."

"Westscott asked me to come to his office," I tell her, straightening my spine. Trying to pretend I'm not bothered by his request whatsoever.

Iris frowns. "Why does he want to see you?"

"I don't know."

"Are you scared?"

My cousin knows me so well.

"No." I shake my head, denying my fear.

"Really?" The doubt in her voice is obvious and I give in.

"Well, I'm a little nervous but what could it be about? I haven't done anything wrong." My laughter is shaky and I clamp my lips shut.

"You haven't?" Iris's brows shoot up.

"What's that supposed to mean?"

"People are talking, Willow. I tried to tell you that yesterday."

We were in the library yesterday catching up on our assignments, and as usual, Iris abandoned me for about thirty minutes, choosing to wander around and talk to everyone else who was in there while I diligently finished my American Government homework. She came back to the table to report that people were gossiping about me. And Rhett.

But they've been gossiping about us for a week, ever since I sat on his lap at that party over a week ago. Nothing else has really happened around campus, so we're still the topic of choice, and it's annoying.

"I doubt Westscott cares about that."

"I don't know..." Iris shrugs. "He's all about appearances."

"We're Lancasters," I say, though she doesn't need the reminder. I'm the one who needs to hear it more often than her. "We're the face of the school."

"He's got a reputation as well. Maybe he's upset that a Lancaster is messing around with his top football player."

"Oh, like he cares." Does he?

"He might. I don't know." Iris backs up, making like she's going to shut her door when she pauses. "Don't let him get to you."

"I won't," I say with as much conviction as I can muster. "I'll be fine."

"You will be. Just—go along with him if he makes any

suggestions, okay? You don't need to be disruptive."

Her words stick with me the entire time I walk to the admin building.

You don't need to be disruptive.

Such an un-Iris thing to say. She's all about disruption. It's her favorite thing. I'm the calm cousin and she's the rowdy one. The troublemaker. She lives to disrupt things.

Why would she say that to me?

By the time I'm in the admin office, my mind is a swirl of confusion and I feel completely unprepared. Untethered. I don't get called to the office to speak to the headmaster. I never have in all my years of attending school. I'm a good girl to the point of annoyance.

"Miss Lancaster, there you are. I'm so glad to see you, and so early." I'm startled by Westscott's voice. He's standing in the open doorway of his office and I realize he's been waiting for my arrival. "Come in."

Without a word I enter his office, swallowing hard when he closes the door behind me. The rest of the admin building is quiet and the desks are empty. It's not even seven-thirty and it appears no one is on duty yet, which is only vaguely disconcerting.

Okay, it's completely disconcerting. I'm half-tempted to text Iris right now and beg her to come to the office immediately.

"I didn't want to miss class," I tell him as I sit in the chair that's across from his desk.

"I appreciate that about you. I've heard from plenty of others that you're a good student." He sits down as well, resting his clasped hands on top of his desk.

"Where did you hear that?"

He frowns. "Excuse me?"

"Who told you I was a good student?"

"Why, my staff has informed me of your studious ways." His smile is gentle. I'd put him at about the same age as my parents, maybe a little older by the looks of the graying hair at his temples.

He's wearing khaki pants and a navy jacket that's similar to our uniform, a white button-down shirt with a hunter green tie.

He could almost—not quite but almost—pass as a student with what he's wearing.

"I care about my grades," I tell him.

"I know." His voice is grave and he nods, somber as a priest in church. "I admire that about you. There are many qualities of yours that I admire."

"Thank you."

"But there is one thing I've heard recently that has me concerned." He tugs at his tie, straightening it. "What is your relationship with Rhett Bennett?"

Alarm races through me, leaving me shaky. "What do you mean?"

"It's a simple question, Miss Lancaster." His tone is faintly condescending. "Are you spending any extra time with Rhett Bennett?"

"I don't see how that's any of your business?" The words leave me without thought and I brace myself, waiting for him to call me out for questioning his authority.

"If you're a student of mine, it's my business." His smile doesn't falter though I see a flicker of irritation in his dark brown gaze. "Answer the question."

I bristle at the demand in his tone. "We're friends."

"That's it?"

"We have a couple of classes together."

"I know." The smile finally fades. "I'm concerned."

"About what?" Oh, my tone is snotty. I never speak like this toward a superior. I definitely shouldn't talk back or ague with him, but it's like I can't help it. I've never had a teacher or counselor or the freaking headmaster ask me about my supposed friends before.

Like how is this any of his business? What does he care if Rhett and I spend time together?

"Rhett Bennett is one of the best high school quarterbacks in the nation. We're expected to win a state championship this season. Maybe even a national one," Westscott stresses. "He needs zero distractions in his life."

"What does that have to do with me? Like I said, we're—friends. I don't think I'm much of a distraction."

"According to a variety of students that I spoke with over the last week, you were seen in a rather—compromising position with Mr. Bennett at a party." Westscott leans back in his chair, the hinges creaking with the movement. He says nothing more, seemingly waiting me out for a response.

"Compromising position?" I choke out.

He nods, his clasped hands now resting on his chest. "You were sitting on his lap."

"I don't see how that's—"

"And you were kissing. In front of everyone," he continues.

"We've never kissed," I say vehemently, because it's the truth.

"I've heard multiple accounts—"

"Your multiple accounts are lying." I'm breathing hard and I press my lips together, trying to contain my shock. My anger. "I don't see how any of this would be a problem."

"You want me to be real with you right now?" His brows lift and I nod mutely, afraid of what he might say. This conversation is surreal. "Rhett is a superior football player and he's also extremely smart. His parents requested that I watch over him when he first started here, and I promised I would do so. Yes, Rhett dates girls. I understand why they're drawn to him. He's charismatic. But we didn't worry about any of them."

Am I supposed to be offended or honored by that last remark?

"You? I worry about." He leans forward, the chair squeaking again, making me wince. "You're beautiful. Smart. A Lancaster."

I don't like that he's calling me beautiful. It's creepy.

"What boy wouldn't want to be with you?" he adds.

None of them do, I want to tell him. And now he's trying to convince me I shouldn't spend time with the only boy who seems interested in me.

"Do what's best for the school, Willow." His smile is small. "Find someone else's lap to sit on."

I blink at him, shocked he would say such a thing to me. "You do realize who you're speaking to."

His smile fades. "If you're trying to pull a 'do you know who I am' type of moment, I'm not going to let it happen, Miss Lancaster. You are a student here, just like everyone else."

"Are you saying Rhett Bennett gets special treatment but no one else does?" I arch a brow.

"There's a reason he receives, as you call it, special treatment. His performance on the field is changing Lancaster Prep's entire image. He's going to leave a legacy on this campus that is unmatched. Can you do the same?"

I leap to my feet. "Your questions are insulting."

"Only because you don't like the answer you might give." He also stands, resting his hands palm down on top of his desk. "Leave Rhett Bennett alone."

"You can't tell me what to do."

"I can make your life miserable if you continue down this path. How does that sound?" He sounds so calm and collected while threatening me.

What a monster.

"I'll tell my parents—"

Westscott's laughter interrupts me and I glare at him, curling my hands into fists. Everyone raves about the new headmaster and how he's changed the school, but all I'm seeing is a deranged nut job who's trying to control every little move on this campus.

"Go ahead and run home to Mommy and Daddy," he taunts. "Tell them how awful I am and how I've mistreated you. They understand the importance of Rhett Bennett's season for this school. After years of dwindling numbers, enrollment is up. Money is being poured into the school from the alumni association, most of it for a new football stadium. The stadium that Bennett built, we all call it. Such a shame he won't benefit from it though."

I don't say anything. I can feel tears prick at the corners of my eyes and I know if I start speaking, I'll end up crying, only because I'm mad. So mad. And I refuse to cry in front of this man.

"Your parents—the entire Lancaster family—all they care about is the bottom line, and right now I'm delivering that. Your brother is benefiting from this as well. Rowan is an excellent football player. He'll go far if he continues down this path. Do you really want to mess everything up for your brother? Don't you have another brother that's going to attend Lancaster Prep eventually? I'm sure he looks up to his big brother and wants to do the same thing as him."

I don't bother telling him that Beau is in youth league football right now, because that would feed right into what Westscott is saying.

"If you want to go ahead and be selfish, then talk to your parents. Tell them everything. I'm a terrible man because I only want what's best for the school. I'm sure they'll agree with you that I'm a tyrant." A door slams from outside the office and Westscott glances toward his closed office door. "You should go. Classes will start soon."

Without another word, I turn on my heel and head for the door, just about to open it when he slams his hand on the door, just above my head. I glance to my right, staring at him mutely, hating that he's so close.

He makes my skin crawl.

"If you're as smart as everyone says you are, you'll heed my advice," he murmurs.

"And if I don't?"

His smile is grim. "Then there will be hell to pay."

CHAPTER TWENTY-TWO

RHETT

I wait for Willow outside of our English class, anxious to talk to her. I haven't seen her since Friday morning when Westscott dragged me away from her. Such a dick move. I messaged her over the weekend and apologized over it, and she was sweet, reassuring me it wasn't my fault. Then we talked about football and the fact that she was home for the weekend, which was a disappointment. I wanted to see her. Was even going to ask her if she wanted to hang out Saturday night, but my plans were crushed by her being off-campus.

We've been vibing all week. I was swamped with school work and football, and she was always patient, always seemingly eager to talk to me. I like that. I like that she's not naggy or demanding, though I never believed she would be. She's cool. I like her.

A lot.

I was completely preoccupied over the weekend anyway, so I didn't have too much time on my hands to feel down that she wasn't around. After our close win, Coach called special practice sessions both Saturday and Sunday because we need to make sure we're up to speed for the first home game this upcoming Friday.

We had an extra practice this morning too—we will all week, just like we did last week. I was up by five-thirty and went for a run. Worked out with weights for thirty minutes and then was out on the field, sweating my ass off despite the cool air and the misty clouds that hung over the stadium.

My energy hasn't waned though. If anything, I'm even more amped up. Excited to see her. Hear her voice. Flirt with her a little bit. Willow Lancaster is nothing but repressed energy, and I can sense there's a bad girl underneath all that innocent shine and she's dying to come out. I can't get the memories of her from that party a couple of weeks ago out of my head, when I kept whispering in her ear. The way she leaned into me. Those breathy sounds she made and how her body trembled.

I look forward to seeing her on campus. In class. Talking to her via DMs when we're not in class and practice is long done. We stayed up way too late Thursday night chatting, which I thought would have me dragging ass on Friday but I was fine. She gives me energy.

Life.

Fuuuuck, she's going to be my undoing if I don't watch it. And I need to stay focused. Football is number one on my priority list. School is number two. Girls—Willow—will have to be number three.

I check my phone for the time. Two minutes or less until the final bell rings. Minus the first day of school in our photography class, she's always early.

Where the hell is she?

The bell is literally ringing when I see her running down the hall, headed straight for me. I push away from the wall, waiting for her, and she comes to an abrupt stop when she notices me standing there. Her shiny loafers squeak as she shuffles her feet along the floor and her cheeks are a dewy pink.

"Rhett!" she chastises. "You should get inside. The bell just rang."

She goes zooming right past me without waiting for a reply and I follow her into the classroom. "Where were you?"

"Running a little late." She practically falls into her desk.

I sit in the one behind her like usual. "You're never late."

"You've known me for a couple of weeks. Meaning, you don't know me that well at all." She sniffs, turning so her back is to me. All that long, glossy dark hair swings and I'm tempted to pull on a strand.

I rear back a little, mulling over what she just said. Her dismissive attitude. What's her problem? I'm filled with the sudden urge to get under her skin—what's fair is fair, right? She's definitely under mine.

"Pretty sure I've got you somewhat figured out, Will. You're an early bird." I give in to my impulses and wrap a thick, silky curl around my finger once, twice, before I give it a hard tug, making her yelp and jerk away from me. "Tell me what's wrong."

Willow sends me a quick glance from over her shoulder, seemingly surprised that I can read her so well. "Nothing's wrong."

"Uh huh." I don't believe her. She's acting weird. "You know you don't have to keep anything from me."

Her shoulders stiffen, and I just know something is bugging this girl. But what could it be?

Mrs. Patel starts taking attendance, but I'm barely paying attention. I'm too caught up in watching Willow. How the tension never leaves her shoulders. How she keeps fidgeting, like she can't get comfortable.

Seriously. What's wrong with her?

Of course, I can't ask her because today's the day our teacher decides to give a big lecture on the joys of F. Scott Fitzgerald and his books. She rambles on about the meaning behind the novel we're supposed to be reading, *The Great Gatsby.*

I haven't even cracked it open yet.

She even has some of us read parts of the book out loud, which means I keep my head down, hopeful she doesn't call on me. I can't concentrate for shit, too wrapped up in the swing of Willow's hair and how I can smell her perfume, that faintly floral scent I remember inhaling Friday night when she sat on my lap. I wish I could bury my face in her neck and breathe deep, imprinting her smell on my senses forever. If I did that though, she'd probably freak the hell out.

Good thing I've got plenty of restraint.

"Willow? Would you care to read a passage?" the teacher asks her at one point.

"Yes, of course." Willow sits up straighter, clears her throat and begins to read while I lean forward across the top of my desk like I'm trying to get closer to her, entranced with the sound of her voice.

I could listen to her all day.

I feel like a lovesick idiot—not that I'm in love with her or anything, but damn. Her voice is soft and sweet, but not too high-pitched or little-girlish. She sounds sophisticated, and she pronounces every word clearly. But I could also imagine her saying something dirty to me and that would be hot.

This girl is hot.

Fuck, I've got it bad.

Next thing I know, the bell is ringing and she's exiting the classroom in a blur of movement, like she's in a race. From not caring if she's late to hightailing her ass out of the room, she's not making any sense.

Weird.

When lunchtime rolls around, I'm entering the dining hall with my friends and my brother when I spot Westscott lingering by the entrance, a faint smile appearing on his face when he spots me.

"Mr. Bennett. A word?" He lifts his brows in question.

"Sure." I follow him as he rounds the corner of the building, coming to a stop near the fence that surrounds the dining hall dumpster. Not that it smells out here. That's the thing about Lancaster Prep. The grounds are manicured and immaculate, and there's never any trash in sight. The entire place is spotless, but that's what money gets you.

Westscott turns to face me, that pleasant smile still on his face. "You ready for this Friday's game?"

"You know it, sir," I say with a firm nod. "Had an intense practice this morning. We'll be keeping it up all week."

"You did great last Friday, though the score was a little closer than I prefer," Westscott says.

He sounds like our coaching staff. They hated how close the score was. I didn't love it either.

"We'll do even better this Friday," I reassure him. "Being on home turf is always a benefit."

"You're right." He sounds satisfied with my answers. "Keep it up."

"Of course, sir. We always want to win no matter what it takes."

"That's the attitude I like to see. Just don't overwork yourself," he warns.

"Never. You have nothing to worry about. We've got this."

"Glad to hear it." He pauses, resting his hands on his hips and glancing around before he returns his gaze to me. I can tell he wants to ask me something else. "Everything going okay for you otherwise?"

"School's good." I don't bother telling him it's boring. Teachers, principals, headmasters—they don't understand.

"Anything else going on?"

Why does it feel like he's digging? "Not much. Just school and football, sir."

"No parties after the game Friday night?"

I shake my head. "We got back to campus so late, all of us were too beat to party."

"Heard about the bonfire last Friday night though," he says casually. Why is he bringing it up now? "Hope there wasn't too much partying and drinking going on then."

The staff tends to turn a figurative cheek when they hear we're partying. It's my favorite thing about Lancaster Prep. Well, that and the hottest girl I've ever met who goes here and just so happens to be a Lancaster.

"I didn't get shitfaced." I grimace the moment the words leave me. Probably shouldn't have said it like that. "Sir."

Westscott chuckles. "Good to know, Bennett. Just—make sure you stay focused. You don't need any distractions in your life right now, especially during football season. You've got a lot on your plate."

"Right." I nod. "No distractions."

"I know how it is. I was a teenage boy once. At this stage in our life, we're all young, dumb and full of cum." Westscott chuckles.

I blink at him, shocked he would say that. I mean yeah, my dad would probably say something like that but in a joking way. And plus, he's my dad. We have that kind of relationship where it's no bullshit. He remembers what it was like when he was a teen, he's told me. He was all over the place and obsessed with two things—football.

And my mother.

But Westscott is the headmaster. He runs the entire school and he has an image to uphold—he's told me that plenty of times. He looked pretty serious saying it too, which is just odd.

"Right," I say lightly, trying to laugh but failing miserably. Instead, I just feel uncomfortable. "You don't have to worry about me, sir. I'm one hundred percent focused on football. We're going all the way. I can feel it."

"Good to know." Westscott claps me on the shoulder so hard I take a stumbling step forward, glaring at him as he turns and walks away.

I watch him go, rubbing the back of my neck, wondering about our conversation. Curious if I'm the only one he says this kind of shit to. When he talks to me like that, he makes me feel like I'm his prized possession, and I don't like it.

At all.

• • •

By the time I'm in our photography class after lunch, I know for a damn fact that Willow is avoiding me. She runs into the classroom right as the bell rings, just like she did in English, earning a stern glare from our teacher who otherwise doesn't say a word to her.

She scrambles to her desk, settling in and keeping her focus off me the entire time, leaving me confused. Everything was cool the last time I talked to her, which was last freaking night. Now she acts like she wants nothing to do with me and I don't get it. Every little bit I get from her is just enough to keep me interested and wanting more.

Maybe it had the opposite effect on her.

If that's the case, man that sucks.

"We're going to work on a project this week that entails you pairing up with another student in class." There's a collective groan from the class and I'm pretty sure I'm the only one who's not complaining. I'd give anything to share the workload with someone else. Makes things so much easier.

"To take away the difficulty of pairing up on your own and to avoid anyone feeling left out, I've already preassigned your partner."

More groaning from the classroom and I brace myself, glancing around the room. There's hardly anybody in this class I want to be paired up with.

Mr. Chen starts rattling off names, going down a list.

"Bennett, you're with Lancaster."

Talk about good luck. I thought for sure I'd have to pair up with that weird brainiac freshman that no one talks to. Poor kid.

Willow's hand shoots up in the air.

"Yes, Willow?"

"Um, maybe I could switch partners?" She still won't look at me, and damn, I'm hurt.

She'd rather work with someone else. Maybe even the brainiac freshman?

Ouch.

"I'm afraid I can't switch you with anyone else. Working with someone you're unfamiliar with is good practice for when you're out in the real world." Mr. Chen's face falls a little. "Well, you'll probably never have to deal with that considering who you are."

Someone giggles. Willow's face turns red.

All I can do is glare at her.

"Okay!" Mr. Chen claps his hands, causing the room to go silent. "We'll be heading outside to work on our first assignment for the week. Please make sure you grab one of the sheets here." He gestures toward his desk. "The instructions are included, but if you have any questions, please let me know. Make sure you grab your belongings. We won't be returning to the classroom before the bell rings and I don't want to make you late for your next class."

I grab my shit and stand, waiting for Willow. Watching as she moves at a snail's pace to gather her things. She finally shoots me a quick glance, her eyes wide. She almost looks like she's afraid to deal with me.

She jerks her gaze from mine and scurries out of the classroom, clutching her backpack in front of her chest. After grabbing our assignment sheet from the desk, I chase after her, calling her name, but she won't look back at me.

If she's trying to fuck with my head, she's doing a damn good job of it.

"Will, come on. Let me talk to you," I call after her.

She comes to a stop and whirls on me when I get close, stabbing her finger in the center of my chest. "You need to be quiet."

"I'll be quiet if you stop running from me," I retort.

"Give me the assignment sheet." She wiggles her fingers at me and I hand the piece of paper to her. She looks it over, her brows drawing together as she keeps reading. "We're supposed to be each other's partner for the next two weeks."

"Two weeks?" If she's going to treat me like shit the entire time, this is going to be torture.

Willow nods, still scanning the paper. "We're supposed to take photos of the same things and then compare our compositions."

"Our what?"

She rolls her eyes and shoves the paper back at me, slapping it against my chest. "No one sees objects or scenery in the same way. We all have different eyes. How we view the world."

I remember her explaining this to me on the first day of class, and how embarrassed she got over it.

"I think that's the point he's wanting to prove with this project. If we work together long enough, maybe we'll see things in a different light. You'll teach me, and I'll teach you," she explains, her lips forming into a frown.

"Sounds like we'll be working closely together."

She nods but otherwise says nothing.

"And you act like that's your own personal nightmare," I continue.

Her gaze is full of misery when it meets mine. "We shouldn't be doing this."

I'm completely baffled by her behavior. "What are you talking about?"

"Working together." She takes a deep breath and straightens her shoulders. "But I suppose we don't have a choice. We'll need to keep this strictly business, okay?"

I'm tempted to salute her. "What the hell happened to you?"

"What do you mean?"

"You're like…a completely different person compared to last night."

"I know," she admits, her voice full of sorrow. "I, um, had a realization."

"What was it?"

"We're not compatible."

CHAPTER TWENTY-THREE

WILLOW

I'm lying through my teeth. We are most definitely compatible. Rhett looks at me and I'm tempted to throw myself at him. He touches me and I swear electricity sparks between us. He seems into me, which is shocking, but then again, it's not. He was waiting for me outside of English class this morning. Adorable in his rumpled uniform and his golden-brown hair sticking up wildly, like he'd run his fingers through it over and over again. I wanted to run to him. Hug him close and tell him I missed him over the weekend, but I did none of that.

Westscott's words ran through my brain on repeat, filling me with guilt. And shame. I can't be a distraction to Rhett. Football is important to him. To his family. I did some googling earlier—I can't believe I didn't do it before. I saw all the news articles about his family and how they're a football legacy. I also saw photos of his father when he was younger, and wow.

Rhett is the spitting image of Eli Bennett.

His mother is beautiful. His sister is too. His grandmother is Fable Callahan. Even I know who Fable Callahan is and it's funny to me that I didn't put it together that Rhett's younger brother's name is Callahan, but then again, I'm not an NFL fan. Fable is married to her husband Drew, who is one of the best quarterbacks to ever play football. Meaning, Rhett comes from a very famous family. An important family in both college football and the NFL. No wonder Westscott is so protective of Rhett.

I'm not about to become the downfall of Rhett Bennett and his football future. No thank you.

Not that I believe I have that kind of power, because I am just a girl who can't seem to get anyone to pay attention to me here anyway—with the exception of Rhett. I wonder if Westscott said something to the other boys about how they needed to stay focused and not get distracted by girls. Did he talk to Rhett? Would he do that?

Doubtful. It's never a man's fault if a woman is involved. In this scenario, I'm the siren who is temptation personified. This is a tale as old as time—straight out of the Bible even. Rhett is Adam and I'm Eve, holding the apple toward him and egging him on to take a bite.

Okay, my thoughts are completely overdramatic, but I can't help it. I've been dwelling on my conversation with Westscott all day.

And on that note, why wouldn't Westscott say something to the teachers so we could avoid situations like the very one we're in currently? I'm supposed to leave Rhett alone, yet I'm paired up with him for the next two weeks? Who assigns a two-week project anyway?

"You don't think we're compatible, huh?" Rhett is smiling, and I can tell he's about to call me out on my lies. Ugh, that smile. Its power is devastating and I lock my knees so my legs don't wobble.

"We're not." My voice is firm. I guess I can be a good liar when necessary. "You said so yourself that you don't do relationships."

"When did I ever say that?"

My mind scrambles—I remember Iris saying something like that, but I don't know if those words ever came out of Rhett's mouth.

"It doesn't matter," I tell him. "I am a relationship girl through and through."

"Oh yeah?" He squints at me, as if he's having trouble understanding. "How many relationships have you been in?"

"Um..."

None. Zero. Nada.

"That's what I thought." His voice is smug.

"Well, how many have you been in?" I throw at him.

"Not a single one," he says without hesitation. "We've already had this conversation. We're just talking in circles."

He's right. I know he is.

"I'm willing to change things up though," he adds.

"Change things up about what?"

"A relationship doesn't sound so bad...with you."

Oh God. Did he really just say that?

"I thought we had something going on the last week, but now you're giving me mixed signals, Will. And I don't get it. What happened?" He sounds genuinely confused and I feel terrible.

The urge to tell him what Westscott said rests on the tip of my tongue, but I swallow the words down. Would he even believe me? Or worse, would he run off to Westscott's office and confront him over it? That would be awful. I'm not about to stir up any trouble because then I would just be proving Westscott's point.

I'm a distraction.

And I refuse to tell my parents about any of this because the headmaster is right—there are more important things to worry about right now in regards to Lancaster Prep than whether I have a crush on the varsity team's top football player. What I want shouldn't matter. Besides, it's our senior year. We're going to graduate and go our separate ways.

From the start, I've told myself I want a high school romance to enjoy during my senior year. A guaranteed date for all of the important events—dances, prom. That's what I was looking for, and yes, it probably would've been fun to do all of that with Rhett, but this is turning into too much trouble.

Trouble I don't want.

"Like I said, I had a realization. We would never work," I reiterate.

"You so sure about that?" Oh, there's that dare in his voice again. The sly smile on his face. It's like no matter what I say, it doesn't deter him. I didn't think he'd be so determined.

"We should focus on our assignment," I say, changing the subject. "Let's find something to take a photo of."

He goes along with my conversation change and we both start walking. "How about one of those creepy statues in the rose garden behind the library?"

I almost want to laugh at him calling the statues creepy. "Most of those statues are of my ancestors."

"No shit?" He seems surprised. "I never really paid much attention to them."

"There are nameplates on almost every single one of the statues." And I've examined every single one of them over the years because I'm related to those people. It's odd, to look at statues and know you come from a long line of Lancasters. That our family name has carried on for generations—centuries. There's so much history there. There are even books written about my family—especially Augustus Lancaster, the first one to make a name in the US.

"And you're related to them all, huh?" We approach the library, taking the sidewalk that veers to the right and leads to the gardens.

"They're all Lancasters and I am too," I say with a nod.

"What's that like, being part of a family that goes back so far?" He sounds genuinely curious.

"It doesn't feel like anything really. Our lineage is just part of my life."

"You make yourself sound like a well-bred dog." He nudges my side with his elbow, and I take a step to the right, vaguely offended. "A cute dog. Like a golden doodle."

I roll my eyes, but I see what he's saying. "It's the word lineage."

"Exactly."

"You come from a legacy family yourself," I remind him.

His brows shoot up in question. "Someone did their research."

"I've heard your family history mentioned before." I shrug, trying to play it off.

"Uh huh. I'm guessing if I checked out your search history, I'd find my name typed in. It's cool," he says when he notices I'm about to argue with him. "I googled you too."

"You did?"

"I was curious." He shrugs.

We're quiet as we enter the rose garden and I take a deep breath, the scent of the roses lingering in the air. I stop at the row of bushes covered in peach-colored flowers, scanning the plaque that sits in front of them.

"*Dedicated to Rose Albright. Forever in our hearts.*" Rhett glances over at me. "You related to Rose?"

I shake my head. "Not really, but kind of? My father's cousin Arch married Rose's daughter Daisy. Rose died when Daisy was twelve."

"Sad." He shoves his hands in his pockets, staring at the flowers for a moment. "I can't imagine life without my mom."

"I can't either," I murmur, banishing the horrid thought. "Come on. Let's go find a creepy statue."

We venture deeper into the garden, the sun beating down upon us, the soft buzz of bees filling the air. I come to a stop in front of one of the oldest statues in the garden, tilting my head back to look at it. It's of Ezekiel Lancaster, Augustus's brother. His expression is stern, his nose prominent and his lips thin. He looks terribly unhappy. I would probably never admit this out loud, but this statue?

It creeps me out a little—well, more than anything, I feel sorry for him.

"Who's this dude?" Rhett asks as he comes to a stop beside me.

"Ezekiel Lancaster is the younger brother of Augustus."

"And Augustus was the one who started all of this, right?"

I nod. "Ezekiel was younger by only a year. Supposedly they were always close, though Ezekiel was also envious of his brother's success. Everything came naturally to Augustus, while Ezekiel worked extra hard and was rarely awarded for his efforts."

"Typical brother against brother shit is what you're telling me."

I turn to look at him. "Are you close with your brother?"

"Cal and I? We get along. Sometimes I think he gets tired of being compared to me, and I don't blame him. That's why he's not a quarterback. He's trying to stand out on his own. He's really good."

I can tell by the tone of Rhett's voice that he likes his brother, and that makes me like him even more, though I shouldn't.

I'm supposed to stay far away from him.

"I know nothing about football, remember?"

"Oh yeah, that's right. I said I'd teach you."

"Which isn't necessary," I'm quick to add, but he ignores me.

"You ever watch a game before?"

"No." I thought I told him that already.

"Your dad not into football?"

"He would watch it when I was younger and I was at home all the time, but I wasn't paying attention."

"Who's his favorite team?"

"I'm not sure."

"College or professional?"

"There's a difference?" I'm teasing him, and after a second of letting my words sink in, he smiles, realizing it.

"You think you're pretty funny, huh, Will?"

"Not particularly." I shrug.

We go quiet again, but it's not uncomfortable. He's standing close enough to me that I can feel the warmth from his body radiating toward me, and when he shifts, his arm brushes against mine. When there's no one else around and we're just focused on each other, I can almost believe we could have something special.

"You are, you know," he finally says.

"I'm what?"

"Funny. Interesting. You're not boring."

He probably remembers when I told him I was boring, and how mortifying is that?

"And I don't know what happened to change your mind from last night to this morning, but something did, and if you're feeling brave enough to tell me about it, maybe I could fix it." He turns to face me, but I remain in the same position, staring up at poor, old, unappreciated Ezekiel.

I can relate to him. Even though I'm the oldest, there are so many Lancasters that are part of my generation, and I feel outshined by every one of them. Or maybe I'm just having a complete pity party and feeling sorry for myself.

"Nothing happened," I murmur. "I just had a realization, which I already told you."

I can feel him staring at my profile and I finally give in, facing him head on, standing up straighter like perfect posture is the proper defense against the powers that make up Rhett Bennett.

"I call bullshit on your realization, Willow, but okay. Whatever. You really believe we're not compatible?"

My nod is as stiff as my posture.

He blows out a harsh breath, resting his hands on his hips. As usual, he's discarded his uniform jacket and I can't help but note the way his shirt sleeves strain against the muscles in his arms. I wonder what he looks like shirtless.

I wonder what he looks like naked.

"Guess it won't matter to you then if I find some other girl to spend my time with."

His words are like a slap in the face.

"And it won't bother you at all if some other girl that's in our class is wearing my jersey on game day," he continues.

"Is that a thing?" My question is a whisper, floating away with the breeze.

"It's definitely a thing," he bites out, his gaze boring into me.

"As a matter of fact, I might ask Iris if she'd like to wear my jersey on Friday. Think she would?"

It would absolutely kill me if he asked my cousin that. She'd tell him no, I have no doubt about it, but knowing he'd ask...imagining her wearing his jersey at the football game and looking cute while cheering him on?

No. I can't stand the thought of *any* girl doing that.

But I can't do it for him either. How obvious would I be, showing up to the game in his jersey—not that he's said he wants me to wear it, but I'm guessing he's implying that—yelling my encouragement from the stands. Westscott able to witness me doing exactly what he told me not to do.

There's just no way.

"We should take our photos," I tell him, changing the subject yet again. I grab my phone and aim it at Ezekiel's statue, snapping a halfhearted photo. I didn't even check if it was in focus so I take a few more, hoping one of them is decent.

Rhett does the same, not uttering a word, and I can tell by the set of his jaw that he's angry. With me. I suppose I deserve his anger. All I have to do is open my mouth and tell him the truth but...

I don't want to cause any trouble. So I'm just going to hold on to it and keep my secret.

Even if it kills me.

CHAPTER TWENTY-FOUR

WILLOW

"You're going to the game, right?"

We're sitting at our usual table during lunch with Bronwyn joining us. We've become a threesome, Bronwyn fitting right into the slot Alana vacated. I like Bronwyn. She's sweet and she's funny and she doesn't seem prone to drama. Not that Alana ever did either, but sometimes I would see this look in her eyes that told me she was envious of Iris and me. I get it. It's not easy being friends with us. We're as close as sisters.

"I don't think so." I smile and duck my head, concentrating on the grilled chicken sandwich sitting in front of me. I grab hold of it and bring the sandwich to my mouth, taking a big bite.

"Why not? Come on, Willow. It'll be fun. Everyone goes to the first home game," Iris stresses.

The idea of sitting there watching everyone cheer Rhett on while I can do nothing but sit on my hands and pretend that he doesn't exist? Sounds like torture. I'm being selfish, but I have to protect myself. This week in photography class has been pure torture, having to work with him. He's given up trying to reason with me and instead we have stilted conversations while we work on the various assignments.

It's awful.

"Not me," I say brightly. "You know I don't like football."

"I don't even watch the games," Bronwyn says. "I'm just there for the snacks and the gossip."

"Yeah, it's not always about the game, though I'm sure our team will bring it." Iris sends me a pouty look. "You wanted to go last week."

"That was last week."

Iris rolls her eyes. "Come on. Go for me."

"You don't need me there."

"I want you there. Big difference. Plus, I need to cheer on Brooks. Don't you want to support him?"

"Brooks? Since when do you cheer on Brooks?"

"He's always been a friend." She shrugs, her expression downright mysterious. "And I like to support my friends."

Huh.

"Everyone is going," Bronwyn says with the utmost authority. As if she's surveyed every student on this campus. "You'll be, like, the only person who's not there."

"And we can't have that. People will start saying you're boring if you don't show up," Iris adds, a devilish twinkle in her gaze.

I shove at her arm. "You said that on purpose."

She knows it's my weak spot. Stupid Alana for calling me that. Guess things are still going strong for her and Silas. They're practically joined at the hip everywhere they go, and he doesn't try and talk to me in English anymore, thank God.

But I don't really talk to anyone in English. Or in any other class for that matter. Some people might call me unapproachable now more than ever, but I'm just protecting myself. Protecting Rhett too.

I miss him terribly.

"I'll be right back." Bronwyn leaps to her feet. "Bathroom break."

The moment she's gone, Iris leans in close to me, her expression dead serious. "You need to cut the crap."

"What do you mean?"

"Something is up. You're all whiny and mopey and don't really talk. I know you, Willow. I've known you my entire life and I can tell something—or someone—is bringing you down." Her expression is fierce. "Tell me who it is."

"It's nothing" is my automatic reply, and she shakes her head, cutting me off.

"Don't give me that bullshit. You're lying to me. Tell me." She grabs hold of my arm, clinging to me. "I miss you. You haven't been the same since you came back from Italy and all I want is for you to be happy, you know?"

I swallow hard, staring into her eyes, seeing all the sincerity in her gaze. "I can't tell you here. There are too many people."

The triumphant expression on my cousin's face is almost comical. "I knew something was bugging you. Come on, let's go to your room. Or mine."

"What about Bronwyn?"

"I'll text her right now." Iris grabs her phone and starts typing.

I check my phone. "We only have a few more minutes left until the bell rings."

"Then we better hurry."

We dash out of the dining hall and practically run back to the building where our dorm suites are. Once we're inside and alone, I come this close to spilling my guts about Westscott's secret meeting before school and how I basically had to turn down Rhett. How, after Rhett and I had that awful conversation, he hasn't tried to talk to me again.

But I don't do any of that. I keep everything that's happened to myself, which is the most difficult thing I've ever had to do, especially with Iris. I tell her *everything*. Instead, I come up with a somewhat fake problem instead.

"I don't think Rhett and I could ever work together and I told him that," I lie.

Iris frowns. "Why would you say that? You haven't even given him a real chance yet, have you?"

"No, but I just…I know it wouldn't work, and trust me, I felt bad turning him down. But it's easier if I just let him down now and get it over with." I shrug, keeping my gaze averted. Looking into her eyes might be truth serum and I can't afford to confess my real issue.

"You turned him down?" There's disbelief in her voice.

"Sort of." I hesitate. "He's not my type."

"Maybe you're making a mistake by not giving him a chance though? You just never know. Sometimes we end up with people we never believed were possible," she says almost cryptically.

I study her, curious by her response. "Are you referring to someone specific?"

Iris flashes me a dazzling smile, and it almost feels like she's trying to distract me. "Oh, my mom always says that to me. She claims Dad was the last person she should've ever ended up with, but she did anyway because they were basically soulmates. I'm not sure if I believe in that sort of thing though."

I do. I believe in it with every part of my being. There's a reason I'm drawn to Rhett despite him not being someone I would've normally picked for myself. Maybe he's my soulmate?

Probably not. And really? I shouldn't think like that.

We hear the bell ring in the distance and I'm already dashing toward the door and opening it. "We need to go."

"What we need is to continue this conversation." Iris follows right behind me.

"There's no point." I turn to face her as the door slams behind her. "Promise me you won't go to Rhett and say something to him."

She gapes at me as if I shocked her with my request. "I would never betray you like that."

She's right. She never would. And I can't believe I said that to her. "I know you wouldn't. I—I'm sorry I said it." I reach for her but she's already pulling me into her arms, giving me a quick hug.

"It's fine. I know you didn't mean it. I just—you'll tell me if something major is bothering you, right?" Iris pulls away from me but keeps her grip on my upper arms, staring into my eyes. "Promise me you will."

"I promise." My smile is weak, my throat aching with the words I should be saying to her. "We should go to class."

"Right." Her gaze searches mine. "You know we swore to each other a long time ago that we'd never keep secrets from one another."

"We were five," I remind her.

"And I still stand by that promise." Her voice, her expression is somber, and I feel terrible that I'm keeping this from her.

"Me too," I whisper.

"Good." She blinks once, twice. "Um, I have a confession to make."

I'm frowning. "What do you mean?"

"My own secret. That I've been keeping from you."

My mouth falls open. "Are you serious? After you just gave me a total guilt trip, you've been keeping something from me all along?"

"I'm sorry! I didn't know how to tell you." She glances around, noting how more and more people are passing us by. "But I'll have to reveal it later, when no one is around."

"And now you're leaving me with a cliffhanger? You're unbelievable."

Iris laughs and I'm so grateful to hear that sound, I nearly sag with relief. "I'm sorry! We can talk about it when we get ready for the game."

"Iris..."

"You're going." Her voice is firm. She's not about to let me out of this. "Whether you like it or not."

A despondent sigh is my only answer and she flashes me a cheeky grin. "See you after school! Meet me in my room."

And then she's gone.

• • •

For the rest of the afternoon, I think about what Iris said, and what her secret could be. I turn over every possibility I can come up with, all of them having to do with boys. Because, seriously, I think that's the only thing she would keep from me.

Who she's messing around with.

She alluded to someone when I first came back, but she never mentioned a name or gave me a clue to who he could be. And I sort of forgot about it, becoming wrapped up in my own drama and problems.

I'm selfish. Here's Iris willing to drop everything to be a good friend to me, and all I can focus on is my own crap.

Photography is easy because Rhett isn't in class. The football team is already out for the rest of the day, preparing for tonight's game. At least I don't have to face him and all the disappointment I see shining in his eyes every time he looks in my direction.

When the final bell rings, I'm hurriedly heading back to my dorm suite, coming to a halt when I see two familiar heads behind a bush. The sound of voices rising as tempers flare.

"You were all over her," I hear Alana say, her tone accusatory. "You know she has a little crush on you. Why are you encouraging her like that?"

Well, at least I know she's not yelling about me. I've avoided Silas all week.

"It's nothing," Silas reassures. "I'm totally into you, babe. You know this."

I make a face. I hate the way he just called her babe, and not because I'm jealous. It just sounded so insincere.

"No. I don't know it because I'm constantly catching you flirting with other girls. It's like you want their attention because it makes you feel better. You make me feel like I'm not enough and that's unfair. You did it with me and Willow, and now you're doing it with Margaret and it's not fair, Silas. If you want to be with her, then go for it. I'm not going to stand in your way."

"I don't want to be with Margaret. She's only a sophomore for Christ's sake," he gripes, sounding totally unlike himself.

But maybe that's the real Silas, what I'm hearing. He was putting on some sort of fake persona to impress me.

Alana goes dead silent and I can practically feel the fury vibrating off her. "Are you saying that because she's younger, you're afraid she won't put out? Is that the issue?"

"One time," he mutters. "One time you catch me fucking around with another girl and you'll never let me forget it."

"I can't forget it! You're not loyal, Silas. As a matter of fact, you're a terrible boyfriend. I don't know why I ever thought this would work. We're done. I mean it this time." Alana storms from behind the bush, and I'm so shocked by their revelations that she catches me standing there, unable to move.

She spots me because, of course, she does, and she comes to a stop, staring at me for a moment before a faintly hysterical laugh leaves her. "I guess you win, Willow. You can have him."

Silas stops just behind Alana, a smile appearing on his face when he spots me. "Oh hey, Willow."

Alana jabs him in the ribs. "She was spying on our conversation."

"I wasn't spying. I couldn't help but hear it, you two were so loud," I retort.

Silas winces. "I guess I don't look so good to you right now, huh?"

"No, you definitely don't. But both of you revealed your true colors to me a long time ago." I wave at them. "Bye."

I rush away from them, eager to get to Iris so I can tell her everything, but I hear footsteps behind me, and oh my God, it's freaking Silas. I come to a full stop and turn to face him, ready to shove at him if need be. I don't want this guy near me.

"Alana is just—jealous," he starts. "Of you. Of Margaret. Of any girl I speak to or even look at. She can't help it. I guess I bring that out of her."

I roll my eyes at his remark. Is he for real right now? "There's no point in you chasing after me or trying to change my mind. I'm not interested, Silas."

"But we could've been so good together—"

"Get the fuck out of here, dude."

We both go still at the angry male voice coming from behind me. Slowly I turn around to find Rhett standing there with a furious expression on his face, which doesn't distract from his attractiveness. No, in this moment, he's even more appealing, rushing to my defense, looking ready to tear Silas apart with his bare hands.

All because Silas won't leave me alone. Rhett is protecting me when he doesn't need to. When he has no reason to. After I've been so dismissive of him lately.

My heart swells with emotion.

"This is really none of your business," Silas starts to say, but he goes silent at the death glare Rhett sends him.

"It's my business. Like I told you before, she belongs to me." Rhett makes his way toward us, stopping directly in front of me, blocking me completely from Silas's view. "So back the fuck off."

"I never see the two of you together—"

"Because we don't need to flaunt to everyone else that we're together, okay, asshole? Now beat it."

They stare at each other, though I can't see Silas, thanks to Rhett standing in my way. My gaze drops to his hands, the way they're curled into fists. Like he wants to use them against Silas, and my heart drops.

Here I am avoiding Rhett completely and I'm still somehow a complete distraction to him. If Westscott saw us right now, he'd blame me, and I guess he'd be right. It doesn't seem to matter what I do. Rhett is still going to run to my rescue. And deep down…

I'm grateful for it.

CHAPTER TWENTY-FIVE

RHETT

Silas is a fucking wimp. I see the flicker of fear in his gaze as I glare at him. The way his Adam's apple bobs when his gaze drops to my fisted hands. I'd use them on him too, but I don't want to risk the game. I can't. Too many people are depending on me tonight.

But damn, the moment I saw this little prick giving Willow a bunch of shit, I had to come over and end it. Fuck this guy. He needs to stay away from her. I don't really care either if Willow is mad that I ran to her defense and called her mine because this fucker doesn't ever seem to take a hint.

Clueless asshole.

I don't give in to Silas, don't even bother to say a word either, and I don't have to. He silently gives in without any more urging from me, turning and slinking away like a beat down dog. Only when he's out of sight do I turn and check on Willow.

"You all right?"

She seems dazed. Even a little confused. "What are you doing here?"

"Walked over here with your brother. Said he had to go to his room to grab something. He's still in there." I frown, wondering what the hell Row needs. I'm sure he told me, but I've forgotten thanks to my all-encompassing rage toward Silas.

Been bored pretty much all afternoon while watching everyone run through drills and practice their asses off. Coach didn't want me working too hard and fucking up my chances for tonight so I was just sitting around and killing time. I jumped at the chance to walk with Rowan over to his special Lancaster dorm building. Was I hoping to run into Willow?

Maybe.

Definitely.

"Oh." She offers me a genuine smile and the sight of it eases my anger some. She hasn't looked at me like that in a week and I've missed it. Missed her. "Well, thank you. I appreciate it."

"You're welcome. That asshole needs to leave you alone."

She laughs. "Tell me about it."

"Why was he chasing after you anyway?"

"I caught him and Alana arguing." Her expression turns sheepish. "I was kind of spying on their conversation."

Now I'm the one chuckling. "I would've too. I bet it was good."

"It was. When she was yelling at him, she even mentioned that he cheated on her before." Will shakes her head, the disgust on her face obvious. "So disappointing."

"What a bastard."

"Have you ever cheated on someone before?"

I'm taken aback by her question. That she actually had the nerve to ask me this.

"First, I've never been in a relationship where it would be considered cheating if I talked to another girl, and second, when I'm all in, I'm all in. I would never cheat," I say vehemently. "I'm the most loyal motherfucker you'll ever meet."

She seems shocked by my admission, and maybe I went a little overboard, but fuck it. I'm tired of this girl constantly making it seem like I'm a problem. I'm not the problem here—she is. I'm ready to be down for her. I've got it so fucking bad for Willow Lancaster and she has no goddamn clue because she hasn't given me a chance to show her.

And man, the things I could show her.

"That's good to know," she finally says, sounding vaguely breathless.

"I get it from my dad. He's worshipped my mother since the first moment he spoke to her." Even worshipped her from afar for about two years, though he admitted he wasn't a saint then. Not like he could save himself for her, he told me, which just made me laugh. And then got me a little grossed out because the last thing I ever want to think about is my parents having sex.

"That's sweet." Willow's smile is as soft as her voice. "My parents are the same way."

That means she might be searching for the same thing I am—hopefully. "You get along with them?"

She nods. "Oh, definitely. I'm really close to my mom. She's like my best friend. Well, besides Iris."

"Does Iris hate me?" I can never get a read on that girl. She's too unpredictable.

Same with the one standing in front of me.

"No, of course not. If Iris hated you, you'd know it."

"Okay." Not sure if I one hundred percent believe her, but I guess I'll take her word for it.

"I've come to realize that you're always running to my rescue," she murmurs.

"Gladly," I say without hesitation. "I will do anything to protect you, Will."

She's frowning, her delicate brows drawing together in confusion. "You don't even know—"

"I know enough," I tell her, cutting her off. "I know you enjoy reading that suck ass book in English and you feel sorry for that dead relative of yours with the creepy statue. I know you like to wear bows in your hair every day and that sexy red lipstick on your mouth and you always look fucking hot. I know you're really smart and you have a great voice and you're genuinely kind. I know you feel invisible sometimes and that's probably because Iris is the louder Lancaster between the two of you, but I *see* you, Willow. I see you and I want to see more of you and I don't know why you keep denying me the privilege. Because that's what it would be—a privilege to be with you. To let everyone know that we're together. Maybe I'm talking out my ass and I'm saying too much but I can't keep it in any longer. I've never felt this way about a girl before."

She's frozen in place. The only thing moving is her chest, which rises and falls at a rapid pace, as if she's breathing heavily. All from what I just said? I guess so. It was a lot. Probably too much.

Damn, I hope I didn't mess everything up.

"I should go." I glance just beyond her shoulder to see Row emerging from the building, a giant smile on his face as he heads in our direction. "Your brother is coming over here."

"Oh." She nods and turns to smile at him, and I wish she'd aim more of that sunshine on me. "Hey, Row. How are you?"

"Great. Ready for tonight's game," he answers with a smile.

"I'd wish you good luck, but I don't think you need it. I'm sure you'll crush them," she says with all the confidence of a supportive sister.

Rowan pulls her into a quick hug, towering over her. They look alike, but not quite. Just enough to know they're siblings. They have the same color hair and eyes. "Thanks. You coming to my game?"

"Of course," she says with an enthusiastic nod. "I wouldn't miss it."

"Awesome. Mom and Dad will be there too."

"They will?" She seems shocked. Like what, her parents didn't let her know they were coming?

"They come to all my games, even the away ones." Row smiles, reaching out to nudge her shoulder, giving her a little push though she doesn't really move. "It's nice to see them in the stands."

"Mom never mentioned it to me. Though I haven't talked to her all week," Willow admits.

"She probably assumed you'd already know because I told

you. I haven't talked to you much either. Too much going on with football," he tells her. "You can sit with them. Or with Iris. You'll probably have more fun with Iris."

"Maybe I'll sit with them during the JV game," Willow says, her gaze shifting to me, lingering for the briefest moment before she hurriedly looks away. "And I'll sit with Iris and our friends during the varsity game."

"Sounds like a plan." Row sends me a quick glance. "We should probably head back, huh?"

"Yeah, let's do it." I turn my attention to Willow, wishing we could talk more after my over-the-top confession, but I'm not about to get all in my feels in front of her little brother, so I keep my mouth shut. "You're definitely staying for the varsity game?"

"Yes." Her smile is small. Real. The sight of it touches my soul, which sounds like a bunch of shit to my logical self, but the emotional part of me believes it wholeheartedly. I needed to see that smile more than anything. "I wouldn't miss it."

"Good. The first touchdown I throw will be just for you."

And with that crazed statement, I leave her where she stands, heading for the field with Row walking along beside me. I can tell he's trying to figure out why I just said all that. His lips part and he clamps them shut repeatedly before he finally just blurts out the question when we're about halfway to the stadium.

"You into my sister or what?"

"Maybe." I shrug. Why deny it? "Yes. Do you have a problem with that?"

I don't mean to sound so hostile, but I'm sick of the roadblocks that are thrown at me from every angle, especially the ones from Willow herself.

"I don't have a problem with it," Rowan says slowly, as if he's thinking over everything I just said. "What does Willow think?"

"She's not into me," I reply.

"Did she tell you that?"

Damn it, yes, she did. "Sort of."

"But she's coming to your game."

"It's a football game, Row. There's nothing else going on tonight. Everyone is coming." I'm trying to rationalize this idea with myself so I don't get my hopes up. Too late though.

They're up. As high as the fucking sky.

"You told her you'll throw a touchdown for her," Row points out.

"That was just some corny shit." I'm trying to play it off.

"Sounded pretty serious to me."

These fucking Lancasters are too smart for their own good. "I'm flirting with her, not that she gets it."

"Well, don't forget to treat my sister with respect," Row practically demands. "She's a good girl."

"I know." I nod as we walk along the path that leads to the stadium, my mind filled with nothing else but her. I can hear Coach blowing his whistle, a couple guys are yelling, and I know my head should be in the game. This is an important night. "I know."

We're quiet for a moment and only when we're walking through the stadium's front gates does Row speak again.

"Want to get in good with my sister?"

"Definitely." This is the type of information I didn't expect and desperately need.

"Get close to our family. It's the most important thing to her. To all of us," Row explains. "You're already ahead of the game since we're friends."

"Yeah?" I slap him on the back, making him grunt. "I appreciate you, man. Truly."

Row laughs. "You owe me."

"I do," I agree without hesitation.

His advice is great and all, but I have an immediate situation here that I need to take care of. All I can think about is Will. I can envision her sitting in the stands, wearing that sweet smile when I look up at her after I throw the first touchdown. She might even be blushing. And I'll be grinning, knowing I did it all for her.

I'd do anything for her.

CHAPTER TWENTY-SIX

WILLOW

I can't stop thinking about what Rhett said to me before my brother showed up. It felt as if he poured his heart out to me, his words raw and his voice hoarse. Like it took everything out of him to make that confession, but he was still brave enough to do it.

The look on his face when he said it is embedded in my memory. The way he watched me, never looking away once. No one has ever spoken to me like that before. Ever.

He was dead serious, and while I sit here and get all dreamy over his romantic declaration, I know deep in my soul that I'll have to reject him yet again. Westscott won't stand for it.

"You're in a weird mood," Iris calls from the bathroom as we're getting ready for the game together in her room.

"What do you mean?" I'm standing in front of her full-length mirror, checking my outfit. Jeans and a Lancaster Lions T-shirt I picked up in the student store earlier today and white Chanel sneakers on my feet because my mom gave them to me for my birthday this summer and I rarely wear them, which makes me feel guilty. She'll be here tonight, so she'll see them and that'll make her happy.

"You seem completely distracted." Iris emerges from the bathroom and I turn to face her. "Sometimes I don't even think you're paying attention to what I'm saying."

Busted. I'm not. She's been keeping up nonstop chatter since she took her shower and opened the door to let the steam escape once she was finished. I told her all about Alana and Silas's fight that I overheard, and how Silas chased after me. How Rhett told him to back off. That earned major points in Iris's eyes.

"Please tell me you're not considering trying to make a go for Silas again, are you?" Clad in only her underwear, Iris goes to her closet and yanks a navy Lancaster Prep crewneck sweatshirt from a hanger and tugs it on over her head. "And don't accuse me of sending you mixed messages. I swear I will never try reverse psychology on you again."

"Good, because that was dumb." I shake my head. "And no, I'm not interested in Silas. Not after I heard what Alana said."

And what Rhett said to me, too. Not that I've mentioned it to Iris. I swear I'll tell her someday, but right now, I need to savor the moment for myself. I don't want anyone else's opinion on Rhett interfering with my own thoughts. I need to make this decision on my own. Not with Iris's input because I have no clue how she might respond.

"Who knew wimpy Silas had it in him to cheat?" Iris grabs a pair of jeans and settles on the edge of her bed, pulling them on. "I didn't think he was the type."

"I agree. He's always been so quiet. Almost shy."

"Those are the ones to watch, I guess. Sneaky." Iris's gaze drops to my feet. "Chanel, Willow? So fancy."

"Says the girl wearing a Cartier necklace," I throw back at her. I kick out my right foot. "My mom gave me these."

"They're cute. Your mom has always been a Chanel devotee."

"It's my dad's fault. He sent her all of those lipsticks." Back when they were seniors and going to this school. He knew then. I've heard the story countless times, noted the glow of nostalgic love in his gaze every time he tells it. When I was little, I loved that story because he played up the fact that Mom didn't like him.

I thought that was funny.

But now…I think about me and Rhett. How I didn't like him much either at first, and how he's worn me down.

We don't know each other well enough that I'm expecting declarations of undying love, and I don't want them because it's just way too soon, but I…

I want to go on a date with him. Spend time with him just one on one. Get to know him better. I'm fairly certain he wants the same thing. So what's holding us back from each other?

Me. And what Westscott said. I should just tell Rhett. He might get mad, but he deserves to know the truth. I should tell my parents too. I'll have my opportunity tonight. My dad will be furious and probably want to come at the headmaster, but Mom will tell him to calm down. I'm sure once confronted, Westscott will play off our conversation as one big misunderstanding and all will be well.

A girl can dream.

"I just want to make sure that you're not down in the dumps over Silas. He's not worth one ounce of your thoughts. He's nothing but wasted emotion." Iris goes to her vanity and sits on the chair, yanking open a drawer and pulling out a bunch of makeup. Not that I have any room to talk. We both own so many products and cosmetics, we probably look like a Sephora store. "I need to look good tonight."

"Why? Are you trying to look good for someone in particular?" I'm teasing her, but she lifts her gaze to mine in the mirror, her expression serious.

"I never did confess my little story to you."

With the drama from Alana and Silas and then Rhett's heartfelt confession, I sort of forgot all about her cliffhanger moment. "Oh my God, you didn't. I need all the details. Now."

"Well…" Her gaze drops from mine and she focuses on piling up a little mountain of cosmetics on top of the vanity counter. "I, um, hooked up with someone this summer. And then I promptly ghosted him."

I'm frowning, my mind scrambling, but I can't come up with a face, let alone a name. "Who?"

"You know him. Very well." She plucks an eyebrow pencil from a cup and starts filling in her brows. They're a golden blonde and she likes to darken them. I've told her time and again to just get them tinted, but I'm veering way off topic here. "He goes to this school. I sort of hate him, but not really."

Realization dawns. "Oh my God, Iris. Is it…"

"Brooks," she supplies for me. My jaw feels like it dropped to the floor. "He's really good with his hands. That's all I'm going to say."

My mind is literally blown. I settle heavily on the edge of her bed, staring at her while she goes about putting on her makeup like she didn't just rock my world with her confession. "Brooks?" I finally ask. "Really?"

"Is it that far-fetched?"

"No." I shake my head. It actually makes all the sense in the world. "You've never given me any inclination that you're interested in him."

"Because I never was. Brooks is always just…there, you know? We've gone to school with him for a long time. I always thought he was nice, but I never looked at him and thought, 'Yeah, I want him to get me off with his fingers in my panties for seven nights straight', which is exactly what happened." Her tone is so matter of fact, as if she's talking about the weather.

"Seven nights straight?" I ask weakly, still trying to wrap my head around this.

"It was magical." A wistful sigh leaves her and she immediately shakes her head, like she's trying to rid herself of every romantic thought she has in regards to Brooks. "And then I ignored his texts, which means he of course sent me countless messages. He was relentless, but he eventually stopped and now here we are. Pretending it never happened."

"Why would you want to do that?"

"I don't know. Brooks Crosby is a big deal." Iris has covered her face with countless dots of foundation and now she starts vigorously blending it into her skin with a brush. "His family is powerful. Political. The perfect match for a Lancaster. My parents would be thrilled to know I'm dating Brooks."

"But you're not dating him."

"No, and I won't. A week-long affair is all we'll ever be. Isn't that romantic?" Another sigh leaves her and I swear her disappointment is a living, breathing thing in the room. I can feel it swirl all around us, but I'm guessing she doesn't have a clue, which is kind of funny. Silly Iris.

"Why are you trying to look extra good for him tonight then?" I'm curious as to her motive.

"To make him want to eat his heart out and see what he's missing." She rolls her eyes at me in the mirror's reflection, but I don't take offense.

"You're the one who ghosted him."

"Right, but since senior year started, he's completely avoided me and pretends that week never happened."

"I'm sure he acts that way because *you* ghosted *him*," I repeat with extra emphasis this time around. "He's just following your lead by pretending nothing happened."

"I suppose so, but I don't know. Maybe I made a mistake. I should've kept it up with him. Wouldn't an illicit affair be so much fun right now? Sneaking around, praying no one catches us? Feels dangerous." Iris's eyes gleam. "I like danger."

She's terrifying when she talks like this. If I ever killed someone by accident, she would be the first person I call to help me bury the body. She'd agree with no hesitation.

"Doesn't Taylor Swift have a song called that? 'Illicit Affairs?' That should be my new theme song." She grabs her phone and scrolls Spotify. A song starts seconds later and I realize it's the very song she just mentioned, which is on my favorite album, *Folklore*.

"Ooh this is moody. Fitting since I'm in a mood and so are you."

"I told you, I'm not in a mood." God, I'm in a total mood, but I don't want to tell her why. If she can keep secrets, so can I.

"Fine, whatever. Keep living in denial." She faces the mirror once more and starts applying blush to her cheeks. "Are you going to wear makeup?"

I shrug. "I'll put on some mascara. That's it. Oh, and lipstick."

"So bare faced."

"I don't have a man to impress."

"Right. Sure, you don't."

What Iris said only a moment ago really hit home. An illicit affair. Sneaking around and how fun that can be. Maybe that's what I can do with Rhett, at least at first. We can build up to being public by taking our time and seeing each other without anyone knowing. It'll be difficult, but I think it's possible.

Will Rhett want to do that though? He doesn't seem like the type to hide much. He's very upfront with his feelings so I assume he'd almost be offended by my suggestion.

Guess it's the chance I'll have to take.

"Are you going to talk to Brooks tonight?"

"Absolutely not." Iris smiles. I think she enjoys torturing him. "That's why I want to look as beautiful as possible, so I can torture him and make him regret every single one of his life choices."

"Oh, Iris. You're beautiful no matter what. I'm sure he's completely smitten with you."

"Smitten? I like that word. So old-fashioned."

"You know me. I'm always full of nostalgia."

"Romanticizing your life, bestie? I know you're all about that too."

There's nothing romantic about keeping my feelings and thoughts about someone all bottled up inside, is there?

Hmm. Maybe there is.

CHAPTER TWENTY-SEVEN

WILLOW

"Hi!" I'm swept up into a bear hug from my father, who holds me close and kisses the top of my head before practically shoving me into my mother's arms. "I've missed you guys."

"We've missed you too, darling." Mom presses her fragrant cheek against mine before shifting away from me, her hands on my upper arms as she holds me there, checking me out. "You look wonderful."

I almost roll my eyes, but I don't want to hurt her feelings and besides, I will take the compliments any time I can get them, I've been feeling so low lately. "You do too. You didn't tell me you were coming today."

My tone is faintly accusatory and Mom frowns, shaking her head once. "I swore I did."

"You didn't," Dad says, his gaze going to mine. "Sorry about that, sweetie."

I smile at the two of them. "I just didn't know, but this is a pleasant surprise."

"We came to all of Row's games last season but you weren't here. I suppose I forgot," Mom murmurs, frowning. "Well, it doesn't matter now. Expect to see us as much as possible throughout the football season, though we won't cramp your style."

"What do you mean?"

"If you want to spend time with your friends or whoever." Mom smiles, her eyes twinkling. "Is there a special someone who's caught your eye?"

"Mom, oh my God." I glance around us but no one is paying any attention. "There's no one. And if there was, I don't know if I'd tell you yet."

We're standing outside of the Lancaster Prep stadium, keeping our eye on the scoreboard across the field, which says we have fifteen minutes until the JV game starts.

"You better not tell me yet because I'd automatically want to break his legs for thinking about getting with my daughter," Dad says fiercely.

I roll my eyes while Mom laughs nervously. He's so over the top. "I'm not a little girl anymore, Dad."

"Oh, trust me, I know. That's why I'd break the kid's legs. That way he couldn't stand near you. He'd be laid up in a wheelchair."

"He'd still have his hands," I point out, thinking of Iris's earlier comment about Brooks and how he was good with his.

I wonder if Rhett is good with his hands. Fingers. Whatever. A shiver steals over me at the thought.

My dad's face turns red and I realize that was probably the wrong thing to say. "I'll break his arms too, then. And every one of those fingers."

"Crew." Mom settles her hand on Dad's arm, her voice calm and soothing because no doubt, Dad needs a little soothing right now. "You're getting all worked up over an imaginary boy. You need to calm down."

"I know how I was at her age." He shakes his head and I can tell he already seems a little calmer. His gaze locks with mine. "Watch out, Willow. We're all motivated by our hormones. I know I was."

"You were the most romantic boy I knew, Crew Lancaster." Mom rises up on her tiptoes and presses a kiss to his lips.

"You weren't living in my head twenty-four seven, thank God,"

Dad mutters.

I ignore their romantic banter, checking out the stadium. It's definitely old like Westscott told me and I'm curious if he was telling me the truth when he said money was pouring in from alumni donations, thanks to the success of the football team. And that they plan on spending that money on constructing a new stadium.

I don't know why he'd lie about that, though as I continue looking around, I realize it's not very busy. Oh, there are a few people milling about, but it's mostly parents or underclassmen.

"It's kind of quiet out here," I note.

"I'm guessing the stands will fill up after the JV game is done," Dad tells me.

"I was hoping more people would come and watch the JV team," Mom says, her voice full of disappointment. "They need support just like the varsity team does."

"Row will be playing varsity next year," Dad reassures her. "Then we won't have to come to these games."

"I think I like the smaller crowds." Mom glances around. "They're so much quieter."

Dad grabs hold of Mom's hand and squeezes it. They're both wearing matching Lancaster Prep Lions T-shirts and jeans, and Mom's hair is in a low ponytail, her lips painted crimson, much like mine. "We should head inside. The game is going to start soon and I want to get good seats."

I follow them through the gates, glancing around in search of Iris. We parted ways once my parents texted to let me know they were on campus, and she went to hang out with Bronwyn and a few other girls when I said I was going to meet up with them.

"I'll come sit with you guys once the JV game starts. I want to see your parents," Iris promised me, kissing me on the cheek before she left.

I checked my face in the mirror once she was gone, not surprised to see the lipstick smear on my cheek along with a hint of foundation. I rubbed it off, grateful she wasn't wearing a darker shade, but the lipstick print gave me an idea. Made me think of those photos I found of my parents—of my dad covered in lipstick prints Mom gave him.

I wouldn't mind trying that with Rhett, but would he let me? He'd probably think it was stupid. Silly. I'm sure he's been with plenty of sexually-experienced girls while I'm over here wearing my imaginary "Hi, I'm a virgin" T-shirt. He has to know. I've basically admitted it to him without actually saying the words.

But he hasn't gone running yet so maybe he doesn't mind.

We find seats halfway up the stands, right on the fifty-yard line, which Dad says is the best view in the house. Our JV team is on the sidelines already, and I note how they're a variety of sizes. Since the team is made up of mostly freshmen and sophomores, they're all at different stages of growing, and some of them are short and slight, while others are tall and lanky, like my brother.

Row towers above most of them, and I watch as he stands next to one of his coaches, listening intently to whatever the man is telling him. He's got those dark smudge marks under his eyes that I've never understood why they do that, his hands curved around the neckline of his jersey. He's nodding along with whatever his coach is telling him, finally smiling at one point, and I hear a girl shout his name from the bottom of the stands.

"Row, I love you!"

Her declaration is followed by a bunch of giggles, and I share a look with Mom, who just shakes her head.

"He has fans."

"Of course, he does. He's an excellent quarterback," Dad says, his voice full of pride.

"I don't think his fandom has anything to do with his football skills," Mom says wryly.

I agree with her.

Once the game starts, I actually get into it. We have the ball first, and while I don't fully comprehend what's happening on the field, I can figure out a few things, and within minutes, our team has already run in a touchdown. The other team seems slower than ours, and they make a lot of mistakes. Dad is shouting at the top of his lungs with every play Row makes, cupping his hands around his mouth so my brother can hear him, I guess. He's gone into full-on sports dad mode and it's almost comical.

"He loves this," Mom admits to me near the end of the first quarter. "I don't think he ever expected to have a football playing son and he secretly lives for it. He's so proud. Beau is most likely going to follow in your brother's footsteps too. He's very good. His first game is tomorrow."

"Are you going back home tonight?" I thought they might stay for the weekend and I was looking forward to it.

"We have to so we can watch Beau's game. I wouldn't miss it." Mom smiles, reaching out to brush a few stray hairs away from my forehead. "This is the time of year where your dad and I are on the go constantly."

"I missed it all last year," I say softly. That makes me sad, but there's nothing I can do to change it, so I banish the emotion. "I'm sure it's fun."

"So much fun." Music starts playing and Mom leans in, whispering in my ear. "How are you, sweetie? Is school going well? Do you like your classes? Where's Iris? Are you two getting along?"

I pull back, smiling at her. "I'm good. School is going well and I like all of my classes, even the tough ones. Iris is with a couple of friends, but she said she'd sit with us for a while because she wants to see you guys. And we're getting along great."

"Good." Mom cups my cheek, staring into my eyes. Hers are a vivid green and I've thought more than once how much I wish mine were green too, but Beau is the lucky one of the three of us to get her eyes. "I worry about you."

"Why?"

"Because I can't help but always worry about you. I worry about all three of you. You're all a piece of my heart, and I just want to make sure you're doing well and that you're happy."

"I'm good, Mom." I grab hold of her wrist and give it a gentle squeeze. "Please don't worry about me."

"And your brother? Should I be worried about him and his fangirls?"

I didn't even know he had fangirls. Row and I aren't talking much right now and I figured that was because he's so busy with football. "I don't think it's a big concern."

"If you say so." Mom drops her hand from my cheek and faces forward, her gaze seeking out and finding Row right away. I find him too. He's on the sidelines, his helmet clasped in his hand and his hair absolutely chaotic. He probably stinks. I don't know how any girl can find him appealing in this moment. To me, he's just my sweaty little brother.

"Hey, guys!" Iris calls as she walks up the steps, her arm above her head as she waves at us frantically. She looks absolutely gorgeous in the simplest outfit, and I wonder why she went to so much trouble applying all that makeup. She doesn't even need it.

"Iris!" Mom yells, waving back frantically in return. "Come sit!"

My cousin squeezes in on the other side of me, and Mom practically shoves me out of the way to give Iris a hug. Once she lets her go, I squirm my way back in between them, turning to Iris. "Where's Bronwyn?"

"She's down there." Iris waves a hand toward the bottom of the stands. "She's got the hots for someone on the JV team. He's a sophomore. I keep giving her shit for liking younger men."

"Who is it?"

"Not your brother, so don't worry." Iris grins and pops the bright blue gum in her mouth, making me grimace. I hate when she chews gum. She's so loud with it sometimes. "His name is Hartford."

"Hartford?" Mom asks, leaning into our conversation. "Is that his last name?"

"Nope, his first name. It was his mom's maiden name I think."

Alarm flits across Mom's face. I don't think Iris notices it, but I sure do. "What's his last name?"

"Morales," Iris answers, punctuating her sentence with another popped gum bubble.

"Wait a minute. Is his mother Natalie Hartford?" Mom's expression is downright horrified and even Dad is paying attention to our conversation.

"I don't know. I think so?" Iris shrugs.

"Oh my God," Mom breathes, turning to Dad. "It's her."

"Babe. Her son started last year. You didn't put that together?"

"I don't pay attention to the student roster. Why didn't you ever mention it to me?" Mom's tone is vaguely accusing.

"I'm sure I did. I wouldn't let that tasty little morsel slip by you." Dad smiles and Mom gives him a gentle shove.

"Who's Natalie Hartford?" I ask Mom.

"Well, her name is Natalie Morales now. She married Eric Morales." Mom is frowning. "She was my worst nightmare back in high school."

"I don't know if I'd take it that far," Dad starts, but Mom silences him with a look.

"It's true," Mom tells me and Iris. "She made my life miserable there for a while."

"I'm sure she regrets her actions," Dad says like he's trying to console her.

"Ha! I doubt it. That girl was a total bitch."

I gape at my mother, shocked to hear her call this Natalie person a bitch. She rarely has bad words to say about anybody, and I suppose if she doesn't like someone, she always keeps her opinion to herself.

Apparently not with this woman.

"Ah, come on now. Who got the last laugh, huh?" Dad leans in and kisses Mom's cheek, but she pulls away from him, scowling.

"This isn't a contest, Crew. I just—I haven't had to think about her in a long time, and I'd prefer to keep it that way." It's as if realization dawns and Mom's head starts swiveling this way and that, scanning the stadium. "What if she's here right now, watching her son play? What if I run into her? I really wish you would've mentioned this to me sooner."

"I didn't think about it because Morales didn't play last year. With the football team's success, they gained a lot more players this season," Dad explains.

"Hmm." Mom crosses her arms, looking put out. "I don't want to resort to violence if I bump into her."

"Violence?" Iris chokes out on a laugh. "Come on, Aunt Wren. You would never."

"I might," Mom murmurs, surprising me.

It's so interesting, seeing this different side of my mother I've never witnessed before. She's feisty, with a determined jut to her jaw and anger simmering in her gaze. Mom rarely lets something ruffle her feathers like this, so this Natalie woman must be awful.

"If you do happen to see her, you'll be polite like you always are and make small talk with her while mentally cursing her out the entire time. Don't worry about it." Now it's Dad's turn to soothe Mom and I can tell it's working. Her body was completely rigid only seconds ago and now she's visibly more relaxed, her shoulders lowering as the tension seeps out of her.

"You're right. That's exactly what I'll do." Mom nods, and this time she's accepting of the kiss Dad delivers to her, right on the lips.

I turn away, shrugging at Iris, who seems highly amused by the entire interaction. I can't blame her. That was a wild moment to witness and shocking to see. But it was also a little refreshing, I can't lie, watching her get riled up about someone from her past.

Makes me think my feelings about Alana aren't unwarranted after all. I'm always afraid of overreacting. My mother's voice is often in my head when I'm in certain situations—how would she react? What would she do? I try to emulate her as much as possible, and I worried my anger and frustration with Alana was just me being petty. Even a little paranoid.

I had reason to feel betrayed. How can I be friends with her again after everything that's happened? Not that she's rushing over to reignite our friendship, but I wouldn't put it past her if she and Silas are truly broken up. She doesn't really have any other friends, and while I feel sorry for her, I don't necessarily want her back in our fold either.

Sitting up straighter, I check the field just in time to watch Row make a spectacular pass, the ball landing in a receiver's hands before the boy runs the ball into the end zone. The entire crowd starts cheering, including me, and I share a smile with Iris, proud of my brother.

Tonight is going to be a good night.

CHAPTER TWENTY-EIGHT

RHETT

"Did you see that play I made?" Cal asks me once he comes off the field, whipping his helmet off and wearing a big ol' dopey grin on his face. "It was fucking magical."

"Good job," I tell him, holding out my hand so we can do that intricate handshake thing we made up when we were little. "You guys are killing it."

"Thank God." Cal groans after taking a giant drink of water. His hair is sticking up haphazardly all over his head and he's sweating like a mofo, but he looks genuinely happy. "We kind of sucked ass last year."

I say nothing because I don't feel like rubbing salt in the wound that is the JV team's disastrous last season. They were an uncoordinated mess and their coaching staff worked extra hard to slap them into shape, especially that last month of summer when they had mandatory practices. We did too but nothing as intense as what they had going on.

"Hey, hey, there's my superstars."

We both turn to watch as our dad approaches us, a big ol' grin on his face and his arms spread wide. He wraps us both up in a three-way hug, Callahan ducking out of it after about five seconds. This allows me to full-on embrace my old man because damn, I'm always glad to see him. Cal is still going through teenage angst bullshit, which means he doesn't want anyone to see him being affectionate with our father.

Me? I'm like bring it on. Eli Bennett is the real superstar and my inspiration since I was a freaking toddler and ran around the backyard with a football tucked under my arm. All I've ever wanted is to be like him so bad. I want everything he's got and more. And he's been right there with me every step of the way as I work toward my goals, encouraging me and believing in me. My mom too. I might've been mad when we moved to the East Coast for my dad to take the new coaching job, but he did it for us too.

"Ready for your game?" he asks me oncc we've pulled away from each other.

I stare at his face, noting for about the millionth time that I look so much like him, it's like staring into a mirror of the future. The only difference is my eyes are a little greener like Mom's and my hair is a little darker, which I get from the Callahan side of the family.

"I don't think I can be any more ready than I am," I admit. My body is vibrating with the need to get out onto the field. We're lucky Coach let a few of us seniors stand on the sideline of the JV game. I pled my case by wanting to watch my brother play and that is ninety percent of the reason why I'm down here.

The other ten percent has to do with me about to do a casual scan of the stands and see if Willow is here like she said she would be.

"You're going to play great," Dad says, the sincerity ringing in his voice, calming my slightly frazzled nerves. We all deserve someone to believe in us like my dad believes in me. "Cal is looking good too. He caught that ball perfectly."

"Yeah, he did." I nod in agreement, quickly glancing over my shoulder. I spot Bronwyn, that chick who's a junior and is always hanging out with Willow and Iris, but otherwise, that's it.

"The QB is pretty good too. Isn't the same one the JV team

had last year. Right?"

"Row replaced him," I say, watching as the JV defensive line holds the other team solidly. "The team is looking way better this season."

"Yeah, they are. This ought to be a good season." Dad smiles. "For the both of you."

We talk for a few minutes, Cal ditching us because he needs to focus on his team and listen to his coaches. Dad starts yapping at one of them and they eat up everything he says because the man brings with him a ton of experience. I'd listen to him too.

I do.

But in this moment, I'm over playing it cool and I blatantly turn around and face the crowd, scanning the stands more thoroughly on the hunt for Willow. I finally spot her about halfway up, sitting with who I can only assume are her parents. The older woman sitting next to her is a dead ringer for Willow and the man sitting on the other side of her gives me Rowan vibes. Iris is sitting with them as well, and she and Will are currently engrossed in a deep conversation.

I watch them, willing Willow to look my way. If she does without any prompting from me, I know we're meant to be together. She needs to feel my vibe. My eyes watching her.

Come on, baby. Feel me.

As if she could hear my thoughts, Will tears her attention away from Iris and looks around, her gaze dropping to the field. To the sideline.

To me.

Our gazes lock and I grin like an idiot, giving her a discreet wave. She lifts her hand in return, the tiny smile curving her lips lighting up her entire face. She's so beautiful she makes my chest ache.

"Who's the girl?" Dad asks, catching me.

I drop my hand and jerk my gaze to his, feeling guilty because I just got caught. I'm tempted to say she's no one important but that would be the biggest lie I've ever told. I decide to go with the truth.

"My future wife," I reply.

Dad shakes his head, chuckling. "Got it bad for someone finally, huh?"

My gaze returns to Will, who's still watching me, that smile still curving her ruby red lips. Damn, I'd love nothing more than to kiss her and smudge that lipstick all over her mouth. Maybe even get some of it on my lips. I wouldn't mind.

It'd be worth it to kiss her. Something I've been thinking about constantly.

"Yeah," I croak, clearing my throat.

"Well, that's a first. You've been a little girl crazy the last couple of years but nothing serious." Dad lifts his gaze to the stands as well, and I hold my breath, praying he doesn't say something stupid. Sometimes Dad doesn't think before he speaks. I share that same trait with him. "She's beautiful."

A grateful exhale leaves me. "I know."

"The blonde sitting next to her is pretty too." He's referring to Iris.

"I don't like blondes."

Dad laughs. "I love a beautiful blonde."

"You love Mom. I get it. I see blondes and think of Kenz." I'm referring to my sister. Yeah, not interested in blondes at all.

"I never realized you were so anti-blonde."

"I like dark-haired girls with red lips." I should change that from plural to singular. There is only one girl with dark brown hair and red lips that interests me. It's only been a couple of weeks, but fuck it. I'm in it to win it. Win this game tonight. Win the whole season.

And win the girl.

CHAPTER TWENTY-NINE

WILLOW

The JV team won their first game and it was so fun to witness the pure joy on Row's face when they ran out onto the field to celebrate their victory. When they all stood in a line in front of the stands and held their helmets above their heads, shouting, "Thank you, fans!" we jumped to our feet and cheered them on. I swear Mom even had tears in her eyes.

I understand the feeling. I was proud of Row too.

Once the teams were off the field for good, the clock on the scoreboard switched to thirty minutes. The countdown is on for the varsity football game to start and it's so weird to feel this way, but I'm anxious. Nervous.

I just want Rhett to do well. I want them to win.

Desperately.

I'm bouncing my knee, making the entire bench we're sitting on vibrate and rattle, and Iris finally settles her hand on my thigh, forcing me to stop. "What's wrong with you?"

"I don't know." I shrug. "I'm nervous. I want them to do well."

"They're going to be amazing," Iris says with all the confidence I don't feel. "You haven't even seen them in action yet."

She's right. I haven't. I have no idea just how good they could possibly be, but the opposing team is out on the field running through some drills, according to my father, and they look huge.

Intimidating.

Granted, Rhett is pretty tall and broad, but I've never thought of any of the other boys who are on the team as particularly intimidating. Well Brooks is tall as well and even broader than Rhett.

I glance over at Iris, who's wearing this serene expression on her face, like nothing is bothering her, and I envy that.

"Why are you looking at me like that?" she asks, frowning.

"You seem perfectly at ease with yourself."

"I am," she says with zero hesitation. "I love going to football games."

"They make me anxious."

Iris laughs. "First one you've gone to and now you're an expert on how they make you feel."

"I'm sure I sound ridiculous but seriously. Can't you feel the anticipation in the air?" I glance around, noting how much fuller the stands are now. And there are so many people flooding the walkway down below, all of them wanting to come sit in the stands as well. I don't know how they're all going to fit.

"The anticipation is a good thing, Willow. It's exciting, watching them play! This is what Westscott was talking about on the first day of school. Making the football team that much better brings a sense of school spirit that Lancaster Prep has never had before. It's so much fun." Iris circles her arm around mine, tugging me in close, our heads bent together. "I had a great time at the games last season, but I was always missing you."

I give her arm a squeeze and rest my head on her shoulder. A part of me likes to hear that I was missed and the other part always feels guilty for being gone. It's like I can't win. I do wish I was here last year and could've experienced what it was like, the campus changing. How exciting it must've been with the football team doing well and everyone getting caught up in it.

But I wasn't here. I don't regret going to Italy either. It was a great experience and I learned so much.

"I don't mean to make you feel bad," Iris admits, as if she can read my thoughts. She probably can, we spend so much time together. "I'm just really glad you're back and we get to experience our senior year together."

"Like that was ever not going to happen." I press my head to hers, making her smile. "You going to talk to Brooks after the game?"

She practically leaps away from me, glancing around like she's afraid someone overheard my question. "Do not bring up his name right now. Anyone could hear you."

"Oh, please." I shake my head. "You're being dramatic."

"I'm always dramatic. You should know this by now." She's smiling, but she's also serious. I can see it in her eyes. "And I already told you I won't talk to him. I don't want to get his hopes up."

"Pretty sure his hopes are completely dashed and burned into the ground after you treated him like this for so long," I point out. "Not that I'm trying to make you feel bad but—"

"No, I get it. You're right." She shrugs, staring off into the distance. "I'm not ready for a relationship."

I say nothing. She's admitted this to me countless times before and I never understand why she feels that way. Her parents are still madly in love after all these years and she comes from a loving, thoughtful household, just like me. Her dad can be a jerk sometimes, but it's mostly out of love for his children—he's way too overprotective.

Though from what my dad said earlier, I'm thinking he's been talking to Whit too much lately. Talk about an over-the-top reaction.

What if Rhett and I do become…a couple? I don't want to jinx myself and think it'll actually happen.

It'll probably never happen.

But what if it did? How would my father react? Would he

even like Rhett?

These are all concerns I can't even wrap my head around right now. There's no point in worrying about something that hasn't even happened yet.

"We should go grab something to eat," Iris declares, leaping to her feet. She wags her hand at me. "Come on. I want pizza."

"Isn't the game starting soon?" I ask, my voice weak. I'm not sure if I want to walk around right now. "And isn't the line probably crazy long?"

"We still have almost twenty minutes on the clock, and there are two snack bars open. We'll go to the one at the top of the stands. It's always got a shorter line and they're pretty fast."

"I want a hot dog," my dad says, reaching for his wallet.

"Grab me a bottle of water, would you, sweetie?" Mom asks me.

Guess I'm going to the snack bar.

I take Iris's hand, snatch the cash from Dad's fingers, and head up the stairs toward the snack bar at the top of the stands, just beneath the game announcers' box. I say hi to a few familiar faces as we walk past, and once we're in line, I breathe a sigh of relief.

I'm worried we'll run into Silas or Alana or the two of them together, and I really don't want to deal. They'll only make me more anxious and I'm dealing with enough.

"Your dad eats hot dogs?" Iris sounds surprised.

"He likes them." I shrug. "Not like he gets them much."

"True." Iris nods. "The pizza here is good. They bring it in from that one Italian restaurant in town."

"I don't think I've ever had their pizza before, though their food is always good."

"You'll love it. Get pepperoni though. The cheese slices are a little bland."

I'm about to answer when I see them. Silas and Alana. Together.

Ugh.

My stomach sinks and I turn to the side, hoping they don't see me. I don't want to get pulled back into their drama yet again.

"What's going on?" Iris asks. "You're getting all weird."

"Alana and Silas," I say out of the side of my mouth. "They're right over there."

"Together?" Iris glances around me, making a face when she spots them. "I guess that little fight was no big deal, huh?"

"Looked like a big deal to me." I scoot closer to Iris and keep my back to the line, and hopefully to Alana and Silas if they happen to pass by. Which they do.

Only to get in line directly behind us.

I share a look with Iris, unsure of how to go about this. Talk about awkward. But then Iris gets this determined look on her face and I know she's going to open her mouth and say something. I brace myself, waiting for the damage.

"Hey, Silas." Oh, Iris's voice is so *so* cold. "Alana."

"Hey, Iris." This comes from Alana, her voice just as cool. "Hi, Willow."

She greets me deliberately and extra loud and I barely look in their direction. "Hi."

We all four go silent and I pray the parents working the snack bar are as quick as Iris promised they would be. I heard the people who work the snack bars during games are parents. I wonder if my parents did that last year, and would they do it again next year? I can only imagine Dad plating pizza while Mom collects the money. It would probably be funny to watch them.

Iris nudges me and I send a glare in her direction, scowling when she has the nerve to look like she's about to burst out laughing. The tension among us is ridiculous. I just want them gone.

"If you want to leave, I've got this," Iris whispers in my ear. "I know they're torturing you."

Sending her a grateful look, I grab her hand and squeeze it. "Thank you. I do need to use the bathroom real quick."

I take off, not saying a word to Alana or Silas, desperate to get away from them. I only breathe easier when they're out of the vicinity and I slip into the bathroom to use it, relieved to find it's mostly empty. But when I'm in a stall, a bunch of giggling girls enter the restroom, talking so loudly I can't help but overhear their conversation.

"Did you see him? My God, he's *so* hot. You think he'll notice me?"

"Maybe if you flash him your tits, he'll notice you."

They all burst into laughter.

"I'm not wearing a bra. Hopefully that'll catch his eye."

Oh God. Who are they talking about?

"Like I said, lift your shirt and he'll definitely pay attention."

"I'm not about to get busted. I don't want Rhett's attention that badly."

More laughter accompanied by running water and shuffling feet. Someone must pull out a perfume bottle because the scent is so strong, it makes my nose twitch and I eventually sneeze.

The girls go quiet and they don't speak until I finally flush the toilet and emerge from the stall.

I don't recognize any of them. They all seem really young and their faces are covered with heavy makeup. The moment they notice me, they completely dismiss me, chatting amongst themselves once again as I go to the sink and wash my hands, contemplating if I should say something to them or not.

"You don't have to worry about trying to get Rhett Bennett's attention," I finally say, the words leaving me without thought.

One of the girls makes a huffing noise. "What do you know about Rhett?"

"I'm his girlfriend," I tell them with a blissful smile, tossing my paper towel in the trash before I exit the bathroom, the door slamming behind me just as I hear them erupt into loud conversation.

Oh my God, it felt good to say that. Even if it's not quite true. What does it matter? Who are they going to tell? They look like a bunch of freshmen anyway.

I make my way back toward the snack bar when I spot Iris

standing just ahead of me, her arms full of snacks and drinks, a cheesy grin on her face. I rush to her and take some of the load she's carrying.

"Want to hear what I just did?" I ask her as we start making our way back to the stands.

"Please tell me."

"I told a bunch of freshmen girls who were talking about flashing Rhett their boobs that he was my boyfriend."

Iris bursts out laughing, which makes me laugh too. "You did not."

"I did. And it felt good to say it too. Shut them right up."

"Look at you." Iris shakes her head.

"What do you mean?"

"I feel like you're making your way back."

"I would've never said that sort of thing before. I don't even know what possessed me." Which is the honest to God truth.

"Maybe you're manifesting it. Putting it out into the world could make it come true," Iris says.

In my dreams.

"Look, there's your boyfriend."

She inclines her head toward the field, and I see that our football team is out there in two lines, running through drills just like the opposing team did during the JV game. My gaze immediately finds Rhett, not that it's difficult for me. I've come to recognize the shape of his body. His height. The breadth of his shoulders.

Helps too that I remember his jersey number. One. Because of course it is.

"We should hurry," I tell Iris, and she laughs when I shoot past her and slide into our aisle. We settle in as the announcer begins to speak, my dad taking a greedy bite of his hot dog while Mom sips on her water. Iris and I split a slice of pizza since they're so huge and I eat my portion but slowly because my appetite has faded, replaced once again with nervousness.

By the time the team is out on the sideline and the national anthem is being sung by a student standing in the middle of the field, I'm giddy with excitement. And when Rhett glances up in the stands, his gaze locking with mine, he holds up his hand, pointing at me.

My heart stutters to a halt before it seems to trip over itself. I smile at him.

He smiles back.

Oh God.

CHAPTER THIRTY

RHETT

First drive of the game and barely two minutes in, I throw a beautiful spiral that Brooks catches, and he runs it straight into the end zone.

Touchdown. All for Will.

We lock eyes as I come off the field once we scored our extra point. I send her a nod of recognition, letting her know that was for her, and she smiles, seeming to bounce in her seat. She's adorable.

Once I secure this win, I'm going to do what I can to secure that one as mine.

The game goes by in a hurried blur of constant motion. By the top of the fourth quarter, we're up by seventeen points and about to score another touchdown. We run the ball into the end zone in the next play and I'm sure we'll win.

It's practically guaranteed.

Our team is playing together like a well-oiled machine. All those months of practice have paid off. The excitement is palpable, the crowd won't stop yelling their encouragement, and goddamn it feels good. The coaching staff allowed my dad on the sidelines because of who he is, and he's shouting at me every time I'm on the field. His words only fuel me though. Make me better.

Knowing Willow is up in the stands watching me is also fuel.

Her parents watching too? I want to impress them. I want to impress everyone.

I'm on a high and I don't wanna come down any time soon.

One of our tight ends catches the next ball while he's basically in the end zone, so it's an easy touchdown. We get the extra point and I'm ready to coast. This team we're playing isn't that good; they're incredibly sloppy. They make a lot of errors that costs them—yardage from penalties, bad throws that turn into interceptions. It's what allowed us to get ahead of them so quickly.

I have zero complaints.

By the time the game is over, I'm eager to go talk to Willow, but I gotta go through all the game day rituals first. A resounding speech from Coach out on the field with the entire team circled around him, followed by us going to stand in front of the crowd and shout our thank yous for their support. Finally, the crowd starts to disperse, most everyone leaving the stands save for family members, friends and girls.

Plenty of girls.

A group of giggling freshmen approach me and I take a quick photo with them, eager to get them on their way. Can't let Willow see me with them and think I'm just some player out to bag a girl for the night. There is no one else I'm interested in.

Just her.

Dad reappears with Cal and Mom, who I had no clue was even at the game. I give her a big hug, clutching her close to me, breathing in her familiar, comforting scent before I pull away slightly to stare at her face.

"I didn't know you were here."

"Your dad didn't mention it?" When Dad just offers her a helpless shrug as his answer, she shakes her head. "Well, here I am. I wouldn't miss this game for the world—we just had to fly in and see our boys play their first games of the season."

Even though Dad is busy with coaching his own football team, they still make the time to come to almost every single one of our games, unless his team is playing an away game. Mom will usually come alone when that happens, though on occasion she's gone with Dad to his away games as well. Like the one that was played in Germany last season.

Can't really blame them for missing our games.

"Hey," I call to Brooks when he's about to walk past me. "Take a pic of me and the fam?"

"Sure." Brooks takes my phone and we pose for him, all three of us guys towering over Mom while she stands in the middle of us, a big smile on her face.

"We're only missing Kenzie," Mom says, referring to our sister, who's away at college and living her best life partying all the time. At least that's what I see on her private stories and her second account on Insta. It's obvious she's keeping this from Mom and Dad, but I'm not about to rat her out. I'll probably be doing the same thing when I'm in college.

"Eli, did you bring the necklace with you?" Mom asks Dad.

He nods. "You want to do this now?"

"I'm sure he's going to hang out with his friends tonight. Right, Rhett?" Mom tilts her head up to look at me for confirmation.

"Yeah, probably." I have no idea what they're talking about.

"I remember what it was like. Your dad and I would hang out after games," Mom says fondly. "Going to parties."

"Sneaking around so we wouldn't get caught together," Dad adds with a sly smile on his face.

Mom shakes her head, ignoring him, her focus on me. "We have something for you."

"Cal!"

We all turn our heads and watch as a group of girls approaches my brother. They're all cute and staring at him like he's a celebrity. The grin on Callahan's face tells me he's eating this shit up.

I don't blame him.

"Go on," Dad tells him. "Talk to your fans."

Mom laughs. Cal's cheeks turn red, but he does as Dad says.

This kid is going to turn into a total player.

"What do you want to give me?" I'm clueless over what this is about. They're acting mysterious. Wanting to give me something out on the football field after a game? It seems kind of odd.

Dad approaches, reaching into his front pocket and pulling out a tiny velvet gift bag. "This is for you."

He hands the black bag to me and I take it, staring at it for a moment. "What is it?"

"Open it and find out," Mom encourages.

I undo the drawstring and reach inside, feeling a chain. Grabbing hold of it, I pull it out to find a gold necklace with a pendant hanging from it.

#1.

"My father gave me that and I eventually gave it to your mom," Dad explains. "Over the summer, your mom found it in her jewelry box and said she wanted to give it to you since you're number one now."

I stare at the pendant lying in my hand. The gold shines brightly against my palm, like it was just polished, and I curl my fingers around it, clutching it tightly. "I love it. Thank you."

"Maybe if you ever meet a girl who steals your heart, you can give it to her like your dad gave it to me," Mom says, her voice soft. She's always been a total romantic. "I wore that necklace proudly for years. Throughout your dad's football career."

I remember her wearing it. I've seen photos. At one point, I even wanted it, but eventually I forgot about it.

"This means a lot." I clear my throat, suddenly feeling a little choked up. "I wanna wear it now."

"I'll help you," Dad says because he's tall enough to do the clasp, and for Mom, I'd have to be on my knees for her to put it on me.

Within seconds the chain is secured around my neck, the pendant outside of my jersey for everyone to see. I reach for it, skimming my fingers over the number one when I spot her.

Willow. She's with her parents and Iris, surrounding Rowan while some random person takes their photos. As if she can feel me watching her, she turns her head to the right, our gazes locking, and she smiles at me.

I smile right back, my heart threatening to gallop straight out of my chest. This fucking girl.

"Who's that?" Mom asks, her voice low.

Guess she caught me staring.

Turning to face her, I admit, "The girl I want to see wearing this someday."

I tap the pendant and Mom smiles, her gaze filled with emotion. "She's pretty."

"She's a Lancaster."

Dad chuckles. "Always aiming high, aren't you, Rhett?"

"I want to meet her," Mom says.

"I don't know if that's a good idea."

"Why not?" Mom appears vaguely offended.

"I don't want her freaking out," I admit. "She's kind of jumpy."

"Oh, don't be silly. She'd probably love to meet us."

"Ava. Baby." The warning tone in Dad's voice is kind of funny. "Don't be too pushy."

"Am I ever pushy?" she asks, sounding put out.

"Yes," we both answer simultaneously.

"You're both ridiculous." Mom rolls her eyes. "Let's go meet her."

She's about to walk over to Willow and her family, but I grab hold of Mom's arm, stopping her. "It's still too new between us. Like, we're not even…anything yet."

Mom considers me, her lips pursed. She looks young tonight, wearing the Lancaster Prep football gear and her bright blonde hair in a ponytail. I can see why my dad fell head over heels for her. Why he's still so gone over her. It's not just because of her looks either. She has a big heart and she loves hard. Puts her family above all else and does her best to make us all happy.

"You'll be something," Mom finally says. "You have that same determined look on your face that your dad always wore when he was in hot pursuit of me."

"I was in hot pursuit?" Dad asks.

"Don't play it cool, Eli. You know you were completely obsessed with me," Mom tosses at him.

"Fair." Dad wraps Mom up in his arms, squeezing her close. "Your mom is right. I was obsessed. Still am."

"Please don't start making out here." I groan, wishing Cal was with me so our protests would shut them down quicker.

But they just laugh at me and Dad kisses Mom in front of God and everybody.

"Hey, Rhett."

I turn to find Rowan approaching us, his parents trailing behind him, along with Willow.

Oh shit. They came over here. That wasn't expected.

"Hey, Row. Good game today," I tell him, even though I already complimented him on his game play earlier.

"Same to you. You were awesome." Row smiles and I swear it's faintly devious. "Wanted to introduce you to my parents. My father was impressed."

From the smirk on Row's face, I get the feeling he did this knowing full well I'm into his sister. Meaning, I owe him one.

"I've been impressed. You've turned this program around, Rhett." Row and Willow's dad steps forward, thrusting his hand toward me. "Crew Lancaster."

"Nice to meet you, sir." I shake his hand and also his wife's when he introduces her to me.

"You look just like Will," I tell Wren Lancaster as I shake her hand, sounding like an idiot.

"Most people say she looks like me," she says, laughing. "You know Willow?"

"I do." My gaze shifts to Will, who's eating me up with her eyes. Making me stand a little taller. "We're—friends."

"I'm Rhett's mother. Ava," Mom says, stepping toward Willow. "It's nice to meet you."

Introductions are made all around, the parents chatting like they're old friends right out the gate. I stand back, happy to see everyone getting along, noting the way my mom glances over at me every few minutes, her expression pleased.

I think she likes Willow. Thank God.

"The kids are headed to the family estate for the weekend," Willow's mom announces, her gaze going to me. "You and your brother should join them. I know Cal was just there. We loved having him."

"I'm all for it," I say without hesitation. "You don't mind having us?"

"The house is huge. We don't know who's there half the time, and anyway, it's not our house." Willow's dad chuckles. "It's my cousin's. But they invite guests all the time. They don't mind a few extra showing up."

"Do we have to run it by the headmaster?" Dad asks.

Oh shit. Westscott has been riding my ass hard all week and I don't need him messing up my opportunity. He better let us go.

"I'll talk to Westscott," Crew Lancaster says. "He'll okay it."

He says this with such authority, my entire body relaxes. And when I glance over at Will, she's already watching me, trying to hide a smile.

Looks like it's going to be an interesting weekend.

CHAPTER THIRTY-ONE

WILLOW

"Please, I'm begging you. Whatever you end up doing with Rhett, don't do it in here," Iris says as we enter her bedroom and she turns on the lamp on her dresser.

I head straight for my bed, flopping on top of the mattress so hard, I swear I bounce. "Like I would. We haven't even kissed yet."

"That's coming, you know. And once that happens, forget it." Iris mimics me, draping her body across her bed.

Rolling over on my side to face her, I prop my elbow on the bed and rest my head on my fist. "What do you mean by that?"

"I mean when you guys finally kiss, and it's so good your toes curl and you're scared you might come on the spot just from his freaking lips, watch out. It's all you're going to want to do. And you won't want to stop. He'll touch your boobs and you'll let him. He'll slip his fingers under your clothes and you won't deny him. He'll push his fingers inside your panties and you'll beg for more." Iris sounds like she's speaking from experience while I'm over here blushing just from her words.

"I don't know…that sounds awfully fast." The idea of any of that used to scare me, but now?

I can't help but find it exciting because it's with Rhett.

"You won't even care. He'll take your virginity and you won't even realize it's happening until he pushes inside of you."

"Iris!" I sit up, staring at her. "What are you trying to tell me?"

A sigh leaves her as she sits up too, tossing her head back to stare up at the intricate crown molding on the ceiling, her hands braced on the mattress. "I suppose I'm saying I'm not a virgin anymore."

"When did this happen?" My brain scrambles to come up with the scenario, but I don't know. I've been holed up in my room nightly this past week. Either doing homework or studying or staring at the wall thinking about Rhett.

"A few nights ago, in my room."

"In your room? You snuck Brooks into your room?" How did I miss this?

"How do you know I lost it to Brooks?"

I gape at her, unable to speak. She leaves me hanging for seconds that feel like hours until she finally bursts out laughing, grabbing a pillow and rolling around on top of her bed like an evil little gremlin.

"You're the worst," I mutter, shaking my head.

"You know who's not?" She doesn't give me enough time to answer. "Brooks. That boy is too good. He knows exactly what he's doing."

"Are you finally going to put him out of his misery and make your relationship public?" I ask, already knowing what her answer is.

"It's not a relationship, so there's nothing to make public. I'm still leaning heavily into the illicit affair label."

"Iris…"

"What?" She sits up again, pushing her hair out of her face. "You can't judge me, Willow, because you don't know what it's like. You're in the early stages with Rhett while I'm over here thinking about how I can get Brooks back into my bed."

I remain quiet, mulling over what she's saying. Knowing she doesn't want my opinion. She just wants to get her feelings out.

"How does he feel about it?" I finally ask.

"He's getting free pussy and blow jobs. How do you think he feels?"

Her casual words shock me, how she describes what's happening between her and Brooks, when maybe it's more than that to him. Or even her. She has to like him somewhat. Otherwise, she wouldn't let this happen. So why is she keeping him at arm's length? Why won't she acknowledge him and their relationship?

It's wild to me.

But I'm also the one who thought about sneaking around with Rhett because I can't acknowledge our relationship, thanks to Westscott. I'm grateful that Rhett is here right now at my family's estate with his brother. No one is around—specifically the headmaster. No one will see us together.

"Iris." I rise from my bed and go to hers, settling in right beside her and wrapping my arm around her shoulders. "I want you to think about this over the weekend. About what you're doing with Brooks and how it might affect him. He probably thinks you're playing games and just using him."

With a sigh, Iris rests her head on my shoulder, quiet for a moment as I snuggle her closer. "What if he's just using me?"

It's almost a relief, getting this glimmer of vulnerability from her. Something she rarely allows anyone to see. "I don't think so. He's going along with your wishes every step of the way."

"Maybe those are his wishes too. Maybe he doesn't want anyone to know we're together." She turns into me, hooking her hand around the back of my neck, her arm draped across my chest. "I don't know what to do."

"Do you like him?"

"I think so." Her voice is muffled against my chest.

"You should give him a chance then."

"You make it sound so easy."

"You're right. It's not. But you'll never know if you don't give him a chance."

"Maybe..." Her voice drifts, and she lifts away from me, her eyes actually shining with unshed tears. "What about you and Rhett? Are you willing to give him a chance?"

"Yes," I say without thinking. Without any hesitation either. "I've wasted enough time."

Iris actually starts laughing. "It's only been a few weeks since school started."

"It feels like it's been years." And it does. The time has both flown and dragged, and I don't know how that's possible.

"You should go meet him. Right now."

My mouth goes dry. "What? No. I couldn't."

"Why not?" Iris leaps from the bed and goes to the window, pushing the curtains back to stare outside. "There's a full moon."

"So?"

"That's so romantic." She turns to face me. "Text him and ask if he'll meet you out on the back terrace right now. I'm sure he will."

"What if he's asleep already?"

"Come on. Even if he's in bed, I'm sure he'd rather see you than sleep." She waves a hand at me. "Go on. Text him."

"I don't have his number," I admit.

"Oh my God." Iris stomps over to where she left her phone and grabs it, tapping away at the screen. Within minutes, she's rattling off Rhett's phone number to me while I hurriedly add it to my contacts, nerves making my skin buzz. "There. Text him."

"Who did you ask for his number?"

"Your brother." Iris's smile is smug.

"You didn't tell him I was the one who wanted it, did you?"

"If you think Row isn't aware of what's going on between you and Rhett, then you're blind." Iris tosses her phone on the bed. "But no. I didn't tell him. You have nothing to worry about."

I open up a new text thread with Rhett's number and stare at the screen, unsure. What do I say to him? Will he even realize it's me? I suppose I should lead with that.

Me: **Hey, it's Willow.**

I send just that text first to test the conversation out. He responds almost immediately.

Rhett: **How'd you get my number?**

My cheeks are hot from embarrassment. Thank God he's not here to witness it.

Me: **Row gave it to Iris.**

Rhett: **Sneaky.**

Rhett: **Are you with her right now?**

Me: **Yes.**

Rhett: **Want to meet up? It's still early.**

It's almost eleven o'clock and normally I'd be tired. I'm not though. Even if I tried to go to bed, I'd be too excited to sleep.

Me: **Okay. Where do you want to meet?**

Rhett: **You tell me. This is your family's house.**

He has no idea where to go. A person could easily get lost in this giant house. I get lost in it somctimes and I've been coming here since I can remember.

Me: **Meet me at the base of the stairs in fifteen minutes.**

Rhett: **Fifteen minutes? Why so long?**

Me: **I need to get ready.**

Rhett: **You don't need to do anything. You're beautiful. Meet me right now.**

I smile at his impatience.

Me: **I want to change my outfit.**

Rhett: **Don't bother getting fancy for me, Will. This house is intimidating enough. I don't need you trying to impress me.**

Me: **But I want to wear something more comfortable.**

Rhett: **Don't let me stop you then. Meet in five?**

Me: **Ten.**

Rhett: **Seven?**

He's making me giggle.

Me: **Ten.**

Rhett: **See you soon, princess.**

CHAPTER THIRTY-TWO

RHETT

I don't even last five minutes. I eventually leave my room—I somehow scored my own while Cal has to share with Rowan—and creep down the hallway, feeling like a spy. A thief. It's dark, and the cavernous house is mostly quiet. There are actual wings in this place and we're in our own, no adult supervision to be found.

That's real fuckin' dangerous if you ask me. These parents must trust their children implicitly.

I stop at the top of the staircase and check out the massive portrait hanging on the wall. There's a small brass plaque at the base of the frame that says Augustus Lancaster on it, and I think it's funny, how his name is on there like we're in a museum versus their family home.

This is the dude who started it all. The original Lancaster who came to the States and made his fortune. He looks like a giant asshole.

I bet he was one too.

Turning away from the painting, I head down the carpet-covered marble stairs, keeping my steps light though they still echo as I walk. Once I'm on the ground floor I walk around the stairs, finding a nook tucked beneath them with a chair and everything, and I settle in, checking my phone.

I have a text from Brooks.

Brooks: **Where the hell are you? I wanted to party tonight and you're gone.**

Me: **I'm at the Lancaster estate with your girlfriend.**

He told me in strictest confidence last night that he and Iris finally did it. I can tell he's totally into her, though he's trying to play it off, which I get. Iris is hard to figure out and she runs so hot and cold. It's driving him nuts.

Brooks: **That is some bullshit. Why am I not there?**

Me: **Come on out. I'm sure Rowan can arrange it.**

Brooks: **I can't just show up there uninvited. Iris will kill me.**

She probably would.

Me: **Blame it on Row. I'll talk to him for you if you'd like.**

Brooks: **I couldn't.**

I wait him out, not responding. He's going to change his own mind in three, two, one…

Brooks: **Talk to Row for me.**

Knew it.

Me: **I will.**

Brooks: **Should I text him? Or will I look too eager? You think he knows I'm fucking his cousin? God, if her big brother ever found out, I would be dead. He'd bury my body so well no one would ever find me again.**

He is completely overreacting. I'm sure Iris's brother could give two shits over who she's fucking.

Me: **Like I said, I'll take care of it. Be prepared to leave early tomorrow morning.**

Brooks: **Will do. Keep me posted?**

Me: **You know it.**

I open another text thread and send a message to Rowan.

Me: **Do you care if Brooks comes out here tomorrow?**

He responds quickly.

Row: **Not at all. Love that guy. I've known him forever.**

Me: **Okay cool. He can stay in my room if it's a problem.**

Row: **Nah, there are so many bedrooms in this place, we'll find him one. Tell him he can drive out tonight if he wants to.**

If I do that, Brooks will drive straight over here immediately. I don't know if I want to deal with him tonight.

Me: **I just texted him. He'll head out first thing tomorrow.**

Row: **Perfect.**

I wait a few minutes before I send a text to Brooks.

Me: **Drive out here tomorrow morning. They'll be expecting you.**

Brooks: **Thanks, man. Will do. Hopefully Iris won't be pissed.**

Me: **I doubt she will. At least then all of us can pair up.**

Brooks: **Meaning you and Willow?**

Me: **Definitely.**

Brooks: **Niiiice.**

I jerk my head up when I hear hurried footsteps coming down the stairs, light enough that I could almost believe they weren't there at all. Slowly, I rise from the chair, pocketing my phone as I carefully slip out of the nook.

It's Willow dressed in all black, her hair flowing down her back and not in its usual ponytail. She pauses on the second to last step, scanning the area, her head slowly moving.

My chest aches at seeing her. This feels like a moment that I've been waiting for forever is finally coming true and I'm suddenly nervous as fuck.

I don't want to blow this—my chance with Willow.

She finally takes those last two steps and rounds the stairwell, her soft voice reaching me.

"Rhett?"

I appear out of the shadows, startling her, but she doesn't make a sound. Her eyes go wide when she spots me, and she reaches for my hand, quietly leading me toward the back of the house. Until we're outside on a massive patio with statues and giant planters full of flowers.

"This house is unbelievable," I murmur as I look around.

"Come on, we'll go downstairs where the gardens are." Willow tugs on my hand and I follow her down the stairs. I can smell the lush fragrance of roses before I even see them, mixing with the nostalgic scent of fresh cut grass.

That smell always makes me think of a football field. When I was younger, there was no better scent in the world.

"Where exactly are you taking me?" I ask Willow when I realize we're still on the move.

"Iris's mom had a maze put into the gardens last spring. I like to get lost in it," Willow explains.

We do exactly that—get lost in the maze. The shrubbery walls tower over us and they're narrow, making me feel boxed in. We come across the occasional bench or statue as we make our way through it, and at one point, I tug on Willow's hand, pressing her against the vegetation wall with my body.

"What are you doing?" She's breathless, her chest rising and falling with each breath, brushing against my own.

"I was about to ask you the same thing." I lean in close, my mouth at her neck as I breathe her in.

Willow's scent is far better than any fresh cut grass.

She rests her hands against my chest, her fingers curling into the fabric of my sweatshirt. "I don't know. Having fun?"

"Torturing me." I pull away from her neck to stare into her eyes, my gaze dropping to her lips. Lingering there. I dip my head, about to kiss her, but she presses her hand against my mouth, stopping me.

"Not yet," she murmurs. "Let's wait until we find the center of the maze."

Somehow, she wiggles out of my hold and takes off. With a groan, I follow after her, dragging my feet, tired of running around in a circle. When we finally do discover the center, she rushes over to a bench that sits right in front of a massive lit fountain, the water gurgling as it cascades down.

"Join me." She pats the empty spot next to her on the bench and I settle right in, stretching my arm across the back of the bench, my fingers brushing her shoulder. "See? Isn't it beautiful? It's worth finding the center."

"How do we get out of here?"

"I'm not sure." She shrugs, seeming at complete ease. "We'll figure it out."

I slowly shake my head as I lift my hand, my fingers tangling in her silky hair. "I like that you wore your hair down."

"I rarely do it."

"I like it. It's pretty."

Her smile is serene. "I like that you're not afraid to give compliments."

"Don't encourage me. I'll start complimenting you so much, you'll beg me to stop," I warn her.

She laughs. "I like how funny you are too."

"You think I'm funny?"

Willow nods, leaning closer to me. "Very."

"Are you drunk?"

"What? No!" She starts to rear back, but I drop my arm to her shoulders, keeping her in place. "I'm just…happy."

"Why are you happy?" I want to hear her say that I'm the reason for her happiness.

"I'm glad you're here." Her hand lands on my thigh, her touch light. As if she's testing me out. "Can I admit something to you?"

"Please."

"I don't like playing games." Willow blinks at me, the moon touching her skin, casting her in a silvery glow. She's beautiful. Sweet and open and fuck, she's going to be all mine by the time this weekend is over. I guarantee it.

"The only game I like to play is football," I say truthfully.

Her smile is faint. "I'm talking about with—relationships. Not that I'm expecting one from you. Not this soon, but just know that I'm tired of pretending that I feel indifferent when it comes to you."

"You don't feel indifferent about me?" I'm smiling.

She slowly shakes her head, her hair spilling all over her

shoulders. I'm tempted to bury my face in it, but I restrain myself. "I like you, Rhett."

Those four words hang between us in the moonlit night, softly spoken and touching the depths of my heart. Sounds corny as shit and I don't normally think like this, but what's happening between Will and me isn't normal.

It feels…life-changing. Earth shaking.

"I like you too, Will." I touch her face, letting my fingers drift across her cheek until I'm touching the corner of her mouth. She parts her lips and I slip my index finger between them, tracing their plump softness, and when I feel her tongue lick my fingertip, I groan.

Cupping her face, I tilt her head back and stare into her eyes. "When I kiss you, this changes everything."

Willow nods, not deterred by my statement at all. "Okay."

"If that Silas creep comes around you again, I'm breaking his legs," I say vehemently.

"I don't want him to come around me," she murmurs. "But I don't want you getting in trouble either."

My smile is slow. Some would probably call it lethal. "He won't be a problem anymore, baby. I promise."

Her frown is slight. "Did you just call me baby?"

"Did I?" I didn't even realize it. "You don't like that?"

"I love it," she whispers, and I swear I can feel her skin grow warm beneath my palms. "I like it when you call me Will too."

"I've been calling you princess in my thoughts lately."

"You think about me?" She sounds surprised.

"Will." I lean in, my forehead touching hers. "I think about you all the fucking time."

She tilts her head back a little, aligning our mouths, and I can feel her breath waft across my lips. Can sense the faint tremble that runs through her. "I think about you too. All the time. It's like I can't stop."

CHAPTER THIRTY-THREE

WILLOW

Something came over me as I hurriedly prepared to meet with Rhett. All of the game playing and pretending that feelings aren't actually there is exhausting. Look at poor Iris. She's trying to play it cool in regards to Brooks—her mode of operation pretty much her entire life—and she's miserable. Unsure. I don't want that. I've dealt with enough uncertainty and misery when it comes to a particular boy—Silas. I vow that I never want to experience that again.

To give myself so freely, so openly to a boy without knowing how he feels about me in return? Sounds like absolute torture.

I couldn't stand the thought of doing it again with Rhett. There is no need for me to play games with him. I like him. He's pretty much admitted that he likes me too. What's the harm in that?

Nothing.

This is why I'm being totally honest with him. Expressing my true feelings about him. I want Rhett to want me as badly as I want him. And I want him so much, my body aches with the need to be pressed against his. I want to absorb his warmth and strength. I want to feel his arms come around me and hold me tight. I want to kiss him until my mouth aches and my jaw is tired and then when it's over, I want to do it all over again.

If Iris heard what I just said to him, she'd probably tell me I'm making a huge mistake. But I don't think so. I think me confessing that I can't stop thinking about him is just what Rhett wants to hear. Needs to hear.

"You haunt my every thought day and night." He turns his head slightly, his mouth connecting with my cheek, and I suck in a harsh breath, tingles sweeping over me at the touch of his lips on my skin. They're soft, and when he speaks, they tickle me. "I think about the two of us alone and I'm doing all kinds of things to you."

Self-conscious Willow would be too afraid to ask what sorts of things but…

"What do you want to do to me?" I slide my hands over his shoulders and around the back of his neck. Up into his hair, which is soft and silky and clings to my fingers. I remember touching his face last Friday night, how he invited me to do whatever I wanted.

"If I told you, you'd probably slap me." His mouth hovers above mine. "All of my thoughts about you are dirty, princess."

I like how he calls me that. "Tell me."

He doesn't tell me. He kisses me instead. His mouth settles on mine, that first electrifying touch sending a sizzle of awareness straight through me, settling between my thighs. I lean into him, my lips parting beneath his, his tongue sweeping in. Searching my mouth, twisting around mine.

The kiss turns heated in an instant. His mouth is greedy. Insistent. I respond to every stroke of his tongue, every groan that sounds deep in his chest when I scoot closer. When I touch him somewhere new. I don't worry about what he might think or if I'm being too forward, or too much. I touch him where I want, slipping my fingers beneath his sweatshirt to touch the bare skin of his stomach. He's hot and firm, and he groans when I curl my fingers around the waistband of his joggers, his hand immediately settling over mine. Halting my progress.

"You want me to stop?" I whisper into his mouth, grabbing his lower lip between both of mine and giving it a tug.

"I want you to slow down." His hand is gentle as it rests over mine, his teeth nipping at my lower lip in response to what I just did to him only a moment ago. "We're not getting naked out here, Will."

My entire body lights up at hearing him use the word naked. "Why not?"

"Anyone could find us."

"No, they won't. We're lost." And that sounds perfectly logical to me.

Rhett chuckles. "This is the first time we've kissed. I'm not taking it much farther than that."

I pull away from him, disappointed. As if he can sense it, he gathers me back into his arms, holding me close, his mouth resting against my forehead.

"You need to learn patience," he says, his deep voice making my skin break out in goosebumps all over. "It'll all be worth the wait."

"I don't want to be patient," I admit, my hands sneaking under his sweatshirt once more. I skim my fingers over his flat, muscular stomach, marveling at how hard he is. Not an ounce of fat anywhere to be found. "Take me back to your room."

"Will." He groans my name, his forehead pressed against mine once again. "You're killing me."

"You know you want to." I take his hand and rest it on the side of my breast, shocking myself.

Shocking him too. I can feel it in the way he goes still, his fingers barely touching me, hovering there. I can sense it as he waits, like he's afraid I'm trying to trick him and am about to push him away.

"I want you," I tell him solemnly, staring into his eyes.

Within seconds, he's on his feet, his hand clasped around mine as he jerks me off the bench. We take off running, moving through the maze, coming to the occasional dead end that makes me giggle while he moans with frustration.

"Get us out of here." He growls at one point, which only makes me laugh harder.

I'm channeling my inner Iris in this moment. Free and reckless and not caring about anyone else but myself. Well, and Rhett of course.

We eventually emerge from the maze and I see the moon has shifted lower in the sky. Its light is so bright I can make out almost everything. Including the look on Rhett's face as he stares at the towering house, his brows drawn together.

Does my family's wealth intimidate him? He comes from money too, and fame. His parents were nice. Looking at his dad was like seeing Rhett in the future. He talks like him too. They have similar mannerisms. And his mother is beautiful. You can tell she loves both of her sons by the way she looks at them. How she says their names.

"If we get caught…" Rhett's voice drifts and he turns to look at me. "Are you going to get in trouble?"

"My parents aren't here." I head for the steps that lead to the terrace, Rhett right behind me. "They'll never find out."

"What about Iris's parents?"

"They're asleep." I glance toward one of the windows that I know is their bedroom and come to a stop when I see the golden light shining from within. "Maybe."

Rhett looms behind me, his hand landing on my waist in a wholly possessive gesture. "We'll have to be quiet when we go back inside."

"I can do that."

"I don't remember where my room is." I glance over at him, noting his sheepish expression. "This house is too damn big."

"I know where it's at." Not too far from the room Rowan uses when he visits. Just down the corridor from Iris's bedroom.

We creep back into the house, our footsteps light, our movements cautious. We practically run up the stairs. They're sturdy and don't creak at all since they were reinforced after the unfortunate accident that caused the death of Sylvia Lancaster.

I only relax when we're in the bedroom corridor, waving at Rowan's bedroom door as we pass by it. "Does any of this look familiar to you?"

"I'm down here. I left my door partially open on purpose."

He finds the room quickly, pulling me inside and closing the door behind us, pressing me against it with his big body. I rest my hands on his chest, everything inside me going tight when I hear him turn the lock on the door.

"Will Iris wonder where you're at?" he asks.

"She already knows," I admit.

His smile is faint. "Can I tell you something in confidence?"

"Of course."

"You can't tell Iris."

An inner war starts inside me. I'm loyal to Iris above anyone else, but now there's Rhett asking for my confidence and I want to give it to him. I want him to trust me. "I won't tell her."

"Brooks will be here tomorrow morning." Rhett leans in, his mouth at my temple. "I know those two are hot for each other."

"They did it," I whisper. "A couple of nights ago."

"Oh yeah?"

"Yes, it's true. He's her first." I snap my lips shut, worried I said too much.

"Will she be mad if he shows up?"

"I'm not sure."

"No one can predict anything when it comes to Iris."

I nod, glad that he gets it. "She's hard to pin down."

"I've realized that." He brushes his mouth against mine, and I can't help but sigh when he pulls away. "We're in dangerous territory, Will."

"What do you mean?" I'm frowning, confused by what he's referring to.

"All alone in this bedroom. No adult supervision. Nothing but long, quiet hours stretching out ahead of us." He's smiling, his expression downright devilish. "We'll probably get up to no good."

"You promise?" That's exactly what I want.

"I can definitely make that promise." He cups my chin, tilting my head back, his mouth on mine once more, and I lose myself in his kiss. The taste of his lips. The delicate yet incessant strokes of his tongue. I can't get enough. I never want him to stop kissing me and it goes on for what feels like hours.

It's both too much and not enough, and when we finally break apart to catch our breath, I say the first thing that comes to my mind. "We'll have to keep this a secret."

I feel his muscles stiffen beneath my hands and he slowly pulls away to study me. "Keep what a secret?"

His voice is careful, but I hear the unease there. My heart trips over itself and my brain scrambles to come up with a reason. I can't tell him the truth.

Can I?

"Don't you think it would be fun?" I try to lighten the mood. I think of Iris and her secret affair and how fun she claims it is to sneak around. "Besides, I have a reputation to uphold."

He completely pulls away from me and I instantly miss his touch, his warmth. "What the hell is that supposed to mean? You don't want to be seen with me? You don't want people to know?"

Anxiety makes my thoughts turn into a jumble of nonsense. I'm handling this all wrong. "I just—everyone knows who Willow Lancaster is. And that she's a good girl—that's my reputation. The teachers, the staff, pretty much every student on that campus—that's how they think of me."

"And what? I'm a bad boy who'll dirty up your pristine reputation? Are you saying I'm *beneath* you?" Oh, he sounds angry.

"No! Not at all." I rush toward him, but he deviates to the side at the last second, escaping my touch. I watch as he makes his way to the other side of the room, propping his shoulder against the wall and curling his arms in front of him. His defenses are totally up. "It's just…"

"Use your words, princess. Go ahead and tell me that you don't want to be seen with me. I'm pretty sure I understand where you're coming from with this." His voice is snarky, with a heavy dose of disgust added in.

My shoulders sag and I close my eyes for a moment, trying to collect my thoughts. To tell him the truth could cause me nothing but trouble and I'm not sure if I want to risk it.

Telling him the truth could also make everything better between us too. I don't know what to do. It almost feels like it's too late. I already screwed everything up.

"You should probably go back to your room," he murmurs, his voice cold as ice.

"You misunderstood me, Rhett, I swear I—"

"Go to your room, Willow." His voice is firm, his face like a mask. "We'll talk in the morning."

I stare at him, the truth on the tip of my tongue, but in the end, all I can do is swallow the words down, offer him a tiny smile before I turn on my heel and leave his room.

The slam of his bedroom door makes me jump, and I scurry to Iris's room, closing and locking the door. Tears are already falling down my face as I make my way to my bed, collapsing on top of it and burying my face in the pillow. I sob and sob, trying to be quiet, but it's no use. I can't contain my tears.

Just like I can't contain my emotions.

Eventually I feel tentative fingers touch my back and I turn on my side to see Iris sitting on the edge of my bed. Her hair is mussed and her eyes glow with concern. She doesn't say a word but seeing her there, knowing she wants to comfort me, makes me cry even harder.

She pulls me into her arms and holds me close while I sob into her shoulder, soaking her T-shirt with my tears. She still doesn't say anything and I remain quiet as well, getting it all out of my system.

I appreciate her silent comfort more than she'll ever know.

CHAPTER THIRTY-FOUR

WILLOW

I wake up to bright sunshine filling the bedroom. The heavy silk white and pink toile curtains are pulled back, letting an abundance of light in, and I swear I even hear birds chirping. Like I'm waking up in a Disney movie full of talking animals and fairy tales.

"You're awake," Iris says when I sit up and shove my hair out of my face. I slept in the same clothes I wore last night, and I feel all grimy and gross. "How did you sleep?"

"Okay, I guess." I glance down at myself, pulling my crewneck sweatshirt away from my chest. "I tossed and turned a lot."

"I'm sorry." Iris smiles at me, but I can't manage to muster one up in return. "Do you want to talk about what happened?"

"I think Rhett hates me," I tell her, pressing my lips together when I feel a sob try to form in my throat. Nope, I refuse to cry over this again. I'm being silly.

"Why would you think that?" She sounds genuinely confused.

I explain everything that happened last night, leaving out a few not so important details to the story. Like how good of a kisser Rhett is. And how I basically threw myself at him.

"And then I said I wanted to keep what we're doing a secret." I bite my lower lip, not about to tell her why I said that. The moment

I tell her about Westscott's threats, she'll blab to everyone—the first person being her dad, who will make it his life's mission to get Westscott fired, which is pointless. God knows what Westscott would tell him about me. I'm sure he'd make up lies and maybe even try to spread rumors about me. I don't know how vindictive this man is.

I can't risk it.

"He was offended by my suggestion and accused me of wanting to hide our relationship like I was ashamed of him. And then when I said I had a reputation to uphold, he became even angrier and kicked me out of his room." A single tear streaks down my face. "See? He hates me."

"You said you had a reputation to uphold?" Iris winces. "Oh, Willow."

"I didn't mean it like that! I don't know what I meant." I throw my arms up in the air, frustrated with the entire situation and myself in particular. I've only made everything worse.

"You're going to have to apologize to him." Iris's expression is somber, and I know she's right. Iris is not big on apologies. She never wants to admit when she's wrong. And she tries to get me to act the same way when I'm the one who's ready to say sorry, even if it's not really my fault.

"I know." I blow out a harsh breath. "I want to. I just...I hope I didn't ruin everything."

"What did you mean by the reputation thing? That's probably what hurt him the most," Iris points out.

"Everyone has all of these expectations for me. They all want me to act and look a certain way. I'm not supposed to cause any issues and I'm always expected to be a—good girl. And I sort of said that to him but without enough context, so he immediately assumed I was saying he isn't good enough to be seen with me."

"Sounds like you'll really need to explain yourself."

"Yeah." I know it's bad when Iris isn't telling me I'll be okay. She's the biggest hype girl around.

"It'll be fine." The false smile on Iris's face tells me everything I need to know. She has zero faith I'll be able to work this out with Rhett. "You just need to get your feelings across to him the best that you can so he'll understand. Hopefully."

"Yes. Exactly." I climb out of bed and go to the window, staring out at the front drive. There's an unfamiliar car idling in the driveway. Sleek and sporty and gleaming black. I watch as Brooks climbs out of the driver's seat and goes to the trunk, extracting a large, black duffel bag out of it.

That's right—Rhett told me Brooks was showing up today. I didn't think he'd be here this early.

"You'll never believe who just arrived," I murmur, eager for the subject change.

"Who?" Iris sounds bored, and she doesn't budge from her bed.

"Come and see."

"Seriously, Willow? Is it that big of a deal?"

"Oh yeah." I keep my back to her, my heart leaping to my throat when I see Rhett emerge from the front door, his brother and mine flanking either side of him. They all go to Brooks and greet him enthusiastically. "You better hurry before he disappears."

I hear much grumbling and cursing as Iris drags herself out of bed and shuffles over to the window. "This better be good."

I hold back the curtain and step away from the window to give her a better view, but otherwise don't say a thing. She shifts closer to the window, her eyebrows drawing together. Her mouth hanging open.

"What the hell?"

"It's Brooks."

"I can see that," she says sarcastically, bracing one hand on the window as she continues to watch them. "What is he doing here?"

"Looks like the guys invited him." I'm not about to tell her that I knew he was coming. She'd probably be furious that I didn't give her a heads up.

Besides, with all my drama and weepiness, I sort of forgot.

"God, he's probably here for the entire weekend. How am I going to avoid him?" She turns to face me.

"Why would you want to avoid him?"

"This is my home. My sanctuary. I'm sure your brother is behind this." Iris marches across her bedroom and goes to her massive armoire, ripping open the doors and scanning the mess of clothing on the shelves. It looks like a bomb went off in there. I see a pile of designer bags stacked on top of each other on the top shelf and wince. My mother would die if she saw that. "I need to wear something spectacular."

I glance down at my sweaty clothes from last night with a frown. "I need to take a shower."

"Hurry and take one then. We need to go down there together as a united front." The determination in Iris's voice is just the fuel I need to get motivated.

She's right. We need to be a united front. And I need to look my best when I apologize to Rhett.

I can only hope he'll accept what I have to say and forgive me.

• • •

Forty minutes later, Iris and I are downstairs, headed for the dining room. The scent of cooked bacon lingers in the air and my stomach growls, despite feeling nauseous.

Iris is wearing a cream knit tank dress that fits her like a glove. She's wearing nothing underneath it because she didn't want lines showing—direct quote. Her hair is in a messy bun and she's got giant gold hoops hanging from her ears. Not a lick of makeup is on her face save for a shiny lip gloss coating her mouth, and she's never looked better.

Brooks is going to swallow his tongue when he sees her.

I'm also wearing a dress. Black and flowy that nips in at the waist and has tiny buttons on the bodice. I left a few undone and somehow, Iris convinced me not to wear a bra, which I regret. My boobs are huge and when they're uncontained, it feels like they're constantly in the way.

But she told me I didn't have a choice. Why I listen to her, I don't know.

"Rhett will realize you're not wearing a bra and he'll get stuck on your tits. You could tell him you're sorry you made him mad, but you're going to have to kill him, and he'd agree because he'd be too caught up in trying to figure out the exact color of your nipples," she said right before we left her bedroom.

That sounded like a far-fetched explanation, but there's not a lot of fight in me, so I decided to go along with it.

We enter the dining room to find all of them already at the table: Rowan, Callahan, Brooks and Rhett. Along with Vaughn and Beau, our little brothers, who are sitting with the older boys, stars in their eyes as they listen to them speak.

My heart aches a little when I see Rhett sitting there, his head carefully averted so he doesn't notice me. Is he doing that on purpose? Is he that disgusted with me that he can't even look at me?

I follow Iris to the sideboard where breakfast awaits, grabbing a warmed plate and serving myself scrambled eggs, two pieces of bacon and a bunch of strawberries. Marta bustles in just as we're about to sit, smiling warmly at both of us.

"Iced vanilla lattes for the two of you, hmm?" She's already got them in her hands, setting them on the table once we sit.

"You're a vanilla latte drinker now?" I ask Iris, my voice low.

She shrugs one shoulder. "I put in my order with her when you were taking a shower. I'm trying to lower my sugar intake."

I send an amused glance in the housekeeper's direction.

"Thank you, Marta," I say, grateful for her attentiveness.

"You're a doll, Marta." Iris practically shouts this as she grabs her glass and sips noisily from the straw, catching the attention from all the boys at the table. She studies them, her lips still wrapped around the straw, her eyes wide before she lets it go to speak. "Oh, am I disturbing you?"

Rhett says nothing. Cal and Row send each other secretive looks while Brooks blatantly stares at Iris.

"Nice…dress," he says, his gaze lingering on her chest.

Iris doesn't miss a beat, thrusting her chest out, her tiny nipples poking against the fabric. "Knew you'd love it, Brooksie."

The younger boys snicker, going silent when Brooks sends them a menacing look.

Rhett finally chooses this moment to glance down the table, his gaze sweeping over me in an almost dismissive manner. My appetite disappears when he resumes eating, shoving a piece of bacon into his mouth, smiling at something Row said to him.

"Men," Iris says out of the side of her mouth.

"They're annoying," I add, nibbling on a piece of bacon. I need to eat something or I'm going to feel terrible for the rest of the day.

"Children!" Iris's mother bursts into the dining room, a big smile on her face. "It's so good to see you all congregated in here."

"Hi, Mom," Iris says while Vaughn waves at Summer.

"We have new people here this morning." Summer's gaze lands on the boys. "Brooks Crosby. I haven't seen you in a while."

"Hi, Mrs. Lancaster." His cheeks are pink and he ducks his head, obviously feeling awkward. Iris snorts, but no one acknowledges it.

"And, Callahan…I remember you were here a few weeks ago. Nice to see you again." Summer smiles at Cal.

"Thank you for having us. This is my brother, Rhett." Cal points at him.

"Wait, you're the quarterback." Summer tilts her head to the side. "The one who's transforming the athletics department at Lancaster Prep."

"I don't know if I'm transforming the entire program…" Rhett starts, but Summer cuts him off.

"I've heard plenty about you and how the football team has helped student enrollment," she says. "We'll have to make sure and attend a game soon."

"I'd appreciate having you in the stands," Rhett says, ever so diplomatic.

Iris kicks me under the table and I glare at her, unsure how she wants me to react.

"The reason I actually came in here was to warn you all that there's a party being held at the house this afternoon for Paris and Pru," Summer explains. "Their birthday is Tuesday but their parents wanted them to have an early celebration this weekend. They're turning thirteen."

Paris and Pru are Carolina and West's twin daughters.

"A party for a bunch of thirteen-year-old girls?" Vaughn tosses his napkin on top of his empty plate. "I'm out."

Hilarious, considering he's the same age.

"Vaughn, you are most definitely not out. They're your closest cousins besides Beau," Summer gently chastises. "The four of you have grown up together, along with Christopher. You are definitely going to this party. You are too, Beau."

Chris is Sylvie and Spencer's only son. There are five of them that are all the same age and they've always been close, just like Summer says.

Both boys actually groan in misery, making me roll my eyes.

"I was hoping you two would help." Summer turns her attention to us. "There will be a total of fifteen girls at the party, along with some family, and I'm sure it will be complete mayhem."

"What do you want us to do?" Iris asks.

"Just be present. That's all I ask. Participate in any of the activities or games."

"There are games?" Iris's expression turns vaguely horrified. "That sounds like torture."

"It won't be so bad." Summer's gaze slides to mine. "You don't mind helping, do you, Willow?"

"Of course not. I'm happy to help and it sounds like fun." As fun as fifteen girls could be—which sounds a little terrifying, but

I don't mention that. "Is there a theme for the party?"

"Everything is pink and girly," Summer says, which causes the boys to groan some more. The withering stare Iris sends in their direction would devastate weaker men, but no one reacts. "Oh, and there will be a fortune teller there too. Though she does things a little differently."

"Ooh, that sounds fun." Iris lightly jabs me in the ribs with her elbow. "How does she read you your fortune?"

"You have to kiss a card with lipstick. She reads lip prints. She's a little quirky but pretty much anyone who tells you your fortune has to be quirky," Summer explains.

"I can't wait." Iris rubs her hands together, her gaze stuck on Brooks, who stares back at her helplessly. "I'm looking forward to what my fortune will say."

"Me too," I murmur, though I'm lying.

It sounds intimidating. What if the fortune teller says something I don't want to hear? I feel bad enough about everything that's happened since last night with Rhett. I don't care about having my fortune told.

I need to fix what happened with him—and hopefully it's not too late.

CHAPTER THIRTY-FIVE

RHETT

We're all sitting out by the pool before lunch, staying out of the way as the event planner and her staff show up to set up for the birthday party. I feel like I shouldn't be here because of it and I even told Rowan that right after breakfast, but he reassured me we can stay. It'll give him someone to hang out with versus having to spend time with a bunch of squealing pre-teens.

Considering the girls are turning thirteen, that means they're actually teenagers, but I don't bother pointing that out to him. He already knows.

Not gonna lie, I'm still pissed about what happened with Willow last night, though my anger has simmered down some. I don't know what she meant by everything she said, but she put me straight on the defensive, and it was like my overstimulated brain and exhausted body shut down. I couldn't talk about it with her anymore.

This morning at breakfast though, she looked hotter than straight fire, which made my brain scramble just staring at her. The black dress she wore fit tight around her tits, and I swear I saw the hard beads of her nipples poking against the fabric. No bra?

Shocking.

Made me instantly regret I didn't feel her up more last night.

Not sure if I'm going to get a chance today either.

Damn.

I could see the worry on her pretty face. Her eyes looked haunted and I caught her staring at me with longing a few times. At least, that's what it looked like. The feeling was mutual. I'm not going to be mad at her just for anger's sake. I'm sure she'll apologize. And I'll apologize too for being a gruff asshole. Hopefully that'll make everything better.

Iris may as well have showed up to breakfast naked. Her off-white dress clung to her like a second skin and it was obvious she wore nothing underneath it. Pretty sure Brooks got a stiffy, considering he didn't budge from his seat at the dining table for a long time. Iris knew what she was doing too. That evil smile on her face said all that I needed to know.

I might be upset still with Willow, but I definitely made the right choice when it comes to the Lancaster girls. Iris is just too much for me. I don't know how Brooks does it.

"Do we really have to hang out at this party?" Iris's little brother Vaughn whines to us. He's currently sitting on a giant white swan floaty and wearing a pair of classic Wayfarer Ray-Ban sunglasses, drifting across the pool with his toes dragging in the water.

"Give me a break. You're dying to go to this party and check out the chicks." This is from Row, who's sitting on a lounge chair and soaking up the late summer sun.

It's not that warm out here, but the sun is shining upon us and it feels good. Plus, the pool is heated, so it won't be that rough jumping in.

"That's my plan," Beau adds. He's Row and Willow's little brother, and he is the spitting image of his dad. Even more so than Rowan. "You know there has to be a couple of hotties showing up."

Row makes a face, exchanging a look with my brother. "Have fun with your jailbait options."

"Says the dude who's also jailbait," I mutter, slipping my glasses over my eyes. Now this is the fucking life. Lounging by the pool and relaxing on a warm Saturday. Servants at our every beck and call, and enough food to keep us fed for the next month. I thought we grew up spoiled—our childhood was nothing compared to this.

I can feel Row glaring at me. "You know what I mean."

"I do, I do." I lower my sunglasses to study him. He looks put out but not really. "Where's Brooks?"

"Said he had to use the bathroom," Row answers.

"That was twenty minutes ago," Vaughn adds.

Row and I share a look before I push my sunglasses back into place. He's most likely hooking up with Iris.

"Hi, guys."

I swivel my head in the direction of that sweet voice greeting us, seeing Willow approach. Her thick hair is piled into a bun on top of her head and she's wearing a short black tank dress that hits about mid-thigh, designer slides on her feet, her toenails painted a vivid red. There are at least four gold necklaces in varying lengths around her neck and diamond studs winking in her ears.

This girl screams money and I had no idea I was so attracted to wealthy girls before, but here I am, lusting after her even though she pissed me off last night.

I make no sense.

When no one responds, she drops the plush white towel she's clutching under one arm onto the nearest lounge chair, unrolling it and placing it carefully across the cushions before she kicks off her slides. My temperature rises when she reaches for the sides of her cover up, pausing when she realizes she has an audience.

Me.

Beau, Vaughn and Row are too busy chatting to notice what she's doing and besides, they don't care. She's family. Their sister, their cousin. While I'm sitting over here remembering what it felt like to have her in my arms last night. The sweet sighs and low moans that sounded deep in her throat when I kissed the shit out of her.

If she's trying to get under my skin by showing up poolside, it's working.

Her gaze meets mine and her mouth curves downward. I'm sure she doesn't love it that I have sunglasses on, but they give me the benefit of looking at her wherever and whenever I want and she can't tell. There's an internal war that seems to be happening within her from the expression I see on her face, and she finally gives in, grabbing the dress and yanking it up and over her head.

Leaving me stunned.

She's wearing a bright green bikini that's not covering much. Her tits are barely contained by the flimsy fabric and yep, those are definitely her hard nipples I see. Her stomach is flat and her waist is tiny, her hips wide and the perfect place for someone to plant his hands.

Me. I'm that someone.

Willow also has good legs and I stare hard at the scrap of fabric that's covering the motherland. I don't even know why I referred to her pussy like that but I'm suddenly dying to see it. Slip my fingers inside it. See if she's wet.

Fuck, now I feel like Brooks. No wonder the guy snuck off with Iris. He's probably fucking her in a closet at this very moment while I sit out here, silently suffering.

Lucky fucker.

"Why isn't anyone in the water?" Willow asks no one in particular.

"I'm in the pool," Vaughn says, still gliding around on the swan.

"But you're not in the water. Swimming." Willow rests her hands on her hips, studying her cousin before she glances over her shoulder, her gaze scanning all of us. Landing on me. "You guys are no fun."

I lift a brow in silent challenge but she doesn't respond, turning to face the pool once more.

She wants fun? I can show her fun.

She's also giving me a perfect view of her ass and it is juicy.

I sound like a dick even in my own head. Objectifying her every body part, but it feels like she's putting on a show just for me and I can't help but notice. I'm an eighteen-year-old male in the prime of my life. Sue me.

Without warning, she dives into the water, barely breaking the surface, it's so smooth. She swims across the pool, popping up in front of Vaughn's swan, wearing a big grin and the water dripping down her face as she tips the swan over, sending Vaughn sputtering into the water.

Row laughs. So does Beau. And so does Willow.

Me? I'm quiet, enjoying this playful side Will is showing me. I don't see this version of her at school. She always seems stressed and serious. Worried. In this moment, she's carefree and I like it.

"That sucked," Vaughn declares when he resurfaces. He cuts his hand through the water, splashing Willow. "Why did you push me off the swan?"

"You looked like you needed to cool off." She shrugs, shrieking when Vaughn lunges for her, and she swims away hurriedly.

Beau jumps into the water, ready to harass his sister, which he does. They're all splashing each other and laughing in the pool while Row and I stay on the loungers. Row is too busy paying attention to his phone, which means I can leisurely watch Willow without any questions or judgment.

She's currently struggling to climb onto the swan, Beau choosing this moment to shove her right off, and when she falls into the water with a big splash, I can't help but laugh. She reappears in an instant, grabbing hold of the swan and swimming away with it, pushing the giant floaty in front of her, the boys yelling at her.

Damn it, I can't stay mad at her. Not when she's awkwardly trying to get back on the swan, laughing the entire time. Eventually Vaughn holds the front of the swan to stabilize it for her and she gets what she wants. Sitting on top of the swan, straddling the swan's neck, lifting her right arm in triumph while Vaughn swims to the back of it and pushes her around the pool. They pass by me and she smiles, her eyes glowing, the look on her face just for me. Silently communicating that she remembers what we shared last night too, and do I want to do it again?

That's the message I'm taking from that look. And my response is yes. Yes, fucking please let's do it again.

"Hey." Brooks magically appears, clad in a pair of pale pink swim trunks and wearing a hideous Hawaiian print shirt he left unbuttoned. He falls onto the lounger next to mine and stretches out his big frame, tilting his face toward the sun. "What did I miss?"

"The question we really should ask is where were you?"

He pulls a pair of sunglasses out of the front pocket of his shirt and slips them on, shading his eyes. "Went to check out my room and change. I'm right next door to you."

Thank God we're not sharing a room. He'd probably kick me out and entertain Iris in it all night.

"Check out your room, huh? That's what we're calling it?"

Brooks remains as cool as ever, seemingly unfazed. "This place is like a damn hotel."

"With free services?" He finally turns his head in my direction. "Come clean, my friend. Where were you really?"

He glances back at Row before turning to face me, his voice going low. "With Iris."

"Doing what?"

"You know."

"Chatting her up?" My tone, my face is pure innocence.

"Sure." His voice is smooth, his gaze shifting down and to the left.

I remember reading somewhere recently that's how you know someone is lying. When they look down and to the left.

"Chatting her up while your dick was inside her?" I ask, keeping it casual.

A strangled sound leaves Brooks, causing him to immediately start coughing, and I just sit there and watch him while he has a complete attack. They even go quiet in the pool, all of them not moving while they wait for Brooks to finish.

"Are you okay?" Willow asks when he's finally done, her voice full of concern.

"I'm fine," he manages to utter, his voice strangled. He keeps clearing his throat, and I have to admit to myself I don't even feel bad for making that happen.

"Must've nailed it," I say only when they all start swimming around again, their constant chatter background noise to our conversation. "Or maybe I should say, you must've been nailing her."

"Look, I don't want it getting around, especially to her family." Brooks casts a worried glance toward the pool before he meets my gaze again. "She'd prefer to keep this a secret."

"Your secret is safe with me," I say solemnly, meaning every word I say. I won't break Brooks's trust. He's my best friend at this school. I won't put that at risk.

"Good." He sits up, turning to sit on the side of the lounger facing me, his bare feet planted on the ground. "I think I'm in love with her."

Now I'm the one coughing, choking on my own saliva because damn, that's a big statement. "Seriously?"

Brooks nods, his face gravely serious. "I can't stop thinking about her. She's all I want to see, to do, to talk to. She keeps pushing me away and that only makes me want her more. It's bad, but I never want the feeling to stop."

"Sounds like you're obsessed."

"That's it. That's the perfect word to describe how I feel about her." He leans forward and so do I, sensing he's going to say something important. "We just fucked for the last thirty minutes in my room. I came twice. I don't know how she does it."

I'm envious. I wish I was the one fucking for thirty minutes straight and it was good enough that I'm coming twice. "Sounds fun."

"It was fun. It's like, life-transforming. What this girl makes me feel…" His voice drifts, and he shakes his head. "Like I said, I think I love her."

"Do you think she loves you?"

"Not at all." He doesn't even hesitate with that response.

I frown. "That sucks."

"It is what it is." He shrugs. "She has a hard time showing her feelings. While all I want to do is express my undying love for her every time we're together. It's not a good mix."

As if conjured up by his mere words, Iris appears, clad in the skimpiest black bikini I've ever seen in my life, her ass cheeks hanging out as she runs toward the pool and jumps in the middle of it. Her perfect cannonball causes giant waves to ripple through the pool and Willow and the boys are yelling at her when her head pops out of the water.

"Look at her. She makes a splash wherever she goes," Brooks says, a dazed look on his face as he stares at the love of his life.

That was the corniest shit ever, but I can see he's gone over her.

"You've got to play it cool."

"What?" Brooks swivels his head in my direction, frowning. "Play it cool?"

He says the words like it's an unfathomable concept.

"With her." I nod, waving a hand in the pool's direction. "She knows how you feel. She's leading you around by your dick and you're letting her."

"Yeah. She's really good at it." He doesn't sound mad about it at all.

"Right. So she's got you where she wants you, and you're letting it happen. She's taken complete control of the situation. She's in charge of your relationship."

"I'm cool with it." He shrugs.

"You won't be when she tells you she can't be with you like that."

Brooks goes completely still, his gaze back on the pool. On Iris. "She wouldn't do that to me."

"She already is."

His frown is deep. "I'll talk to her tonight about it."

"Really?" I sound doubtful. I *am* doubtful. My friend doesn't want to mess up a good thing. And I suppose I can't blame him. Why make waves when he's getting everything he could want? A beautiful girl letting him fuck her every which way he can, whenever he wants for the most part.

But isn't there more to life than just constant sex with no feelings involved? Or in Brooks's case, one-sided feelings? I'd hate to be in his position.

My gaze drifts to the swan. Now Iris is somehow sitting on it too, directly behind Willow. Her arms are around her waist, her cheek pressed against Willow's shoulder and they're laughing. Iris's gaze meets mine and her arms tighten around Willow, a smirk appearing on her face. She's sending me a message. Not sure how I know this, I just do.

You want her—you better treat her right.

That's what she's telling me without saying a word, and I realize…

I need to talk to Willow as soon as possible. I can't let Brooks and Iris be the only ones having a good time behind closed doors this weekend.

CHAPTER THIRTY-SIX

WILLOW

Iris and I eventually leave the pool and boys behind, heading up to our shared room so we can get ready for the twins' party. Summer let us know when we first entered the house that they'll be here within the hour and all their little friends will start showing up soon after, which we took as our hint to take a shower and change.

"That was fun," I tell Iris once we're inside her room.

"Showing off your hot bod for Rhett? I'm sure it was a blast," Iris teases, immediately undoing the string at her neck so that her bikini top falls forward, exposing her chest.

I avert my gaze, going into the bathroom and grabbing my brush. My hair is a tangled mess and I can't just jump in the shower like this. I already called dibs on showering first. "I wasn't showing off."

"Whatever you say," Iris calls, her voice full of doubt.

I peek my head around the open doorway. "He didn't even notice. He was too busy talking to Brooks once he showed up."

The satisfied smile on Iris's face tells me everything I didn't ask. They disappeared at the same time for at least a half hour, maybe longer, and I assumed they were together. I'm sure I was right.

"He was paying attention to you."

"No, he wasn't."

"Yes, he was. I saw him staring at you. And don't deny that you look hot because you do. I'm proud of you for wearing the bikini in front of him."

I had nothing to lose and everything to gain. That's why I wore it. Plus, there's something about this bright green two-piece that fills me with confidence every time I wear it. I bought it when we were in Europe, and the first time I wore it on the beach in the South of France, my father demanded I cover myself. Mom had to calm him down and remind him that his daughter isn't a little girl anymore, which from the look on his face, he hated to hear.

Mom never complaining about the bikini made me feel like a grown-up. Like she was on my side and saw nothing wrong with me wearing it. Ever since that moment, this swimsuit has become a total confidence builder.

And fine, I did notice Rhett looking my way a few times while we were in the pool, but I told myself I was probably overreacting. I wanted him to look at me so badly I took any glance in the pool's direction as him ogling me.

Maybe he actually was.

"What are you wearing to this party?"

"Something cute and with easy access. A dress." Iris disappears into her walk-in closet, and I can hear her rifling through her clothes. "What about you?"

"I didn't bring anything cute enough to wear to the party." I wasn't aware there was even going to be a party today. I knew the twins' birthday was coming up, but normally our family has their party the weekend after the date, not before.

"You have a couple of dresses in here," Iris tells me.

I abandon my brushing session to go into her closet, checking out my options. One dress is old. A blue floral sundress that I wore a couple of years ago at some sort of formal event that was being held here.

"I don't think this will fit across my chest anymore." I pull the dress out and hold it in front of me.

“You’d look like a little girl in it anyway. You need something more sophisticated,” Iris says.

“I don’t own anything sophisticated.”

“Oh, come on now. Of course, you do.” Iris joins me, sifting through the meager options I have hanging in her closet, pausing to pull out a specific dress. “Now this could work.”

It’s pink and short, with straps for sleeves that tie on top of the shoulder and cutouts on either side, right at the rib cage. The skirt is tiered with white ribbon trim and it hits at about mid to upper-thigh. One strong breeze and I’d be exposed. Speaking of exposed, the back of the dress is totally open, with a band of pink stretched across mid-back and open both above and below it. I probably can’t wear a bra with it.

“My boobs are probably too big.”

“No way. We can shove them in there.” Iris presses the dress against the front of me, her gaze assessing. “You could borrow my off-white strappy sandals.”

We may not have the same body type, but we share a shoe size, which comes in handy in times like these.

“Isn’t it too…sexy for this party?” I wrinkle my nose, grabbing the dress from her and approaching the full-length mirror hanging on the wall. “My dad might flip.”

“Is he coming?”

I send a quick text to my mom asking if they’re attending Prudence and Paris’s birthday party.

Mama: **Unfortunately, we can’t make it this year. There’s an art exposition opening tonight that your father and I RSVP’d to months ago. We don’t want to miss it. We sent the girls presents though! You’ll have to tell me if they like them.**

“They’re not coming,” I announce to Iris after reading the text. The relief I feel knowing that my father won’t see me in this dress is monumental.

He’d freak out. I know he would.

She grins. "Perfect. Go take a shower and get ready. I'll help you with the dress if you have trouble getting your tits in it."

I burst out laughing. "Gee, thanks."

After I take a shower—where I carefully shaved everything because you just never know—I lather on the expensive lotion Iris's mom gave me last Christmas, then slip on a pair of lacy white panties before I pull on the dress. It's a struggle to get the top over my boobs, but I make it work without Iris's assistance. The only issue I have is being able to reach to pull up the zipper that rests on my lower spine. I call her in for help and she zips it up with ease, our gazes meeting in the mirror.

"He's going to die."

"I hope so," is my response, making us smile.

I still feel guilty about last night, and that we never got a chance to talk so far today. Maybe after the party? I have no idea what Summer wants us to do, but I'm sure she'll keep us busy for hours.

I blow dry and style my hair while Iris is in the shower, and once she's out, she slicks her hair back into a sleek bun, adding thin gold hoop earrings to complement the look. "I'm keeping things simple," she tells me after she's slipped into a body-hugging black knit dress that's similar to the cream-colored one she wore this morning. "Less is more."

I think of how she piled on the makeup just last night for the game, but I keep those thoughts to myself.

We head downstairs after we're done, and Summer puts us right to work. Despite all of the servants bustling around and the event planner's staff, we don't mind helping out. She puts us in charge of answering the door to the parents dropping off their children to the party, and we greet the other guests as well. Some of our family members show up, including Charlotte and Perry, who have their own daughter close to Pru and Paris's age, though Juliette just turned twelve.

It's fun, greeting everyone, especially the older relatives. My grandma eventually shows up, accompanied by her much younger "companion" as she calls him, Geoffrey. My grandfather died when I was little, and I've heard enough stories over the years to know he doesn't sound like a very nice man. Once he passed though, my grandmother became much kinder, according to Mom.

"My darling girl, look at you," my grandma says when she sees me. She stops in front of me, grabbing both of my hands and stretching my arms out wide as she turns to look at Geoffrey. "Isn't she a delight?"

"It's nice to see you, Willow," Geoffrey says, inclining his head toward me. He's in his fifties with a full head of hair and his gaze is always admiring when he stares at my grandmother.

"Grandma, you're making me self-conscious." I pull her in for a hug and her gentle hands pat at my bare back, exposed thanks to the dress. "But thank you."

"Is your father here?" The amusement on her face is obvious. "Has he seen you in this dress yet?"

"No and no. He's unable to make it," I tell her with a mock sad face.

"Lucky for you," she murmurs as she goes to embrace Iris.

Once everyone has arrived, Iris and I make our way outside where the festivities are being held. Pru and Paris are truly the spotlight, their friends surrounding them as they move about the terrace like a swarm of bees, buzzing and talking and laughing. I spot the boys sitting at a nearby table. Row and Callahan both look like they'd rather be anywhere but here, while Beau and Vaughn sit on the edge of their seats, watching the girls with stars in their eyes.

It's kind of amusing.

I don't see the older boys yet, which only makes me nervous. Iris is fidgety too, her head whipping this way and that as she scans the area, trying to play it cool while I know she's in search of Brooks.

"Girls, come have your fortune told." Summer appears in front of us, holding her arm out toward where the lip print reader has set up her little booth. "The younger girls are scared to do it. They want you to go first."

"No problem." Iris shrugs and we both head over to the area where the woman has set up. The three tables are set up in a U-shape, and they're covered in vivid red, gauzy tablecloths. On one of the tables is a stack of white card stock accompanied by a display full of various shades of lipsticks.

"Welcome," the woman says, a friendly smile on her face. Her lips are full and slicked with red. "Care to have your lips read?"

"Yes," Iris says, stepping forward. I already told her she should go first. "What shall we do? I'm wearing clear gloss."

The woman plucks a tissue from the box on her table and hands it to Iris. "Wipe your lips clean and choose a lipstick shade. Whichever one you want. Please hand it to me when you're done and grab a blank card. I'll need you to kiss it twice."

Iris does as she's instructed, choosing the darkest red she could find and smearing it on her lips in an extra thick coat. I choose my shade as well, going for a soft but obvious pink, studying myself in one of the mirrors that sits on the table as I carefully apply it. I grab a piece of card stock and kiss it twice, taking my time while Iris is already seated in front of the woman, who introduces herself as Linda, eager to hear what she has to say.

"Do you mind if your friend listens in?" Linda asks Iris, referring to me.

"She's my best friend and my cousin. We have no secrets," Iris tells her.

Hmm, not so sure about that, but I keep my mouth shut.

"Very well, then." Linda takes the kiss-covered card from Iris and sets it in front of her, dropping her head to examine it carefully. She even pulls out a small magnifying glass, squinting into it as she scans it over the first lipstick print, then the second one. "Hmm."

Iris and I share a look, Iris appearing like she might burst out laughing, and I send her a quick headshake. I don't want her disrespecting the poor woman who seems to take her job very seriously.

"See how close your lips are?" Linda taps the thin slide of open space between the kiss print. "You tend to be closed off—mysterious."

"Accurate," Iris says with a laugh.

"And the diamond shape." Linda traces the shape between Iris's lips on the card. "While you're mysterious, you also crave attention. You want everyone to notice how you sparkle and shine."

"It's true. Right, Willow?" Iris looks to me for confirmation.

"Very true," I say, glancing down at my own kiss card, which looks nothing like Iris's.

Linda goes on to feed into Iris's assumptions about herself, and I wonder if Linda is telling the truth, or if she's done her research before arriving and figured out Iris's personality just from her social media profiles. I start to tune out what they're saying, watching the younger girls move closer to us in a pack. Spotting Beau and Vaughn in the near distance following after them.

My gaze stops on Rhett, who's standing on the edge of the terrace with Brooks and Row on either side of him. All three of them are wearing khakis and button-up shirts that are open at the collar. Rhett's shirt is white while Brooks's is pale blue, and Row's is a darker blue. I wonder if Rhett borrowed that shirt from one of them because how did he know to bring something a little dressier?

It doesn't matter. He looks amazing. His hair is relatively tame, though the ends flare up as the breeze ruffles through it. He's got his shirt sleeves already rolled up, exposing those sexy forearms of his, and my mouth goes dry when our gazes meet.

His lips curl into the faintest smile, but he looks away when Brooks speaks to him, breaking our connection. I return my attention to the lip print reader and realize Iris is rising from the chair, a big smile on her face when she faces me.

"Your turn!"

I settle into the chair, my stomach churning with nerves as I hand over the kiss card. Linda immediately examines it, holding it up in the air, squinting at it.

"What's your name?"

"Willow," I answer, clearing my throat.

She offers me a gentle smile. "Are you nervous?"

"A little." I twist my hands together.

"Don't be. This is for fun. Nothing too serious." She sets the kiss card on the table and picks up the magnifying glass, carefully scanning both of my lipstick prints. "I like your choice of color. Very pink and soft. I take it you're a quiet person."

"Quieter than Iris," I quip.

Linda offers a polite smile. "Indeed."

She's silent as she continues to study my lip prints, her brows drawing together as she leans in closer. I fidget in my seat, wishing I'd never done this, almost afraid of what she might say. I'm taking this far too seriously.

"The space here." She taps at the white space between my lips. "Your cousin's was narrower, while yours is more open. This means you're friendly and you value the relationships you have with those you're closest to. You're close to your family?"

"Yes," I admit.

"I can tell. But you're also shy. A bit reserved. It's in the depth of your kiss. See how light the pigmentation is?" She points at the pale pink on the cardstock. "The lighter the color, the shier you are, but you also have strict boundaries. Look at the outer edges of the print. They're firmly defined. No one can take advantage of you."

"Okay." I nod, liking how everything she says sounds.

"And the lines in your lips. These?" She drags her finger along each tiny line in my upper lip print. "Mean you're a creative soul. You think outside the box."

I'm not sure how accurate that is but I'll go along with it.

"Your lips are very balanced too. They're almost the same size. This means you're a balanced person in real life as well. And that you're looking for a partner who's the same. Do you have a boyfriend?" I shake my head. "Someone you're casually seeing or that you're interested in?"

"Well…yes." I may as well be truthful.

"You'll want him to be the same." Her gaze dances with mischief when it meets mine. "Think any of the young men in attendance will participate in this little activity?"

Laughing, I shake my head. "Doubtful. You probably wouldn't catch any of them dead in lipstick. Even for a few seconds to kiss a piece of paper."

"That's a shame," Linda says with a sigh, leaning back in her chair. "I get the sense that the boy you're interested in is here this afternoon."

"He is," I admit.

"A great romance is in your future." Linda's gaze locks with mine, as sincere as the sound of her voice. "I can also read people's energy. You are on the cusp of falling in love."

"I am?" My voice squeaks and I clear my throat, feeling foolish.

"You are," Linda says firmly. "He's here. I can feel his energy too. Something monumental is going to happen tonight."

I swallow hard at her words.

"I can feel it."

CHAPTER THIRTY-SEVEN

RHETT

I can take staring at Willow in that dress for only so long before I give in to my every urge and need and finally approach her. She's kept her distance the entire afternoon as if she knows how much she's torturing me and I can't stand it any longer.

She's on the other side of the pool, standing by the balcony that overlooks the expansive gardens below and the ocean just beyond the green. She was just talking to an older woman who scooped her up in a hug before walking away. Meaning, she's all alone.

It's my chance to swoop in.

I approach her from behind, taking in how the dress exposes the smooth expanse of her back. How the dress sits low at the base of her spine—if it dipped any lower, I could probably see her ass crack. She looks as sweet and as innocent as sunshine with her hair flowing down her back, the front pieces pulled into a cream-colored silky bow, and matching cream, heeled sandals on her feet, which make her a little taller.

Easier to kiss maybe.

All the girls went nuts over the lady reading their kiss prints. At one point the fortune teller tried to get us to do it too, but we all refused. I'm not going to put on lipstick and kiss a piece of paper for her to tell me some bullshit about my personality or future.

No thank you. That lady looked right at me when she was talking to us, pointing at me with her index finger.

"The love of your life is here tonight," she told me. That's all she said.

Brooks had slapped my chest. "What was that about?"

I had no idea.

Is this girl I'm sneaking up on the love of my life? Sounds dramatic. And maybe it's some bullshit, but I don't know.

We're gonna find out.

"Whatcha doing out here all alone?" I ask her.

Willow startles and turns to face me, her wide eyes meeting mine. "Oh. Hi." She rests her hand on her chest, her palm pressing against her cleavage. "You scared me."

"Sorry." I slip my hands into my pockets so I don't reach for her. I'm still supposed to be mad at her, but the anger has waned as the day has gone on.

"I was talking to my grandma. She was leaving."

"Where's your mom and dad?" I haven't spotted them yet, but there are a lot of people here.

"They couldn't make it." Her smile is small, her gaze unsure. "Are you having fun?"

"It's all right." I shrug. "For a kids' party."

"If my cousins heard you, they'd be devastated. Paris and Pru are feeling very grown-up," Willow says.

"You're looking pretty grown-up in that dress." Okay, that sounded lame.

"Oh." She glances down at herself before lifting her head to meet my gaze again. "It's kind of scandalous."

"I like it."

"You don't think it's too much?"

I slowly shake my head. "You look amazing."

Her cheeks turn the faintest shade of pink. "Thank you."

We stare at each for a moment and I see the uncertainty flicker in her gaze.

"I'm sorry for what happened last night. I didn't mean to insult you or hurt your feelings." Her voice is soft, making it hard to hear her clearly.

I take a step closer to her, resting my hand on the balcony's ledge. "I was kind of a dick."

"No, I was rude. I don't know what I was trying to say, but I'm not embarrassed to be seen with you, Rhett. It's just—there are other circumstances preventing me from being with you." She covers her face with her hands. "Oh, that was so presumptive of me. I don't expect us to be together. I don't even know how you feel about me."

Well, that's total crap because I've told her how I feel about her multiple times, but maybe she needs to hear it again.

Shifting closer, I circle my fingers around her wrist and tug one of her hands down, causing her to drop the other. "Tell me what's going on, Will. I feel like you're keeping secrets from me."

"Can I tell you later?" It's her turn to come closer, her body colliding gently with mine, sending an electric shock spiraling through my blood, settling in my dick. "I don't want to ruin tonight. Will you accept my apology?"

I can hear the agony in her voice, see the swirl of emotion in her eyes. She hated that she made me angry. "Yes." I slip my arm around her slender waist, my fingers landing on the bare skin that's exposed by the cutouts in her dress. Her skin is warm and smooth and God, her smell. I can't get enough of it. "Think we can ditch the party?"

She rests her hand lightly on my chest, her touch like a brand. I'm hers, whether she realizes it or not. And she's mine. "I don't think I want to. Not yet, at least. Is that bad? Let's wander around together. Please?"

"Want to feel like a couple, Will?" I put it into words, knowing she wouldn't dare say it out loud. And from the way her cheeks turn redder, I'm thinking I hit it right on the head.

"I do," she whispers. "Again, I'm making assumptions but…"

I cut her off with my lips, delivering a soft kiss. Keeping it light because the second we take it deeper, I'm not going to be able to stop. And I'm not about to devour her in front of a bunch of thirteen-year-old girls and her family. "You're not making assumptions. I want the same thing."

"You do?" She sounds giddy. She even laughs. "We barely know each other. It's only been—"

I deliver another kiss to her lips to shut her up. "Sometimes when you know, you just know. Right?"

She nods, her fingers drifting down my chest, her light touch making me shiver. "That's what my father has always said."

"Seriously?" I'm frowning.

"Yes." Willow plucks at the front of my shirt, keeping her gaze on her hand. "He used to tell me the story of when he met my mother and how they fell in love. She hated him at first, but he told me he just…knew. Even though he was in denial and told himself that he didn't like her either, he wasn't being truthful. He was drawn to her from the start."

"My dad admitted to me that he saw my mom in the stands of a football game and fell in love with her that day. He never even talked to her for the next two years," I confess. "Her older brother played the same position as my dad at their rival school. They were enemies. He likes to give my uncle Jake shit to this day, but they like each other. I think."

"That sounds so romantic," Willow whispers, her lips curving upward. "I think we both come from a family of romantics."

"You're probably right." I touch her hair, pushing a strand behind her ear. "I wouldn't call myself a romantic, though."

"Really? You've been pretty romantic toward me," she whispers.

"I'm only a romantic for you," I murmur, leaning in to press my lips to her cheek. Her ear. "I can't wait to get you alone."

A shiver moves through her, so strong I can feel it. She pulls away from me, a knowing smile on her face as she grabs hold of my hand and tugs. "Not yet, Rhett Bennett. We're going to make the rounds first."

"Oh, yeah?" I go along with her as we walk away from the pool and head for where the party guests are congregated.

"Unfortunately, my grandmother already left for the evening or I would've introduced you. She'd love you. I just know it." Willow laughs. "I'll introduce you to the rest of my family that's here though."

A month ago, this would've made me freak the fuck out. I'm not about meeting some girl's family. Not normally. But that was before I met Willow.

Now, I'm in. I've already met the parents and she's met mine. Only a few weeks in and we're past the major hurdles. It's all moving so damn fast, but I'm all for it.

I haven't forgotten what she said though. I want to know what circumstances aren't allowing her to go public with me. Sounds bogus. If she's just stringing me along for some weird reason, I'm going to be pissed.

But I'm still gonna go along with it anyway.

CHAPTER THIRTY-EIGHT

WILLOW

I have the best time taking Rhett around the party and introducing him to everyone I know. Everyone I'm related to. I even introduce him to the twins who giggle and carry on and ask if Rhett is my boyfriend. He answers yes before I can respond, sending a thrill through me that has my heart beating extra hard.

It's the perfect night. The air is cool but not too cold, and the moon shines its silvery glow down upon us. The food is delicious, and Summer and Whit hired a DJ, who's playing a mixture of current hits and oldies that gets everyone—including the parents and grandparents—out on the dance floor. Even Linda the lip print reader is dancing, her hands in the air as she moves to the beat.

We catch Iris and Brooks kissing behind a massive planter that's taller than Brooks, which is saying a lot. Brooks appears sheepish, his hands springing away from Iris's waist when we come upon them, but Iris just grabs one of his hands and settles it right on her butt.

"They know we're fucking around, Brooksie. We don't need to hide," she says with a smile, just before he kisses her again.

It's kind of romantic, how she spoke to him. How he looked at her. As if the sun rises and sets on her pretty little head.

I want Rhett to look at me like that.

We eat some food and watch the twins cut their birthday cake. Their mom Carolina delivers sparklers to all of the girls' friends and they wave them in the air, the music playing extra loud as slices of cake get passed out by the caterer's staff.

"This party is like a freaking wedding," Rhett says at one point when he's handed a plate of cake. We find a table to sit at and he immediately digs in while I watch him. "You're not going to have any?"

I slowly shake my head. I'm too nervous to eat anything sweet, which is a shame because I absolutely adore cake with thick frosting on it. I've always had a sweet tooth. "I'm not hungry."

"You're watching me like you're dying to snatch the fork from my fingers and steal this bite for yourself." He pauses, holding the fork in front of my mouth. "You sure you don't want some? I can share."

I shake my head. "I'm fine."

He shoves the bite into his mouth, savoring it, humming his pleasure. The sound makes my body light up, ultra-aware of every little thing he does. "You're missing out."

His reaction to the cake is making me forget my nerves. "Fine. Feed me a bite."

Pleased with himself, he cuts me off a big chunk and holds the fork in front of my mouth. "Open up."

I part my lips, all the air leaving my lungs when he slowly slides the tines of the fork into my mouth. The sugary goodness of the cake melts on my tongue and I wrap my lips around it, murmuring when he pulls the fork from my mouth. His gaze darkens, his focus solely on my mouth and nothing else, and awareness crackles in the air between us.

I chew and swallow, shocked that Rhett feeding me a bite of cake in the middle of a birthday party could be so…sensual.

"Good?" His voice is rough, his gaze fiery.

Nodding, I rub my lips together, getting one last taste of the sugary sweetness. "Delicious."

"Want another bite?" His brows lift in question.

"I probably shouldn't." I shake my head.

But I don't mean it. He feeds me a few more bites between his own, the two of us leaning toward each other more and more, until I'm close enough that I can easily crawl into his lap. I'm tempted to do it. To curl up close and feel those big arms come around my body, cradling me.

My phone buzzes and I check to see who the message is from.

Iris: **Meet us at the hot tub in one hour.**

"Iris wants us to meet her at the hot tub," I tell Rhett.

"With Brooks?" he asks.

Me: **Is Brooks with you?**

Iris: **Duh. I found a bottle of Veuve Clicquot. We want to share it with you guys.**

"She has champagne." I lift my gaze to find Rhett already watching me. "Do want to hang out with them?"

"I'd rather hang out with you. Alone." His voice deepens, the look on his face almost feral, making me shiver.

"We can hang out alone for a little bit," I whisper. "She wants to meet us in an hour. I'm assuming that's when the party should end."

"We can do a lot in an hour, princess."

An incessant throb starts in my belly. Lower. What he's suggesting…

Am I ready for it?

My phone buzzes in my hand again.

Iris: **So????????**

I start typing.

Me: **We're in. Do you think the party will be done by then?**

Iris: **It better be. I want everyone out of here. Might go a little longer though. Are you still hanging out at the party?**

Me: **Where are you?**

Iris: **Um…in our room. With Brooks.**

"Iris is in the room we share with Brooks," I murmur.

"We can go to my room," Rhett suggests.

I keep my focus on the phone, thinking. If my parents were here, I'd never have the guts to sneak into Rhett's room. But they're not here. Summer and Whit are too preoccupied by the party. So are all of my aunts and uncles who are in attendance. No one is paying attention to us.

Lifting my gaze to Rhett's, I murmur, "Okay."

• • •

It took us at least fifteen minutes to say our goodbyes to various people at the party, including Iris's parents, who both asked me if I'd seen her—talk about making me anxious. I hate lying but I just blew them off, claiming Iris was most likely in the kitchen. Why I said that, I don't know.

I never claimed to be a good liar.

By the time we're entering the house, I'm a frazzled mess. Well, inside at least. Outwardly, I'm trying my best to keep my demeanor calm. Almost nonchalant. Like it's no big deal that I'm going to a boy's room all alone on a Saturday night.

This is a huge deal. And it feels like we're running out of time. Tonight, this weekend. I don't know how long this is going to last with Rhett. It could all come crashing down around our heads tomorrow night. Monday morning. Just thinking about it fills me with agitated nerves accompanied by a wave of nausea.

Shoving the thoughts out of my mind, I focus on this moment. Right now. The way Rhett looks at me. How he touches me. Currently his hand rests on my lower back, his wide palm and long fingers pressed against bare skin thanks to the open back of my dress. He doesn't say much, but I can feel the urgency vibrating off of him. He's eager to get me alone.

I feel the same about him, though I'm probably more nervous than he is.

"Do you ever get lost in this place?" he asks, frustration lacing his tone as I verbally guide him toward the stairwell that leads us to our bedroom wing.

"I have," I say with a laugh. "Plenty of times. When I was around six, I got so lost, I cried and cried for my mama. Iris's dad found me in the butler's pantry, sitting on the floor crying as hard as I can ever remember. It was a traumatic moment."

Considering my upbringing and how loving our household is, that counts as one of the most terrifying moments of my childhood. Lost in this place.

"Sounds like it." His tone is vaguely sarcastic and I ignore it. I'm sure he's had a privileged upbringing as well.

I decide to change the subject.

"There are ghosts here you know," I say as we come upon the staircase.

"Ghosts?" Now he sounds amused. "Like who? The creepy statue on campus?"

"Yes!" I laugh, increasing my pace to get ahead of Rhett, reaching out to grasp the intricate iron railing. "He's definitely one of them. Ezekiel died young."

"How?"

Biting my lower lip, I turn to face him, standing on the second step, which puts me at perfect height with him. I might even be a little taller. I can see the top of his head, his mussed golden-brown hair. How it waves at the ends. "He killed himself. Jumped off the roof of this very house."

"What?" His eyes go wide and he glances around, his expression unsure. "Are you serious?"

I nod. "There used to be a terrace up there. They had parties much like the one tonight. They did it for the view, and of course, the higher you are, the richer you feel." My uncle Grant told me that once. But then he also added, *The higher you are, the harder you fall.*

That always stuck with me.

"Okay..." He steps closer and I rest my hands on his broad

shoulders, staring into his hazel eyes. The green in his gaze seems more intense tonight. "I can tell there's more to this story."

"Oh, yes." I am relishing this moment. No one is around and I have Rhett Bennett's undivided attention. This might be a stall tactic on my part, but it's also fun. And I think he's enjoying the story too. "The night it happened, there was a party. His younger brother was engaged and the family was celebrating, with the exception of Ezekiel. He was morose the entire evening. Snarly and snapping at everyone, and no one could figure out why. And when the party was long over, in the middle of the night, Ezekiel jumped from the roof and landed in the circular drive."

I shiver at the mental image and Rhett's brows are drawn together.

"Creepy," he says. "No wonder that statue has always bothered me."

"Why he did it isn't creepy, it's tragic." I pause, because another thing my uncle Grant taught me is that a solid pause in the middle of a story always makes it more engrossing. "He left behind a note. He was in love with his brother's new fiancée, and couldn't go on living if he had to witness her marrying his brother."

"Was she in love with him?"

"She was seeing Ezekiel first, but then she met Thomas Lancaster. His younger and much more charming brother. It was never that serious, what she shared with Ezekiel, but her abandonment devastated him," I explain. Oh, I love Lancaster family lore. It's so intricate and dramatic and interesting.

"What happened after he killed himself? Did they get married?" Rhett asks.

"Yes. They pushed back their wedding date due to the funeral and the time of mourning for the family, but six months after his death, they were married. They ended up very happy together and had six children. Their youngest boy they named Ezekiel, after his dead uncle."

Rhett actually chuckles. "That's a little morbid, don't you

think? He was in love with her. Killed himself at the loss of her, and they named their kid after him?"

"Thomas loved his brother. He was always plagued with guilt, but I suppose love wins over blood in the end?" I shrug, sliding my hands to the back of Rhett's head, burying my fingers in his hair. I love how soft it is.

His lids lower, as if he's enjoying me playing with his hair. "That's kind of fucked up."

I lean in close, pressing my cheek to his so I can whisper in his ear. "My entire family is kind of…fucked up."

Rhett rears back, his shocked gaze meeting mine. "Did you just say fuck, Willow Lancaster?"

I nod, pressing my lips to his to keep him quiet. It's a playful gesture, but when I try to pull away, his hand cups the back of my head, keeping me in place as he deepens the kiss. His tongue searches my mouth, making me whimper.

A loud noise booms somewhere in the depths of the house, startling me, and Rhett growls, grabbing my hand and leading me up the stairs. I follow after him, hurrying to keep up, both of us silent as we move down the corridor, passing by Iris's closed bedroom door.

I swear I hear her giggling, followed by a very male groan.

Oh my.

We stop in front of the guest bedroom door Rhett's staying in and he rests his hand on the handle, pausing to turn toward me.

"You're sure?"

He doesn't say any more, but I know what he's referring to, and I nod firmly.

"Yes."

CHAPTER THIRTY-NINE

RHETT

I drag her into the bedroom and shut and lock the door, pressing her against it, pinning her there with my body. Her yes was all I needed to hear and now I'm not going to let her get away from me.

Not until I touch her. Slip my hand beneath her dress. Maybe slip my hand beneath her panties too. Whatever she'll let me do, I'm going to do because fuck. I want her.

Bad.

Willow tips her head back, her gaze heated, her mouth swollen from our earlier kiss on the stairway. I reach for her face, tracing my fingers along her delicate jaw. Her chin. Her lids lower, her lips parting on a sigh. And when I drag my thumb across her lower lip, she tilts her hips, pressing her lower body against mine.

My dick reacts, getting hard in an instant. I've had sex a handful of times with no one that special. The first time I did it was just to get the act out of the way. The next few times it was always with a girl I was attracted to during a drunken moment, sneaking away during a party or after a football game. Nothing serious.

Ever.

This feels serious. Monumental. Yes, we snuck away from a party, but it was a family party and I just...don't really go to those with a girl. I feel like I've met pretty much every Lancaster in existence tonight, and I'm not tempted to go running scared out of here. I liked all of them. I watched Willow get her kiss print read by some whack fortune teller and I could tell she enjoyed every second of it. I even swiped her kiss card off the table when she wasn't looking and it's currently in the back pocket of my borrowed khakis. Probably bent to shit but I don't care.

I wanted to keep them. A memory of this day—of this night.

"You have a sexy mouth," I whisper to her because fuck, she seriously does. Her lipstick is long gone and I miss the scarlet red mouth, but her natural lips are a vivid pink. Plump and damp and sweet. I remember watching her eat those bites of cake earlier and that was about the sexiest thing I've ever seen her do.

Wild but true.

I lean into her, acting like I'm going to kiss her but dodging to the side at the last minute, pressing my face against her neck. She tilts her head back, her hair rustling against the wooden door, and I inhale her candy sweet fragrance. It's like a drug, her scent, and I'm getting high the deeper I inhale her.

She rests her hands on my chest, her fingers hooking on the shirt pocket, tugging lightly. I borrowed the shirt from her brother because she was right—I didn't have the right clothes for the party, but Row hooked me up. Next time I come here, I'll make sure I bring clothes for every fucking occasion.

These damn Lancasters, they're pretty fucking fancy and I can't lie—being in their world is intoxicating. Almost as intoxicating as the girl I've got in my arms. The opulence, the history, the absolute joy they all have in celebrating each other in a giant way—it's unmatched. My parents and family, we get along great. But we're all scattered to the wind as careers and lifestyles have sent us to all parts of the country. I miss spending time with my cousins and my aunts and uncles. We need to do it more.

We need to do it up right like the Lancaster family.

But I shove all thoughts of family and parties and celebrating away when I feel Willow shift in my arms, her hands going to the center of my shirt, her fingers pausing on the top button. Hesitant. Asking a silent question.

I'm impressed by her bravery. This is a very un-Willow move, but I'm not about to stop her as she slowly but surely unbuttons my shirt, until it's hanging open and she's pushing the fabric aside, her hands landing on my ribs, her fingers splaying. As if she's trying to touch every inch of my skin she can reach.

"You're so warm," she whispers. "And hard."

My dick gets harder at hearing her say that word and I kiss her. Devour her with my mouth and tongue and even my teeth. Nipping at her lips, sucking on her tongue, tangling mine with hers. She moans, the sound soft and sweet, sending a ripple of awareness through my blood. I drop my hands lower, reaching for her, and she immediately understands what I want, going with me as I lift her up, my hands cupping her ass. She winds her legs around my hips, anchoring herself to me and I shift closer, pressing my erection against her so she can feel what she's doing to me.

"Oh God," she gasps against my lips, tilting her hips upward, the fabric of her dress riding up.

I break away so I can see her, my gaze eating her up. Whatever panties she's got on aren't much. The fabric is thin and drenched. I can feel her wetness rub against the front of my pants and fuck.

I want to take them off.

Instead, I kiss her for long, tongue-filled minutes, letting my hands wander all over her. The dress she wore tonight should be fucking criminal. Innocent and sexy all at once, which is the perfect description for Willow. At one point, I gently tug at the front of her dress, my fingers curling around the neckline, brushing against the soft skin of her tits, and she pulls away from my lips. Her breaths are coming fast, her entire body trembling, and when I press my index finger into the hollow spot where her breasts meet, her eyes fall closed, her voice so quiet I almost can't hear her.

"I-I've never done this before."

Her confession and how nervous she sounds is sweet. It also fills me with the need to make this moment special for her. A night she'll never forget.

"I won't do anything you don't want to do," I reassure her, removing my fingers from the front of her dress to cup the side of her face. Her eyes crack open, her gaze dazed and full of wonder when I lean in and brush her lips with mine. "Tell me to stop and I will."

"I don't think…I want you to stop anything," she admits.

Those are words she should say cautiously. The wrong guy would have her bent over the bed and fucking her from behind without hesitation. Not that I don't want to do that, I fucking do, but I'm not going to rush this.

"What have you done, princess?" I kiss her cheek. Her jaw. Her ear, her neck—that spot where it meets her shoulder, where her pulse thrums wildly. "Tell me."

"Nothing." Her hands slide down my chest, landing on the waistband of my khakis. She hesitates there before curling her fingers around the front beltloops and giving them a tug. "Kissing, but it's never felt like this. That's it."

Just kissing. Meaning, she hasn't done shit.

"Can I ask you a question?" When she nods, I forge on. "How did you get to eighteen and there hasn't been one guy who's tried to feel you up?"

She laughs, the sound soft and almost shy. Maybe even a little embarrassed. "I don't know. I don't think guys are attracted to me. At least, not the guys I've been around."

I actually snort. "I don't believe it."

"Maybe I scare them? Being a Lancaster also has disadvantages." She sounds sad about that tiny fact.

Me though? I love that all of these assholes haven't tried anything with her. Their opportunity lost is my advantage gained.

"I'll go slow." I kiss her again, unable to resist her plump lips. I could kiss her all night. She'd probably be more than okay with that idea, but I also want more.

So much more.

"I know you will." She pulls away some, a tentative smile on her face. "How much more time do you think we have?"

I frown at her, confused. "What are you talking about?"

"We're supposed to meet Iris and Brooks at the hot tub. Do you think they're there already? You have a view of the backyard." She shoves lightly at my chest and I let go of her, her feet dropping to the floor as she slips from between me and the door, heading to the window.

I watch her go, resting one hand on my hip while I run my other hand through my hair, trying to calm my racing heart. She pauses in front of the window, pushing back the curtains with both hands, the light from outside outlining her figure. My greedy gaze drinks her in, how her skirt is slightly wrinkled and rises higher than normal, offering me a glimpse of the back of her thighs. The very thighs I had my hands on not even seconds ago.

I want to get my hands back on them again.

"The party is clearing out," she announces, her gaze stuck on the terrace below. "Looks like most of Pru and Paris's guests are gone."

Is she so nervous that she's stalling? Probably.

"Do you see Iris or Brooks?"

"No." She shakes her head but doesn't look at me, her gaze still stuck on the window. Her hands still curled around the silk curtains, keeping them apart. "I thought I heard them in Iris's room when we walked past the door."

I heard that too. The giggle and the groan. I'm sure they're having a great time alone together. The hot tub meeting might even end up forgotten if they get too carried away.

"Should I text Iris?" she asks.

"No," is my immediate response, making her glance over her shoulder at me. "We should probably leave them alone. Would you want Iris texting you right now?"

"I don't know." She visibly swallows and returns her attention to the window.

Oh yeah. This girl is definitely stalling. The nerves are getting to her.

I consider taking my shirt off but leave it on, approaching her carefully. Slowly. Until I'm standing directly behind her, settling my hands on the gentle swell of her hips, pressing my fingers against her flesh. I'd love to get rid of the dress. Get rid of my clothes. Pull her onto the bed and slide right into her, but that is moving way too fast.

I might have to settle with some dry humping, and I can do that.

I'll do anything for this girl. I wonder if she realizes that yet.

CHAPTER FORTY

WILLOW

I am so nervous, I'm visibly shaking. The only reason I've got the silk curtains in a death grip is because I'm hoping it's not obvious how much I'm trembling. I'm too much in my head, thinking all of the thoughts that go along with the situation I'm currently in.

Are we going to have sex tonight? Is it going to hurt? He promised to go slow. I felt his erection and it was…larger than I thought it could be. That struck terror in my heart and filled me with worry. Is this possible? Will he fit? Will he stretch me so wide that I'll cry?

Oh God.

See? This has the potential for disaster—my thoughts. My worry.

But then he rests his hands on my hips, shifting ever so close to me, and I close my eyes, grateful for his nearness. The solid weight of his body seems to keep me propped up and I lean into him, letting my muscles relax. Trying my hardest to shut off my overworking brain.

It's tough though. Those thoughts are on repeat and refusing to stop.

"Are you freaking out?" Rhett shifts even closer, his arms wrapping around my middle. He rests his hands on my stomach, my back plastered to his front, and I lean the back of my head against his chest, savoring the warmth and strength of his touch.

"A little," I admit, wanting to be truthful with him.

"Don't." His voice is low, rumbling along my nerve endings, settling them. Somewhat. "I've got you."

His mouth drifts across the side of my face, his lips feather soft and barely there. I lean my head into his, about to release my grip on the curtains when his command stops me.

"Don't let go."

I go still, uncertainty making me freeze. I don't know what he wants. Waiting for a signal from him. But he doesn't give me one. Instead, he moves his hands so that they rest on my hips, his fingers curling, slowly gathering the fabric of my skirt. Lifting it up, the cool air hitting my legs, making me tremble.

"What's happening now?" he asks, his tone conversational, his hands working magic on my skin. They slip under my dress, rough fingertips brushing along my outer thighs. "Outside at the party?"

"Oh." I choke on the single word when his fingers slide up, brushing over the thin waistband of my panties. "Um, most of the guests are gone. The catering staff is cleaning up."

"Think they can see you?" He slips his fingers beneath the waistband, touching the bare skin of my hips. "Standing in the window?"

"I-I don't know." I sway when he traces the waistband of my panties from my hips to my backside.

"Do you want them to see you?" Oh, his voice is a sensuous dare, one I've never heard before, and I feel as if I'm in a trance. Lost in the sensation of his touch, the words he's saying to me.

"Maybe," I whisper, nearly stumbling when he glides me closer to the window, my body pressed to the cold glass. It's a shock to my warm skin and I suck in a sharp breath, closing my eyes when he tugs on my panties, yanking them down my butt cheeks. Exposing me.

"This dress..." His voice drifts and he shoves at the fabric of my skirt, bunching it around my waist. My butt is completely exposed to his gaze and I'm both mortified and completely aroused at the same time. I don't know how that's even possible. "It's been driving me crazy all night."

"Really?" My voice squeaks with surprise. I felt good in it, but I wasn't sure if he really noticed.

"You ask that like you're shocked. Come on, Will. You know what you do to me." He presses his torso against my butt, letting me feel exactly what I do to him.

He's hard. Huge. My legs wobble at the sheer size of him and I hang on tighter to the curtains. His right hand slips around, cupping the front of my panties, his mouth right at my ear. "You're wet."

Embarrassingly so. His fingers gently press against my flesh, saturating my flimsy panties with my own wetness and when he starts to rub, my head falls back against his shoulder once again. I close my eyes, lost in the sensations of his busy fingers, and when he presses against a particularly sensitive spot, it's as if sparks light up my skin, spreading everywhere.

"Do you ever touch yourself like this?" he asks, and oh my God, how do I answer him? With the truth? "You can trust me, Will. I won't reveal your dirty little secrets."

"Y-yes-s." The word stutters out of me like I can barely speak. Or maybe that's because he's increased his speed, touching me harder. Faster. It feels so much better when he does it. When I can feel him pressed against me, his mouth at my cheek, my ear. His hot, panting breaths. He's enjoying this maybe almost as much as I am.

Or maybe not, because the way he's stroking me feels amazing.

"This morning in the shower, I jerked off while thinking about you," he admits, his deep voice vibrating within me. I'm tingling everywhere, imagining him touching himself. "I imagined doing exactly this with you. Making you wet. Making you come."

Oh. My clit is throbbing from his words and touch. I'm going to come. I'm so close.

"Spread your legs, baby," he demands, and I automatically do as he says. "And don't let go of the curtains."

He spins little circles atop my clit with his thumb. His index finger. And then he stops, sliding his fingers through my slick folds, his middle finger testing my entrance before pushing inside. I hold my breath at the sensation of him inside me. Even if it's just his finger, this feels like a moment. I remember vaguely what Iris told me. How there's no going back after this. The more you give them, the more they want, and eventually, you don't even care. You want to give them everything.

"Fuck, you're tight." His voice is harsh, his control remarkable. I don't know why he hasn't just flipped me over his shoulder and carried me back to the bed already. But it's kind of exciting, standing in front of the window with Rhett's fingers under my panties, searching me.

About to make me come.

I hang on the precipice, a moan leaving me when he withdraws his finger from where no one has ever been before. He returns his attention to my clit, rubbing it in quick little circles that has me panting, the tension radiating throughout my body making it a struggle to breathe. I tilt my hips upward, seeking more, needing more, and he gives it to me. His mouth is crushed against my ear, his breaths harsh, his fingers frenzied. I'm close. So close…

His mouth somehow finds mine in a sloppy kiss and the moment his tongue strokes mine, I'm coming. I gasp and moan against his lips, my head falling back as he presses against my clit. Wave after wave of sensation slams into me, making me weak. Dizzy. I let go of the curtains in freefall for only a second before his arms tighten around me, keeping me on my feet.

I sag against him once my orgasm subsides, trying to catch my breath when I hear both of our phones ding with a notification.

"I bet that's Iris," I murmur, allowing Rhett to turn me to face him, his hands on my hips. "She probably wants to meet us now."

Rhett glances down at himself and I follow his path, my eyes widening when I see his erection straining against the front of his pants. "I don't think I can go out like this."

A giggle escapes me when I picture him showing up at the hot tub with a tent in his swim trunks. I'm sure Iris would find it hilarious. And then she'd probably call me a lucky bitch.

I can literally hear her say exactly that.

"Do you need my help?" I reach out to touch him, drifting my fingers across his impressive length. He hisses in a breath at first contact but that only makes me bolder. I touch him more firmly, curling my fingers around him, trying to learn his shape despite the thick material of his pants.

"Willow..." His voice is a warning, one I don't take. With my other hand, I reach for the button, undoing it before I pull down the zipper, my hand automatically going to the front of his black underwear. He's even warmer with only the cotton barrier preventing me from touching his actual flesh, and I glance up at him, feeling powerful.

I did this to him. I made him hard and aching for me. The agony on his face is obvious and he grabs hold of my wrist, stopping me from further exploring.

"You don't have to do this."

"I want to," I say without hesitation. "Let's go to the bed."

"Should we check our messages?" His voice is weak. I want his resolve to be as well. I want him to do what I want, so I can do what I want to him.

"They can wait." I remove my hand from inside his khakis and shift away from him, heading for the bed. "Are you coming?"

My voice is a tease, as is my choice of words. He follows after me without hesitation, both of us sitting on the edge of the mattress, me lunging for him, my mouth finding his. I kiss him with everything I've got. All the pent-up emotion and passion I've felt throughout the night. The gratitude I want to show him for giving me my first orgasm brought on by someone else.

It was a delicious, life-changing moment. One I want to repeat with him as often as possible.

We kiss and kiss, rarely breaking apart, but somehow, he ends up with his khakis down around his ankles and my hand beneath his boxer briefs. Learning the shape and size of him and what he might like. Currently it's anything I do, but I'm sure he has preferences. Spots that feel better when touched than others. I want to learn them all.

I want to learn everything about him.

"Will you come like this?" I whisper against his always seeking lips. My hand is wrapped around his length and he's leaking all over my fingers. I don't know why, but I didn't realize men could be as wet as women before they actually come.

"Squeeze a little tighter and move a little faster—that'll make me come," he says.

I do as he suggests, my fingers grasping his shaft harder, sliding up and down. Our mouths fused, his hand on my breasts, tugging at the front of my dress with enough force that eventually they pop out. I can feel his fingers on my nipples. Teasing them. Pinching them and I swear I'm wet again.

"Oh fuck." He moans when I rub my thumb across his tip, my fingers squeezing. "Just like that."

I keep doing what he likes, his entire body going still—to the point that I swear he's not even breathing. I increase my pace, my movements jerky. Not practiced at all but I don't think he cares. He even settles his hand over mine, demonstrating what he wants me to do before he lets go and I mimic him, pulling away from his mouth, glancing down to watch.

When I imagined doing something sexually with a boy for the first time, I never thought I'd want to actually see anything. I figured I'd keep my eyes tightly closed and concentrate on feeling.

But there is something almost beautiful in witnessing this moment—the one I'm sharing with Rhett for the first time. How vulnerable he is, how real and raw and beautiful. His eyes crack open as well, his gaze meeting mine, and we stare at each other while I stroke him, our gazes both dropping when I feel that first spurt of liquid on my fingers.

He's coming all over my hand, groaning from the force of it, his body wracked with shudders. I watch in quiet fascination, my hand going slower and slower as he leans back, his hands braced on the mattress behind him, his erection still in my hands, pulsating.

When he's done, I carefully remove my hand, bringing my fingers to my face so I can smell his semen. This experience feels like a mystery revealed, a moment etched in my brain, one I will never be able to forget.

There's a knock on the door. A pounding really. It startles us both, our heads whipping in the direction of the door, and the handle jiggles, as if someone is trying to open it.

"We know you're in there, you perverts," Iris seems to breathe through the wood. Is she speaking into the crack between the door and the frame? Trying to see inside? "Stop fucking around and meet us in ten."

"I had nothing to do with this," Brooks calls as Iris gives the handle one more shake before giving up.

We remain quiet for a moment, sharing a look only when we assume they're gone.

"Your cousin is fucking insane," Rhett mutters.

"I know," I whisper with a giggle.

"You going to clean that up or lick it off?" Rhett arches a brow.

My cheeks burn. Even after what just happened and how bold I acted, I am blushing like a virgin. Which after all, I still am one.

Probably not for long though.

CHAPTER FORTY-ONE

RHETT

Twenty minutes later and we're in the hot tub with Iris and Brooks, who are both watching us with suspicious gleams in their eyes, sharing secret looks with each other every few minutes. They are sitting across from us, the warm water bubbling all around us, the lights from within the tub changing colors every few seconds.

Any remnants from the birthday party are gone, like it never even happened. The house is mostly quiet. No one else is outside with us. All is peaceful tonight, including me. Everything just feels right in this moment and I fucking love it.

Willow is planted firmly at my side, wearing another swimsuit. It's hot pink, not as skimpy as the green one she wore earlier, but it's still giving me all sorts of ideas. Those strings everywhere that I can undo. At her neck and back. Upon each hip. A few tugs and she'd be naked, and fuck, I'd like to see that.

Not right now though. With Iris and Brooks as our audience. No thank you.

"You two were gone a long time," Iris says, not about to let this situation go. "What were you up to, hmm?"

"Like I'm going to tell you." Willow cuts her hand through the bubbling water, splashing Iris, who only laughs. "You've disappeared with Brooks today more often than not."

"That's because I'm letting him fuck me every chance he gets," Iris says with a straight face.

Brooks says nothing. Just slides down the side of the hot tub, submerging himself completely underwater.

"You're embarrassing him," Willow chastises right as Brooks's head pops back up, water streaming down his face. He scrubs a hand across his mouth, sliding it up to push his hair back.

"It's cool. Whatever." Brooks leans back, spreading his arms out wide across the edge of the hot tub, his fingers toying with Iris's hair. There's an ease about them that makes me think they might've established what they are to each other, but who knows? They could be living in a bubble this weekend, and come Monday, it'll be back to reality. Back to Iris ignoring him or treating him like garbage, and Brooks begging for scraps.

I send a quick glance in Willow's direction, noting the contented expression on her face. I hope like hell that won't happen to us, but it could. There's something going on with Will, and she's not telling me what it is. I don't want to get too bogged down in those details either. Making myself depressed is not the move at the moment.

Guess I'll wait until we're back at campus. Maybe both Brooks and I are going to get dumped on our asses.

"You're quiet." Iris points at me, a smirk on her face.

"And?" I ask, keeping my voice even. Iris loves to call out people and make them squirm. I'm not falling for her shit.

"You're too quiet." She turns her fingers into a gun, making like she's going to shoot me. "I don't trust boys who are quiet."

"I'm quiet," Brooks reminds her.

"No, you're really not." Forgetting all about me, Iris turns her back on us and climbs onto Brooks's lap, rolling her hips against him. I swear Brooks's eyes practically roll into the back of his head. "Sometimes you're a little too loud, Brooksie."

Willow and I share a look and I grab her by the waist, making her squeal when I haul her into my lap, though I don't have her straddle me.

That'll send me straight into Bonerville.

"Do you think they're going to have sex in the hot tub with us?" I wrap my arms around Willow and hold her close, my mouth close to her ear as I whisper my question.

"I hope not," she whispers back, sounding vaguely horrified. "That is something I don't want to witness."

"We can hear you," Iris calls, her back still to us as she basically humps Brooks. "And no, I'm not going to fuck him in the hot tub. Not with you guys in it. Gross."

Willow glances up at me and I can't help myself—I kiss her. She responds automatically, her lips parting, allowing my tongue entry, which I take. I don't mean to get carried away but I do, and the next thing I know, my hand is beneath her bikini top, my fingers pinching her nipple—

"We can see you too," Iris calls. "Stop mauling her, Bennett."

I release my hold on Willow's nipple, removing my hand from her top completely while she readjusts it. "Sorry."

"I got carried away too," Willow murmurs, her entire face pink but I can't tell if that's from embarrassment or the steamy heat of the water.

"Ah, young love," Iris singsongs, leaning back against Brooks's arm. Her gaze shifts to me. "You better not break her heart."

"I think she's the one who's going to end up breaking mine," I drawl, dragging Willow closer to me. Her butt is nestled perfectly against my junk and I can still see it in my mind. Curvy and round and utterly squeezable. I didn't squeeze it enough when I had it bared in front of me earlier. Hopefully I can rectify that later.

"No, I won't," Willow says, but her voice is weak and I can't tell if she really means it or not.

I'd prefer to pretend she totally means it. That she won't destroy me because she could now. After what we shared, after what we did—I'm a goner. There will be no one else who could even spark my interest. All that matters is her.

We make small talk for a while and eventually, Iris brings the bottle of champagne out of hiding. Brooks opens it, the cork shooting into the air, making Iris squeal, and then she's drinking straight from the bottle, guzzling it before she hands it over to Brooks.

Once he's done, he passes it to Willow, who slowly shakes her head. "No, thank you."

I don't push Willow into taking a drink. I'm not about to make her uncomfortable. Instead, I take the bottle from her and take a long pull, the bubbles tickling my throat, the slightly bitter yet crisp taste lingering on my tongue.

"Why aren't you drinking?" Iris asks as she takes the bottle from me.

"I don't know." Willow shrugs, her gaze going to mine before skittering away. "I don't want to forget anything about tonight."

Iris grins. Brooks acts like he didn't hear her.

I gawk at her like an idiot, oddly touched.

She doesn't want to forget a single detail about this night with me, which reveals more than what she could ever say with words. She wants to remember this night, this moment.

I do too.

When the bottle is returned to me, I take a small sip, nuzzling my face against Willow's once I've passed the champagne on to her cousin.

"I don't want to forget anything either," I tell her, my voice low, my words sincere. I hope she realizes it.

Willow turns in my arms, facing me, her lips right at level with mine. Brooks turns up the speed on the hot tub, the bubbles coming louder and faster, and I realize I can't hear a damn word they're saying.

Not that they're talking to us. No, currently Iris and Brooks are wrapped around each other, full-on making out. I saw tongues and everything.

"Maybe we should leave so they can have some alone time." Willow sounds amused, though her gaze is vaguely worried.

I'm sure she doesn't want to witness anything either.

"We probably should," I agree, wrapping my arm around her shoulders. Her skin is smooth and wet, and I'd give anything to slowly strip her of the sexy bikini and worship her with my hands. My mouth. I'd go down on her if she let me. Eat that sweet little pussy until she was crying out, grinding her juicy cunt on my mouth and chin, her fingers tugging on my hair.

I'd do anything to make that fucking happen.

"There are towels in that deck box right over there." Willow inclines her head to just behind me and I look over at where she indicated, noticing the box. "We could run over there, grab some towels and go."

We both swivel our heads in the direction of Brooks and Iris, who are still wrapped up in each other. They're not noticing shit.

"Let's do it," I tell Willow.

Within seconds we're out of the hot tub, both of us shivering as she leads the way to the deck box. She flips open the top, pulling out thick, cream-colored towels, and hands one to me before she wraps herself up in one. They're huge, giving me the coverage I want since it's cold as balls out here and I'm shivering.

"Can we go into the house like this?" I ask. We're dripping wet.

"No one minds. Besides, we might dry off some by the time we're inside," Willow says. "Come on."

Within minutes we're creeping up the stairs, my heart in my throat because I don't know what she's going to do or say next. Tell me good night and go back to the room she shares with Iris? Follow me and let me guide her back into the guest room I'm staying in?

If she chooses the latter, she has to know what might happen. We might not do the actual deed yet, but I'm going to do something to her again. Whether it's with my fingers or my mouth or my dick, I'm going to make this girl come again.

I'm dying to.

CHAPTER FORTY-TWO

WILLOW

I can sense Rhett is waiting for me to make a decision—and I appreciate that he's leaving it all up to me. He doesn't try to coerce me into going into the room with him—instead he's giving me the power to make my own choice. And it's not like it's something he's *giving* me either. He respects me and my decisions, and I appreciate that more than he'll ever know.

It's almost as if he was made for me. Only me.

Some would call me spoiled, and I wouldn't argue with them. I understand that I live an incredible life of privilege, where I never have to worry about money or getting what I want—for the most part. But those are material things. When it comes to people, it's harder to trust, to share parts of myself without fear of judgment or worse, someone wanting to get close to me only because of my family and the wealth that comes with it. It's difficult to know who has your best interests at heart. I think of Alana and how quick she was to turn on our friendship for her own happiness. And now look at her, most likely miserable with Silas.

I suppose that's what she deserves.

Mulling over this makes me understand Iris's behavior even more now. Why she's so afraid to trust. To readily give her heart to someone—to break down those walls and let Brooks in. That's all he wants. He seems to accept her for who she is, but she still has difficulty seeing that and I finally get why.

Letting down our guard and letting someone into our private world isn't easy. People want to use us for what we can give them, for our status. If you're sincere, starting a relationship with a Lancaster can't be easy.

My gaze finds Rhett, my heart swelling the longer I study him. I trust him. I adore him. It's only been a few weeks that we've known each other but there's not a doubt in my mind that he would ever hurt me. I care about him, and the idea of that is thrilling and scary and exciting and terrifying.

"Can we go to your room?" I ask shyly, smiling.

The pleased look on his face makes my heart beat harder. "Is that what you want?"

I go to him, letting my towel drop with a wet plop onto the floor, and he opens his towel up, pulling me in closer and wrapping me up in his arms. I feel nothing but damp skin and hard muscles and I rest my hand on his stomach, noting how the muscles jump there.

"It's what I want," I whisper.

In a flash he's hurriedly escorting me to his room, opening the door with jerky movements and practically shoving me inside. I go willingly, turning to face him when he enters, reaching behind him to twist the lock into place. He tosses his towel onto the connected bathroom floor, stalking toward me with a serious look on his handsome face. His mouth is pursed, his eyes are sparkling with mischief, and I can't help it.

Squealing, I try to run, but it's no use. He catches me with ease, his arm hooking around my middle, hauling me close to him. I savor the press of his skin against mine, how hot he is, and when he bends down, he scoops me completely into his arms, cradling me as he walks me over to the bed.

"Put me down," I tell him, trying to put up a struggle, but it's pitiful at best. I'm enjoying it too much.

Rhett does as I ask though, dropping me onto the bed and

following after me, caging me with his big body. I'm pinned to the mattress by his bulky frame and I love it.

Winding my arms around his neck, I tangle my fingers into the damp hair at his nape, toying with it as I stare up into his face. He's so handsome he makes my heart ache. I touch his cheek and let my hand drift down, my fingers streaking across his mouth. He kisses my fingertips, the gesture sweet, and I rear up, pressing my mouth to his in a simple kiss.

"What was that for?" he asks after I pull away, dipping his head to nuzzle my cheek with his nose.

"I like you," I whisper, and it's true. "I like how you treat me."

"How do I treat you?"

"Like I'm breakable, but that's okay because you're there to put me back together if necessary." I smile.

Rhett does too. "I like how you put that."

"Was it corny?"

"No. It was kind of romantic." It's his turn to kiss me. "Are you implying that I'm the only one who can put you back together?"

"You're the only one who knows my exact fit." Oh, that sounds silly. I'm being silly, but it truly feels like that with Rhett.

Like he's the only one who understands me. Who sees me for who I really am.

"I'm totally rushing things, aren't I?" I ask, a little embarrassed. "Maybe we should change the subject."

"No." It's his turn to touch my face, his fingers firm when they wrap around my chin. "I think we're both rushing things."

I blink up at him, my heart in freefall. I want him to be truthful with me, but I also don't want him to say we should slow things down. I'd automatically assume that means he doesn't feel the same as I do and in this very moment, I'm overwhelmed with emotion. For him.

"Is that bad?" I whisper, fear tightening my throat, making it difficult to breathe.

Rhett slowly shakes his head, his sexy lips curved into the

faintest smile. I will remember that look on his face for the rest of my life, I tell myself. The way his eyes light up and that barely-there smile. "I feel the same way."

I kiss him again like I can't help it, my mouth finding his, my tongue sweeping in. The more I'm with him, the bolder I feel and I can tell he likes it from the groan that leaves him. His hand cups the side of my face, tilting my head back, allowing our kiss to deepen and I'm lost. Lost in a tangle of limbs and breathless sighs. My teeth nipping his lower lip—tugging and pulling. He seems to savor me, his tongue searching my mouth, circling around mine, his hips starting to move, surging against me.

He's hard and thick, and I automatically spread my legs, allowing him to settle more firmly against me. His erection nudges a spot beneath my bikini bottoms, making me see stars, and I lift my hips, seeking more. He responds, and in seconds we're grinding against each other, the friction driving me wild. Making me want more.

Too fast.

The words flit through my brain and I pause for a moment. Catching my breath, gathering my thoughts. Rhett kisses along my jaw, down my neck, nibbling and licking my sensitive skin. I'm trembling from his attention, from nerves, from the cold fabric of my bikini.

Rhett lifts his head, studying me. "Are you all right?"

I offer a quick nod. "A little nervous."

He rises up, his mouth finding mine again, kissing me lightly before pulling away. "I won't push. Whatever you want to do, Will, that's what we'll do."

"I know." A shuddery breath leaves me and I touch his face. "I'm getting too in my head again."

He kisses me. "We should try and fix that."

"And I'm cold," I add.

"Is that why you're shivering?"

"It's one of the reasons." I bite my lip.

"Let's warm you up." He drops his hand to my waist, smoothing his palm along my side before sweeping back up and over my chest, cupping my breast. "Your top is wet."

"I know."

"Should we take it off?" He's asking permission, his fingers massaging my flesh, and of course I nod my answer.

Reaching behind me, he grabs hold of the string tied at the back of my neck, gently tugging on it. It comes undone with ease, my top loosening, and within seconds, it's gone. Leaving me completely exposed to him.

"I imagined this," he admits, his gaze roving over my naked breasts. I've always considered them a burden. They're large, they're heavy, and my mom always sympathizes with me when I complain about them because I inherited them from her.

But the way he's looking at me right now, as if I'm the most beautiful thing he's ever seen, I don't mind them at all. And when he cups one in his hand, rearing up to press his mouth to mine while his fingers work my nipple, I cry out against his lips. A jolt runs through me from his touch, from my breast to my core, and I lift into his touch, seeking more.

He gives me what I want, sliding down my body, mapping my skin with his mouth. Kissing my neck, my shoulder, my collarbone. Across my chest and downward, running his lips over one breast, then the other, avoiding my nipples.

Driving me out of my mind with need.

When he kisses my stomach, a surge of moisture floods my bikini bottoms, and I imagine him kissing me down there. Licking me. Searching every part of me with his tongue. A shudder moves through me and I spread my legs even wider, accommodating his body as he lies there between my legs, tracing a circle around my navel with his tongue.

Teasing me again, he shifts back up, his mouth finding my right nipple this time, pulling it into his mouth. He sucks it deep and I clasp his head against me, my fingers buried in his hair. He teases the bit of flesh with his tongue, pulling away to deliver the same attention to my other nipple. Alternating between the two, licking and sucking and nibbling, making me writhe beneath him.

I want more. I feel empty, like I need him inside of me. Running on pure instinct, I slide my hands across his shoulders. Down the smooth expanse of his muscled back. His skin is hot and firm, and when I reach the waistband of his swim trunks, I only hesitate for a moment before I slip them beneath the damp fabric, pressing him closer to me.

He groans into the valley between my breasts, lifting his head to study me with lust-filled eyes. I'm sure I have the same look of dazed wonder on my face, my chest rising and falling in tandem to my rapid breathing. "I don't want to get carried away—"

I cut him off. "Don't worry. You're not."

Rhett returns his attention to my stomach, his mouth gliding across my skin, making my inner walls clench. He drops tiny kisses along the top edge of my bikini bottoms and I'm shivering. Dying for him to put his mouth on me. I didn't think we'd actually do this tonight but if he stops? I'll be disappointed.

I don't ever want him to stop.

He shifts downward, his hands going to the inside of my thighs, spreading me even wider and then his mouth is there, kissing one inner thigh, then the other. I can smell myself, and I know he can smell me too. I'm so turned inside out for him, I'm afraid I might come on the spot when he finally puts his mouth on me.

But he's a tease. Kissing the inside of my knees before he lifts up, rising on his knees over me. I open my eyes to stare up at him, my gaze dropping to his erection straining the front of his trunks. Reaching out, I touch him. Draw my fingers along his length lightly before I wrap my fingers around him and he undoes the string of his swim trunks, reaching inside to pull his erection out.

I stare at it, shocked by its size. The wide head and the pearl of pre-cum filling the slit. I touch it, swipe it up with my finger and bring it to my mouth, tasting him for the first time. It's faintly sour and I lick my lips, making him groan.

"You're fucking killing me, princess," he mutters, reaching for my bikini bottoms and tugging. "Let's take these off."

It's a blur after that. We both end up naked and when he lies on top of me once again, we're like a perfect fit. I can feel him nudge against me, seeking entry and again, I spread my thighs, allowing him to settle more firmly against me. He lifts up, curling his fingers around the base, and he drags his cock up and down, pressing against my clit.

"Oh God," I choke out.

"Feel good?"

"Do it again," I demand.

He does, sliding up and down, over and over, before he tries to slip inside. I tense up, my hands flying to his shoulders, holding him off.

"Not yet," I whisper, my gaze finding his. "Do you have protection?"

Rhett winces. "No."

"That's okay." I take a deep breath, exhaling slowly. "I don't know if I'm ready."

"You want to stop?" He sounds pained. He looks pained.

I shake my head. "We can do…other stuff."

"Yeah?" His pain switches to hope.

"Yes."

There's no hesitation. He resumes his search of my body with his mouth and I feel like I'm melting into the mattress, it's so good. He kisses me everywhere he can reach, touching parts of my body that I didn't think were erotic, but oh my God, it feels so good. The inside of my arm. The side of my rib cage. At one point he grabs my wrist, licking each of my fingers, and I want to die from how good it feels. From the look on his face. It's as if he wants to devour every part of me and I'll gladly let him. I want to be devoured. Worshiped.

Loved.

Maybe love isn't part of the equation yet, but I can feel myself falling for him and I'm unable to stop it. I don't want to stop it.

"You smell so good," he murmurs against my lower stomach, his mouth close to where I want it. I don't die of embarrassment when he says those words either.

And when he drifts his mouth lower, his tongue finding my heated center, a long, shuddery sigh leaves me. I'm such a cliché but…

I feel like I've died and gone straight to heaven.

CHAPTER FORTY-THREE

RHETT

Willow is so responsive. Her head thrashes back and forth as I continue to give long, wet licks on her pussy. And she tastes good, especially when I suck on her little clit. I've never gone down on anyone else before so this is a new experience.

I'm glad there's been no one else. Just Willow.

Working on instinct, I search her everywhere I can, teasing her entrance. Circling her clit. Licking her as far back as I can go without freaking her out because I don't want to go too far or do something that'll make her anxious.

She moans and shifts beneath me, her hands in my hair, guiding me where she wants me. I take her subtle hints, focusing my attention on her clit. Slipping a finger inside her but not going too deep. Testing her.

Pretty sure she loves it all.

It doesn't take long for me to bring her to orgasm, and when it happens, I pop my eyes open, watching her. Savoring the way that she lifts her hips and smashes her sweet pussy against my face. She's completely uninhibited, her keening cries letting me know she's coming, her entire body shivering from her orgasm. I keep licking and sucking until she's pushing me away with faint, almost incoherent protests.

Once I lift away from her, she rolls over on her side, her back to me, her body still shuddering. I grab my dick, giving it a few quick, short strokes, hissing in a breath. I'm so hard it's painful, and if this is it for the night, I'm gonna have to go into the bathroom and give myself some release. No way am I coming down from this any time soon. I'm as hard as a fucking rock.

"You okay?" I touch her smooth shoulder and she rolls onto her back with ease, smiling up at me.

"Yes," she whispers, flinging her arm over her face, covering her eyes. "That was…intense."

"Oh yeah?" I lean in and kiss her, and she touches my face, keeping me there so she can kiss me again.

"I can taste myself," she admits, her voice a low murmur that has my cock surging.

"Do you like it?" I lick my lips, then lick hers.

She nods. "I've never come that hard before."

"I've never gone down on a girl before."

Willow pulls away slightly so she can stare into my eyes. "Really?"

"Yeah, really. Did I do it okay?"

Her laugh is sweet and reassuring. "Definitely."

We're smiling at each other and somehow, I don't notice when she reaches for my dick, her slender fingers wrapping around my shaft and giving me a squeeze. Squeezing a groan right out of me, though I rest my hand on top of hers, keeping her still.

"You don't have to."

She flexes her fingers beneath my touch. "I want to." Her grip tightens. "Does this hurt?"

"Yes," I admit without hesitation.

Her expression switches to concern. "Seriously? Am I doing something wrong?"

I'm laughing, shaking my head. "No. It's just—when I get really hard and don't come, it becomes painful."

"You need to come then."

I'm impressed she's so causally talking about coming. I didn't figure she'd be that way. She's always so reserved. "I do."

"I can help." Her smile is sly. "Tell me what you need."

"Whatever you want to do to me, I'll take," which is the goddamn truth. I'm not picky.

Willow begins to stroke me in earnest, her movements jerky at first until she establishes a steady rhythm. When she's not looking at me, she's watching herself, staring at my pulsating dick like it's some sort of miracle conjured up by her vivid imagination. Or maybe that's my own vivid imagination talking.

It goes on for minutes before she lets me go, sliding down so that her mouth is at dick level, her tongue sneaking out for a lick. Just the tip.

My guttural groan is loud, causing her to glance up, her lips parting as she pulls the head of my cock into her mouth. I immediately break out into a sweat, imprinting this moment on my brain for all eternity. This sweet, sexy girl pulling me into her mouth for the first time. Her beautiful naked body on display, just for me. All of this is for me.

How'd I get so damn lucky?

She has no idea what she's doing so I encourage her, telling her to suck harder. Take it deeper. I push her hair away from her face, holding it there so I can watch because oh, what a fucking sight this is. My balls tighten and a tingly sensation starts at the base of my spine. I'm going to come. I'm close.

So fucking close.

When she takes me deeper than she's ever done, she hesitates, her tongue lashing around my dick, her gaze lifting to meet mine. I can feel her throat relax and then she takes me farther, until I swear I'm bumping the back of her throat. I jerk my hips, desperate to go deeper, and she suctions her mouth around me.

That's it. I come like a fucking geyser, unable to warn her when it just…happens. She doesn't move away or release me from her mouth. Instead, she takes it, swallowing it down, shocking me.

This girl is a constant surprise.

"Wow," she murmurs when the remnants of my orgasm are mostly gone. I'm still wracked by the occasional shiver and I roll over on my back, staring up at the ceiling as I try to control my breathing. My wildly beating heart.

"That was," I take a deep breath, releasing it as steadily as I can. "Fucking unbelievable."

She's bouncing next to me, pouncing on top of me with a big smile on her face. "Really? It was good for you?"

"The best." I smooth her hair away from her face with my hand, staring up into her eyes. Finding myself getting lost in them. They're so vividly blue and full of happiness. "I'm tired."

Her laugh is soft. "Me too. We should go to sleep."

"Stay with me?" I feel so fucking raw, asking her that. It's an unfamiliar sensation for me—vulnerability. I don't leave myself so open to other people, especially girls. I haven't met one who was special enough yet.

Until this girl.

Her nod is slow, her expression turning shy. "Yes."

We pull the covers over us and she snuggles close, her head on my shoulder, her hand resting lightly on the center of my chest. Right at my heart. We're quiet in the dark, my eyes falling shut, my breaths evening out.

"I don't want to go back to campus," she admits so softly I'm not sure if I actually heard her at first. "I don't want this weekend to end."

I feel the same exact way. Reality is right in front of us and I'd love to avoid it too.

But we can't.

Leaning down, I press my mouth to the top of her head, breathing in her delicious scent. "Me neither."

There's a hesitation in the air and I wait for her to say something, but in the end, she doesn't, and I can't help but wonder what that was about. What did she want to tell me? We never did discuss why she can't be seen with me on campus—she mentioned extenuating circumstances but what the hell was that about? I have no idea.

Honestly? I don't want to know. I want to live in my Willow Lancaster bubble forever. Even though I know that's impossible.

Fucking real life sucks.

CHAPTER FORTY-FOUR

WILLOW

Sunday night and I'm holed up in my dorm suite alone, thinking about tomorrow. How I'm going to have to pretend I don't care about Rhett. Anxious over how I'm supposed to reject him without hurting his feelings.

It's going to be impossible.

Only hours ago we woke up together and messed around in the early morning light. Making each other come with our fingers and mouths. Kissing each other so much, my mouth still aches and my body is tender. I miss him.

He's going to hate me.

And it feels like I don't have a choice.

I'm a distraction. I'll ruin him. I can see it now—it's painfully clear. He's completely gone over me. I sound awful, like my ego is ginormous and I'm thrilled by this turn of events, but I'm not. I almost wish I hadn't seen that dazed look in his eyes earlier, when he walked me to my room and kissed me soundly. I begged off spending time with him tonight, claiming I had a paper to write for American Government, which is partially true.

I just couldn't stand the thought of spending time with him in my room. The two of us alone. I know what would've happened. If he had condoms? We would've had actual sex. Intercourse. I would've given him my virginity freely with zero regrets.

But I couldn't do that to myself. To have him here and then push him away tomorrow would've been terrible. Spending time in my room after? Like torture. It's best that what we shared happened at the Lancaster estate. Not ideal, since I'll be going there for the rest of my life and the ghost of him will linger in the hall. In the guest bedroom. In the hot tub. At least I don't spend every single day there.

God, none of this is easy. Tears spring to my eyes and I close them tightly, fighting an internal battle. I will not cry.

I will not.

Eventually I unpack my bag and stow it away in my closet. I open my laptop and read over the rough draft of the paper that's due at midnight, tweaking it here and there before I send it off. I take a shower and wash my hair, wincing when I touch myself between my legs. It hurts, but not in a bad way. More like it's just a reminder that I had Rhett between my legs countless times and he made me come.

I want to feel him again. One last time because I just know that this is it. He'll be angry with me, but I refuse to be his downfall. I thought Westscott was exaggerating when he said I would be the biggest distraction for Rhett and he wouldn't be able to play well. At the time, his warning was almost ridiculous. I didn't think I was important enough in Rhett's life to actually be considered a distraction.

But it's true. I can feel it. I shouldn't have done what I did with him this weekend; I was being selfish. I wanted to know what it was like, to be the center of Rhett Bennett's world. And it was exactly like I thought it would be.

Magical.

Around nine there's a knock on my door and I go still, standing in the center of my suite. I was about to go to the bathroom and brush my teeth and pretend to go to bed, already knowing I wouldn't be able to sleep. There's too much on my mind. Too much to worry about.

Swallowing hard, I stare at the door, praying it's not Rhett. Secretly hoping it is. I'd let him come in. I'd let him kiss me. I'd let him take off my clothes and touch me everywhere and I'd probably even let him have sex with me. And I'd be a willing participant every step of the way because I care about him that much. I want him that much.

When it comes to this boy, I'm weak.

"Willow! Open up!" Iris bangs on the door, her fists heavy, and I rush toward it, turning the lock and letting her inside. She's muttering as she strides in, wearing a long silk nightgown like she's the heroine of some long-ago gothic love story.

She whips around to face me, the ivory silk skirt spreading outward, making her movements dramatic. So fitting. The moment she sees my face, she points at me. "What's wrong with you?"

"Absolutely nothing." I put on a bright face, but it feels so incredibly false. I let my smile fall almost immediately. "I'm just tired. What's going on with you?"

She forgets about my troubles and I'm grateful. I'd rather she focuses on herself right now. I need the distraction. "I've had a revelation."

Iris throws herself on my bed, gathering her legs underneath herself, her skirt swirling outward, covering most of the comforter.

"What's your revelation?"

"I'm in love with Brooks Crosby." It's a declaration, said loudly. Like she needed to do that to prove a point. "I am. I'm totally in love with him and I want everyone to know it. Even my parents. Even my *dad*."

The last sentence is the kicker for me that says she's dead serious. "Even your father?"

Iris nods, her expression solemn. "I want them to know. They might already know after this weekend."

"Did you talk to them?"

"A little." She shrugs one shoulder, her gaze growing distant as she stares at the ceiling above me. "I told my mother that I liked Brooks. That we were somewhat…involved."

"And what did Summer say?"

"She asked if I was using protection." Iris rolls her eyes. "All she cares about is that I'm not going to have a baby. Heaven forbid she becomes a grandmother at her age."

"I'm sure that's not the whole reason she said that. Besides, you don't want to be a mom."

"You're right. I can barely take care of myself." Her sigh is overly dramatic and so very Iris. "But wouldn't Brooks's baby be adorable? All of that dark hair."

Her dreamy voice and the equally dreamy look on her face has me shook. "You're in love with him."

She blinks, the dreaminess gone. "I already told you that."

"I can see it." Oh God, are those tears in my eyes? I try to blink them away but instead, they fall down my cheeks. "I'm so happy for you."

"Why are you crying then?" Iris's lower lip trembles. She too appears on the verge of tears.

"They're happy tears. I promise." More tears slide down my cheeks and then I'm crying even harder. She's crying too. I go to her and wrap her in my arms, squeezing her close. "Your mom said that to you because she was distracted. She had an entire party going on at her house and you hit her with, 'I like Brooks.' What is she supposed to say?"

"I don't know, but you're probably right." Iris sniffs, pressing her runny nose against my sweatshirt, and I try not to be grossed out. "I miss him."

"You rode back with him." We all rode back together, me and Iris crammed into the back of Rhett's Porsche, Brooks's big body folded into the passenger seat. At least Rhett didn't drive like a wild man, which I appreciated. I was nervous about it too because I remembered how he tore out of the driveway the first time I met him.

That moment feels so long ago. But so much has changed in such a short amount of time. Even with Iris.

"I know, and he said he had a paper to write for American Government. I don't know if I believe him." Iris pouts.

"I had to write the same paper. He's telling you the truth. Don't you have to write that paper too?"

"Maybe? I can't remember. It doesn't matter." She rises to her feet and starts spinning around, her skirt swirling about her legs. "I feel free and in love and it's the best feeling ever!"

"I'm happy for you." I try to infuse joy in my voice but…it's difficult when I'm feeling so melancholy.

Iris stops spinning, staring at me. "Are you sure you're okay? You look sad."

I promptly burst into tears at her questioning and she wraps me up in her arms, consoling me with soft murmurs while running her fingers through my hair. When I've composed myself somewhat, she pulls away slightly, her hands gripping my upper arms while she studies my face. "What happened? Tell me everything. Did Rhett do something?"

"N-no." I shake my head, a fresh set of tears flowing. "He's p-p-perfect."

"Then, what is it? I don't understand." Her confusion is evident on her face and I want to tell her so badly what's going on, but I can't have her marching over to Westscott's office to scream at him. I just can't.

"If I tell you, you have to promise not to do anything but listen." I stare into her eyes. "Can you promise?"

Her expression turns wary. "I don't know. Can I?"

"Probably not." I sigh and shake my head. "Then I can't tell you."

"Come on, Willow. You need to get it off your chest. Something is clearly bothering you. Just tell me."

I consider my options. Keep this secret inside of me until I burst and possibly tell the wrong person? Go to my parents? That won't make me feel any better.

Grabbing Iris's hands, I squeeze them in mine, putting on my most menacing face, which isn't that menacing at all. "Swear on Brooks's body that you won't tell anyone what I'm about to tell you."

Iris seems alarmed by my demand. "Swear on his body?"

I nod. "You have to, or I'm keeping my mouth shut."

"Oh, come on, Willow."

"Nope." I shake my head. "Swear on it."

"Fine." She sighs. "I swear on it."

"Say it."

"I swear on Brooks's sexy body, especially his massive penis." Iris throws her hands into the air. "You happy now?"

"Yes." Though I didn't need to hear about his massive penis, my God.

I launch into the story, telling her every single thing Westscott said to me that morning. How I am a potential distraction and he can't take the risk. How he threatened me to stay away or he'd make my life miserable. As if I'm not as important as the athletic program at the school. The more I say, the angrier Iris gets, and now she's the one who looks like she's going to burst when I'm finished with my tale.

"I cannot BELIEVE you've kept this from me." Iris's hands are curled into fists as she paces back and forth in my room, her face red, her mouth curled into a snarl. "Westscott is a fucking snake!"

"You're shouting," I tell her, my voice calm. "And there's nothing we can do about it."

Iris comes to a stop, glaring at me in disbelief. "You're kidding me. There is definitely something we can do about it. Does he know who he's messing with? We're Lancasters!"

"Right, and he's the headmaster who's trying to turn this school around. Do you know that before he started, it was on the verge of becoming a financial drain? They were losing money every year for the last five years." I did a little research on my own and discovered that interesting tidbit. "They were even contemplating shutting down the school."

Iris's mouth drops open. "This place is legendary. An institution!"

"It had become a financial burden. Westscott turned it around, specifically by bringing Rhett into the football program. Other families are now lining up to have their children go to the school and be a part of the program. Admissions are up. Tuition is up. Westscott is the reason for that. He's untouchable," I stress.

"He is not," Iris retorts. "Fuck that guy. I don't care if he's turned the school around and is making our family millions of dollars. He has no right to threaten you or tell you what to do."

"I don't want to hurt Rhett's potential career." I shake my head. "I could put it at risk. He needs to focus on football and nothing else."

"After what happened between the two of you over the weekend, do you really believe he's going to let you go so easily?" At the doubt that crosses my face, Iris snorts. "No, he's not. He's so gone for you, Willow. I saw the way he looked at you, especially today. Nothing is going to stop that boy from wanting to spend time with you. Not even you."

She's right. I know she is. "What am I supposed to do then? Push him away? Get Westscott in trouble and then Rhett will be mad I didn't come to him in the first place? I can't win in either scenario."

Iris appears genuinely stumped and I know it's because what I'm saying is true. I don't know how to win at this, not that *win* is the right word. This isn't a game, it's my life. It's Rhett's life too.

"You need to tell your parents what happened with Westscott," she finally says, her voice eerily serious. As serious as I've ever heard her. "They won't stand for it. What he did, and how he spoke to you, isn't appropriate."

She's right on that point. "Do you think he'll get fired?"

"Maybe." Iris shrugs. "He deserves to be."

Does he really though? He's a man in a panic, dealing with a teenaged girl whose family owns the entire school. He took a risk by threatening me, and it actually worked.

"I don't know how to tell them," I say, shaking my head. Now I'm the one pacing around the room.

"You pick up the phone and tell them everything, just like you told me. Or you FaceTime them." We both grimace. "Yeah, call them. It's easier if you don't have to look them in the eyes."

I check the time on my phone, looking for any excuse. "It's late though. I'll call them in the morning."

"It's barely eight o'clock. You know they're still up." Iris waves a hand at the phone I'm clutching. "Call them. I'll stay if you want me to. Or I can go. It's up to you."

"I hate that you came over here for advice and I made it all about me instead," I admit, feeling awful.

"Oh please. You didn't make it all about you. You have a legitimate problem and I just want to help you fix it. Besides, I didn't need advice. I just needed to tell someone that I'm in love with Brooks."

Her face, her entire being, appears to go soft with the admission. Like she's turned into a big fluffy white angel cloud now that she's in love.

"You really do love him, huh?"

She nods, her eyes wide and shining bright. "It's terrible. He's all I think about."

"It actually sounds wonderful." I think of Rhett. If I'll ever have the chance to fall completely in love with him. I'm already on my way there. But have I ruined everything?

"It is wonderful," Iris admits, glancing down at the floor for a moment before returning her gaze to mine. "Don't sit on this any longer, Willow. Tell your parents. And then go to Rhett tomorrow and tell him everything. You'll feel better telling the truth."

I know she's right and I nod my agreement, even though I'm still reluctant. And scared.

So scared.

• • •

"Darling, why didn't you tell us this sooner?" Mom sounds incredulous and I can hear Dad's deep yet ragged breathing. Like he's trying to get his emotions under control. "How dare that man speak to you in such a manner!"

"I understand why he did it though." I don't know why I'm defending Westscott—what's wrong with me?

"Do you? He has no business talking to my daughter like that." My father's voice is tight. I can feel his anger through the phone.

My parents are on speaker, taking my call together like I asked them to. And while it was terrifying to tell them everything, I also do feel better now that the truth is out.

"You're right. He shouldn't talk to any student like that, whether they're a Lancaster or not," I say.

"But you are a Lancaster. The school belongs to us. All of us. Our parents—your grandparents—have mostly retired, leaving the decision-making to us. Your uncle Grant is on the board of trustees. Once he hears about this, there will be hell to pay," Dad explains.

I close my eyes, dreading the idea of Uncle Grant hearing this news. He's extraordinarily grumpy, much like Whit, and he sees things as either black or white. No gray in between.

"Does it have to get to that point though?" Mom asks Dad.

"Of course." His voice is gruff. "What else is supposed to happen?"

"Perhaps you can talk to him and set him straight. You have such a persuasive way with words. Better than Grant or Whit," Mom tells him.

I hold my breath, waiting to hear my father's reply.

"I can speak with him. Want me to do it first thing tomorrow?"

"Only if you promise not to fire him," I say. "You can't deny he's been good for the school."

"Willow, why in the world are you so set on him staying after the way he spoke to you? It makes no sense." Mom sounds truly bewildered, and I suppose I can't blame her.

I don't know why I want to keep him here either. Maybe I don't want that responsibility of him losing his job hanging over me. I would feel terrible—terribly guilty. He truly did seem to be watching out for Rhett's best interests, though truly, they're Westscott's best interests as well.

"What he did was wrong, but I don't think it's worth losing his job over. I'm only eighteen, what do I know of these things? But it doesn't feel right. He's just trying to do what's best for the school."

"And for himself," Dad says grumpily.

"Right. For himself too, and for Rhett."

"You like him, don't you?" Mom says.

I swallow past the sudden lump in my throat. "So much. I care about him a lot."

My father actually growls. "He breaks your heart, I will break his wrists. I mean it."

"Crew!" Mom chastises. "You can't go around threatening the boy your daughter is dating."

"I can and I will. That little punk won't destroy my daughter's dignity if I have anything to say about it. I was a teenaged boy once and a rightful asshole about it."

Mom actually laughs. "Yes, you were, but you were terribly sweet. You didn't break my heart."

"Once I knew I had it, there was no way I would break it."

Oh my God, they're having a total moment right now.

"Guys, I love how romantic you two are, but we need to focus on the issue at hand," I remind them. "And please, whatever you do, whatever Rhett does to me, don't break his wrists. He needs them to play football."

"That's why they're the first things I'm going for if he does anything to you," Dad says vehemently.

"Crew..."

"Fine." He blows out a harsh breath. "I'll call Westscott first thing in the morning and let him know that I know. And that he needs to watch what he says and leave you alone."

"Thank you," I whisper, closing my eyes.

We talk for a few more minutes and then we finally end the call with plenty of "I love yous" and promises to talk later this week. I know Mom is curious about my relationship with Rhett and I'm sure she'll reach out sooner versus later. I don't mind talking about it with her, but I still feel so unsure. Things could change by tomorrow. I hope not, but they could.

Once I'm in bed and scrolling social media, I receive a text from Rhett.

Rhett: **I miss you.**

Smiling, I quickly respond.

Me: **I miss you too.**

Rhett: **Want to meet in the dining hall tomorrow for breakfast?**

Should I? Hopefully my father won't forget to call Westscott. I'm sure he won't—Mom won't let him. Meaning, it shouldn't matter if I spend time with Rhett or not. There's nothing the headmaster can do about it.

Me: **I'd love that.**

He doesn't respond for at least five minutes, making me nervous. And when he does finally reply, I'm surprised by his answer.

Rhett: **Turns out I can't. Forgot I have weight training and early morning practice tomorrow. But I'll see you in class? Maybe right before school starts even?**

Disappointment fills me, but I push past it. This is important to him. Football. Practice. Weight training. All of it. It's making him a better player and I need to support him in his passions.

Me: **I totally understand.**

Rhett: **Still miss you.**

Me: **I miss you too.**

Rhett: **You'll have to sneak me into your room one day.**

Me: **I'm sure you'd love that.**

Rhett: **Actually I know you'll love it more.**

He then sends me the tongue sticking out emoji.

My face goes hot and I smile.

We're going to be just fine.

CHAPTER FORTY-FIVE

RHETT

"Thank you for coming by so early in the morning to see me," Westscott welcomes me as I stride into his office. "Please. Sit down."

"I'd rather stand." My impatience is showing and I feel like a jerk, but I can't help it. This meeting was called at the last minute via a text from the headmaster—which never happens. I was tempted to say no, but how can I say no to my biggest advocate on this campus?

No way could I turn him down.

I check my phone yet again for the time, hating how this impromptu meeting is eating into my morning. I need to go to weight training. Warned Coach I'd be late because I was meeting with Westscott, and he was cool with it, but I feel bad. Plus, I don't want to let the rest of the team down. I have to lead by example. Meaning, I should be there.

"Anxious to get to practice?" Westscott seats himself behind the desk, leaning back in his chair as if he has all the time in the world.

"Yeah. I never want to miss it." I stress those last words, but he acts oblivious to my urgency.

"You're a great example to the team, Rhett. How was your weekend?"

I frown. Why are we making small talk? "It was good. Busy."

"Where were you?"

His tone is friendly, but there's something else to it that I can't quite explain—and it seems kind of hostile. Like how is it his business where I was this weekend? I checked out of school like I was supposed to. I'm not about to break any rules right now. Everything is riding on football and there's no chance I'm going to fuck it up by doing something dumb.

"Visiting friends." I hesitate, noting the flicker of annoyance in his gaze. "I followed the rules for check out, sir. Even my parents okayed it since they were here Friday night for the game."

"Of course, of course. I'm not saying you broke any rules or did anything..." His words die and he considers me for a moment. "May I be blunt with you?"

I flick my chin at him. "Go for it."

"You were with Willow Lancaster, weren't you?"

I blink at him, surprised he knew. How did he find out? "I was actually with Rowan and Brooks Crosby."

"You're suddenly friends with Rowan." The doubt in his voice is obvious.

"There's no sudden about it. He's the JV quarterback, I'm the varsity quarterback. He looks to me for guidance and I give it to him. We've grown closer because of it." I seriously shouldn't have to justify my friendship to this guy.

"I see." Westscott drops his gaze to his desk, his mouth working from side to side like he's got some sort of weird tic going on or something. "But Willow was there too."

I'm quiet for so long that he lifts his head, pinning me with his stare. "She was."

"Meaning, you spent time with her."

The words explode from my mouth as if I have no control over them. "What does it matter if I was with her? Like I said, she was there, yes."

He doesn't even seem that pissed that I sort of yelled at him.

I think he's pleased that I confirmed she was there. "Are you two—seeing each other?"

"How is that any of your business?"

His expression smooths out completely. It's downright creepy, how blank he looks. "It's my business because you're a student at this school, and a very important one at that. What you do and who you see matters to me. It's my business because *you're* my business, as is the football team."

"If this has anything to do with football, I don't see how." I'm shaking my head, baffled by the balls on this guy. "I'm doing what I'm supposed to do, so don't worry about me. In fact, the only one who's keeping me from my team currently is you for calling this meeting. Now if you'll excuse me, I need to go to weight training."

"No."

I'm already in front of his office door when his denial actually sinks in. My hand rests loosely on the handle as I slowly turn to face him once more. "What did you say?"

"I said no. I'm not excusing you. You're going to listen to me." He rises to his feet, bracing his hands on the desk. "Everything this school is doing right now hinges on your performance on the field. I'm not about to let my star player get distracted by a beautiful girl—a Lancaster—and mess up his chance at getting a full ride to a D1 school. This season is important not only to you, but to Lancaster Prep as well. Admissions are up thanks to you. Every teenage child from the wealthiest families across this country and the world want to play football—just like you. They want to *be* you. You've transformed the landscape of our athletic department, and I'll be damned if some girl who readily spreads her legs for you is going to distract your ass from playing quality ball."

Westscott is so worked up I swear to God he's frothing at the mouth like a rabid dog. He's even breathing hard, his hands splayed across the desk, his shoulders rigid with tension.

But I don't even care. My mind is still stuck on what he said about Willow.

Some girl who readily spreads her legs for you.

"Take that back," I say through clenched teeth. "What you just said about Willow. Take it back."

He pushes away from the desk, crossing his arms in front of his chest. He's a big man but I'm stronger and faster. I could totally take him. "I will not take back what I said because it's the truth. I know for a fact you returned Sunday afternoon and had Willow Lancaster in the car with you. That Rowan and your own brother rode in a separate car—driven by the hired help from the Lancaster estate."

I say nothing. The man is right. That's exactly how it went down.

"I've seen it on camera—the four of you spilling out of your vehicle. You, Willow, Iris Lancaster and Brooks Crosby. You and Crosby had your hands all over those young ladies." The disgust on Westscott's face is obvious. "How could you jeopardize yourselves in such a way? Tossing aside valuable practice time to spend it with *girls*."

He says girls like it's a dirty word. "What I do in my free time is none of your business."

"You're wrong." Westscott pounds his fist onto his desk, making the entire thing shake. "*Everything* you do is my business. My reputation is on the line, as is yours. I'd advise you to clean up your act and keep your dick out of Willow Lancaster until the season is over."

God, the way this man is talking to me. Talking about Willow...

Fuck this.

"Or what?"

He goes still, staring at me. "Or what?"

"Yeah, or what? What are you going to do if I don't stay away from her, huh?" I'm taunting him. Daring him. He's going to make me do something I'll probably regret, but I don't give a damn.

Fuck this guy. He can't do this. Boss me around and tell me who I can or cannot spend time with. Especially a girl who wouldn't harm a fly, who would feel tremendous guilt if she knew she was called a distraction. Who'd probably try to turn me away if Westscott ever approached her—

Wait a second.

It all comes together like the last remaining pieces of a puzzle, locking into place. Anger makes my chest tight and I curl my hands into fists, wishing I could pound his face in.

"You spoke to her about me, didn't you?"

There's that blank expression again. "What are you talking about?"

"I know what you did. I know what you're doing. You talked to Willow Lancaster and told her to stay away from me, didn't you? Did you try to make her feel *guilty?* Did you call her a *distraction?*"

My breathing is ragged, I'm so worked up. Just like he was only a few moments ago.

Westscott's face turns bright red, his eyes bulging. The man is seriously pissed.

"She told you, didn't she? I told her to keep quiet, and she went to you anyway and ratted me out. A girl like that can't be trusted, Rhett—"

"She didn't have to tell me. I figured it out on my own. Just now." My voice drips with disgust and this time I do open the office door. I can see his assistant sitting at her desk just outside his office, along with other office staff getting ready to start their day, and I pause, saying loud enough for them to hear, "And you won't have to worry about me anymore, because I fucking quit."

I slam the door behind me, so hard the windows rattle and the ladies jump in their seats. I walk past them, nodding in their direction, muttering a half-hearted *sorry* before I bail out of the office. I don't stop walking until I'm halfway across campus, stopping in the middle of the sidewalk, nothing but expansive green lawn surrounding me. There still aren't many people out here yet because it's so damn early and I've already rocked my fucking world with a couple of shitty choice words for the headmaster.

Fuck me, what did I just do?

With shaky fingers, I pull my phone out of my jacket pocket and hit the first number on speed dial. When I hear the familiar voice in my ear, I briefly close my eyes, grateful he answered on the first ring.

"Dad? I think I'm in trouble."

CHAPTER FORTY-SIX

WILLOW

By the time I'm headed to our English class, the rumors are running rampant around campus. Westscott and Rhett argued in Westscott's office. Rhett screamed *fuck you* at him before leaving his office. They got into a fist fight and the headmaster is now sporting a black eye. Rhett quit the football team, quit Lancaster Prep in general.

I don't know what to believe, but it's the last rumor that has me the most worried. Rhett leaving Lancaster Prep, leaving the football team?

I feel somewhat responsible for that. Would he blame me? Is that why I haven't heard from him? Is he in trouble? Did he actually hit Westscott?

No, he would never. He's not dumb. But would he quit the football team? That's the most important thing to him, hands down. It's what he's been working toward his entire life, so to throw it away by quitting the team, I just find it unbelievable.

What makes everything worse is there's been nothing but silence on Rhett's end. I haven't heard from him since late last night, when we texted for a little bit. I sent him a text after Iris informed me of the rumors she'd heard, but he never responded.

I'm completely in the dark and I hate it.

The halls are abuzz with chatter, and I swear Rhett's name is mentioned every other word. Mouths are moving and the rumors are growing, and I do my best to tune them out, but it's difficult. Worry gnaws at me and I regret eating that pesto bagel for breakfast. It sits in my stomach like a lead weight, dragging me down.

When I enter the classroom, it's mostly empty. The disappointment hits me like a punch to the jaw and I frown, glancing around the room like I might find Rhett sitting in the corner, waiting for me.

But he's not here.

I settle into my desk and check my phone for about the hundredth time, but there's no texts from anyone. Not even Iris. Sighing, I slip my phone into the front pocket of my backpack, my gaze jerking to the classroom door when I see someone standing there.

It's Silas.

He enters the classroom, his gaze on me the entire time as he approaches. I brace myself, fully prepared to fight back because I just know he's got something to say to me and I really don't want to deal with him right now.

"Hey." His voice is low, his gaze full of fake sympathy. "You doing okay?"

I smile brightly at him. "I'm great. Why do you ask?"

No one knows Rhett and I are together—and Silas definitely shouldn't know.

"You're…friends with Rhett Bennett. I heard he got expelled for punching Westscott in the face." Silas settles into the desk next to mine, shaking his head. "So stupid."

The rumor is so laughable that I do just that—laugh. And the way Silas is watching me, like I must've lost my mind or something, just has me laughing even harder. It takes me a bit to compose myself and once I do, I call him out.

"First, the story you've heard is just that—a story. Fictional. There is no way Rhett would punch our headmaster. He would never put his football career at risk like that," I say with all the confidence in the world.

"He quit the team. I know that much is true." Silas pulls his phone out of his pocket and taps at the screen, then holds it out for me to read.

It's a private story on a social media site from a student, who I can only assume is on the team with Rhett.

It's true. He quit this morning. We're fucked.

Rearing back from Silas's phone, I face forward, trying to hide my anxiety. "I won't believe it until I hear the words come from his mouth."

The classroom is slowly filling up, and Rhett isn't anywhere in sight. My disappointment grows, my stomach cramping with the realization that he's not coming, when the bell rings and Mrs. Patel practically comes running into the classroom.

"Sorry I'm late," she calls, zooming toward her desk.

Alana scurries in after her, glaring at me sitting right next to Silas before she settles into a seat in the front of the row. Mrs. Patel frowns at Alana.

"Are you changing seats?"

"I can pay attention much better up here," Alana says, loud enough for us to hear.

Whatever. I'm not even interested in Silas. I wish he wasn't sitting next to me.

Mrs. Patel starts lecturing us about *The Great Gatsby,* and I realize I haven't read a word of the book in days. I try to pay attention, but my focus keeps straying to the open door. I swear I see someone walk by that looks like Rhett.

Sitting up straighter, I keep my gaze focused on the hallway. A shadow appears and then I see Rhett's head, peeking around the edge of the door.

He's looking right at me.

Come out here, he mouths.

My gaze shifts to Mrs. Patel, who keeps talking like she's

never going to stop. I start tapping my foot on the floor, anxious to get out of here. I'm extra fidgety, to the point that the people sitting by me are sending me odd looks, and finally I can't take it anymore. I shoot my arm into the air.

"Yes, Willow?"

"Do you mind if I go use the bathroom?" I paint on my best smile.

"Of course. Go right ahead."

I leave my stuff behind except for my phone, slipping it into my jacket pocket. My gaze accidentally finds Silas and he's watching me with a disappointed expression, which makes me think he saw Rhett outside waiting for me.

Well, too bad.

Within seconds of me leaving the classroom, Rhett appears at my side, grabbing my hand and jerking me into a janitorial closet. The scent of antiseptic and bleach is strong enough to make me wrinkle my nose and it's so dark in here, my butt hits a rack just behind me.

"Rhett, why did you—"

He gathers me in my arms and kisses me, cutting off my protests. I immediately lose myself in his lips. His tongue. The thorough way he kisses me. He ends the kiss as abruptly as he started it, pulling away, raising his arm to pull on something.

A single bulb illuminates the closet, and I glance around before my gaze meets his. He looks very pleased with himself, which for whatever reason, irritates me.

Maybe it's because I've been worrying about him all morning. Or because I haven't heard from him and I've been quietly freaking out, thanks to all the outrageous stories spreading around the school.

Without warning, I give him a shove, and he goes stumbling backward, reaching out and bracing his hand on the wall to keep himself from falling into a giant garbage can full of mops and brooms.

"What the hell was that for?"

"I've been worried sick about you!" I take a deep breath, mentally telling myself to calm down. "Where have you been?"

"I'm sorry. I didn't mean to worry you. I just—" He snaps his lips shut and runs his hand through his already messy hair. I get the feeling he's been doing that a lot today. "I had to get my shit straight first."

"What happened? I've heard every story you can imagine. None of them I believe though."

"What have you heard?" He frowns.

"That you've been expelled, that you punched Westscott, that you quit the football team. Those are the worst of the rumors spreading."

He slowly shakes his head, scrubbing the back of his neck. "I didn't punch him, though I wanted to. And I definitely wasn't expelled."

"Did you quit the team?" My whisper is raspy, my throat closing up with fear. I noticed how he didn't acknowledge that particular rumor.

Blowing out a harsh breath, Rhett grips the back of his neck with both hands, his elbow bumping into a bottle of cleaner and almost knocking it over. "Sometimes I'm too impulsive."

"You quit?" Shock courses through me and my head goes fuzzy. "Oh my God, Rhett! Why would you do that?"

"I told Westscott I quit. Then I called my dad and he told me to go straight to Coach, which I did. I let him know what was going on."

"What exactly is going on?"

"I don't want to tell you." He shakes his head. "Makes me too fucking mad still when I think about it."

"Rhett." I take a step closer to him, resting my hands on his chest as I stare into his eyes. "What did Westscott tell you?"

His mouth thins into a straight line, his lips almost disappearing, he looks so angry. "He didn't have to tell me anything. I figured it out myself. He went to you, huh? Told you to stay away from me? Called you a distraction?"

I nod, swallowing hard. "Yes. He did."

"Why didn't you tell me?"

"I didn't know you that well," I start, but he cuts me off.

"You know me pretty damn well, princess. We've gone way past the point of casual friends."

"I know, I know." I take a step back, my butt hitting the shelves again, making everything rattle. "I tried to stay away from you like Westscott told me to do, but I didn't know how to tell you to leave me alone. Well, I tried but you were persistent."

His smile returns, and it's such a relief to see it. "When I want something, I go after it."

"I know," I whisper, smiling at him. The tension between us seems to dissipate, slowly but surely. "You can't quit the team, Rhett. They need you and you need them."

"I don't know what's going to happen with the team. Or with me." He winces. "I might get suspended."

"Why?"

"I cursed at Westscott. Said I fucking quit before I stormed out of his office, and man, he didn't like that. Plus, I talked back to him. I shouldn't have done that, but the questions he asked me..." His voice drifts and he shakes his head. "He had no right to dig for that information. He's crossed lines."

"Will he get in trouble?" I think of what I told my parents and how I didn't want Westscott to get fired.

"Maybe. I don't know. The whole situation is a mess. My dad wants to meet with him. My parents are coming this afternoon and we're all going to talk. I'm not sure what's going to happen." He grabs my hands, clasping them in his, interlocking our fingers. "You're not a distraction, Willow. Not even close. If I stopped seeing you right now, I don't think I'd be able to concentrate on anything else but you and how I could get you back."

"You haven't lost me." I rise up on tiptoe, pressing my mouth to his in a soft kiss. "I'm not going anywhere."

"I need you in my life." His voice is hoarse, as if it took a lot for him to say that. "I've never felt like this about a girl before. You're the first."

I throw myself at him, curling my arms around his neck, clinging to him. His arms come around my waist, pulling me even closer, and I kiss him with everything I've got. He returns the kiss with the same enthusiasm and we get a little carried away…

Until we practically fall into the shelves behind us, knocking a few cleaning supplies over.

"You need to get back to class," he murmurs against my neck.

"I don't want to."

"You have to." He pulls away slightly, slipping his fingers under my chin to tilt my face up, our gazes locking. "Gotta keep up that good girl image."

I roll my eyes. "I should've never said anything like that."

"Too late. You did." He kisses my forehead. "Don't listen to any of the rumors going around school. It's all a bunch of lies. I'll let you know what happens as soon as we get out of the meeting with Westscott."

"Are you nervous?"

"A little," he admits. "Dad told me to stay out of class today. Keep a low profile until we figure everything out."

"That's good advice."

"I think so too." He spins me around by my shoulders, reaching out to open the door. "Go back to class. Tell Silas hi from me."

I glance over my shoulder. "You saw him sitting next to me?"

"Yeah." His expression turns grim. "Tell that fucker to stay away from my girl."

"I can't say that." I loved how he just called me his girl.

"You can't? Fine, I'll tell him then." Rhett gives me a gentle shove and I exit the closet with him following after me. "Like I said, don't listen to the rumors. People will be talking mad shit about me."

"They already are."

"Right. Only believe what you hear from me." He hooks his arm around my neck and hauls me in close, kissing my cheek. "I'll see you later?"

"Yes," I whisper, smiling at him. "Text me."

"I will."

I watch him walk away from me, calling out, "Good luck!"

He flashes me that cocky smile. The one he gave me the first day I met him, out in front of the house. "With you on my side, I don't need any luck."

I smile, wishing I could tell him how I really feel, but this is way too soon. I can't be in love with him already.

Can I?

CHAPTER FORTY-SEVEN

RHETT

We're in a neutral space—my dad, mom and me, along with Westscott and a representative from the Lancaster family—Whit Lancaster, Iris's dad.

He's an intimidating motherfucker, sitting at the head of the table in one of the meeting rooms in the admin building. Mom and Dad are completely unfazed by him, making small talk while Westscott sits on the other side of the table, looking like he's sweating profusely. His face is red and his lips are tight, like he might have trouble speaking.

Whatever. I'm still so pissed at him I can hardly see straight when I look at him, so I avoid doing that at all costs.

Lancaster checks his phone, frowning as he taps out a quick response before he smoothly puts his phone in his pocket. Dude showed up in a three-piece suit while Dad is in his Nike track pants and a polo shirt with the NFL emblem on both. Not sure if he wore that on purpose or left work looking like this, but I don't mind. I like the reminder. My dad is a badass. So is my mom. She told me before the meeting that she was mad at Westscott and he took things too far.

Glad to know my parents are on my side.

"I thought my cousin Grant would be able to make the meeting, but it turns out he had an unexpected meeting, which means I'm the only Lancaster representative here today." He sits up straighter, a single brow rising as he contemplates Westscott. "Would you like to explain yourself, Claude?"

Damn what a shitty name. I'd want to be known as Westscott all the time too.

"You already know how I feel, Whit. This young man is important to our athletic team and the school in general. And while I understand that he believes I overstepped my boundaries and spoke to him in an inappropriate manner, I sincerely had his best interests at heart. Nothing more," Westscott explains.

"I believe you overstepped your boundaries as well," Dad tells him. "You have no business asking my son those personal questions. You can't tell him what to do during the weekend either."

"That's incorrect," Westscott says, his voice cool. "Any time a student is on the Lancaster Prep campus, I have the authority to discipline them as I see fit."

"You see, Claude, that's part of the problem. Mr. Bennett here was on my property for the weekend," Whit says, inclining his head toward me. "When he's off campus, he's not your issue."

Westscott clamps his lips together, like he's trying to prevent himself from saying something stupid. "Can't you see that everything I'm doing is for the betterment of this establishment? I'm trying to turn this place around and make it a better school. You are a part of that plan, Rhett, and you're an excellent athlete and student. You're a great representation of this school. I'm only trying to watch out for you."

I dare to look at him, fighting the disgust I feel when I do.

"You told Willow that my parents asked you to do this," I throw at him, letting my anger show. That's one of the many things he said that bugged the shit out of me. "Which is a straight-up lie."

"I spoke with your parents privately, right before the school year." Westscott's gaze goes to my mom and dad. "Back me up here. This conversation did happen."

Dad exhales roughly, rubbing along the side of his jaw. "Yeah, we spoke to you. But you initiated the call and you told us, you assured us, you would watch over him. We didn't tell you to be his watch dog and decide who he can and cannot spend time with."

"You lied to her," I say again, because it makes me so fucking angry he tried to intimidate her. Actually, there's no trying about it—he did intimidate her. And that's some straight-up bullshit. "You said Willow was just some girl who would spread her legs for me. And you threatened her by practically daring her to go to her parents and tell. That they would do nothing anyway because all the Lancasters care about is the bottom line and you were delivering exactly what they wanted."

"You threatened Crew Lancaster's daughter?" Whit Lancaster's voice is casual, but I see the flash of anger in his blue eyes that are like ice. "You know her father is here on campus. Want me to pull him into this meeting?"

Fuck, this guy is cold.

Westscott's face turns pale. "I didn't threaten her."

"Sounded like what Rhett repeated was a threat. Are you calling him a liar? Are you calling Willow Lancaster a liar?"

I can practically feel Westscott scrambling to come up with the right answer. "No, of course not. They just—she just misunderstood me."

"Seems like there's been a lot of misunderstanding from you lately," Dad says, leaning forward to prop his arms against the edge of the marble boardroom table. "You know, I thought my son coming to this school would be good for him and everyone else too. Looks like that has come true, but I'm guessing with all of this attention the school is getting, you're power-tripping. Believing you're solely responsible for all of it."

"I do believe it," Westscott says with a sniff.

"And that just goes to show me how you don't know what it's like to be part of a team. You can't do this alone. There are so many moving parts. So many members of this team who've made this school better. But you can't even give them any credit. You want all the accolades and fuck everyone else." Dad shoots a look in Whit Lancaster's direction. "Sorry."

"No need. That was perfectly said." Whit leans back in his chair, his gaze never straying from Westscott. "You've really stepped in it, Claude. I'm afraid we're going to have to put you on administrative leave while we finish this investigation."

"Administrative leave? Investigation? What the hell are you investigating? What a great job I'm doing? How much attendance is up? How much more tuition the school is taking in? Don't even get me started on alumni donations. The money is pouring in by the millions every month. We'll be able to start construction on the new stadium in the spring!"

"Keep this up and there won't be anything else to investigate. You'll be fired." Lancaster glances over at us. "I'm sorry this happened, and that you just had to listen to that little tirade. The board of trustees will investigate this matter further and let you know what we've decided. Rhett, you'll still be on the football team if you want to be."

"I want to be," I say without hesitation. "But am I going to get into any trouble?"

"Trouble?" Whit asks. "Why would you be in any trouble?"

Mom sends me a look, one that says don't open your mouth, and I take it to heart.

"Just asking." The relief that hits me has me slumping in my seat. "I'm good. We're good."

We all shuffle out of the meeting room, leaving Westscott in there alone with Whit, and the moment we're outside, Dad is breathing a sigh of relief.

"I wouldn't want to be that guy, alone with Whit Lancaster." Dad mock shivers. "He's scary."

"He's not that bad," Mom murmurs. "Very handsome."

"Oh, you like that type now?" Dad wraps his arm around Mom's shoulders, hauling her in close. She digs her elbow into his side, pretending to try and get away, but she gives in quickly, letting him wrap her up in his arms. "He's intimidating."

"He is," I agree, ignoring my parents. They always do this sort of thing. I just never expected them to act like this while we're walking across campus, but whatever. "I seriously thought I was going to get suspended."

"Glad you kept your mouth shut." Mom sends me a pointed look.

"Yeah, good call."

We make small talk as I walk with them out to the guest parking lot and Dad promises to talk to my coaches. Mom gives me a big hug when we stop by the rental car they drove over. They have a flight they need to catch in about four hours so they need to get going.

"Are you sure you're okay with us leaving?" Mom stands in front of me, standing on her tiptoes to brush the hair away from my forehead since she's such a shrimp.

"Yeah, Mom, I'm not a baby." Though I gotta admit, I kind of like it when she babies me. "I'll be fine."

"You like this girl, don't you?" Mom murmurs. It's not a question. She can see it. Feel it.

"I do." My chest gets tight just thinking about Willow. "I hate how he talked to her. And about her."

"It wasn't right," Mom agrees. "I like seeing you rush to her defense. How protective you feel. Reminds me of your father. He was the same way. Still is."

"I'm what?" Dad asks, approaching us. "The love of your life?"

"Yes, that's true, but you've always been very protective of me." Mom circles her arm through Dad's, leaning her head on his shoulder. "And I've always loved that."

"I protect what's mine," Dad says, his gaze sliding to me. "I'm guessing you're feeling the same way about that girl?"

Mom lightly slaps his arm. "She's not just that girl. Her name is Willow."

"I care about her, yeah," I say, my throat thick with a weird emotion. I swallow it down, rubbing at my chest. "I care about her a lot."

"Have you told her that?" Mom asks.

"No." I'm a little uncomfortable talking about this—about Willow. Maybe because I never really have yet. "It feels too early."

"It's never too early," Mom says. "If you feel a certain way about her, you should tell her."

"Are you for real right now?" Dad asks, sending her a questioning look. "You were always trying to push me away at first."

"You scared me with your big feelings and I didn't know how to tell my family we were seeing each other." Mom shrugs. "It's mostly Jake's fault. I didn't want to make him mad."

"Motherfucker," Dad mutters, shaking his head. His so-called rivalry with my uncle is family legend. They still play it up all these years later and I think it's kind of hilarious.

"Look, I'll talk to Willow when it feels right," I tell my parents. "That might be soon. That might be later. I'm not sure yet."

"Don't wait too long," Dad says, his demeanor turning serious. "Listen to your mom. It's better to be straight up from the start than keep things from her. What if you miss your chance?"

His words send a streak of terror through me and I stand up straighter, having a total realization. "I'm not about to lose my chance with Willow."

Dad smiles, and for a second there, I feel like I'm looking into a mirror. "That's my boy."

CHAPTER FORTY-EIGHT

WILLOW

It's after school and I'm doing something I've never done before. Going to football practice.

Thankfully, I'm not going alone. Iris is tagging along because of course she is. She and Brooks are basically out as a couple. He sat with us at lunch today and they walked to classes together holding hands. If that isn't telling the world that you're together, I don't know what is.

I wish Rhett and I could do that. Maybe we will here soon. He needs to show up for class though first.

One step at a time, I guess.

We climb the bleachers and sit about halfway up, right on the fifty-yard line. There aren't as many girls here as there were when school first started and I'm relieved. I don't want to fight for attention amongst the Rhett Bennett fan club, but I do have the advantage of being the only girl he's interested in, so I try my best to remember that.

Even if there are a couple of girls surrounding us who are cheering him on. I can't get mad or jealous.

Okay, I'm not mad, but I am the teeniest bit jealous.

Iris kicks back, propping her arms and back onto the bench above us and stretching her long legs out as she keeps her gaze focused on the field. "I can't believe I'm dating Brooks Crosby. I used to draw monster pictures with crayon in elementary school and then name them Brooks."

I burst out laughing. "You did not."

"I so did. He drove me bonkers. He still does." Her smile is soft, her gaze going hazy. "He's such a good kisser though. Who knew?"

Shaking my head, I scan the field until I find Brooks, who's currently doing some sort of weird dance that looks extra goofy considering his size. "He's silly."

"He makes me laugh." Iris is watching him too. "I like that he's silly."

"You need silly. Sometimes you're a little too serious." I pause. "Well, serious isn't the right word. You're too..."

"Dramatic," she supplies for me. "He takes me down a notch, which I need. I like that about him. I like a lot of things about him."

I make like I'm going to cover my ears with my hands. "If you say anything about particular body parts or how good he is with them, I'm going to scream."

"Ha! I won't torture you out here in public." She glances around at the smattering of girls and guys sitting in the stands. "I don't want anyone knowing how good I've got it. He seems to cruise under the radar. Unlike your guy."

My heart warms at hearing Rhett referred to as my guy, though I don't love everything she said. Not like she's lying though. Rhett definitely brings a lot of attention on himself. He's the current face of the athletic department. Feels like everyone is watching him at all times, and I wonder if he hates that.

I'm sure he does. It's a lot of pressure.

"Where is he?" Iris asks when I remain quiet. "I figured he'd show up to practice. If he doesn't, those quit the team rumors will really gain some legs."

"I'm surprised there aren't more people out here to see if he'd show up," I mumble.

"You didn't answer my question."

A sigh leaves me and I lean in close, lowering my voice. "He had a meeting with Westscott and his parents. Oh, and someone from the board of trustees."

Iris's brows shoot up. "I wonder if it was your uncle Grant. He is the president, you know."

"I'm not sure." I didn't even think about that. Uncle Grant is just as grumpy as Iris's dad. Together those two are a force most don't want to reckon with.

"I bet Westscott gets fired."

"I would feel bad if he did."

"Look, Willow, you're not responsible for his behavior. He's the one who threatened you. Who butted into your personal business and tried to tell you what to do. He has no right to do that, and if he gets in trouble and gets fired, then that's on him. Not you." Iris's eyes blaze with anger, and I can't lie, I'm shocked by her outburst.

But I'm also realizing she's just speaking the truth.

"Fine. You're right." My gaze goes to the sidelines, wishing Rhett was standing there. I need to see him. I go a couple of hours without him and I feel like a junkie needing her fix. "He's a jerk."

"That's putting it mildly."

"And if he gets fired, I have nothing to do with it." I'm saying this like I need to hear it, which I do. "He brought it on himself."

"Exactly." All the boys on the field start yelling and we both turn our heads to see what's going on.

My heart trips over itself when I see who's joined them out on the field.

It's Rhett. All of his teammates surround him, celebrating his return, even though he never really left, and I can't help but smile as I watch him. He's smiling and laughing as they all crowd him, one of their coaches eventually blowing his whistle to get them to break up and get back to practice.

Within minutes he's out on the field, throwing the ball to Brooks, who catches it with ease. I watch them, impressed with how far he can throw the ball, and how Brooks catches it every time. They're good together, which is kind of fun.

Me and my best friend have fallen for best friends. How convenient is that?

"I love watching them play together," Iris murmurs, like she's in my head and knows what I'm thinking.

"I do too." I send her a quick smile. "They're good."

"So good." Iris nods. "You going to talk to Rhett after practice?"

"Definitely."

"I'll distract Brooks so you can have Rhett all to yourself."

"I think you're making that offer because you want Brooks all to yourself."

Iris giggles. "Busted. You caught me."

"I don't blame you." My gaze returns to the field.

I want Rhett all to myself too.

• • •

I wait for him by the stadium gates alone. Iris and Brooks already left together, and Brooks let me know Rhett was talking to the coaching staff, but he'd be out soon.

Girls study me with curiosity in their eyes as they reluctantly leave the stadium, and I know they're wondering why I'm here, and why I'm waiting. They have no idea how important Rhett has become to me in such a short amount of time, and I can't wait to let everyone know we're actually together.

Hopefully, Rhett wants the same thing. I'm pretty sure he does, but there's always that hint of doubt that lives inside me. I worry a lot about everything, and most of the time, it's like I can't help it.

Leaning against the chain-link fence, I check my phone, bored. Anxious. Eager to see him. And when he finally appears, clad in a pair of navy sweatpants with the Lancaster Prep logo stitched on it and a gray T-shirt that says Lancaster Lions across the front, the relief that floods my body at seeing him leaves me weak.

And excited. So, so excited.

When he spots me, a slow, confident smile spreads across his handsome face and I don't even think. I just run toward him, breathless when he pulls me into his arms and holds me close, his hands landing on my butt and hauling me closer. I'm laughing, and then he's kissing me, not caring if there are people around, not giving a crap who might see. I return the kiss with all of the emotion I can pour into it, wanting him to know how much I missed him, even though I saw him only a few hours ago.

It still felt like a long time, with uncertainty hanging over us, and I hated that.

"Someone's glad to see me," he murmurs against my lips once he breaks the kiss.

Reaching up, I touch the corner of his mouth, unable to resist. "I could say the same thing."

He squeezes my butt, somehow pulling me even closer to him. "Felt good to be out there, knowing you were watching me."

"Did it? You saw me?"

"Baby, I couldn't miss you. My eyes go to you every time we're near each other. Don't you realize that?"

His words make my heart feel like it's going to take flight straight out of my chest. I wrap my arms around his neck, pressing my lips to his skin, breathing him in. "You say the best things."

"Just telling the truth." He kisses my cheek and then pulls away. "Want to get out of here?"

I frown. "Where do you want to go?"

"I was thinking your room." He shrugs, playing it cool. "If you want."

I want, I want, I want.

"Sure." I pull out of his arms and grab his hand. "Let's go."

Much like Iris and Brooks walked around campus hand in hand, Rhett and I do the same. It feels good, having his fingers curled around mine, occasionally bumping into each other as we walk like we can't help ourselves. Which I can't. I want to be close to him always.

By the time we're walking into my dorm suite, I'm full of anticipation, dying to feel his hands and mouth on me again, but instead, he starts wandering around the room, checking everything out.

"You're not messy," he observes as he studies the top of my desk, where everything is neatly in its place. Much like the rest of my room.

"I leave that up to Iris."

He goes to the window and stares out at the view of the caretaker's cottage and gardens in the distance. It's a great view—not that I'm trying to spy on the caretaker, but I love all the roses that bloom there. They're as beautiful as the ones in the garden behind the library.

"I bet you're sad you can't see any statues out there," he says, turning to face me with a big smile on his face. "You miss Ezekiel?"

"Absolutely not." I lunge for him like I have no control over myself, throwing myself at him and tugging his head down so his mouth is on mine. "I missed you though."

"I missed you too."

We lose ourselves in the kiss, our tongues sliding against each other. He groans. I whimper. His hands are everywhere, mapping my body, trying to touch actual skin. Without hesitation, he slips his hands beneath my skirt, palming my panty-covered butt, and I end the kiss, trying to catch my breath.

"Sorry," he says, not sounding sorry at all. "I get you alone and this is all I can think about."

"What exactly are you referring to?" I'm pretty confident I know what he means. I just need to hear him say it.

"Getting my hands on you. Stripping you naked." His smile is sheepish. "But if you're not ready for any of that…"

I step forward, clapping my hand over his mouth and silencing him. "I'm ready for it."

When I drop my hand from his face he asks, "Are you sure?"

Nodding, I go to my nightstand and pull open the top drawer, pulling out a box of condoms. “I’m fully prepared.”

The expression on his face tells me I shocked him. “Where did you get those?”

“Brooks. Well, Iris got them for me. When she told him they were for us, he gave her an entire box.”

Rhett doesn’t come closer. It’s almost as if he’s keeping away from me on purpose. “Are you sure, princess? We can do other stuff if you want.” His grin is wicked. “I’m always up for the other stuff too.”

I am as well, but…

“I’m ready.” My voice is soft. I’ve never been surer of anything in my life. “I mean, we need to lead up to it. I don’t think I want you to pounce.”

He smiles. Kisses me.

And then he pounces.

CHAPTER FORTY-NINE

RHETT

We end up on the bed together, Willow pinned beneath me, our mouths fused, my hands wandering all over her. I want to touch her, consume her, make her come, see that pleasure wash over her face when the orgasm hits her. I want all of it, right now, with Willow.

The day was torture. I feel like I've lived a thousand lives since I woke up this morning to a text from Westscott asking if we could "chat for a minute." Everything that's happened since has blown my mind. My parents were even here for a bit.

Wild.

Can't think about any of that right now though. Not when I've got the girl of my dreams in my arms, her sexy as fuck body wiggling beneath mine. She's still in her uniform, even the jacket, and I lift away from her, tugging on the sleeve.

"We need to get all of this off of you," I demand.

She lifts up, contorting her body into awkward positions to get the jacket off, and when she does, I'm flinging it onto the floor, diving in for another kiss while my hands fall to the front of her button-up shirt. With fumbling fingers, I undo each one, my fingers brushing against her skin, making her shiver. When I've finally got the shirt open, I pull away so I can look at her. How beautiful she is, her white, lacy bra barely containing her breasts. I trace a finger along her cleavage, slipping it beneath the fabric of her bra, and she tilts her head back, her eyes falling closed.

"You're gorgeous," I whisper, mesmerized by the texture of her skin. I want to touch her for hours, learn every single little part of her.

Goosebumps rise on her skin when I run my finger along the lacy edge of her left bra cup, then the right. And when I slip my hand beneath her back and undo the clasp, she helps me get rid of it, hurriedly detangling the straps from her arms before she lies back onto the mattress, on full display for me.

Her rosy nipples are hard and I bend my head over her chest, licking at one, then giving the same treatment to the other. She whimpers, thrusting her chest upward, seeking more and I give it to her, sucking one nipple deep into my mouth, swirling my tongue around it before I gently clasp it in between my teeth and press down.

She hisses in a breath and I release it immediately, sucking and nibbling on her other nipple, dividing my attention equally between both breasts. I could do this for hours too, encouraged by her responsiveness. She likes it. She has to from the way she's grabbing at the back of my head, her fingers tugging on my hair, holding me close to her. I run my hands down her sides to her legs, flipping the heavy wool material of her skirt up, gliding my fingers along her smooth, soft thighs, and she automatically spreads them.

My girl knows what she wants. And I'm more than willing to give it to her.

Sliding down, I kiss her stomach. Along the waistband of her skirt, all while I've still got my hands beneath her skirt since the fabric fell back into place. I curl my fingers around the flimsy fabric of her panties, tugging on them before I slip my fingers into the front, encountering nothing but wet heat.

"Fuck me." I'm in awe of how wet I make her, how responsive her body is. Somehow, we get rid of the panties and I'm sliding my fingers between her thighs, stroking, the creamy sounds filling the otherwise quiet room and I concentrate my efforts on her clit. The more I rub it, the more she makes those needy sounds, and I lie there watching her face. Her eyes are closed and her hair spills all around her, her lips parted as she pants each breath. Her cheeks are pink, as is her chest, and I swear I feel a fresh gush of wetness coat my fingers when I slide one inside her body.

She's tight. And a virgin. I don't want to hurt her, but I assume I will.

Need to get her nice and ready for me.

Without warning, I shift lower, my hands sliding under her plump ass, pulling her to me as I settle my mouth on her pussy. She cries out, slapping her hand over her mouth as I lick her everywhere I can, my tongue searching every little part of her. Her clit throbs against my tongue and I draw tiny circles around it before I go lower, tongue-fucking her, my gaze going back to her face to find she's watching me.

I pull away slightly, giving her an exaggerated lick on her clit and a low moan sounds in her chest, her entire body stiff. Almost unyielding. I think she's close.

It goes on like this for long minutes. I add more fingers to it, fucking her with them, stretching her wide. Wider. She's absolutely soaked, and I hope like hell all of this helps when I finally enter her for the first time because I'm aching to know what it's like, to come inside of her.

"Rhett," she whispers, and just her saying my name encourages me to go faster, desperate to make her come. To know I'm the one who has this hold on her. This power over her. "Oh my God, right…"

"Right what, baby? Right here?" I suck her clit extra hard, two fingers inside her, and that's all it takes.

She's coming all over my face. My fingers. Her body quakes with the force of her orgasm, her soft cries making my dick ready to bust out of my sweatpants, and I keep my attention on her for as long as she can stand it before she's pushing me away.

I lift away from her, remembering how sensitive she was after I made her come the last time, and I climb off the bed, getting rid of my shirt. My sweats. Keeping my boxer briefs on to contain the beast so to speak, because I don't need to look like I'm going to fuck her immediately. I can wait. I'm patient.

Somewhat.

I rejoin her on the bed, watching as she gets rid of the rest of her clothes until she's completely naked, making me think of a flushed, naughty angel. I gather her in my arms, savoring the sensation of her skin against mine, and I let my fingers drift up and down her back, making her shiver.

"Was it good?" I ask, needing a critique.

"So good," she whispers against my neck, kissing me there. I grimace, reaching for my dick so I can readjust it. I'm throbbing, dying for some relief, but I need to wait.

No matter how difficult it is. I can do this.

"I'm sure you're suffering though." Her hand finds my cock, her fingers drifting over the front of my boxer briefs, and I grab her wrist, pausing her exploration.

"I am," I bite out. "You sure you want to go there?"

Willow lifts her head, her mouth finding mine in a quick, tongue-thrusting kiss before she pulls away to whisper, "Definitely."

That's all the encouragement I need to hear.

We resume kissing, her hand delving beneath my boxer briefs, fingers closing around my cock. I let her play with it, not giving her any guidance because I will take her touching me however I can get it. When she starts to stroke and eventually find a rhythm that has me rocking against her hand, I make her stop.

"Wha—" she starts, but she goes quiet when I lean over and grab the box of condoms that sits on her nightstand, tearing it open. "Oh."

Rising onto my knees, I open the condom packet and roll it on, grimacing when my fingers brush my sensitive, extra hard dick.

A shuddery breath leaves me and I tip my head back, closing my eyes. Trying to regain some sense of control. I think of boring things. Classes. Math. History. English. That dumb book we have to finish reading.

But then that makes me think of Willow sitting in front of me in class and how I dreamed of this moment. Now that it's finally here, I'm trying my best to prolong it, but I'm failing miserably. This is too much.

She is everything I could ever want.

When I crack my eyes open and level my gaze onto her face, I find her watching me, her teeth buried in her lower lip. She looks nervous.

"I'll go slow," I promise as I guide my cock toward her entrance, pausing there for a moment before I drag just the head up and down, like I did to her last time, which she seemed to like.

Willow doesn't look away as I tease her clit with my dick. She spreads her legs wider, scooting closer to me, and I know now is the time. I need to enter her as slowly as possible so I won't hurt her, though I doubt I'll be able to avoid it completely.

"Just do it," she encourages, her voice trembling. "Don't prolong it."

Under her encouragement, I push inside her, pausing when just the head is in. I'm immediately enveloped in tight heat and I wait there, letting her adjust, letting me regain some control so I don't do something stupid like come all over her thighs.

Fuck, this is rough.

Eventually I push in farther, inch by excruciating inch, trying to savor the sensation of her squeezing me tightly. Trying more to resist the urge to come. This girl has me wound around her finger and I don't know if she realizes just how much I would do to make her smile. Hear her laugh. Hear her moan. I would do anything for this girl.

Anything.

Even if she wanted me to stop right now, I would. It would be difficult but I'd do it.

For her.

I should tell her how I feel. How much I care. How I think I'm falling in love with her. It's all happening so fast but I remember what my parents said—the last people I want to think about right now but here I am, doing exactly that—how I shouldn't hold back my feelings. I need to come clean, but will she freak out?

God, I hope not.

CHAPTER FIFTY

WILLOW

I will my body to relax as I feel Rhett enter me for the first time. Closing my eyes, I breathe deep, wincing as he slowly pushes inside, pressing my lips together when I feel the pinch and sting. I've never felt so full, so connected to another human being before, and when I shift my hips, it only sends him deeper, making him groan.

He presses his forehead against mine, like he's trying to regain some control, and I wait for him, allowing myself to get used to the sensation of him being inside me. It's odd and wondrous and amazing and awkward, all at once.

"I need to take this slow," he bites out. "I don't want to come too fast."

I frown, settling my hands at the back of his neck, toying with the curling damp hair there. His entire body is covered with a thin sheen of sweat. "Could you come right now?"

He nods. "Don't want to."

"But you could."

"Yeah," he grits out. "And if we keep talking about it, I will."

I kiss him, silencing us both, silencing the thoughts running through my brain as well. The worry and the nerves and the fear of this being extremely painful. It's not that bad. Not at all. Especially with how careful he's being, which I appreciate.

Once he's gained some control, he begins to move, pulling almost all the way out before he pushes back in. I shift my position on the mattress, again sending him deeper, and I rest my hands on his shoulders, clinging to him. Watching him. His eyes are closed but he has this look of pure determination on his face. Like he's concentrating so hard, trying to make this good. For me?

I assume so. He's so thoughtful. Putting me first.

Testing it out, I curl my leg around his, making him groan. Press my foot into the back of his calf, marveling at how hard it is. He is nothing but solid muscle and I love the weight of him on top of me. I slide my leg up, hooking it around his hip, and oh that position change is good. Like he's touching some part of me deep inside that I've never experienced before.

I want him to do it again.

Eventually I have both of my legs around his waist and he's moving faster. I flex my hips, trying to send him deeper and every time I do it, he groans, our foreheads pressed together just before his mouth finds mine. The kiss is wild, completely out of control, and when he reaches in between us, his fingers finding my clit, I'm flying.

Coming.

My inner walls contract, milking him, and with a strangled groan he bucks against me, his body going tense right before he falls completely apart. He's coming, thrusting once. Twice. Three times before he collapses on top of me, a panting, shuddering mess.

My heart races scarily fast and I close my eyes, stroking his hair. Running my fingers over his shoulders as he lies extraordinarily still on me. I try to soothe him, noting how he shivers when I stroke my fingernails across his skin so I keep doing it, knowing that he likes it.

"Are you okay?" I ask him, still stroking his back.

"Shouldn't I be asking you that?" He lifts away from me so he can look into my eyes.

I stare up at him, a little shocked that we actually just did what we did. I had sex with Rhett Bennett. And it was amazing. I've always heard first time horror stories but that wasn't terrible. Not even close.

"I'm definitely okay." I smile and stretch beneath him. "It only hurt a little bit."

He's studying me, slowly shaking his head. "You amaze me, you know that?"

"I do?" My smile fades. "How?"

"There is no one else like you, Will. You surprise me constantly. I think you're going to react one way and you never do. You go in the complete opposite direction every damn time. Not that I'm complaining." He kisses me, his lips soft and oh so sweet. "You are a constant contradiction and you keep me on my toes."

"And you like that?" I sink into his kiss, my body reacting almost immediately, but he ends it too soon.

"I love it." He gives me a quick kiss on the lips. "I…I'm in love with you."

I'm stunned silent by his declaration. Did he really just say that?

Did he really just admit that he loves me?

"Did you hear what I just said, Will?" He's sweating this. I can tell. And I immediately feel bad.

"I heard you." Lifting my head, I brush his mouth with mine, touching his cheek while I stare into his beautiful hazel eyes. "I'm in love with you too."

A variety of emotions crosses his face. Relief. Happiness. Even a hint of lust. His kiss turns fierce, and I can feel all of his feelings and more in his persuasive lips. "Think we're moving too quickly."

He doesn't even ask it as a question.

"Probably." I smile against his still seeking lips. "But I don't care."

"I don't either." His expression is deadly serious when he pulls back and stares into my eyes. "I've always been told that when you know, you know."

"My dad used to say that too," I admit, letting all the love I'm feeling shine in my eyes, just for Rhett. "I wasn't sure if I ever really believed it though. I wanted to, but as I got older, I started to doubt him."

I blamed it on my unrequited crush on Silas. I realize now I was just focusing on the wrong person. The right one is here with me now. In my bed. And that feels like a very grown-up thought, but it's true.

"I didn't really believe it either," Rhett admits. "But I do now."

I smile at him, my heart squeezing. "I do too."

• • •

"You secretive little bitch," Iris breathes when I open the door to her hours after Rhett snuck out of my dorm. "I know what you did."

She barges into my room, walking right past me while I slowly close the door. I remember at one point when I was with Rhett, I smacked my hand over my mouth for fear someone—Iris—might hear me moan but then I sort of forgot myself.

I decide to play dumb.

"What are you talking about?" I blink at her, trying to keep a straight face.

"Oh please, you whore. I saw Rhett leave your room a few hours ago and you didn't bother texting me. You didn't call. You didn't DM me, nothing. And I just know that you two did it."

My mouth hangs open for a moment before I snap it shut. "Wait a second. Did he tell you that?"

"Ha!" She snaps her fingers and points at me. "Caught ya! I didn't even speak to him but I didn't have to. He was *whistling* when he left your room. Who whistles? Guys who just got laid do, that's who."

I'm slightly mortified but then again, I'm not because this is Iris that I'm dealing with. She would make this moment a big deal no matter what.

"Fine, you caught me." I flop onto my bed, staring at the ceiling. I made the bed after he left but I swear I can still smell him on my sheets. The comforter. I did take a shower, though I did it with regret. I don't know why, but I liked being able to smell him on my skin.

"Is that where it happened?" Iris flicks her fingers at me and the bed. "Are you currently lying in your own sex filth or did you at least wash the sheets?"

"I took a shower, but I didn't wash the sheets or comforter. Meaning, I'm lying in my own sex filth and I can't lie, I'm enjoying it." I send her a withering stare. "Did you come over here to give me a hard time about this? Or did you actually need something?"

"Look at you. You finally have sex and now you're feisty." Iris rests her hands on her hips, watching me. "Actually, I came over here to make sure you're okay."

Aw. "I'm more than okay."

"Plus, I was curious and I wanted to ask how it was. Magical? Or terrible?"

I sit up, pushing my hair out of my face. "It was…magical."

"Seriously?" Iris seems shocked, but pleased. "He knows what he's doing then."

"He does." It's like I can't stop nodding. "He definitely does."

"Brooks was pretty good too. The first time. Though we did plenty of other things before that."

"Same."

"Lucky bitch." Iris is grinning.

"Right back at you." I'm grinning too.

She joins me on the bed, her butt perched on the edge of the mattress as she slips her arm around my shoulders. "My little girl is growing up."

"Oh my God." I groan, but I rest my head against hers, glad

that she came over. I like that we're talking about it, but she's not pushing for too many details. And while it feels like so much is changing for all of us, I still have her. My cousin. My best friend.

"We'll have to go on a double date sometime," Iris suggests. "The homecoming dance is coming up soon."

"Homecoming dance?" I'm already groaning. Yet another change. "We never had one of those before."

"Right, because this school was lame. But we had one last year and we had so much fun. Nominees will be announced soon."

"Seriously? Like for queen and king?" I knew this was a thing at high schools all over the United States but we've never done it at Lancaster Prep.

"Yes. And then there are princes and princesses for the other classes. Your man is a shoo-in for king this year. I wonder if that means you'll be nominated too." Her smile is sly when she glances down at me. "Guess I'll be campaigning against you."

"Will you be nominated too?"

"Of course, I will. We're Lancasters, darling. We rule the school."

We both laugh and cling to each other, then sit in silence for a moment. I can't help but think of Rhett, and wonder what he's doing right now. Is he thinking about me?

I hope so.

"He told me that he's in love with me," I admit, my voice soft.

Iris shifts, and I pull away from her so we can face each other. "Oh my God. What did you say to him?"

"I told him that I loved him too."

"Seriously?" Her voice is a squeak. "Do you think you actually love him?"

I nod. "I know I do."

"But it's so soon…" Iris shakes her head. "I haven't even told Brooks I love him yet."

"Has he ever said it to you?"

"No, and I don't expect him to." She peers into my eyes, like she's trying to figure me out. "How do you know that you're in love with Rhett? What does it feel like, to be in love?"

"I don't know. It's hard to describe." I shrug. "It's just…it's a feeling. One that's something I can't contain. It's overwhelming, but not in a bad way. He's all I can think about. Like, it's almost obsessive, how much I think about him. And he truly seems to feel the same way about me. I'm pretty sure he's just as obsessed with me as I am with him, and that's such a great feeling, you know? I don't feel like I'm alone or wasting my time."

It made the moment we shared earlier that much more special too, knowing that we're in love with each other.

"You mean it, don't you?" Iris sounds truly surprised. "You're in love with him."

"I'm in love with him," I say firmly. "I'm in love with Rhett Bennett."

My phone buzzes in the pocket of my sweatpants and I pull it out to see I have a text.

Rhett: **I miss you.**

Rhett: **I wish we were together right now but I'm dealing with Brooks and his lazy ass. He says hi.**

Rhett: **I love you.**

Rhett: **Had the need to tell you that again. Feels more real when I see it actually written out.**

Rhett: **I love you Willow Lancaster.**

Rhett: **I hope I'm not scaring the shit out of you. I probably am huh?**

I'm laughing, all of these texts coming at me, one after the other. I send him a quick reply.

Me: **You don't scare me.**

"Who keeps texting you?" Iris asks.

"It's Rhett. He's with Brooks, who says hi."

The mischievous look that appears on my cousin's face tells me she's scheming. "They should come over."

"It's so late though." My protest is weak. I definitely want them to come over.

"Please. It's not that late. Tell him to come over and bring Brooks with him."

Me: **I love you too, Rhett Bennett. Want to come over?**

He responds immediately.

Rhett: **I'll be there in less than five.**

Me: **Bring Brooks with you. This is Iris's only request.**

Rhett: **Will do.**

He sends me the saluting emoji and I sigh with happiness.

I love him. And he loves me.

So much.

CHAPTER FIFTY-ONE

WILLOW

HOMECOMING NIGHT

I stand just outside the auditorium by myself, taking deep, cleansing breaths. Reminding myself that I can do this alone. Walk into that room with my head held high and everyone's eyes on me while the announcements are made. It'll feel kind of weird doing it alone, and I'll miss him, but it's okay. The dance was already running late and they had to start it before the game was even over.

The roar from the stadium nearby makes me glance over my shoulder. I wish I was watching the game, but Iris's dad—who is the interim headmaster after Westscott was fired, no freaking joke—gently told me I needed to make an appearance at the dance as part of the homecoming court. Even if my king is still out on that field playing in overtime.

I wish I was out there, cheering him on, but I'm sure he understands. We discussed the possibility of this happening earlier today. It's like he knew he'd miss out.

"Hey."

I turn to find Iris exiting the auditorium, the music blasting from within cut off completely when the door slams shut. She's wearing a cute burgundy-lace, off-the-shoulder dress that clings to her like a second skin and black Valentino platform shoes on her feet, her hair falling around her face in loose blonde waves, and her lips painted the same color as the dress. She looks amazing.

"Are you ready?" she asks me when I still haven't said anything.

Nodding, I glance down at myself, readjusting the white sash that I slipped on only a moment ago. It says in sparkly blue lettering, *Homecoming Queen*.

"I still can't believe I won," I murmur, reaching up to readjust the tiara on my head.

Iris bats my hand away and fixes my crown. "There you go. Now it's straight." She takes a step back, taking me in. "Oh, Willow, you look beautiful."

I feel beautiful, especially when I remember the look on Rhett's face when he saw me out on the football field at halftime during the crowning ceremony. The boys all stood in a line waiting for us while our fathers escorted us out to the makeshift stage, including Iris's. The king was announced first, my knees almost buckling when the announcer said Rhett's name. Thank goodness I had a firm grip on my father's arm or I might've collapsed.

And when my name was announced as the homecoming queen, I actually started to cry. Me, the girl who made fun of the fact that we were actually having this silly ritual at our school after never doing it in the history of Lancaster Prep. I cried like a baby when they dropped the sash over my body and set that crown onto my head, Iris screaming her encouragement the entire time. My father looked so proud as he watched us, but I could see there was a bit of sadness lingering in his gaze too.

His little girl is all grown up. I know that's what he was thinking.

Now here I am about to make my appearance at the homecoming dance without my king.

"Thank you," I tell her, reaching out to clasp her hand and give it a squeeze. "I wish you would've won."

"Liar," she whispers, making us both laugh. "You deserved to win. The crown looks good on you."

I smile at her, feeling like I might cry all over again, which is dumb. I swear the only reason I'm so emotional is because I'm hormonal. Or maybe it's because all of these moments we're experiencing feel so final during our senior year. After this, we go on to college or a gap year or whatever plan we might have for our future. That's why I need to live in the now and enjoy every single moment before it's gone for good.

The music stops from inside the auditorium and the DJ starts talking.

"I think that's our cue to go inside," Iris says, slipping her arm through mine. "Come on. I'll be your escort."

We rush into the auditorium, the DJ passing the mic to Whit, who starts talking about creating new traditions at Lancaster Prep. We stand off to the side with the rest of the homecoming court, Iris my unofficial escort, just like she said, and when I glance over at her, I see that she's repeatedly shaking her head.

"I can't believe my dad is doing this. I can't get away with shit at this place now," she mutters.

It takes everything in my power not to burst out laughing, but I somehow manage to remain quiet.

Whit introduces each couple. The freshman prince and princess, then the sophomores, and then the juniors. His gaze catches mine as he says, "And finally we have the senior queen and king..."

His voice drifts, and he does a double take when he sees his daughter. "Make that just the queen since our king must still be out on the football field. Willow Lancaster!"

I walk onto the stage, smiling at Whit, who kisses me on the cheek before I turn to the crowd, smiling. I spot a few familiar faces. Bronwyn is smiling at me, offering a little wave. I spot Alana who looks bored, standing beside Silas because those two can't seem to stay away from each other.

I'm so glad I didn't insist on pursuing Silas. He is so not the guy for me.

Whit says a few more things and then we all exit the stage, me fighting the wave of disappointment that Rhett wasn't able to make it. We walk down the steps and onto the floor, the DJ starting up a new song that's slow and romantic. Of course. Couples shuffle out onto the dance floor and I watch them all embrace each other and start to sway to the beat.

My heart aches at Rhett not being here. He's going to miss the majority of the dance, and I glance toward the double doors, contemplating if I should head back down to the stadium and watch the last minutes of the game.

The guilt that swarms me over not being there and supporting him is all-encompassing. The last month that we've been together has been the best days of my life. We spend almost every waking moment together. I go to sleep smiling, thinking of him, and I wake up excited in the morning, eager to be with him. I didn't know it could be like this, and I'm so grateful he's mine.

And that I'm his.

I stare at the doors, and it's almost as if I willed them to swing open, revealing Rhett and Brooks still in their uniforms, looking dirty and tired. I stand there frozen, unsure of when or where I lost Iris, but I don't even care anymore. Her boyfriend is here.

And so is mine.

CHAPTER FIFTY-TWO

RHETT

I'm out of breath and my entire body hurts after that fucking brutal game but in the end we won, and then Brooks and I hauled ass running up the hill to get here, hoping we didn't miss the homecoming ceremony they planned on having during the dance.

Damn, looks like we just missed it.

But there's my girl, standing alone wearing the homecoming queen sash and the tiara on her head, looking fucking gorgeous in that black velvet dress, a matching thin black velvet choker around her neck. Her dark hair spills down her back in soft waves, clipped back with a black velvet bow. She's wearing shiny black Chanel Mary Jane shoes on her feet, and I only know they're Chanel because she told me.

Her lips are painted a deep red and they slowly part, revealing her teeth in a beautiful smile. I walk toward her, feeling like I'm in a teen movie with the music playing in the background and the couples swaying. Me in my dirty football uniform while my girl is stunning in her beautiful dress.

"I missed it, huh?" I say to Willow when I'm close enough that she can hear me.

She nods, her smile turning tremulous, her eyes shiny. She better not cry. I feel like I'm gonna die whenever she sheds tears, not that she does it often. "Did you win?"

"Yeah, baby, of course we did." Unable to resist, I sweep her into my arms and off her feet, making her squeal as I swing her around. "I'm sorry I wasn't here for the ceremony."

"Don't apologize. You had a game to play and besides, we were together for the most important ceremony out on the field." She kisses my cheek and I feel that innocent touch of her lips on my skin all the way to my bones. "I'm so proud of you."

"I can't stop looking at you." I set her on her feet and take a step back, admiring her. Willow is too beautiful for words, I swear. I get overwhelmed when I look at her and end up feeling like a chump who can't speak. "That dress."

It hugs all of her curves. She's the sexiest woman I know. And she's all mine.

"The way you look at me makes me feel beautiful," she whispers, grabbing my hand and rising up to press a kiss to my cheek.

I can feel the lipstick staining my skin, and she examines it, making like she's going to wipe it away when I take a step backward, dodging her. "Keep it there."

"But I left a lipstick print on your face." She frowns. "You can't walk around like that."

"I sure as hell can." I wave a hand at her. "Take a picture. I left my phone in the locker room."

Like some sort of miracle, her dress has pockets and she pulls her phone out, standing next to me and taking a few selfies of the two of us together before she shows them to me. "Aw, we look cute."

I admire the photo of the two of us, me looking like a lovesick dope with Willow's lipstick print on my cheek, her smiling into the camera. We're fucking happy is what we look like. "Yeah, we do."

"Should we dance?"

"You don't wanna dance with me like this. I'm still in my pads." I've got all the equipment on. So does Brooks. We look ridiculous but man we booked it to get here. Coach didn't even care that we ran out before he could give the team speech.

"That doesn't bother me. Dance with me, Rhett."

Without hesitation I pull her into my arms and we join the rest of the crowd on the dance floor, shuffling to the music. I spot Brooks dancing with Iris as well, the two of us rolling our eyes at each other, but he looks happy too.

It's been a good night. A good week, celebrating homecoming. I have zero complaints. I don't know how I got so lucky to win homecoming king, the girl of my dreams and the game, but here I am, living my best fucking life.

Willow's arms are slung around my middle, her fingers slipping beneath the waistband of my uniform pants.

"Hey, watcha doing?" I ask, hoping like hell she's not going to feel me up out here. Iris's dad is watching the dance floor like a hawk. I know he's paying more attention to his daughter and Brooks but still. That guy scares the shit out of me.

"What is this?" She tugs on something. A piece of cardstock, and I realize a second too late that she's discovered my good luck charm. "Why do you have a piece of paper stuck in your pants?"

"Uhhh." I don't know what to say or how to explain it without looking like a stalker. I mean, I know I'm her boyfriend and it's okay to keep something for myself that originally belonged to her, but she might find this a little weird.

She unfolds the worn and creased paper, frowning before she holds it out to me. "Wait a minute. This is mine, isn't it?"

I nod, wincing. "Maybe?"

"Maybe?" She stares at the lipstick prints on the paper, then glances up at me. "Is this from the lip print reader? The fortune teller lady?"

"Yeah."

"And you kept it?"

"You left it on the table so I figured it was fair game. I took it before it got thrown away."

"You've kept it all this time?"

"It wasn't that long ago." I shrug. Almost a couple of months.

"I like to have it with me during games."

"Why?" Her voice is soft, her eyes glowing.

"It's my good luck charm," I admit.

"Oh my God," she murmurs, carefully folding the paper back up and clutching it in her palm. "This is the sweetest thing you've ever done."

"Yeah? You really think so?" I reach beneath my uniform shirt and the equipment I've got on, pulling out my other good luck charm. "Hate to break it to you, but I need the paper back, Will. And I'd rather give you this."

I let the number one pendant dangle from my fingers, the gold glinting in the light.

"I can't take that. It belonged to your dad," she says, her eyes wide when they meet mine.

"And I want you to have it. You're the number one most important thing to me. You deserve to wear it." I reach behind me with both hands and undo the clasp, carefully removing the chain from my neck before I hold it in front of her. "Turn around for me?"

She does as I ask and I slip the chain around her neck, fumbling for a few seconds before I get the clasp into place. She's got her head bent, her fingers stroking over the pendant, and I lean forward, whispering in her ear, "My dad wore it because his dad gave it to him, and when he was with my mom, he gave it to her. She wore it for years, whenever he played football, but once he was done, she wanted me to have it and he agreed. They said it would be my good luck charm now. But you're the one who brings me luck, Willow. And happiness. You're my number one and I want everyone to know it."

Willow whirls around and hugs me, burying her face against my chest. "I love it. I love you. Thank you."

I hold her close until the song is done, another one starting right up, and it's faster. Everyone floods the dance floor, and I take Willow's hand, pulling her off and away toward a dark corner where we can be more alone.

"You can have this back." She hands me the piece of paper with her lipstick prints on it. "Though I can make you more if you want."

"I kind of like this one best though." I return it to my hiding spot, the tiniest makeshift pocket on the inside of my pants that's only there because of an undone seam. It's the perfect place to stash it.

"You're the sweetest." She's watching me like she can't believe I'm hers.

I know the feeling all too well.

"Pretty sure you're wrong, Will. You've got me beat on the sweetness part. There's no one sweeter than Willow Lancaster," I drawl, appreciating the pink flush that coats her face at my words.

We stare at each other for a moment, lost in our own little world. I could watch her for an eternity and never get tired of looking at her.

"You know all of my kisses are for you, right?" Her gaze goes to the one on my cheek. "You own all of them."

"Good, because I need every one that I can get for luck." I chuckle and she laughs and we lean into each other, our mouths meeting. Melting. "I love you."

"I love you, too," she whispers. "Want to get out of here?"

Those six words are like freaking magic. I'm already impatient and eager to leave. "You sure?"

She nods, slowly pulling away. "Where are my parents?"

"With Row at the field."

"Where are your parents?"

"With my brother. Also out at the field."

"No one is paying attention then." Her smile turns sly.

So does mine. "Nope."

"Let's ditch this dance."

"You got it, baby." I grab her hand, about to hightail it out of there, but she doesn't budge.

"Maybe I can give you more kisses. On your skin." She lowers her voice to the barest whisper. "All over your body."

"Promise?"

She tips her head back, her laughter reaching deep inside me and never letting go. "Yes, Rhett. I promise."

CHAPTER FIFTY-THREE

RHETT

I'm spending my first Thanksgiving holiday away from my family and it's a different vibe, hanging out with the Lancasters.

Dad has a Thursday night football game to coach and Mom is with him because she didn't want to leave him alone for the holiday. Callahan is with them as well, because he wanted to go to the game, and Dad promised him he could get him down on the sidelines at one point, so I don't blame him for going. They asked if I wanted to attend too, but I turned them down, much to my mother's brief disappointment.

When I told her I was invited to spend the Thanksgiving weekend with Willow's family, Mom brightened right up. She likes the two of us together—she told me so. And I have to agree.

I like the two of us together too.

Iris's family house is under an unexpected and extensive renovation thanks to a once in a century—that's how the weather forecasters described it—and extremely early snowstorm that came through the area. A small part of the roof caved due to a weak structural part and the heavy snow sitting on top of it. Considering the roof fell through where the kitchen and dining area is, they had to cancel their annual Thanksgiving plans.

And now the family event is at Willow's family house.

Their house is huge too, and crowded with Lancasters everywhere you look. I've come here before but it was always a brief stop before going over to Iris's house—it's bigger and full of all of those old money Lancaster vibes that this family seems to get off on.

Not that this house isn't full of old money vibes. They just don't have a ballroom—that is literally one of the only differences. Well, that and all the old-timey portraits of various Lancasters from over the years. Every one of those dudes looks like he'd gain pleasure out of stringing me up by my balls.

The portraits—much like the statues on campus—seriously creep me out.

Currently I'm on my way upstairs, trailing after Willow, who is wearing a black dress that is borderline criminal. It gives the illusion of being modest thanks to it covering up the majority of her body—it's got long sleeves and a high neck with a collar and a white ribbon tied in a bow at the center. Where the collar buttons at the back of her neck is the only flash of skin I can see. The tiniest slit offers just a tease of skin.

The issue I have is with the skirt. It's fuckin' short. No other words for it, and as my girl climbs the stairs, I can see the bottom half of her ass cheeks peeking from beneath the skirt with her every step. Yes, I'm practically on top of her and looking for that glimpse of ass cheek, but damn.

The skirt is dangerously short and she looks dangerously hot.

Doesn't help that her hair is pulled into an elegant knot on top of her head and she's got these giant pearls in her ears. The cute little white socks and heeled Mary Jane shoes offer a sweet and innocent touch. She loves playing up this girly side of herself. I love it too.

Behind closed doors, though? The innocent act flies right out the window. She's always just as hungry for me as I am for her. Sometimes maybe more so.

Like tonight.

Halfway through dinner she rested her hand on my thigh—we were seated right next to each other. Her grandma was talking to her about some art gallery she went to in the city and how much she wanted Willow to go too, all while her precious granddaughter was feeling me up at the dinner table.

It was hot, I can't lie.

Now she's going to show me her room. That's what she told her parents, who weren't really paying attention. There's so much family to distract them, and Willow is taking full advantage of it.

I am too.

"I can see your ass," I whisper to her once we're finally at the top of the stairs, my hands on her hips as I pull her into me. "Your skirt is too short."

"You were so close I could practically feel your breath on the back of my thighs," she says, amusement tingeing her voice.

"You liked it." I kiss the side of her exposed neck. I usually like her hair down but when she wears it up, I can't deny it gives me easier access.

"I definitely did." She comes to a stop, causing me to bump into her plump ass and I choke down a strangled groan. "I'm not wearing panties."

I let the groan fly because fuck me running, this girl loves to torture me every chance she gets.

Within a minute we're stumbling into her room, my hands on her waist and about to pin her to the door so I can kiss the shit out of her when I realize we're not alone. There's someone in her room. Two someones.

"Oh my God, is nothing sacred?" Willow practically wails at Iris, who is currently wrapped up in Brooks's arms on top of Willow's bed.

Brooks scrambles to get off of his girlfriend, but Iris just lies there in the center of the mattress with a blissful smile on her face. "You have such a comfy bed."

"You chose my room because you knew no one would come

look for you here," Willow accuses.

Iris stretches her arms over her head before she sits up, pushing her hair away from her face. "You're right. Hey, at least we're not naked."

"Iris," Brooks warns, though he sounds pained.

"Calm down, Brooksie." She hops off the bed, patting me on the arm as she walks by. "Have fun with your girlfriend."

They're gone in seconds, and Willow makes sure and turns the lock into place on the door. "I'm sure they've had sex in my bed before."

"Why do you say that?"

"I don't know. Just a hunch." A tiny shiver runs through her as she approaches me, her lips curling into a seductive smile. "We can forget about them though."

She reaches for me but I rest my hands on her hips yet again, stopping her. "I want to see your room first."

The disappointment on her face is obvious. "What do you mean?"

"I've heard enough about this room over the last few months. I want to see it." It's true. I want to check it out, even though I'm not a big art advocate or whatever you want to call it. But I know enough to realize that she's got some valuable art pieces in here, and her mom told me she's an eclectic collector.

My girlfriend is a mystery. She keeps me guessing. She surprises me with every little bit she shares about herself, and I'm pretty sure I fall more and more in love with her every day.

I'm a lucky man.

I wander around her massive bedroom with her following close behind, examining the paintings on the wall. The photos tucked away in the corner of the mirror that sits above a vanity table. One of the photos is of us from homecoming night, me still in my uniform and her looking like the goddamn queen she is wearing her crown. There's another photo of me and her and Iris and Brooks from the annual Halloween party.

And my new favorite photo of us after we won our latest playoff game. I'm a sweaty, dirty mess and she's beautiful, pressing her cheek to mine for a selfie, the both of us smiling and looking so damn happy.

"Come see this piece." She grabs my hand and drags me away from her mirror, stopping in front of a massive painting. As I study it though, I realize it's not a painting at all. It looks like someone kissed a canvas over and over again in different shades of lipstick. "This has hung in my room since I was a baby."

"Did your mom make this for your dad?" I send her a questioning look.

"No." She shakes her head, grinning at me before she turns her attention to the piece. "It was created by someone else. A woman kissed this canvas repeatedly for the artist, with every shade of Chanel lipstick that exists. My mother fell in love with it when she was young, and she told my dad about it."

I grab her hand and pull her so she's standing in front of me, her perfect ass snug against my dick, the both of us facing the art piece. "Does it have a name?"

"It was called *A Million Kisses in Your Lifetime*, and when my mother first wanted it, it belonged to someone else who wasn't willing to sell it. Once my father found out that she wanted this piece, he made them an offer they couldn't refuse. He got the piece for her and gave it to her on her birthday, which is on Christmas," Willow explains, leaning her head against my chest.

"How much did he spend?"

"Over a million dollars."

I whistle. That's a lot of money—and competition. How can I live up to that? "When exactly did he give it to her?"

"When she turned eighteen."

I'm incredulous. I can't imagine spending that kind of money on a gift for Willow because I don't necessarily have that kind of money—my parents do. But I'm not a Lancaster so there's the difference. "Are you serious?"

She laughs. "My dad is all about the grand gesture."

Now we're talking mega competition. "I love a grand gesture."

"Do you now?"

I start kissing her neck while she keeps staring at the art hanging on her wall. "Definitely."

"I wanted to take it to school and hang it in my dorm suite, but my parents said absolutely not. I suppose I don't blame them, but I miss looking at it every day."

An idea forms in my head but I keep it to myself. "I wouldn't let you take it to school either if I spent a million dollars on it."

"It's worth more than that now."

I pause, my lips still against her neck. "Like how much?"

"Closer to five."

I pull away from her so I can look into her eyes. "You've gotta be kidding me."

"I'm not." She slowly shakes her head, smiling.

"You've got five million dollars just hanging on your wall. A canvas with lipstick all over it."

"It's so much more than that." Willow turns to face me, slinging her arms around my neck. "It's a representation of my parents' love. That my father was and still is willing to do whatever it takes to make my mom happy. She told me when she received that gift, she knew they would be together forever."

"Aw, so romantic." I wrap my arms around her waist and kiss the tip of her nose. "They're setting standards that are impossible to meet, you know."

She laughs. "I don't need a five-million-dollar art piece, Rhett. I just want you."

"And I can give you me." My lips find hers, lingering for a bit before I eventually pull away. "All night long if you want."

I kiss her again, getting lost in her taste. The glide of her tongue against mine. The low sounds she makes in her throat when I slip my hands beneath her skirt and grip her ass cheeks in my hands. I can feel the heat of her pussy pressed against my erection, and somehow I've guided her over to the door, where I've got her pressed firmly against it. I slip my hands beneath her thighs and she goes with me when I lift, wrapping her legs around my waist, her shoes falling off her feet and landing on the floor. I push her into the door, letting her feel what she does to me. Feeling what I do to her because I can tell. My girl is wet and ready for me.

"We probably shouldn't do this," she whispers against my lips at one point and I pull away, giving her the power and control to end it right now. We can straighten ourselves up and head back downstairs. Hang out with the family and watch the game on TV because it's going to come on soon and I promised my dad I would watch it.

But then Willow sneaks her hand in between us, her fingers fumbling to open my khakis, and I don't bother helping her. She'll get them undone. And when she slips her fingers into my boxer briefs and curls them around my aching dick, I forget about everything else, even football, and concentrate on the sensation of her fingers squeezing my cock.

Before I completely lose it, I shove her dress up, exposing her bottom half, my fingers slipping between her thighs. She's hot and wet, and from those whimpers that I keep hearing, I'm guessing she wants it as bad as I do. I shove my khakis down with her help and within seconds I'm pushing inside of her, a muffled groan leaving me when I feel all of that tight wet heat surrounding me.

Pausing, I press my forehead to hers and breathe deep, trying to gain some control. She's on birth control so we're not using condoms anymore and I'm still not used to how fucking amazing it feels, being inside of her like this. Nothing blocking us—just skin on skin.

"Hurry," she encourages. "They might start looking for us."

That's all I need to hear. I fuck my girl hard and steady, keeping up the rhythm I know she likes best, angling my hips and aiming for that secret spot deep inside her that makes her moan. I find her clit and rub it, my mouth fused with hers, my thrusting causing her body to knock against the door every few seconds. We're so caught up in it all that I don't even care if anyone can hear us, and I don't think she does either, which is really fucking dangerous.

It's only when we've both come and we're clinging to each other, me panting into her neck, when we hear a tiny voice sound from the other side of her door.

"You okay in there, Willow?"

I meet Willow's gaze, my heart stopping. "Who the fuck is that?" I whisper at her.

"Um, I'm fine!" Willow calls, her eyes wide and full of panic.

"I thought I heard something knocking."

"I dropped something and it, uh, hit the door," Willow explains, sounding completely out of breath.

"They're going to serve pumpkin pie soon! Come downstairs when you can. Tell your boyfriend too."

We hear footsteps grow distant, until they're completely gone.

"I think that was my cousin. One of the twins." Willow makes a face. "Oh God, what if she tells someone what she heard?"

"That won't happen," I reassure her with all the confidence I can muster but come on.

She might tell someone. Meaning, we need to head to the dining room. Now.

• • •

We cleaned ourselves up and made it downstairs in record time, entering the dining area just as Willow's mom brought out a pumpkin pie, Iris's mom following right after her with an apple pie. I take a slice of both and head for the game room as they call it, where there's a massive big-screen TV and the football game is currently playing.

"That your dad right there?" Willow's father points his fork at the screen.

"Yeah." I smile when I see him standing on the sidelines holding his clipboard in front of his face so no one can figure out what he's saying.

"So freaking cool that your dad coaches for the NFL." Willow's youngest brother Beau's eyes light up.

"It's pretty freaking cool," I agree, settling onto the couch right next to Iris, who is cozied up with Brooks. "I need to talk to you," I tell her.

She's frowning. "What about?"

I can see Willow talking to her mom and aunt, her expression radiant, her hair appearing ready to fall out of the bun. I would do anything for this girl, and I'm about to prove that very fact.

"A present for Willow. I have this idea..."

EPILOGUE

WILLOW

Rhett is being weird and I can't stop thinking about it. He's acting mysterious. Maybe even a little bit…

Sneaky?

Yes, definitely sneaky.

School is winding down for the semester and winter break is almost here. Everyone who wants to go to college has turned in their applications, even Iris, who did it reluctantly but she also admitted that she wanted a back-up plan. I have a feeling if Brooks ends up going somewhere, she'll follow him. They're in love. Madly, passionately in love.

Just like Rhett and I are.

I'm boggled by how mysterious he's being. What is he hiding from me? What sort of plan does he have in place? Because that's what it feels like. He's planning and plotting something, and I can't figure out what. I thought it might be related to Christmas, but it's too soon for that. Christmas isn't for another two weeks, and besides—how much does he need to plan for a Christmas gift?

Though I do know my boyfriend is a "go big or go home" kind of guy, so maybe this shouldn't surprise me. I need to ask Iris if she knows anything about his weird behavior.

I'm at Sunday brunch with my cousins, which is the perfect

opportunity to question her. It's a new thing that we've started over the last month—a way for us to connect with each other and catch up on what's going on. Currently in attendance is me, Iris, Row and even…August. He just got out of college for the semester and agreed to coming to brunch with us only because Iris begged and pleaded.

"He loves to be begged," Iris told me right before we entered the restaurant. "I feel sorry for the woman he ends up with. He'll probably have her constantly on her knees."

"Ew, Iris, why did you have to go there?" My disgust made Iris laugh. I'm sure she's on her knees for Brooks.

I know I'm on my knees for Rhett so…

"None of you are having a drink?" August asks once the server drops off his mimosa.

"We're all underage," Iris reminds him.

"Right," he drawls before taking a healthy sip. "Why am I here again?"

"To bond with your family." Iris smacks August's arm, earning a deathly glare. "Oh stop. You act like such a prick all the time. Aren't you exhausted?"

"This is my personality, so no. I'm not exhausted," August utters, his voice dripping with his disgust.

Iris rolls her eyes at me while Row starts talking.

"I have an issue." We all go quiet when he says that. My brother is probably the most easygoing one out of all of us. He rarely has an issue with anything.

"Is it school?" I ask.

Rowan shakes his head.

"Football?" August asks, though he says the word like a curse. He's not into football. Thinks it's lame that his cousins and little brother plays.

"The season is over, remember?" Ooh, Row's tone is just as jerkish as August's. I'm proud of him. "It's—a girl."

Iris sits up straight, rubbing her hands together. "Tell us

everything. Let me play matchmaker."

"I don't like her." Row's voice is firm. "It's not like that. She drives me crazy. I want advice on how to get her to stop talking to me."

"How exactly does she drive you crazy?" I ask.

"Like I said, she won't stop talking to me. We have a lot of classes together and it's just…nonstop." He rolls his eyes. "And she talks about stuff I don't care about."

"Tell her that," August says, earning a hard stare from both me and Iris. "Or maybe not. Though that's the easiest way to get rid of her."

"That's mean," I stress. "Don't do that."

"She probably likes you," Iris adds.

Row grimaces. As if the concept is foreign to him. "No way. She doesn't like me. Not like that."

"Then why does she keep talking to you?" Iris asks. "That's a sign that she might be into you."

"I think it's a sign that she can't stand me so she keeps up the chatter to get under my skin," Rowan says, grabbing his menu and opening it, even though he told us only a few minutes ago what he wants to order. "This conversation is going nowhere."

Because he's not listening to us. If he treats this poor girl like that, no wonder she keeps talking to him. And I'd guess Iris is right—I bet this girl does like him. Poor thing. She's dealing with someone who's absolutely clueless.

August and Row start talking about the latest Formula 1 race and I turn to Iris, lowering my voice. "Do you know what's going on with Rhett?"

Iris frowns. "What do you mean? Please don't tell me there's trouble in paradise. You guys are the only reason I believe in love."

"Oh, that's such crap and you know it," I tease. "You are so in love with Brooks it's almost pathetic."

"I'm offended." From the tone of her voice, I can tell she's not offended whatsoever. "How is Rhett acting weird?"

"He seems very.. secretive. Like he's hiding something from me. Nothing bad," I rush to say when Iris's mouth pops open. "I'm just guessing that something is going on and I wish I knew what it was."

"I know nothing," Iris says, her expression solemn. "And if I did, I'd tell you."

My cousin is right. She would totally tell me.

"I know you would." I offer her a small smile, fighting the frustration filling me.

Guess I'll have to figure out this mystery on my own.

• • •

"What are you doing tonight?" Rhett asks me during lunch on Wednesday.

"Studying for finals," I remind him, sending him a look. "You should be too."

He rolls his eyes. "Do the teachers pay you to say that shit to me?"

I nudge him in the ribs, leaning into him because he's solid and warm and I can't get enough. "No. I'm just trying to help you out and keep you on track."

"Do my parents pay you, then? No wonder they love you so much." He slings his arm around my shoulders and tucks me even closer into him, his mouth landing on my forehead. "I wanted to get together with you tonight."

"I'll be at the library after school and I don't know how long it's going to take." I've been practically living there all week. "You should join me."

The disappointment on his handsome face is clear. "The library, princess? Really?"

"Only a couple of more days." I brush my mouth along his jaw, breathing in his delicious spicy scent. "And then we're free for two whole weeks."

We're together for the majority of the holiday break. I'm going with him to spend a few days at his parents' house before heading home for Christmas. On the twenty-seventh he'll join my family and we're all headed to Aspen for New Year's. It's the first time we're going out of town to celebrate that particular holiday and I'm really looking forward to it—especially ringing in the new year with Rhett.

"It's dragging on forever," he groans.

"You sound like Iris," I tease.

"We're more alike than you realize," he says.

I lean back to stare into his eyes. They're greener today. They seem to always be greener when he looks at me. "Maybe that's why I like you so much."

"I am nothing like Iris," he gripes. But his satisfied smile makes my heart race.

A couple of boys stop by our table to offer their congratulations to Rhett and Brooks, which they both accept graciously. They won the state championship game at the beginning of December and the fact that they're still being praised for it says a lot. So many people worship the football team—even Iris's dad. He held a special rally for them and everything, giving Rhett the first ever Lancaster Prep MVP award. How sweet is that?

The rest of the day goes by in a blur. Our schedule is changed thanks to finals and we only have one class after lunch. I take my final and we're let out early so I rush to the library, not even bothering to go by my room to drop anything off. I have my laptop with me and there's a meeting scheduled with my advanced calc group at three-thirty so we can go over the study sheets our teacher gave us to prepare for the final tomorrow.

Ugh, math. My least favorite subject and one of the last finals I have to take. I'm not looking forward to it.

I spend the rest of the afternoon in the library, first with my calc group, and then on my own, finishing up a project that's due tomorrow for American Government. Rhett never shows up. Neither does Iris.

I'm kind of irritated. I've told them numerous times that this semester is important because colleges will look at our grades closely, but they both blow me off. Rhett because he's got a stellar football season that's most likely going to get him in wherever he wants, and Iris because she's Iris and doesn't care.

By the time I'm trudging my way back to my dorm suite, I'm even a little angry. The weather doesn't help. The wind is blowing and it's downright bone-chilling. After those early storms that dumped a bunch of snow, we haven't had any since, but one is definitely coming tonight. I can feel it.

I enter the building to see Iris lingering there, pacing the floor while tapping away on her phone. The moment she hears the door clang shut, she lifts her head, smiling at me. "There you are."

"I told you I was going to the library." I start to walk past her and she falls into step beside me.

"What, are you mad?" She sounds amused.

"No." I blow out a harsh breath, hating how tired I suddenly feel. "I'm just over this semester."

"I've been over it since about two weeks in," she jokes.

She's not wrong. I remember her complaining about it.

"What are you up to now?" she asks me.

"Going to my room, taking a shower and collapsing into bed."

"Sounds like an exciting night." She smiles, waving at me as she stops at her door. "See ya later."

"Bye." I head for my door and hit the key code, opening the door to find…

Rhett standing in the middle of my room, looking nervous.

I let the door shut behind me, blinking at him. "What are you doing here?"

His smile is…nervous? "I wanted to surprise you."

All my earlier frustration at him not showing up at the library evaporates. "Well, you did. I'm glad you're here."

I gave him the key code to get into my room a while ago, not that he shows up unannounced or goes into my room when I'm not there. In fact, he's never done this sort of thing before.

"I have something for you." He shoves his hands in his sweats' pockets. He's changed out of his school uniform and is wearing a gray Lancaster Prep hoodie with matching sweatpants. "An early Christmas gift."

"You do?" Maybe I was right. That's why he's been acting so mysterious lately. "What is it?"

"You don't see it?"

I glance around the room, searching for a wrapped box or gift bag, but there's nothing like that anywhere. "No."

"Keep looking." He sounds amused.

I do as he asks, slowly turning in a circle in the middle of my room when I spot it. Hanging on the wall and centered in between two windows.

A large canvas covered in a variety of multi-colored kisses.

Shocked, I turn to look at him, noting the sheepish expression on his face. "Where did you get this?"

"I made it." He shrugs.

"You *made* it?" I approach the canvas, surprised and impressed by how many kisses there are on the canvas. All the different colors of lipstick. Wait a minute…

"Did *you* kiss the canvas?" My gaze goes to his again and his cheeks are ruddy.

"You were sad that you couldn't bring that art piece here so I thought I'd make you your own Million Kisses."

"You bought a bunch of lipsticks to do this?" Rhett actually wore lipstick to create this replica?

"I bought a few. Borrowed a bunch from Iris. She helped me out. Pretty sure she got incriminating photos of me too with lipstick on." He winces. "It wasn't easy making this. I got lipstick on my nose. Some of that shit stays on for pretty long too. I think Iris gave me those on purpose. She wanted me to look like—"

He doesn't get the next words out because I tackle him and kiss him at the same time, wrapping my arms around his neck and putting my all into the kiss before I end it.

"I can't believe you did this for me." I smile at him, touching the side of his face. "I absolutely love it."

"You do?" He sounds relieved. "I figured you'd think I was an idiot for going to so much trouble."

"I think you're the best ever for going to so much trouble. It's the most thoughtful gift anyone has ever given me." I withdraw from his embrace and take his hand, leading him over to the canvas so we can both stare at it for a while. "It's amazing."

"I tried to copy it as close as possible." He shifts so he's standing behind me, his arms circling around my waist. "I'm glad you love it."

"I definitely love it. It's beautiful." A sigh leaves me and I lean my head against the solid wall of his chest, pleased when I feel his arms tighten around me.

"I love you, Will."

I turn in his arms and kiss him again. "I love you too."

"You still promise to give me all of your kisses, princess?" he murmurs against my lips.

"All of them." I kiss him again. "Every single one."

ACKNOWLEDGMENTS

Here's where I admit something - I had no plans on writing a Lancaster Prep next generation series. After Arch's book, I was ready to put the series to bed. I wanted to do something different, but then my agent came to me and said, "Your UK publisher wants more Lancasters," and I was like, "I'm over it…unless they might want a next gen series?" My UK editor said YES WE WANT IT, and the rest is history. So for this book and the whole next gen series, we need to give thanks where it's due - to my UK editor Rebecca Hilsdon at Michael Joseph/Penguin Random House UK.

Once the next generation was put into place, I knew who I wanted to pair Willow up with - Rhett Bennett, son of Eli and Ava Bennett from the Callahans and College Years series. I have created a lot of characters over the years, and I know some have more love than others, but there is just something about Eli Bennett to me that makes him a personal favorite. His son has similar vibes and I adore that. I adore both of them. I hope you adored Rhett too.

My agent and publicist Georgana helped me name most of the next generation and we owe her credit for coming up with Callahan Bennett (so freaking good, IYKYK) and Beau Lancaster (Beau as in Beaumont as in Wren Beaumont, LOVE). Naming everyone is fun but sometimes it's stressful, especially after you've written as many books as I have…

I want to thank the readers because without you I'm literally nothing. I appreciate you reading my books, talking about them, making gorgeous photos, edits, creating replicas of *A Million Kisses in Your Lifetime* (those always blow me away), just... everything you do, know that I appreciate it. And you.

Everyone at Valentine PR, I need you. Please never leave me. Georgana, Kim, Valentine, Daisy, Sarah, Meagan, Josette, Kelley, AMY (my kid, ha) - you ladies are the best! Readers, you need to thank Georgana for demanding more of Rhett and Willow's story. I added more chapters due to her suggestions and I extended the ending. G, your notes always make my books better.

A massive thank you to my editor Becky and my proofreader Sarah. You both keep me straight (timeline issues are real and I have them) and help me polish my stories until they shine. I love working with you both so much!

p.s. - If you enjoyed **ALL MY KISSES FOR YOU**, it would mean so much if you left a review on the retailer site you bought it from, or on Goodreads. Thank you!

AMARA
an imprint of Entangled Publishing LLC